The Consulting Detective Trilogy

Part III: Montague Street

Darlene A. Cypser

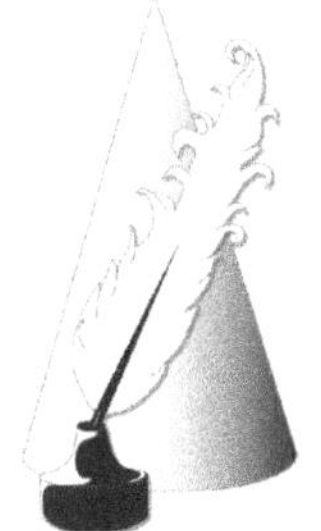

Foolscap & Quill

The Consulting Detective Trilogy Part III: Montague Street

© 2024 Darlene A. Cypser

03212026

Set in Baskerville Classico and Baskerville BT

www.theconsultingdetective.com

ISBN 978-1-938143-45-8

Foolscap & Quill, LLC
151 Summer Street #1018
Morrison, CO 80465-5018
www.foolscap-quill.com

Contents

Preface
Prologue
Chapter 1   Sawdust
Chapter 2   The Stage
Chapter 3   Scandals
Chapter 4   Irregularities
Chapter 5   The Long Wait
Chapter 6   Trials of Spring
Chapter 7   The Tobacconist
Chapter 8   Ashes, Ashes
Chapter 9   We All Fall Down
Chapter 10   Crime & Crutches
Chapter 11   The Blackheath Burglar
Chapter 12   Corpses & Chemistry
Chapter 13   Tiaras & Slippers
Chapter 14   The Tarleton Murders
Chapter 15   The Wine Merchant
Chapter 16   The Musgrave Ritual
Chapter 17   The Old Russion Woman
Chapter 18   Francesco Nicoletti
Chapter 19   The *Matilda Briggs*
Chapter 20   Connections
Chapter 21   Studies
Acknowledgments

Preface

This book concludes a series of four books including *The Crack in the Lens* and *The Consulting Detective Trilogy*.

The Crack in the Lens recorded the background and character of the young Sherlock Holmes, and the traumatic events of 1871 that changed his life and sowed the seeds of his future career.

The Consulting Detective Trilogy stretches from 1871 until his meeting with Dr John H. Watson in 1881. It records his challenges at university, and the events related to the *Gloria Scott* that led to his resolution to become a detective, and his initial studies in that direction in *Part I: University*.

The Consulting Detective Trilogy Part II: On Stage tells the story of Holmes' brief career as an actor, and the adventures and criminal investigations that came his way during that time.

The Consulting Detective Trilogy Part III: Montague Street completes the story as his acting career ends and Holmes begins in earnest to establish his practice as a detective. This book sets out Holmes' initial struggles to find clients, and his earliest cases, including many of the "untold tales" of adventures before he met Dr Watson.

Prologue

After supper Sherlock Holmes retired to his cabin thinking perhaps he was chasing a will o' wisp. He played his violin for a while and then grew drowsy and set it aside. He closed his eyes and slept. He had no idea how long he slept, but he opened his eyes to find the face of Walter Blanchard, a carpenter and handyman of the Corycian Company, staring down at him. Blanchard was leaning with his full weight on his hands which were grasped about Holmes' throat, not only choking his breath, but constricting the blood flow to his brain.

Holmes knew he had mere seconds before he would lose consciousness and that would be a sleep from which there was no waking. The carpenter had strong hands and Holmes could not pull the man's grip away from his throat. The berth was wedged against the wall and Blanchard was on the other side. There was no room to roll and throw the man off. Holmes flailed his hands about for some weapon and one fell upon the neck of his violin. He hesitated a fraction of a second as spots were forming before his eyes. Then he gripped the neck of the instrument and slammed it as hard as he could against Blanchard's head. The blow was sufficient to startle his assailant into loosening his grip long enough for Holmes to gasp a single breath. He aimed the second and third blows at the man's face.

Even as Holmes was physically fighting for his life, another part of his brain was cataloguing the damage to the violin based on the sounds it made. The instrument sang a low pitched protest ending in a sickening crack as the back concussed against his attacker's head on first blow. With the second blow, the back gave way in a chorus of splintering sounds accompanied by a 'sproiing' as the strings were released from their tension. On the third strike the neck snapped and the strings whipped like metal tendrils towards the man's face. By instinct Blanchard's hands had flown to his face, releasing Holmes' throat. While drawing rapid painful breaths, Holmes jabbed at the man's eyes with the broken neck of the instrument and threw himself upward as the man backed off. Soon the two of them tumbled to the deck and were struggling on the floor attacking each other with the fragments of the violin.

Then there were footsteps outside the cabin and Anthony Dewitt entered and pulled Blanchard away. Blanchard immediately wrenched himself free from Dewitt's grasp and bolted out the door. Dewitt ran after him. Holmes inhaled slowly as passengers drawn by the fracas gathered outside the cabin. Several members of the Corycian Company entered as he sat up amidst the strings and scraps of wood that had been his violin.

"Are you all right?" Michael Sassanof asked.

Holmes nodded and swallowed, his throat was too sore yet for speech.

"Liar. He nearly made mincemeat of your throat. Up on the berth. Get the ship's doctor in here."

Dewitt returned to the cabin out of breath.

"Gone," he gasped.

"Gone where?" Langdale Pike asked.

"Overboard."

"He jumped overboard?"

"No," Dewitt said finally catching his breath. "He ran up on deck. I followed but he was running like a mad man. He slipped in the dark and fell over the rail. I looked but could see no sign of him. The crew is searching."

"Why did he attack you?" Sassanof asked.

Holmes shook his head.

Why had Blanchard attacked him? Was it because he was investigating Devigne's fall? Was he responsible for Devigne's fall? If so, why?

Dewitt's words stuck in his mind: "a mad man."

Was it just a coincidence that two men who had tried to kill him in the last two years were described as mad men?

In any case he could not continue his questioning now. Sassanof was correct. Despite the attentions of the ship's doctor, Holmes was unable to speak for several days. Otherwise the results of the battle were scratches on his face and hands and bruises around his throat that all healed in a few days and left no scars. But the destruction of the violin inflamed old scars buried deep beneath the surface.

The following night Holmes stood against the rail looking out at the luminous waves in the dark. Somewhere beyond the horizon was England. In his hands he held a box with the remains of the violin. His mother had insisted that he learn how to play while they were living in France. This violin had been purchased there. How long ago? Nine years? His teachers had been excellent. His mother had urged him to practice frequently after they had returned to England and often asked him to play at family gatherings. She had encouraged him to take it with him to Cambridge. Little did she know that within three years after they returned to England he would play it at her funeral, or that three years after that the violin would save his life.

He recalled the incident on the way to her grave. His father had turned him away due the rain. He was right, but somehow her death had seemed less real as a result. He had never gone to the burial plot afterwards, never seen her tombstone. He had said at the time that he felt nothing about her death and that was true. But even a vacuum where little had been noticed before is a change. He lifted the box and dumped the contents overboard, a burial at sea.

For three days afterwards he stayed in his cabin. He sent out notes that excused his absence by his lack of voice, but there was more to it than that. After he regained his voice the first mate came to the cabin to take his statement about the incident. Blanchard was never found and they discovered nothing of interest among his effects. No one knew why Blanchard had attacked him and possibly Devigne. They might never know. However, they had to file a report.

"You are travelling under the name of William Escott. Is that your real name?"

"My name is Sherlock Holmes, and I am a private consulting detective."

He explained in a few more words what had happened and signed the statement the first mate wrote up, but his own words were ringing in his ears. Sherlock Holmes, consulting detective....

He knew what he must do. He had learned many useful things the past two years, but now it was time to move on.

He approached Sassanof.

"I would like a word, in private, if I may," Holmes said.

"Then come along, Mr Escott."

"I'm going to be leaving the company when we arrive in England," he said once they were alone.

"I hope this attack—"

"It is not that."

"Have you received another offer?" Sassanof asked.

"No, sir. I am leaving the theatre altogether. There are other worlds calling me," Holmes said.

"It is hard to argue when you put it like that," Sassanof said.

"You can tell the company when you please, but I would prefer it be after I left. I don't want to make a big show of it," Holmes insisted.

"I'll respect your wishes, Mr Escott. I can't deny that you have made me a pretty penny and I'd like to make some more. But I sense your determination and I don't think your heart would be in it even if I talked you out of going. A man should throw his whole heart and soul into whatever he wants to do."

"Thank you," Holmes said and shook his hand.

The night they reached London, William Escott died. Sherlock Holmes had intended that Escott die that night, but it happened in a different manner than he expected.

The ship had entered the Thames Estuary late at night. It arrived at the London docks in the wee hours of the morning before even a promise of dawn. The rest of the passengers were asleep, but Holmes had been pacing the deck for hours, impatient to be off. While the gangplank would not be put into place for hours, Holmes was willing to sling his bag on his back and descend to the dock via a rope ladder. He left instructions for his trunk to be sent to Montague Street.

He made his way across the slumbering city and let himself into the rooms with the latchkey. He crept through the sitting room in the dark to his room, threw himself upon the bed and fell asleep. Many hours later someone was shaking him awake. He rolled over to blink at his brother Mycroft.

"Good morning, Mycroft," he said shutting his eyes again.

"It's evening," Mycroft said. "I noted your presence this morning but decided not to wake you then."

Sherlock opened his eyes again.

"And why now?" he asked.

"I thought you might want to read this," Mycroft said holding out a newspaper.

There was something about his brother's manner that made Sherlock sit up and take the paper. It was folded back to an interior page and a small paragraph was circled. The headline read: "Actor Drowned." Sherlock frowned and read on: "Police have reported that a body was pulled from the water near the London docks this morning. It seemed to have been in the water a number of hours which made identification difficult. However, sources believe that it may be the body of a young actor by the name of William Escott. He is reported to have left a recently docked ship before dawn and has not been heard of since. The body is of a young man of similar type. The police reported no signs of foul play. 'He had talked of ending his career when we returned to London,' said the manager of the acting company which just returned from a tour of the States, 'but I had no idea that's what he had in mind.' Police are continuing to investigate."

"You do seem to have a talent for making dramatic exits," Mycroft said.

"Even when I don't intend to, it seems," Sherlock said. "I knew nothing of this. I have no idea whether this poor fellow was in the water anywhere near where I passed or whether it was at all close in time. What time is it now?

"Half past six," Mycroft said.

"Thank you for bringing this to my attention. If I write up a note could you see that it is sent while I clean up? I need to set things straight."

"Certainly."

Holmes wrote a note addressed to Lord Cecil at his club.

Heard about Escott. Must speak to you. Meet at the Criterion Bar at half past seven. Bring Sassanof. No one else.

He left it unsigned certain that the young lord's insatiable curiosity would bring him around and left it to his devices to round up the manager. Having handed the note over to his brother who dispatched a servant with it, Sherlock Holmes shaved off his beard and began trimming his hair.

"So Escott dies anyway," Mycroft observed.

"Well, yes, that was my intent, but not quite like this. I'm not going to revive him merely to kill him again. However, I think I owe it to Sassanof to tell him that it wasn't me. There. I think that will do for now. I will have a barber touch it up later."

"You are looking well," Mycroft said.

"Thank you. It has been quite an adventure."

"As your letters seemed to indicate," Mycroft said.

"Now I've saved enough to pay my debt to the college and embark on my real career."

"Sherlock, you might want to read this," Mycroft said handing him a letter.

It was on Sidney Sussex College letterhead and was signed by the Master.

Dear Mr Holmes:

I am writing to acknowledge receipt of the final payment due upon your debt to the college. I wish you success in your endeavours.

The letter was dated the previous January.

"You paid my debt to the college," Sherlock said to Mycroft.

"Yes, I did," Mycroft admitted. "I knew that you would make good on it, but I was concerned that if it were drawn out too long that they would contact Father about it. So I paid it and have been applying the money you have been wiring to me to repay that loan. It has not been any hardship for me. I am well-paid and my needs are few."

Sherlock shook his head.

"Thank you. I will pay the remainder to you tomorrow when I unpack my bags," Sherlock said. "Right now I need to attend my own wake."

Sherlock Holmes pulled the brim of his top hat down over his face as he approached the Criterion. He noted Sassanof and Lord Cecil, who was also known as the actor Langdale Pike, sitting at the bar as he entered. He sidled into a booth in the corner, ordered a pint, and asked the bar maid take them a note. He looked down at his drink as they approached.

They sat down.

"So what's this you need talk about—," Sassanof began.

Holmes looked up.

"I'll be danged," Sassanof finished, sitting down, and staring at Holmes.

Lord Cecil did not miss a beat. He held out his hand.

"Sherlock, it is very good to see you again!" he cried. "It's been a long time, hasn't it?"

"Yes, indeed," Holmes replied with a twinkle in his eye.

"Have you met Sassanof, here?" Langdale said.

"We've met, but I don't think we were properly introduced," Holmes said.

"Ah, well, I can fix that. This is Michael Sassanof, the manager of the Corycian Company. Sassanof, this is my old college chum, Sherlock Holmes."

"Pleased to meet you," said Sassanof still somewhat in shock. "So that wasn't you?" Sassanof asked in a whisper.

"No. I didn't even hear about it until this evening. I slept all day. My brother woke me to show me the paper. I thought I should set things straight."

"We're mighty glad to know it wasn't you. But then who was it?" Sassanof asked.

"I have no idea. I didn't see anyone like that when I left the docks," Holmes said.

"What if the poor bloke has family looking for him—with the corpse misidentified—the face was all bloated and well, nibbled on," Sassanof shuddered.

"I thought about that. I have an idea. You can go back to the police and tell them that you thought of something else that would make it certain. I have a large scar on my ankle from a nasty dog bite during college. See?" Sherlock said exposing the scar where Victor Trevor's dog had bitten him.

"I remember that," Pike said.

"Or Pike can do it. Tell them that you just remembered it and wanted to look to be sure. When they say no, then you can say then it can't be Escott."

"I can do that," Pike said.

"Just don't raise a hue and cry over what became of Escott. He's gone, and I'd rather he stay that way."

"I appreciate you setting us straight," Sassanof said.

"Well, I thought I owed that much to you, and I knew that Pike would recognize me if we ran into each other on the street, and you might, too, since this is how I looked when we first met."

"So now you are going to concentrate on the detective business?" Pike asked.

"Yes," Holmes said.

"Ha. See, there's the solution," Pike said with triumph. "If anyone is too nosey about Escott, we'll tell them that we hired a private detective named Sherlock Holmes who traced him and found out that he just had taken up a new career out of the limelight."

Holmes laughed.

"You do that," Holmes said.

They had a couple more pints and talked for a while longer.

"I should be going. Pike, we should keep in touch. Here's my card," Holmes said giving one to each of them. "I shall keep an eye on your company and be a patron when I can afford it, Sassanof. If you ever know of anyone who needs to consult a detective, I would be pleased with the referral."

With that, Sherlock Holmes tipped his hat and left them and his career in the theatre behind.

There were mysteries to solve.

Chapter 1

Sawdust

"The stage lost a fine actor, even as science lost an
acute reasoner, when he became a specialist in crime."
Dr John H. Watson, "A Scandal in Bohemia"

Sherlock Holmes stepped down from the hansom cab, tossed a coin to the cabby, and mounted the steps to the rooms at 24, Montague Street. It was a pleasant evening for November. There was a slight chill to the air, yet fog had not settled. After nearly a year in America, the commonplace noise, smells, and bustle of London embraced him: Four million people rubbing elbows with nearly as many secrets. How many crimes were being plotted? How many being carried out? He was still learning his way around the great metropolis but he knew this was the time and place to begin his work as a detective.

Mycroft was setting aside his brandy and rising as Sherlock entered and hung his overcoat upon the rack.

"I suppose you will be sitting up?" Mycroft asked.

"Yes. I brought back the evening papers."

"Good night then," Mycroft said and lumbered off to his bedroom.

Sherlock set aside his frock-coat and donned his dressing gown. He lit a pipe and settled upon the sofa to read the papers. Mycroft had adamantly refused to save the London papers while he had been in America. Sherlock had brought back a few clippings for his collection from American papers, including some reports of English crimes. For the rest he would have to resort to the newspaper collection at the British Museum to read up on crimes he had missed while he was out of the country. He would begin by acquainting himself with the fresh criminal news. He began wading through the stack of papers he had brought home.

An hour and a half had passed when someone began hammering at the door. Sherlock jumped up from the sofa and unbolted the door. As he did, Lord Cecil bounded in, much changed from when

Sherlock had left him at the Criterion Bar two hours before. The normally dapper and blasé young lord was wild-eye and dishevelled. He grabbed Sherlock by the lapel.

"You must come at once!" he cried.

"Where? What has happened?" Sherlock Holmes asked.

"To the theatre. It's ablaze!" Lord Cecil cried.

"What?" Sherlock cried.

He tossed aside his dressing gown and took up his frock-coat, overcoat, and hat again. Lord Cecil continued to talk breathlessly as he did so.

"Less than a day after we return to London it goes up in flames? I cannot believe this is a coincidence," the young lord rattled on. "They will talk of the Corycian curse again, but I think there must be some nefarious human agency at work. I want to hire you to find out who, and how—"

Holmes pushed Lord Cecil out the door and locked it behind them. As they stepped outside, an acrid smell attacked Holmes' nose. The smell became more marked as they gained the street. To the northwest he could see an awful orange cloud billowing high into the night sky.

The Corycian Theatre was not far away. The two young men covered the distance on foot, running part of the way. A cab would have been impractical in any case as Tottenham Court Road was clogged with people and vehicles. They fought their way towards the theatre through the gawping crowds being held back by a line of constables. They could see other people standing on rooftops and leaning out of windows in their nightclothes to catch a glimpse of the fire.

As they neared the theatre the heat became oppressive. Sherlock Holmes looked up. No more dramatic sight had ever graced the Corycian's stage than the flames that now towered behind its façade. The men of the Municipal Fire Brigade were helmeted silhouettes against the flames.

The fire was devouring the building and reaching hungrily towards its neighbours. The fire brigade tore at the burning sections with pick axes. They used their steam-powered fire-engines to draw water from hydrants to spray on the theatre from every vantage point.

The roar of the fire, the shouts of the brigade, and the chugging of the fire-engines overwhelmed the murmur of the crowd of spectators.

Sherlock Holmes knew the building well. He noticed the fire seemed to be concentrated on the north side of the building, towards the back, away from the street. Perhaps that was an indication of the point of origin, though it was obvious to him that the fire had long since reached the workrooms at the top of the building. The hiss and crackle of the flames was accented occasionally by the sound of the skylights crashing into the room where the backdrops had been painted. The tints of the paint added odd colours and smells to the conflagration.

While Holmes was observing the fire, Lord Cecil was carrying on a running monologue. The din of the fire, the brigade, and the crowd made it easier for Holmes to ignore his words than to understand them. Finally, Lord Cecil grabbed his sleeve and shouted into his ear.

"Have you been listening?"

"No," Holmes shouted back.

Just then the face of a man in the crowd caught Holmes' attention. Something about it was familiar. As the man turned more directly towards them, Holmes pulled Lord Cecil back among the other spectators.

"Do you know that man?" Holmes yelled at him.

"Which one?"

"The thickset man wearing expensive clothes and massive rings on his fingers with a young woman on each arm."

"Yes, of course," Lord Cecil shouted back.

"Who is he?"

"Baron von Marienburg, Sassanof's partner in the Corycian Company. You've never met him before?"

"I don't believe we were ever introduced."

At least not under that name, Holmes thought. *Where did he remember him from?*

"He's seen you right enough, or rather your alter ego Escott, upon the stage," Lord Cecil continued in a quieter tone next to Holmes' ear. "Though I suppose like everyone else he thinks Escott is dead. I haven't had time to correct that."

"It is best he continues to think so a while longer, and the company as well," Holmes replied, contradicting what he had said a few hours before.

"Why?"

"I've seen him before," Holmes said.

"At the theatre?"

"No," Holmes replied, deep in thought.

Then the link forged in his mind. He remembered where he had seen that face, or at least variations of it, and the context. The context was summed up in a single word. Then he made another connection, and another, and another. His mind was racing. Suddenly the nagging mysteries of the last two years fell together as pieces of a single puzzle. Sawdust! Why had he not understood the significance of the sawdust? There were a few pieces still missing, but the picture was plain, and he knew where he could find some of the missing pieces.

Yet Sherlock Holmes said not a word. He had learned from recent adventures the hazards of sharing his theories with others before he had his case complete. It had nearly cost Jonathan Beckwith his life. Holmes had also learned the importance of gathering the proofs. He knew the police would treat his theories with scepticism until he could bring them evidence. All this went through his mind as Lord Cecil continued to talk. In the light of the fire, Lord Cecil noticed a change in Holmes' countenance. His eyes shone, his jaw set, and a bit of a smile rose to his lips. This was not the brooding actor or the solitary student. This was a different Sherlock Holmes.

"What's come over you?" Lord Cecil asked.

"Sawdust," was all Holmes said before he turned from Lord Cecil and began pushing his way through the crowd away from the burning theatre.

"Holmes!" Lord Cecil called after him.

Holmes ignored him, but someone else watching the fire did not. A tall, flaxen-haired man turned at the name and grabbed Holmes by the arm as he passed.

"Mr Holmes, so I find you at the site of another conflagration," said Inspector Tobias Gregson.

Suddenly the upper story of the building collapsed onto the lower, causing everyone to turn and look, including the Scotland Yard detective, though he did not release his grip on Holmes. The marble columns of the facade now stood taller than the smouldering debris behind, like ruins from ancient Greece. With the remains of the structure now at their level, the men of the brigade redoubled their efforts saturating them with water.

"Mr Holmes, what are you doing here?" Inspector Gregson asked.

"I was brought here by a member of the Corycian Company to investigate the fire," he responded truthfully. "The building was already ablaze when I arrived."

"Last I heard you were in New York," Gregson said, releasing his hold.

"I returned from the States early this morning. What brings you here, Inspector?"

"I don't mind saying 'cause you'll hear soon enough. They found a body in the fire. Been taken off to the morgue."

"In the northeast corner of the building?" Holmes asked.

"Yes. How—"

Holmes whistled.

"That means something to you?" Gregson asked.

"It means you should keep an eye on that tall, thickset man over there. He's not who he says he is. I should be able to tell you more by morning."

With that, Holmes trotted off as fast as he could push his way through the throng, leaving the inspector calling his name after him, as he had left Lord Cecil.

Once clear of the crowd, Sherlock Holmes ran the whole way back to the rooms in Montague Street. In his bedroom, he began to sift through the papers accumulated there. At last, he found what he was looking for. It was a broadside folded in quarters buried among his notes from the trials at the Old Bailey he had observed in September of 1874, just months after deciding to become a detective. He tucked it in his pocket. He consulted a reference book in the sitting room and was off again.

He had to walk back to Oxford Street to find a cab at the hour. But he was soon on his way to Throgmorton Street. According to the book he had consulted, while he was out of the country, the hall of the Worshipful Company of Carpenters had been damaged in a fire and been demolished to make way for a new building. Their records were being stored temporarily at another location. He arrived at that building just before dawn and waited impatiently for the arrival of a clerk who could provide him the information he desired: the address of Lionel Palgrave. Then he was off in the same hansom he had come in, having induced the cabby to stay with a generous tip and promise of more.

Sherlock Holmes arrived at the home of Lionel Palgrave as the professional carpenter was breaking his fast. Holmes was escorted into the breakfast room by a maid. Palgrave was a tall, broad man with a mane of wild, reddish brown hair. He was eagerly consuming a large breakfast of ham, eggs, kippers, and toast.

"Good morning, Mr Escott. I am very surprised to see you. Would you join me?"

"Just a cup of coffee, if you please, Mr Palgrave. While you knew me by my stage name of Escott, my real name is Sherlock Holmes. I am a detective."

Palgrave did not blink an eye.

"Indeed? I rarely cross paths with detectives. What can I do for you, Mr Holmes?"

"You haven't heard of the fire?"

"What fire? I haven't yet opened my paper."

"At the Corycian Theatre."

"Good heavens!"

"It is likely to be a total loss," Holmes said. "The fire brigade was still at work when I left there."

"At least they can't attempt to blame that on me," Palgrave said bitterly, "I have not been near the place in close to a year."

"You were falsely blamed for the failure of the stage floor," Holmes said.

"That's the bloody truth," Palgrave grumbled. "That stage was perfectly sound. Someone sabotaged it. It must have been cut through, but von Marienburg would not allow me go below to prove it. He had me escorted from the building, and threatened to call the police to remove me if I did not leave at once."

"Do you recognize this man?" Holmes asked unfolding the broadsheet he had stowed in his pocket.

"If I'm not mistaken that's the scoundrel himself. Younger and the name's different, but I recognize those eyes."

"I think I can give you an opportunity to vindicate yourself and help bring this man to justice, if you will come to Scotland Yard with me."

"I'd like nothing better. You cannot imagine how such an accusation can destroy a man's opportunities. I've seriously considered an action for slander."

"I believe if you come with me this morning we can settle this without engaging the lawyers."

It was still early morning when Holmes and Palgrave arrived at Scotland Yard. Unfortunately, Inspector Gregson was not in and they were forced to wait. Holmes paced up and down the hall and in time the carpenter grew impatient.

"Mr Holmes, while I want to see justice done and all, I have other business to attend to," Palgrave said.

As Holmes was about to respond, Gregson arrived.

"Inspector, we must speak to you at once," Holmes insisted.

"Well, come along then," he said and they followed him to his office.

"Mr Holmes," the Inspector said as he sat down behind his desk. "I had a mind to send a constable after you last night and have you detained."

"It is as well you did not, for I would have missed an enlightening conversation with Mr Palgrave here this morning."

"Who are you?" Inspector Gregson asked.

"I am Lionel Palgrave. Until a year ago I was chief carpenter at the Corycian Theatre."

"And what have you to do with this murder?" Gregson asked.

"Murder?" Palgrave exclaimed. "Mr Es—Mr Holmes said nothing about murder."

"Once you hear Mr Palgrave's story you will understand the connection," Holmes said, "and why I need to get into the ruins of the theatre."

"Mr Holmes—" the inspector began.

"It is vitally important that it be done before the evidence is destroyed," Holmes insisted.

"And this will explain your comments about the gentleman last night?"

"Yes, though it is likely that we will need to visit Pentonville before you will be completely satisfied."

"Mr Holmes, if you continue to speak in this manner, you are more likely to visit Bedlam," Inspector Gregson said.

As he was speaking there was a knock at the office door.

"Come in!"

The door opened and a constable stepped in.

"I'm sorry, sir, but his lordship insisted on seeing you at once."

Lord Cecil strode from behind in his most aristocratic attire. The constable bowed out shutting the door behind him. Inspector Gregson stood. Lord Cecil looked at an empty chair and chose to remain standing, but he gestured with his handkerchief for the Inspector to sit, and dropped his visiting card upon the desk.

"How may I help you, your lordship?" Gregson asked as he retrieved the card.

Lord Cecil gave the Scotland Yarder his most condescending look.

"I was told I could find Mr Holmes here," nodding Holmes' direction.

Inspector Gregson squinted at him.

"Your lordship was at the theatre fire last night."

"Yes. I brought Mr Holmes there, though I lost him in the crowd. I am familiar with his work in other cases. I have an interest in the Corycian theatre and I hired Mr Holmes to look into the fire."

"Begging your pardon, your lordship," Inspector Gregson said. "It would be best to leave such matters to the professionals."

"I have every confidence in Mr Holmes' superior abilities. He may seem a bit mad at times, but there is method in it. I hope that

Scotland Yard will extend every courtesy to him."

"You can be assured we will give him all due respect."

"Very good."

"We were about to hear Mr Palgrave tell what he knows of the matter," Holmes said.

"Then proceed," Lord Cecil said with of wave of his hand, privately imagining what a grand tale this would make to share at his club.

Now all eyes turned back to Lionel Palgrave who had watched this performance with wide eyes, but said nothing. He recognized Lord Cecil as the actor he knew as Langdale Pike, but who was he to say that any of the preceding was not true? He'd heard rumours before that Pike was from a noble family. With actors one never knew.

Inspector Gregson sighed at the irregularity of it all, but decided to proceed.

"Mr Palgrave, tell us your story."

"When Mr Sassanof and Baron von Marienburg decided to reopen the Corycian Theatre as part of their new venture, they hired me to evaluate the theatre and bring in men to repair and reconstruct it as necessary. It was a lovely old theatre and some parts were very sound, the proscenium and the stage especially, no sign of insects or rot there. Afterwards I stayed on as chief carpenter because they were going to need elaborate set pieces for their productions and it was steady work.

"No doubt you heard the rubbish in the newspapers of a curse on the theatre last year. I can't speak to all of the things that happened, but I know about some of them. Juliet's balcony, for instance. That was no accident or 'curse.' I examined the remains of the balcony afterwards. I tried to warn Mr Sassanof that it was sabotage. The wood was cut to weaken the structure. It would only hold a person's weight for a few minutes. He thought I was trying to cover for shoddy work."

"Did you have a suspect?" Inspector Gregson asked.

"Could have been any one of the workmen, or one of the stage hands. Anyone with a saw could have done it, though it would take an experienced man to do it so it would hold up for a while."

"Could it have been someone from outside the theatre?" Gregson asked. "Could someone have broken in while the theatre was closed and done it?"

"No," Holmes said shaking his head. "It could only have been done between rehearsals and the performance. Frank would not have allowed a stranger in during that time."

"Who is Frank?" Gregson asked.

"He was the guard at the stage door."

"Yes, well, that's another mystery. We have been unable to locate him," Inspector Gregson said.

"Perhaps he was involved?" Palgrave asked.

"I doubt it," Holmes said.

"Who do you suspect, Mr Holmes?"

"Walter Blanchard," Holmes said.

"Who is he?" the inspector asked, making a note of the name.

"An assistant carpenter," Palgrave said. "He certainly could have done it, but why would he?"

"I think we need to speak to Mr Blanchard to find out," Gregson said.

"You can't," Holmes said.

"Why is that, Mr Holmes?" the inspector asked.

"Because he fell overboard in the middle of the Atlantic after making a murderous attack upon me."

The inspector shook his head.

"Now you are back in the thick of it, Mr Holmes. Why were you on a ship with this Mr Blanchard and why would he attack you? Did you suspect him of something else?"

"I suspected everyone. There had been two previous attacks on members of the Corycian Company on board the ship. I was attempting to narrow down the suspects at the time."

"You believe that is why he attacked you?"

"In part. I think he had a broader motive. He was part of a scheme that connects to the firing of the theatre last night."

"Which may be related to the murder?"

"Murder?" Lord Cecil exclaimed, "Connected to the fire? I've heard nothing."

"It missed the morning papers. I suspect they will get wind of it soon. A body was found by the fire brigade. It has been identified as the stage manager, Michael Sassanof," the inspector explained.

"Good heavens!" Lord Cecil cried.

Palgrave whistled.

"Have they found his valise?" Holmes asked.

"Not that I have heard. What did it look like?"

"It was a black valise with chrome hinges and corners," Holmes said.

"You think it might have been at the theatre?"

"It might have been there or at his home. It is also possible Sassanof deposited it with his bank."

"What was in this valise?"

"Thousands of U.S. dollars," Holmes said.

"Indeed? We return to the States," Inspector Gregson said with raised eyebrows. "You did not answer my question as to why you were on the ship with Mr Blanchard."

"Because I was a member of the Corycian Company which was returning from a tour of the States."

"Your position with the company?"

"I was an actor. I told Mr Sassanof before we made port that I was leaving the company when we reached London."

"That sounds familiar. We have not been idle, Mr Holmes. We have been collecting information about this company since last night."

Inspector shuffled some papers on his desk.

"Here it is. A report about a drowning in which Mr Sassanof is quoted as saying that an actor named Escott had said he was leaving the company and was later found drowned. Is that a coincidence, Mr Holmes?"

"Yes and no," Holmes said.

"Which is it, Mr Holmes?" Gregson asked impatiently.

"I was performing under the stage name of William Escott, as Lord Cecil and Mr Palgrave can attest."

"Yes, that is true," Lord Cecil confirmed.

"Obviously the drowned man was not me. That was a mistake. I left the ship shortly after it docked and went to my brother's rooms. He can attest that I was there—"

"Mr Sherriford or Mr Mycroft?"

"Mycroft. I knew nothing of the misidentification until yesterday evening. I met with Lord Cecil and Mr Sassanof to explain."

"I confirm that, inspector," Lord Cecil said. "We agreed to inform the police of the error in the morning. This morning, in fact."

"I will see that is done. But there is another matter, Mr Holmes."

The Inspector picked up another paper.

"Here is a complaint sworn out by a Mr Sherlock Holmes against a John Travis for attacking him with a knife outside the Corycian Theatre on two occasions."

"Yes, and Lord Cecil was present on both those occasions as well."

"Yes, Travis is a nasty drunkard," Lord Cecil confirmed.

"Perhaps, Mr Holmes, you decided to quit the theatre for a less dangerous occupation?"

Sherlock Holmes laughed.

"No, I decided to concentrate on my true calling."

"Being the detection of criminals?"

"Yes."

Inspected Gregson snorted, but continued with his questions.

"How was Mr Travis connected with the theatre?"

"He had been an actor," Lord Cecil said, "until Mr Sassanof gave him notice."

"Why did he attack Mr Holmes rather than Mr Sassanof?"

"Because Mr Holmes had taken his roles," Lord Cecil responded.

"I think he was part of a fraudulent scheme which would fail if the Corycian Company made a profit," Holmes said. "That gave him another motive for attacking me."

"A scheme involving the gentleman you indicated last night?"

"Yes."

"And the deceased Mr Blanchard?"

"Yes."

"What is the nature of that scheme, Mr Holmes?"

"The man I directed you to is a confidence trickster with a long criminal history who was defrauding the investors in the Corycian Company."

"Baron von Marienburg?" Lord Cecil asked with surprise.

"Yes," Holmes replied.

"That is a serious accusation, Mr Holmes," Inspector Gregson said.

Sherlock Holmes drew the broadside from his pocket and unfolded it. In the centre was a sketch of a man surrounded on both sides by drawings with different hair and whiskers. In large letters above said FRAUD. The words below described how this man had defrauded a widow by courting her, convincing her to hand over funds for investment, and running off with her jewels. It also listed prior convictions for theft and confidence games. The name on it was Reginald Dowson, also known as Royal Reggie.

"Change the glasses and add three stone and there is your 'Baron,'" Holmes said.

Lord Cecil took the paper from him and examined it.

"Good heavens, there is a strong likeness," he said.

"I thought the same," Palgrave said.

Inspector Gregson took the broadsheet and scowled at it. He rang for a constable and sent for the criminal register books containing Dowson's records.

"Mr Holmes' accusation does not surprise me," Palgrave said. "That 'baron,' or whatever he is, is a sneaky, low worm of a man. He dismissed me on a false accusation. I've been to solicitors about it, but they've told me there wasn't enough to take him to law."

"What was this false accusation?"

"That I failed to notice a weakness in the stage floor that led to the collapse of a section of it during a performance. He wouldn't even allow me to go below to inspect the hole. He had me escorted from the building when I suggested it and threatened to call the police."

"I witnessed that argument," Lord Cecil said. "I told you about it, Holmes."

"Not the details!" Holmes exclaimed. "If I had known the exact words exchanged I might have known all."

"Inspector, Lord Cecil and I were both present when the stage collapsed," Holmes said.

"Yes, I shall never forget," Lord Cecil said. "There were tremors on the stage and then Hallows, Leydon, and Wyatt vanished in a cloud of sawdust."

"Sawdust?!" Palgrave exclaimed.

"Yes, sawdust! I saw it, too," Holmes agreed. "I did not realize the significance until last night."

"What is the significance of sawdust?" Inspector Gregson asked.

"There should have been no sawdust," Palgrave said. "Sawdust, as the name implies, is created by the saw biting into wood. Some insects like termites can create similar debris, but old, rotten, or weak wood cracks and splinters. It does not create sawdust. The stage had been sound. I stake my reputation on it. It had been in place for decades. We replaced a few boards on the stage after the balcony collapsed and scarred them, but all that had been cleaned by the stagehands. There should have been no sawdust near the stage."

"I saw sawdust when the balcony collapsed as well," Holmes said.

"I did, too, and I saw the cuts in the wood. I warned Sassanof," Palgrave said.

"But if the stage was rebuilt while the company was on tour, wouldn't all the evidence have been destroyed?" Lord Cecil asked.

"I don't believe the stage was rebuilt," Holmes said. "I believe the fire was set to hide that fact, as well as Sassanof's murder. That's why it happened yesterday, before any of the company set foot in the theatre. Sassanof must have met von Marienburg there. How was he killed?"

"Cracked in the skull with something," Inspector Gregson said. "Police surgeon said he was dead before the fire began."

"I think you will find the fire started in Sassanof's office."

"That has yet to be determined."

"If the theatre was not repaired, what did von Marienburg do with all the money?" Lord Cecil asked.

"Undoubtedly stole it," Holmes said. "That is why we need access to the ruins. From what I saw last night it seemed likely that the fire was set in Sassanof's office and spread first to the work rooms above. I believe the stage may still be intact under the debris. If we can reach the stairs that go under the stage, Mr Palgrave could assess its status. If the hole is still there, then we have cause to charge the 'baron' with fraud and murder."

"These are very deep waters, Mr Holmes," Inspector Gregson said.

He was not yet convinced, but Holmes had supplied enough information to require further investigation.

When the constable brought the criminal registry books, Gregson also gave him a note addressed to Captain Eyre Massey Shaw, the Chief of the Metropolitan Fire Brigade, requesting he meet them near the remains of the theatre in an hour.

"See that this is delivered straight away."

The two books the constable had brought were the smaller, duplicate volumes from the Habitual Criminals Registry. The master files were immense brown albums each containing 6,000 photographs which never left the registry rooms. Hundreds of thousands of records were kept in the registry, mostly illustrated by full and side face photographs, kept up-to-date with scrupulous care. These smaller volumes, containing only five hundred records each, were used by detectives working with witnesses to identify criminals.

Inspector Gregson leafed through the books until he found Dowson's photograph taken at the end of his most recent stay in prison. It was similar to that on the broadsheet and similar to the man he had seen last night, similar enough to question him. But murder was a more serious charge, and the evidence, if there was any, in the ruins of the theatre was not likely to last.

"There does seem to be some basis to your suspicions that this 'Baron' and this Dowson may be one and the same. However, we do need to examine the theatre before we proceed further. Mr Palgrave, I'd appreciate it if you would come along with me."

16

Chapter 2

The Stage

"This, then, is the stage upon which tragedy has been played."
Sherlock Holmes, *The Hound of the Baskervilles*

Holmes shared a cab from Scotland Yard to the theatre with Lord Cecil.

"I am still in shock," Lord Cecil said. "We were with Sassanof a short time before."

"Yes," Holmes said grimly.

"Here," Lord Cecil said, drawing a purse from his frock-coat and handing it to Holmes.

"What is this?"

"I was serious about hiring you," Lord Cecil said.

"It is not necessary. I will follow this to the end in any case," Holmes said.

"You may have resigned your position with the Corycian Company, but this fire has deprived me of mine. It does not put me in any financial hardship, but I take it personally. And now, Sassanof—Take it. You have done much already to throw light on the matter. You need to become accustomed to working for clients if that is how you intend to earn your bread and cheese. Let me be the first."

The hansom stopped as close as it could to the remains of the theatre and they descended. In some ways the view was more traumatic in the light of day than it had been the night before. The flames were gone. The stone façade and marbled front foyer still stood, stained with soot and covered with ash. The stone Muses stood like chief mourners covered in cloaks of ash. Beyond them was a tangled mass of charred wood and twisted pipes. More of the south side of the building stood than the north, suggesting that the fire had started on the north side, as Holmes had told them in the inspector's office.

Members of the fire brigade still wandered about the ruins with their pickaxes, looking for embers. They would not leave until they were certain that the fire would not reignite. Directing them was a tall, thin man in a crisp uniform dotted with ash, and a silver helmet on his head.

"That's Captain Eyre Massey Shaw," Lord Cecil said. "He is a friend of Bertie's."

"The Prince?"

"Indeed. Quite the social darling. Did you see the picture Vanity Fair published of him a few years ago? He completely reorganized the brigade. I suppose the entire area could have burned if it were not for some of his innovations."

Inspector Gregson arrived shortly thereafter with Palgrave and a few constables in tow. Holmes and Lord Cecil approached the carriage as it arrived. The Fire Brigade Chief joined them.

On closer inspection, Captain Eyre Massey Shaw was a remarkable man. He was tall and thin though quite muscular. He had deep-set, hooded eyes over a razor-sharp nose, topping a straggly moustache and goatee, which would have given him a harsh aspect if not for the smile partially hidden underneath. He pulled off heavy gloves as he greeted them.

"Inspector Gregson?" Captain Shaw said.

"Yes," Gregson said taking his hand.

"I've been here since last night. Your message was forwarded to me from headquarters. How may I be of assistance?"

"Captain Massey Shaw, may I introduce, Mr Lionel Palgrave."

"Sir," Shaw said shaking Palgrave's hand then turning to the person next to him. "I've met the loquacious Lord Cecil before."

Lord Cecil laughed.

"And so you may again, perhaps under better circumstances, Eyre."

"And this is Mr Sherlock Holmes," the inspector said.

They shook hands.

"Now, gentlemen, how may I help you?" Shaw asked.

Inspector Gregson responded.

"Captain, Mr Palgrave here used to be the chief carpenter of the theatre. He and these young men believe there is evidence in the lower level of the theatre that would provide a motive for the fire and the murder of the stage manager. They are concerned that the evidence will be destroyed. I have here a warrant to search the ruins."

"Inspector, I am not certain the ruins are safe to be searched," Shaw said. "The lower levels are undoubtedly flooded with the water poured on the fire. We have not yet pumped them out. The structures still standing could collapse, and there is the danger of reignition."

"I accept that there is some risk involved but we also risk allowing a murderer to go free."

Captain Shaw looked at the group.

Lord Cecil threw up his hands and backed away.

"Not me. I shall leave the hazardous work to others."

That left the Inspector, the carpenter, and Holmes.

"If there is fraud involved the insurance companies will want to know about it as well," Captain Shaw said thoughtfully.

Holmes knew that fees and rates paid by insurance companies supported the fire brigade.

"There are some members of the salvage brigade working here. I'll recruit a few of them to go with us. You must allow me and the salvagers to lead."

They donned mackintoshes, rubber boots, and helmets provided by the salvage brigade. They approached from the alley to the south of the building, as the actors were accustomed to do. The frame of the stage door still stood, though the door was stained and pocked. The salvagers wedged the door open and the group passed cautiously through the frame. They worked their way inward, moving obstacles as necessary. Palgrave directed them to where the door should be to the stairs that led below the stage. The salvagers cleared charred beams and debris that had fallen from above to reach it. They forced the door open. Shaw aimed his light down. The stairs were clear.

They descended into what now seemed to be a drenched cellar. Water stood several inches high on the floor and still dripped from above. They flashed their lights right and left, but mostly above their heads. If the stage had been damaged in the fire, it was possible it could collapse on them. But what they saw above were heavy oak beams which showed no sign of charring. The beams were drenched and water continued to drip from them, but they looked sturdy enough.

"See, gentlemen, there is no rot here, no signs of termites or other insects," Mr Palgrave said. "This is good solid oak that withstood even the collapse of the upper floors on top of it."

They sloshed forward. Besides the water, the space they crossed seemed mostly clear from debris. They continued to occasionally shine their lights up, checking the condition of the stage floor above them, which supported the theory that the stage floor was sound, as it also supporting the charred remains of the theatre above their heads. Holmes aimed his light at the water they were wading through.

"Sawdust," he said as he saw some float by.

"Proves nothing," the inspector said. "Could be from reconstruction."

Holmes pressed forward ahead of the others until his foot struck something under the water. He stopped. He pointed his light down and then ahead. Before him was a conical litter of debris. It was composed of ropes, pulleys, curtains, and bits of wood and gas piping. He followed the pile upward with his light to where it pierced the stage.

"I think this demonstrates that the hole in the stage was never repaired," he said.

"How do we know that it wasn't caused by the fire?" Inspector Gregson asked coming up behind him.

"That determination requires a closer inspection," Captain Shaw said.

The Fire Brigade Chief sent a member of the salvage brigade back up for a ladder. A couple of members of the fire brigade came down with him carrying one. At the direction of the chief, they cleared a space at the edge of the debris and set up the ladder. Chief Shaw scrambled up. He had the men move the ladder a few times as he continued his examination. Palgrave watched with earnest and Holmes waited impatiently.

"This hole was not caused by fire," Chief Shaw said as he examined the wood. "There is no charring on the floor like you would expect if fire had caused the collapse. It is clear that the wood was cut partially through a number of months ago and splintered the rest of the way."

"A year ago?" Holmes asked

"Quite likely," Captain Shaw said.

"The pile of debris fell through the existing hole during the fire last night," Holmes said.

"Yes."

"Then why didn't it set fire to the stage?" Inspector Gregson asked.

"The fire started above in Sassanof's office," Holmes said, "and the proscenium held up until the fire brigade was actively fighting the fire. In fact, it is likely you and I witnessed its collapse when we were talking last night. By then the stage area had been so soaked by the efforts of the fire brigade that the proscenium was not on fire when it fell. It was the weight from the burnt upper stories that brought it down rather than the fire itself."

"That is quite astute of you, young man," Captain Shaw said. "I don't know that I could have described it any better."

"Allow me a look," Palgrave said.

The fire chief came down the ladder and Palgrave climbed up. He came down in a few minutes satisfied with his vindication.

"There is no doubt in my mind that this hole through the stage was not caused by fire and is at least a year old. You can see the saw marks," he said.

Sherlock Holmes climbed the ladder to see for himself.

Gregson declined.

"Don't care for ladders. I have the word of two experts that this hole through the stage was not caused by the fire and is at least a year old. Is it also your opinion that this was sabotage?"

"It is obvious that someone intentionally cut through the boards around the hole. They broke the rest of the way when there was enough weight on them," Palgrave said.

"I agree with that assessment," Shaw said.

"I will need you gentlemen to sign statements to that effect."

"Gladly," Palgrave said.

"You may be called to testify at the inquest."

"Certainly," the carpenter assented. He was eager to air his vindication in a public forum.

The fire chief assented as well.

Holmes came down satisfied that the evidence confirmed his theory. The ladder was taken down and the men made their way back as they had come.

After they exited the stage door, they walked down the alley to the street, and began to shed their wet outer garments. Sherlock Holmes removed his, and then looked across the street to where Lord Cecil awaited their news. As their eyes met, the young lord nodded over to his left. Holmes saw the rotund man much on their minds helping a tiny frail woman in fur and lace down from her carriage. The man and the woman turned toward the ruins of the theatre and saw their little group. It was not Holmes von Marienburg locked eyes with, but Palgrave. The "Baron" dropped the woman's arm and took to his heels with Holmes in hot pursuit. Holmes heard the screech of police whistles behind him as Gregson realized what was afoot. The portly man could not outrun the young detective. Holmes tackled him and they were shortly surrounded by constables with Inspector Gregson coming up behind.

As Holmes stood up, he said, "Inspector, allow me to introduce you to Baron von Marienburg, also known as Reginald Dowson, or more familiarly 'Royal Reggie.'"

As "Baron" Dowson stood and dusted himself off, he squinted at Holmes.

"Escott? I thought you were dead," he said.

"T'would've been better for you if he had been," Inspector Gregson said. "I am Inspector Gregson of the Metropolitan Police and you are under arrest—"

"You would allow this impertinent young man to assault me and slander me and then you arrest me?" Dowson thundered.

"—on the charge of murder and arson, and a few other things we might add later," Gregson finished. "Not that they matter since murder will get you the rope."

"I assure you, Inspector, this is all a mistake," Dowson attempting reclaim his charm.

"That's for the law to decide. I must warn you that anything you say will be taken down and used against you."

Gregson directed the constables to take von Marienburg or

Dowson, or whoever he was, to the Bow Street Station. Holmes returned to the road before the ruins of the theatre. The woman that he had seen with Dowson was now on Lord Cecil's arm. She was short and frail with paper-thin, wrinkled skin, silver hair disappearing into a mink hat, and tiny hands covered with kid gloves were just visible in mink sleeves edged with lace.

"Where did the Baron run off to?" she was asking.

"The police have arrested him," Holmes said as he approached.

She turned watery blue eyes towards him.

"Arrested? Whatever for? And who are you?"

"Lady Lewina, I would like to present Mr Sherlock Holmes. Mr Holmes, Lady Lewina, Dowager Duchess of Exeter," Lord Cecil introduced them.

"Your Grace," Holmes said, removing his hat and inclining his head. "I am afraid they have arrested him for murder."

"Did you find what you expected?" Lord Cecil asked him.

"We did."

"Oh, Mr Holmes, come closer," Lady Lewina said, "Let me see you. My eyes are not as good as they once were and I don't have my opera glasses with me. Why surely you are Mr Escott without the beard?"

"Yes, m'lady, but I beg you keep my secret for I have left the theatre."

"Not dead?"

"No, quite alive," he responded.

"Such things that go on in the theatre. Oh, Cecil, don't think you fooled me acting under that silly name. I've known you since you were in skirts. When are you going to stop this foolishness and make up with your father?"

"I think we will need to leave where my foolishness lies to another day. Mr Holmes is a detective."

"A policeman?"

"No, no, not a policeman. A private detective," Cecil said, "I've hired him to look into the fire at the theatre."

"How good of you! It is perfectly dreadful. All that money I invested with the Baron gone up in flames."

"So you invested in the theatre?" asked Inspector Gregson as he approached.

"This is Inspector Gregson of Scotland Yard," Lord Cecil said. "He is a policeman. Inspector Gregson may I present Lady Lewina, Dowager Duchess of Exeter."

"Your Grace," Gregson said.

The dowager duchess scowled at Inspector Gregson and responded to Lord Cecil as if he had asked the question.

"Indeed I did. A good investment it seemed. Very good actors, but they encountered so much bad luck. Of course, you know all that, Cecil."

"When they had bad luck, the Baron came to you for more money?" Holmes asked.

"Yes, of course, he did. I had to protect my investment. The Baron was always so sweet, so apologetic, and full of pity for those young actors he was helping. Of course, he would do it all himself if it wasn't for all his funds being tied up in that land dispute on the Continent. Lawyers can just drain away your income."

"Did he say where the land was?" Holmes asked.

"Where? Oh, I don't remember. Near his ancestral estate, most likely," she responded with a wave of her hand like dismissing a fly. "I don't see what all this has to do with the awful fire."

"Mr Holmes is just very inquisitive," Cecil interjected.

"I suppose that is a good trait for a detective, as long as he doesn't poke about in people's personal business. I didn't ask about where your family came from, Mr Holmes."

"His family has an estate in Yorkshire, your Grace. It is a very old estate," Lord Cecil responded.

"Well, then," the duchess responded as if that settled everything.

"My apologies, Duchess," Holmes said. "One last little question, not to pry too much, but we were trying to estimate how great the loss was—for the insurers, you understand—do you recall how much you invested?"

"Well, no, not offhand. My secretary would know. Hundreds, probably, nothing serious. More after the floor collapsed."

"Thank you."

"It is such a shock," she said shaking her head. "The theatre gone. The baron arrested. Escort me home, Cecil, won't you?"

"Most certainly."

The young lord assisted the duchess into her carriage and boarded after her.

Holmes turned to Inspector Gregson as the carriage pulled away.

"We will speak to her secretary," Gregson said.

"It is likely there were other investors. However, we ought to go to Pentonville to interview John Travis."

"The man who attempted to stab you outside the theatre?" Gregson asked.

"Yes."

"You think he knows something about this business?"

"Yes."

"Perhaps along the way you can explain to me better how you got mixed up in all this before I decide we need a cell for you too."

The hansom Holmes and Lord Cecil had arrived in was still waiting at the curb not far from where they stood. Holmes and the Inspector climbed aboard and directed the driver to Pentonville Prison. With Tottenham Court Road still partially blocked by the Fire Brigade, the driver turned the cab about and headed for Oxford Street then in to Grays Inn Road, northward to Kings Cross and over Regent's Canal with its crowd of factory chimneys, then past a series of suburban terraces, with little strips of garden, or grass-plots in front of each house. Immediately beyond the railway viaduct stretching across the road was a large building walled all round. At the front stood a tall gateway jutting from the main entrance of the building with a little square clock-tower just peeping up behind it. The front contained a number of signs leaving no doubt that this is Pentonville Prison.

They descended from the hansom and Inspector Gregson pulled a bell. He had been here a number of times. The gateway door was opened by a warder. He wore a single-breasted, police-like frock-coat, with a bright brass crown bulging from its stiff, stand-up collar. Around his waist was a broad leather strap holding a shiny cartouche-box at his back. The Scotland Yard inspector explained their purpose. The warder examined their credentials and had them sign the visitor's log before ushering them across a small paved court-yard, and up a broad flight of stone steps to the large glass door leading to the passage to the prison itself.

As they went through each door it was locked behind them. Inside the prison they were led to the interview room at the end of a passage. It was a small room, without any furniture other than a little desk and a few chairs.

On the inside, Pentonville Prison did not fit the public's imagination of a prison. The part Holmes walked through looked like any government office: clean and utilitarian. Through the window of the interview room, he could see figures silhouetted against a bright light.

"Where does that corridor lead?" he asked Inspector Gregson.

Gregson stood up and came to the window to look out.

"That's the centre corridor. The end of it is the middle of the prison. Four other corridors radiate from the centre like spokes on a wheel. They are each three stories high and lit by skylights."

"That's why they seem so bright from here."

"Saves a lot of money on lighting, I hear," Gregson said as he sat down again.

Sherlock Holmes saw two figures starting to separate from the light as they came toward the room. One was a warder. The other was a prisoner dressed in brown flannels. His hair was cropped short and he was remarkably sober, but it was John Travis.

Holmes leaned against the wall as the door opened and shut.

Travis looked around the room, spying the inspector first and then Holmes.

"What are you doing here?" Travis challenged Holmes. "Aren't satisfied with stealing my situation and throwing me in prison?"

"There was more to it than that," Holmes said.

"Don't know what you mean," Travis said as he sat down.

"Dowson offered you money to attack me, didn't he?" Holmes said.

"Don't know any Dowson," Travis said.

"He called himself Baron von Marienburg," Holmes replied.

"What if he did? Why should I tell you? What's his complaint with you?"

"Nothing personal at that time," Holmes said. "It was an attempt to stop the successful run of *Richard III*."

"Dowson's not very fond of you now," Inspector Gregson said to Holmes.

"Why's that?" Travis said.

"Because I turned him over to Scotland Yard," Holmes said.

"What for?"

"Murder and arson for starters," Gregson said.

"Murder? Him? He hasn't the nerve to do anything himself."

"Tell us about him," Gregson said, "and we will give you a good character with the warden. Might get you out of here sooner."

Sherlock Holmes was not especially keen on assisting with the early release of the man who had twice tried to stab him, but Travis was due to be released in a number of months in any case and his evidence could fill in the gaps.

"You are from Scotland Yard?" Travis asked nodding toward Gregson.

"Yes, Inspector Gregson."

"I don't know why I shouldn't. He's done no good to me since. Didn't even offer to bail me out before my trial. The Baron—didn't know what his real name was and didn't care—he said it was a quick way to earn a few quid. He said we could keep draining it for a year or two and then we'd just let it fold. He considered Sassanof an excellent dupe because he really believed that he could make a successful company from that motley crew. The Baron didn't believe it, but that was part of the plan. As long as the plays failed the investors would not expect their money back. They had no idea where it was going, which was mostly into the Baron's pocket. I was in it from the start and the Baron was slipping me some banknotes as we were doing the rehearsals. It just couldn't be too good, you understand?"

"All that cash in your pocket was too much of a temptation to stay off the bottle," the inspector said.

"In any case, once I got fired I wasn't very useful to the Baron, or anyone else for that matter, because I had a hard time getting another job in the theatre after that. Then one day he sends me a note and says he has a job for me. By then I was ready to do anything just for a drink, which he supplied when we met. He told me how you'd taken over my role as Tybalt and all my other roles, and were making quite a name for yourself. He convinced me all that success should have been mine. Maybe he got me riled up into thinking that was true, but I should have known better. He did not hide his own motivations. I knew the confidence game depended on the plays failing and you were helping them succeed. If I had been the one reaping the curtain calls he would have found a way to stop me, too. But the drink was doing the thinking by then and he said I could get paid while getting my revenge. He told me that you were often one of the last actors out of the theatre at night. I am not sure how he knew that. He may have had a member of the stage crew working with him. He gave me the knife. He gave me an advance and promised a lot more afterward. He even promised to get me out if the police nabbed me, but here I am."

"Did he ever mention how he planned to end the game and get away without getting caught? Holmes asked.

"No."

"Did he mention any plan to kill Sassanof or to burn down the theatre?" Inspector Gregson asked.

"No. I don't believe he could kill a man in cold blood, but if he was cornered he might do anything."

"Thank you for your cooperation," Inspector Gregson said.

"You'll talk to the warden?"

"I'll speak to him."

Inspector Gregson did speak to governor of the prison before they left Pentonville. However, everything Travis told them had to be verified.

From the Pentonville Prison they headed to the West End via Marylebone Road.

A maid answered when they rang the bell at Exeter House. While it was undoubtedly a more fashionable address than the Pentonville Prison, it bore much more resemblance to a feudal keep than the prison had. On the outside the old grey stone was unbroken by ironwork or other decoration. Inside it was covered with heavy tapestries of medieval battles. If he had been told there was a dungeon with shackles on the wall, Holmes would not have been surprised. When the maid returned, the strawberry blond head of Lord Cecil bobbed along behind her.

"I have promised Lady Lewina to take care of everything," Lord Cecil explained. "The excitement has given her a headache. If you could take their coats and hats, Mary?" He smiled brightly at the maid. One of the secrets to Lord Cecil's endless supply of gossip was maintaining good will with the servants at all the houses he visited. The house staff was nearly invisible to people in the upper echelons of society and they spoke freely before them. But Lord Cecil knew that servants talk.

As the maid moved off he lowered his voice and spoke to Gregson and Holmes confidentially.

"I have three names for you. Lady Lewina said she introduced them to the 'baron' and they may also have invested."

"Very good, sir. Thank you," Inspector Gregson said.

A middle aged woman was coming down the hallway. Lord Cecil addressed her.

"Meredith, these gentlemen are Inspector Gregson of Scotland Yard and Mr Sherlock Holmes. The Duchess authorized you to speak to them regarding her investment in the Corycian Theatre. If you could take them to your desk and give them some understanding of how much she invested."

"And when the investments were made," Holmes interjected.

"That would be very helpful," Inspector Gregson said.

"Come this way, gentlemen," the secretary said.

A half hour with the secretary was all that was necessary to determine that the duchess had invest thousands of pounds in the theatre and that the timing had coincided with the "accidents" publicly attributed to the curse.

"Once again, Mr Holmes," Inspector Gregson said as they left the old mansion, "you have helped me unravel a case that was much deeper than it initially seemed. We would probably have gotten there eventually but your insights shed light on details faster. There are still some loose threads like the missing doorman and the missing valise.

We will keep working on those details. I can't speak for the prosecutors, but I think we have a nice case against Dowson already."

"Thank you, Inspector," Holmes said.

The hansom dropped Holmes off at Montague Street and then continued on to Scotland Yard.

Sherlock Holmes picked up a newspaper from a boy on the street. He entered the flat and settled down in the sitting room to read it. The housekeeper had just come in to tell him that his brother would be late returning home and ask when he would like his supper when a telegraph boy knocked on the door.

"If you could hold for a moment," Holmes said as he tore open the wire and read it.

Join me at my club at 8 and explain it all to me, it said.

As peremptory as the summons seemed, it was true that Lord Cecil was his client.

"Mrs Denton, Lord Cecil has invited me to join him at his club so you needn't trouble yourself about my supper."

"Very good, sir," the housekeeper said and left.

Holmes wrote a short reply on a form and gave it to the boy with payment. He had a bit of time to wash and change before hunting up a cab to take him to Lord Cecil's club.

Sherlock Holmes remembered when he first mounted the steps to the club in January of 1875 for the breakfast meeting that would lead to his nearly two-year career on the stage. He had passed through the double doors a few times since then, once encountering Henry Irving and other actors from the Lyceum. The interior was as luxurious as ever, but familiarity made it a less impressive experience than that first time.

The hall porter recognized him and led him to the dining room lined with the portraits of great men who had been members. Lord Cecil reigned over a table. The courses had been ordered, and arrived in a timely fashion. As the first course arrived Sherlock Holmes realized he was very hungry. The solution to the Corycian mysteries had given him an appetite that he had not had in weeks. He also answered Lord Cecil's questions between bites.

"I thoroughly enjoyed the time in the inspector's office," Lord

Cecil began.

"The snooty aristocrat remains your best role," Holmes said.

"Not surprising, since I was trained for it from birth. I don't believe I've met a member of the Yard before. Inspector Gregson seemed to know you. How did you come to meet?"

"We met when my nephews were kidnapped. He was in charge of that case."

"Ah. Well, as I understand it—correct me if I err—your theory is that this Dowson began a confidence game as Baron von Marienburg that involved draining funds from investors in the Corycian Company."

"Correct."

"Was Sassanof involved?"

Holmes shook his head.

"No. I believe that Sassanof was devoted to the theatre. I think that Dowson met Sassanof somewhere and they started up a conversation about the theatre and Sassanof's dreams of starting a new company. Dowson may have been working on another scheme at the time or casting about for a mark. He soon recognized the value of Sassanof's story. He tested it on a few of the more gullible marks and found them immediately interested in investing."

"Are the other names I gave Inspector Gregson useful?"

"Yes. Gregson and his men will follow up on them."

"What difference does it make now if he is to be hanged for Sassanof's murder?"

"Gregson has doubts that we have enough to convict him of murder without proving the fraudulent scheme. The defence will argue that he had no motive for the murder."

"But Sassanof would have exposed the fraud!"

"Possibly, but Sassanof is not here to testify. They may argue that Sassanof himself was behind the fraud and died setting the fire."

"But there is Travis' word."

"A convict."

"Palgrave."

"Merely has evidence that someone was defrauding someone. He believes it is Dowson because Dowson fired him."

"You are punching holes in your own theory."

"Only because the legal defence is likely to."

"What about the valise of American money?"

"It has not been found yet. They are searching Dowson's home and bank, as well as Sassanof's."

"And Blanchard?"

"I suspect all the evidence against him went overboard with him. Nothing was found on the ship and he left nothing back in London. If the police can trace the other investors, create a timeline of their investments and compare them both to Dowson's expenditures and the accidents at the theatre, the prosecution may be able to convince the jury that Dowson had gotten himself in too deep and resorted first to violence and eventually murder."

"Why the accidents?"

"As long as plays kept failing or the company struggled along on only *Romeo and Juliet* then he could keep asking the investors for more money and they expected no return on their investment. But when the company was gaining success with *Richard III* and *King Lear* some disaster was planned. The information from the duchess' secretary confirmed that her investments each came right after one of the accidents, even when the accident did not cause substantial financial hardship to the company."

"Why wouldn't he want the company to do well? Why didn't he just pay them a dividend?"

"My theory is that he had oversold the shares in the company several times. Gregson should be able to confirm that when he collects information from other investors. Whether he sold 120% or 200% of the company does not matter. The company could never afford to pay them a return because it would drain all the funds, even if Dowson had not pocketed them himself."

Lord Cecil's eyes opened wide.

"In that regard, it is similar to the *Post* scandal I read about in New York," Holmes continues. "In an effort to pay the debt he had incurred purchasing the *New York Post*, Ezra D. Winslow sold more *Post* stock certificates than the total capital stock allowed. Winslow was a business man who resorted to fraud after suffering a stroke of bad luck. Dowson, however, may have planned the over-sale from the start.

"As in the *Post* case, once you fall short you can only dig in deeper. Winslow resorted to forgeries that eventually exposed the whole scandal. Dowson needed the Corycian Company to keep failing as long as he was milking it. He quickly went from fraud to sabotage to assault—as long as someone else was doing it. Travis admitted Dowson put him up to attacking me, though he was all too willing. The balcony was another attempt. Unless Dowson speaks, we may never know how he recruited Blanchard. I am uncertain whether the failure of the gas fixture was an accident or Blanchard did that, too. Based on what I saw last night and this morning, I think Dowson still thought he could continue the game, using the destruction of the theatre, and even Sassanof's death to draw sympathy and further investment from the duchess and others."

"So Dowson never intended to fix the hole in the stage?"

"He may have at one point and changed his mind. As long as we were in the States he could draw more money from the investors even though the company was actually supporting itself by our receipts. When he heard we were returning he instructed Blanchard to attack Devigne, Sassanof, and myself on the ship."

"Why those three?"

"Sassanof was an obvious choice," Holmes said, "if he wanted to bring the trick to a conclusion without paying out any profits."

"I can imagine it: 'Unfortunate loss of his partner. Can't go on. All the money lost.' What of you and Devigne?"

"I think those attacks were always to reduce the company's income. He had already decided to set fire to the theatre. He had to once he decided not to repair the stage. He was afraid that Sassanof would come up with another way to keep the company working. He probably was pleased with the announcement of Escott's death and may have attributed it to Blanchard if he had not yet heard of Blanchard's death."

"The myth of the curse would cover nearly everything among superstitious theatre people. But not you."

"I knew something was not right, but I couldn't be certain that all the accidents were connected. Once I saw the Baron and recognized him, the pieces fell into place. The plan may have always been to set fire to the theatre. Perhaps he expected Blanchard to do it upon his return but once he heard Blanchard was lost at sea he was forced to do it himself. Perhaps Sassanof caught him in the act."

"Do you think Sassanof had gone by the theatre before he met with us?"

"If so, why didn't he mention it to us? Based on my experience on the trip to Paris, Sassanof could be quite loquacious if something related to the company was troubling him. Perhaps he just went to his office. If the stage was dark, he might not have noticed."

"But what of Frank? Wouldn't Frank have told him that no work had been done?" Lord Cecil asked.

"That's likely, but the police have been unable to locate Frank. I find it difficult to believe he would have been able to bribe Frank. Perhaps Dowson did away with Frank shortly after we left for the States, leaving Blanchard, Palgrave, and Travis as the sole witnesses. He could not reach Travis because he was in prison, but he promised him money if he kept his mouth shut. Once it was obvious that was not going to be forthcoming, Travis told all.

"I think Dowson never expected anyone connected with the theatre to talk to Palgrave after he fired him. That was a mistake. I believe he understood that when he saw Palgrave at the ruins of the theatre. That's why he ran. It wasn't me or the Inspector he was looking at. It was Palgrave. He knew the game was up."

"'Suspicion always haunts the guilty mind,' as the Bard said," Lord Cecil quoted.

"Aptly put," Holmes agreed. "Dowson will go on trial for Sassanof's murder. If convicted of murder he will hang and there will be no need to try him on the other charges. If he slips through on that, then there are plenty of other charges to bring," Holmes concluded suppressing a yawn.

"You seem worn out," Lord Cecil.

"I haven't slept in twenty-four hours. I fear it is catching up with me."

He returned to the Montague Street rooms. Mycroft had already retired. He went directly to his bedroom, removed his boots and his clothes, and fell into his bed.

Chapter 3

Scandals

"He threatened to raise a scandal which would convulse the nation."
Alexander Holder, "The Adventure of the Beryl Coronet"

Sherlock Holmes slept for the next thirty hours uninterrupted. When he awoke much invigorated, he joined Mycroft for breakfast, to the delight of their housekeeper, Mrs Denton. The irregularity of Sherlock's hours always troubled her.

"I've seen the fruits of your labours," Mycroft said. "It has been making quite a sensation in the papers. Only one mention of your name."

"That's hardly surprising," Sherlock responded helping himself to some eggs, rashers, and toast. "I should be glad enough for one this time."

"What are your plans today?" Mycroft asked.

"I will be off to the agency to place advertisements for my services. Then I shall organize my clippings."

"Excellent. Then I shall see you this evening."

After returning from Fleet Street, Sherlock Holmes dove into his travelling trunk. He knew there were clippings at the bottom that he had saved from the American newspapers. In unpacking the trunk, he came upon a copy of his version of *Richard III*. He placed it in the post with this cover letter:

Dear Mr Irving,

I have enclosed my playbook to the production of Shakespeare's Richard III as I drafted it in 1875. I have retired from the stage and have no further use of it. If you should find it worthy of production, I would appreciate a box to view it. I do not wish to have my name connected to it. I added no lines to the Bard's own words.

Sincerely,
Sherlock Holmes
fka William Escott

Sherlock Holmes then pulled out his commonplace books and

began organizing the American clippings. Some of them were reports of American crimes and criminals; some were reports from England and other parts of the world. He also had clippings in a drawer in his bedroom that he had saved before he began acting. He assembled those. Then he took out the paste pot and scissors and began arranging the clippings in the books. He left space for annotations. He did not have the Yard's Habitual Criminal Registry, but he expected these records would be useful to him in the future.

That evening Mycroft arrived home from Whitehall and began reviewing the letters that had arrived in the post. He set aside several envelopes and picked out a fat one from their brother Sherrinford. He took it to his chair to read.

Shortly he said, "Here's one for you" and threw it Sherlock's way.

"From Yorkshire?" Sherlock asked as he caught it.

"Yes. It was inside Sherrinford's letter addressed to me," Mycroft said.

Sherlock opened the envelope. Out fell several newspaper clippings from northern newspapers. The note inside said:

Dear Sir:

I hope you are well. I understand from your brother that you have started your own detective business. The time I spent in your service left me with an interest in crime that is difficult to satisfy on the manor. Things are quiet here. However, I collected these articles about the murder of Police Constable Cock while I was travelling with your brother earlier this year. I thought you might find them of interest.

Your most humble servant,

Jonathan Beckwith

Jonathan Beckwith was currently Sherrinford's valet. He had been Sherlock's servant for a few years prior to that.

Sherlock began reading the clippings. The facts seemed sparse enough. A member of the county constabulary named Nicholas Cock had been shot and killed not far from the gates of Manley Hall in Whalley Range, a suburb of Manchester, the early hours of Wednesday August 2nd. An inquest had been held on the 3rd and Irish brothers named Habron were charged with the crime on the 4th.

The papers reported that Constable Cock had met a young solicitor named Simpson who lived at Manley Hall while walking his beat and they had talked for a while. A few minutes after they parted, Simpson heard shots behind him and turned to see the constable fall to the ground. Despite being taken to a surgeon, the constable lived but a short time, though long enough, it seemed, to make some statements to Superintendent Beat. Those statements were being withheld by the police. However, on the strength of them Superintendent Beat had arrested John, Frank, and William Habron. The Habrons were Irish nursery men who resided at Chorton-cum-Hardy. The evidence against them was all circumstantial and tenuous, but the police were "vigorously investigating the matter further," which Holmes interpreted to mean that they were trying to find more evidence to implicate the Habron brothers.

The bullet extracted from the deceased constable was examined by a gun-maker named Griffith who said it was a .442 bullet. No firearms were found in the Habrons' abode, and other than the fact that the deceased had brought two of the Habrons before the magistrate for drunkenness recently, nothing had been found to connect the young men to the crime. According to the newspapers, the boots of the prisoners had been compared with some footprints found nearby.

What did 'found nearby' mean? Holmes wondered.

It seemed a scattering of odd information which may or may not all be relevant. The police were holding back the dead man's words which could be very significant, and which could have been misinterpreted by the police. The case against the Habron brothers seemed thin enough and seemed likely to break down at trial.

Sherlock Holmes was uncertain what had piqued Jonathan's interest in this crime out of the assortment to be found in any newspaper. However, one sentence in a clipping caught his attention: "The occurrence has caused a great sensation in the neighbourhood of Whalley Range, as it is not many months since two policemen were stabbed by a burglar who was trying to escape."

If he were investigating the shooting of Constable Cock he would look into the stabbing of the two policemen and the reports of burglaries near Manchester. However, he was not investigating the shooting of Constable Cock. Mrs Denton was at the door with their supper and he planned to limit his investigations to that for the time being.

The brothers ate in silence, which was not unusual between them. Sometimes they were each so buried in their own thoughts that conversation would be an effort on which neither of them wished to waste energy. After the things were cleared away, Sherlock added the new clippings from Jonathan to his commonplace books. He left space near them for he felt this case would have new developments.

By the second day of this he'd had run out of space in the books and went out to purchase more. When he returned with the package of purchases under his arm, he tapped on the housekeeper's door to ask if there had been any visitors, letters or telegraphs.

"No," Mrs Denton said. "However, your brother Mycroft's home now preparing to go on a journey."

"Where to?" he asked.

"He won't tell me," she sniffed.

Sherlock Holmes entered the flat.

"Hello, brother, what is this I hear about you travelling? Is the end of the world nigh?" he asked.

"I shall be out of the country for several weeks, perhaps several months," Mycroft said ignoring Sherlock's attempt at humour.

"Business or pleasure?"

"I do not count being crammed into small moving boxes among pleasures," Mycroft grumbled.

"Where are you going?" Sherlock asked.

"For the moment that is confidential, though I suspect it will become obvious eventually."

"What of your usual work here?"

"There was quite a battle over that subject earlier today, other departments insisting that they cannot spare me—I suppose that is somewhat gratifying—but the foreign office won the day."

"And the exclusive use of your services."

"For a time. They have been taking much of my time already, though 'using' it might not be the correct term."

"I wish you a pleasant trip."

"It is quite a bother. You know I don't like to travel. Try not to burn down the flat while I'm gone," Mycroft said.

"Or blow it up," Mycroft tossed over his shoulder as he headed to his bedroom to sort among the clothes to be packed.

Sherlock Holmes chuckled as he sat down to unwrap the scrapbooks.

He soon heard Mrs Denton come in to offer Mycroft assistance followed by the two of them squabbling over what needed to be done. In time the luggage was packed and a cab called. Mycroft tapped on Sherlock's door before leaving.

"Remember what I said: no explosions while I am gone," he called through the closed door.

"I shall keep them to a minimum," Sherlock responded. "Try not to be miserable."

"Some sacrifices must be made for Queen and country. Goodbye," Mycroft responded, and then he was gone.

Sherlock Holmes returned to his commonplace books. He still had a stack of newspapers that had accumulated since he had returned to England to peruse. It would give him something to do while he waited for responses to his advertisements.

The theatre schedule had made him accustomed to late nights and late mornings. He worked on the commonplace books until after midnight on Friday. He was sitting at the table Saturday morning in his dressing gown nursing a cup of coffee and smoking a pipe when there was a rap on the door. When Sherlock pulled it open a messenger stood before him.

"Urgent message for Mr Sherlock Holmes," the young man said. "To his hands only."

"I am Sherlock Holmes."

The messenger handed an envelope to him.

"I have a cab waiting, sir," he said.

"Abrahams & Roffey, Solicitors," Sherlock read aloud as he examined the envelope.

Sherlock opened and read the message to himself still standing at the door sill.

Dear Mr Holmes,

Please excuse my intrusion. I would like to consult with you on a highly confidential matter of the utmost urgency. Could you return with my messenger?

Michael Abrahams, Esq.

"I will be with you shortly," he said to the messenger.

Sherlock pulled off his dressing gown as he headed to his bedroom to finish dressing. Then he joined the messenger in a hansom cab. The address of the firm of Abrahams & Roffey was 8, Old Jewry, a street in the City of London. It was not a long drive from Montague Street, just a few miles along the Holborn Viaduct. Old Jewry was a few blocks of imposing edifices stretching between Gresham Street and Cheapside, not far from the Bank of England. Yet it was a scant half a mile west of the squalor of Whitechapel. The bells of Mary-le-bow Church began to ring the hour as the messenger showed him into Mr Abraham's office.

It was what you would expect of a successful solicitor's office, all oak and leather. Walls lined with leather-bound law books surrounded a large, finely-carved oak desk with matching comfortable leather chairs. While some books were on more general legal topics, the majority dealt with finance and bankruptcy, the bookends of capitalism.

Mr Abrahams was a thin man in his early fifties. It was difficult to say that he looked like anything other than what he was. There was a touch of grey at the temples and bags under the eyes from long nights over briefs. The cut of his coat, the gleam of his watch chain, and the weave of his shirt spoke of financial success in the understated manner of a solicitor. Sherlock Holmes concluded that if he ever wanted to impersonate a well-to-do lawyer, he would take Mr Abrahams as his model.

"How do you do, Mr Holmes?" Abrahams said as they shook hands. "Be seated. I am pleased you could come on such short notice. I must admit you look a bit younger than I had expected."

Mr Abrahams was a very still man, except for his hands. His hands moved when he talked. He did not play with objects as some men did, but rather punctuated his sentences with gestures. The fingers were long, pale, and thin, except knobby where he gripped a pen, though no ink stains were there. He was a careful man, a precise man. At the same time he was making these observations and inferences, the soon-to-be-twenty-three-year-old Sherlock Holmes bristled at the mention of his youth.

"It was my understanding that you were interested in my skills and experience," he responded rising. "If age is the deciding factor, then I should take my leave."

"Sit down, Mr Holmes. It was merely a statement of surprise. It could be an asset in this case. My clerk, James Midwinter, recommended you because he had not seen your name before. I need an agent who is not well-known to Scotland Yard. We made some quick enquiries about you and were satisfied."

Sherlock Holmes was curious what those enquiries had told them about him. Perhaps that was best left unexplored. He was here, which is what mattered in the instance.

"I have some small connection with the Yard," Holmes said.

"With whom?"

"Inspector Gregson, principally."

Abrahams dismissed Gregson with a wave of his hand.

"He is not involved in this case."

"What is this highly confidential and urgent matter?"

Abrahams leaned forward and gave him a piercing glare which made Holmes think that perhaps this man should have become a barrister.

"Would you have any qualms about following a policeman and possibly exposing police corruption?"

"Not in the least," Holmes replied. "Indeed, earlier this year I did some preliminary observations of police activity for Wilson Hargreave of the police department of the City of New York. He believed there was some lack of enforcement of certain laws related to confidence games. They did not want to open an official investigation until they had more information as to who was involved and how widespread it was."

"We have a similar situation. We think enforcement is going awry, but we are uncertain who is at the bottom of it. We also do not know whether it is a matter of corruption or incompetence. At this stage I deem an outside observer essential.”

“That was precisely my role in New York.”

“You understand that everything I tell you is of the strictest confidence.”

“Yes.”

“You agree to tell no one any details about this case.”

“Yes.”

“You are to report to me and no one else.”

“Understood.”

The solicitor opened a portfolio on his desk and glanced down at the papers before him. He looked back up at Holmes.

“This firm has offices in London and Paris. The Comtesse Marie Cecile de Goncourt is one of our French clients. In late August, the Comtesse received a copy of the August 5th edition of *The Sport*, a newspaper about horse racing.”

The solicitor slid the publication across the desk for Holmes to review.

“It was printed in Edinburgh and posted from a London address with a cover letter in French and translation into French of one of the editorial articles.”

Abrahams handed Holmes the two documents.

“Do you read French?”

“Yes,” Holmes confirmed.

“As you can see, the article claimed that a Mr Montgomery was so skilful at picking winning horses that bookies would no longer give him fair odds. As a result, he was seeking individuals to place bets for him. Montgomery would provide cheques for parties to place bets on horses he chose and then send him the winnings. He would pay them a commission out of the winnings.

“The Comtesse was intrigued. She wrote back and Mr Montgomery sent her a cheque for £200 with instructions to place a bet with a Mr Jackson, an English ‘sworn bookmaker’ in London. The horse won and in due course the Comtesse received the winnings. She sent them to Mr Montgomery who in turn sent her commission. Next Montgomery sent a cheque for £1000 for a bet with a different bookmaker and suggested that she venture some of her own money because this bookmaker would not accept bets less than £2000. The Comtesse agreed. Then she was offered the chance to have her bet insured if the bet was at least £4000. The Comtesse obliged and the horse won the Great Northern Handicap and the Comtesse was paid substantial winnings with a cheque from the Royal Bank of London, a bank that does not exist. However, one important provision of this scheme was that the participants were told that English law required them to hold the cheques for three months before converting them into cash. There is no such law. The purpose was to delay the discovery of the fraud as long as possible.

"The Comtesse sent in another £5000 and won again. Over time, she sent in a total of £10 300 and received back fraudulent cheques worth over £80 000. She had at this point exhausted her liquid resources and was still holding the fraudulent cheques. She asked her banker for a loan of an additional £30 000. Her banker was suspicious and asked our firm for advice. We made enquiries and determined that the scheme was fraudulent.

"On September 25th, I personally met with Superintendent Williamson at Scotland Yard and explained the situation to him. Mr Williamson assigned the case to Inspector Druscovich who visited me at my office on the 26th. We went to Marlborough Street to obtain warrants to search the premises listed in the letter and the publication, and arrest the men involved. Mr Knox declined to grant the warrants in the first instance. He wanted additional evidence, Inspector Druscovich made a further application the following day and the warrants were issued."

"Unfortunately the addresses associated with the business, 2, Cleveland Row, 11, King Street, and 8, Northumberland Street—the last of which is only a hundred paces from the back of Scotland Yard— had all been abandoned a few days before they were searched. It could have been a coincidence, but I don't like coincidences, Mr Holmes. It could have been that they got the wind up from some other quarter. Yet it struck me as a bit queer that they took flight directly after I consulted with Scotland Yard."

"What of your office?" Holmes asked.

Mr Abrahams smiled.

"Excellent. Leave no stone unturned. I considered that, even though I have complete confidence in my people here. Only one clerk in these chambers, Mr Midwinter, had this matter in his hand, and only my son Fred here, my partner in Paris, and his chief clerk knew about it. In addition, we had been investigating the matter for some weeks. If they received a warning from inside our firm why wouldn't the criminals have fled earlier? I was puzzled.

"Nevertheless, Scotland Yard continued working on the case. Inspector Druscovich spoke to the landlords. The offices at Northumberland Street had been let for a firm that called itself Brooks & Co., of Glasgow by a person going by Arthur Chapman, but no one could get a lead on him. The landlords at Cleveland Row and King Street said their rooms were let by Andrew Montgomery and Jacob Francis respectively. In the case of King Street, Chapman arranged it claiming to be the secretary of a man named Jacob Francis. The description of Andrew Montgomery was nearly identical to that of Chapman. The bookmaker Charles Jackson had lodgings in St James's Place which were also vacant. We began to suspect all the names were aliases and it was difficult to determine how many men were involved.

"The landlords described other persons who were present at different times. Two were rather distinctive. One, who was probably Jacob Francis, was a short, delicate man with small hands and feet. He dressed elegantly, wore diamond studs, and spoke English with a French accent. He also was somewhat lame, sometimes using crutches and sometimes two walking sticks. That's the best description we had of anyone. The other man was very tall and barrel-chested with a round face. We don't know if any of those names fit him."

"One occurrence on the 28th that may or may not be significant: Superintendent Williamson went on holiday for a month, leaving Chief Inspector George Clarke in charge. It is my understanding that this holiday had been planned substantially before I had first spoken to him—and it was not surprising because the man seemed utterly exhausted. I was, however, disappointed because my expectation had been that he would be overseeing the investigation. Inspector Druscovich seemed to be diligent, if a bit nervous, and at that time I had no reason to doubt him other than the flight of the criminals from the locations."

"At that time?" Holmes said,

"Yes. We will get there directly, Mr Holmes. In any case Super-intendent Williamson had left Inspector Druscovich instructions to clean up this matter before he returned. By this time other complaints were coming in from France. Those complaints were also handed over to Inspector Druscovich. He informed me at one meeting that they were forming a great pile on his desk without providing any new clues. Many of those complaining did not realize that everything from the newspaper to the translation was a fraud.

"Bills were printed and sent out with the descriptions we had, as well as the names, but they were not very hopeful. Inspector Drus-covich spoke to the postmasters for those addresses to have them in-tercept any mail. He found that the mail for all of them had been for-warded to Newmarket to be held until called for. We were hopeful that we could snag at least one of the gang when they came to collect the mail. Then on September 29th the Newmarket postmaster received a telegram from London telling him to forward all the mail to Ports-mouth. This seemed to upset Druscovich for some reason though to my mind it merely shifted the location to observe."

"Unless they had an associate in the post office in Portsmouth."

"A possibility. In any case, Scotland Yard eventually sent an of-ficer there to retrieve the letters rather than wait for someone to claim them. There were other avenues of investigation. The drafts written by the Comtesse on the Credit Lyonnais had been cashed at Rein-hardt's, the moneychanger in Coventry Street, for English bank notes. As you may know English bank notes contain serial numbers which allow them to be traced. The serial numbers and the banks they were drawn on were obtained from Charles Reinhart and the banks were contacted to put a stop on them. On October 3rd, Inspector Druscov-ich learned that some of the notes had already been submitted for ex-change at the Clydesdale Bank, in Glasgow, Scotland. Druscovich sent a letter to the Glasgow police warning them. The letter was not re-ceived until after the conspirators had exchanged a number of the notes and left the area. When I heard about this I asked why he had not telegraphed. I did not receive an answer I considered satisfactory.

However, Druscovich did travel to Glasgow on October 4th where he was told that the transactions had been traced to a man named Coster, whose description matched that given by the landlord of the book-maker Jacob Francis.

"Enquiries were made at railway terminals for any information on the movements of a small, dark, somewhat lame man who walked with two sticks and spoke English with a French accent. The Glasgow police were able to trace Coster/Francis to the Midland Railway train that arrived at St Pancras Station from Scotland at 8 o'clock the morning of the 4th. A Midland Railway constable identified two cabs, a hansom and a four-wheeler, booked from the station at that time, both bound for Stoke Newington. The driver of the four-wheeler, Robert Rose, took on the suspected passenger but reported that his horse fell lame climbing Pentonville Hill and they flagged another cab which took him the rest of the way. As a result he did not know the final destination. They were able to update the description of the man they identified as Coster, alias Jacob Francis. Scotland Yard issued this reward notice seeking the second driver," Abrahams said handing the notice to Holmes.

8.30 a.m. on Wednesday, the 4th inst., a man, 36 years old, 5ft 4 in or 5 in. in height, and of Jewish appearance, hired a passing cab on Pentonville Hill. A reward of £2 would be given to any one giving information as to where the fare was set down, supposed to be in the neighbourhood of Stoke Newington. Information to be given to Superintendent Williamson at Scotland Yard.

Holmes shook his head.

"Bunglers," he said. "They should have investigated discretely. This notice told the gang that they were getting close. They mostly likely fled."

Abrahams smiled again.

"Very astute of you, Mr Holmes."

"A notice with the updated description was circulated to police stations," Mr Abrahams continued, handing Holmes a copy of the notice.

Jacob Francis, alias Coster, growing whiskers, very thin, cut on the *side of the left eye, arrived at St Pancras 8 a.m. on 4th, took a cab, discharged it on Pentonville Hill, took another passing, carried a small bag; special enquiry to be made to find second cab.*

"On the other hand, neither Druscovich, nor anyone under his direction, made any attempt to question the other cab drivers working near St Pancras Station. Mr Midwinter did so. We found the second cab driver and the destination but the man was no longer there.

"My son, Fred, also had the idea of talking to the publishers of the sporting newspapers. He talked to people at *The Sporting Times*, *The Life*, and *The Sportsman*. It was the editor of the latter, Charles Hitchen Ashley, who suggested a name for one of the other gang members. The name was William Kurr. Ashley said that Kurr hung around the track at Sandown Park and Newmarket. He also said he suspected Kurr had been involved in other frauds before. Kurr was the first one he would suspect in this kind of operation. He described Kurr as a tall, round man.

"I relayed this information to Inspector Druscovich at our next meeting. He was not happy that we were continuing to investigate on our own. He said it rendered his enquiries more difficult. I expressed my concerns with the progress of the investigation. Well, let's just say we had words."

"What was the date?"

"October 30th."

"Eleven days ago."

"Yes."

"What has been done since?"

"Superintendent Williamson returned from his holiday about that time. I met with him and expressed some of my concerns. He assured me that he would speak with Inspector Druscovich.

"On November 8th I offered a reward of £1000 for any information relating to Andrew Montgomery, Jacob Francis, Charles Jackson, and the other associated names, and descriptions. It was published in the newspapers and circulated to banks and post offices."

Sherlock Holmes was for an instant puzzled as to why he had missed it. Then he realized that he had been resolving the Corycian Theatre case that day and had not yet finished going through the newspapers.

"In general, I do not favour such rewards. They give too much information to the criminals," he said.

"I am aware of the risk," Abrahams said. "It had to be balanced against the risk that the criminals would escape detection. Scotland Yard's efforts were proceeding too slowly. Yesterday, the pace of the investigation seemed to accelerate. Superintendent Williamson received some information in a letter from Mr Rayner, the postmaster at Shanklin on the Isle of Wight about a man who went by 'Yonge' whose description fit Jacob Francis and Coster. It was my understanding from Inspector Druscovich that he was going to Shanklin. However, I found out that he sent Inspector George Greenham, who seems to lack... subtlety, instead. I think he rushed his enquiries in Shanklin. He spoke to a servant girl of that Yonge as well as the postmaster and returned to London. I still believe there is more to be mined there and in Portsmouth."

"Where is Inspector Druscovich?"

"An excellent question. I received this wire from him this morning," Abrahams said handing the yellow slip of paper to Sherlock Holmes.

It was a telegram from the post office in Edinburgh.

"He's in Scotland."

"As you see, he claims to be on their trail."

"You suspect Inspector Druscovich of being in league with the gang?"

"Yes, Mr Holmes. Signs point that direction. Coincidence has become strained. Incompetence does not seem to explain everything. Don't you agree?"

"Yes. There are many pieces missing to the puzzle, but Inspector Druscovich seems to be the key. I should go to Scotland."

"Yes. Find Inspector Druscovich. Figure out what he is doing. Find out if he is in touch with the gang members. See if you can trace any of them. Finding Druscovich should not be difficult. He is tall, with thick black hair and a heavy moustache. He has a foreign accent even though he was born in London. His father was from Moldovia and he spent part of his youth on the Continent. Druscovich is also very nervous-looking. I don't know if that is his usual state or if it is unique to this case. My primary goal, Mr Holmes, is to prosecute the criminals who took advantage of my client. My secondary goal is to ascertain whether our laws are being enforced properly by Scotland Yard."

Abrahams picked a few papers from the portfolio.

"I have written a concise summary of the case for you here. It contains all I have told you and some additional details. Here is a bank draft to cover your first week and this is for your initial expenses."

Holmes folded the papers Mr Abrahams had given to him and placed them in his pocket book along with the draft.

"Very good," Holmes said tucking the silver away in the pocket of his frock-coat and rising to leave.

Abrahams offered his hand and he shook it.

"Thank you, Mr Holmes. You give me confidence. Do send a wire with any information we should follow up here. We will have someone here at all hours awaiting your news."

"One more thing. Is there a rear exit to this building?" Holmes asked.

"Yes. Do you think you were followed here?"

"No. However, I wish to be certain that I am not followed from here."

"I will have Mr Midwinter show you the way."

On the cab ride to Montague Street he planned. In New York City Holmes had used his acting skills to blend into the human environment while not changing his appearance much. There he had been a stranger who expected to leave the city in a few months. That provided him with greater anonymity than he would have here in London. There was the risk in London of Holmes being recognized not only as himself, but as a doppelganger for the more famous William Escott whom many people had seen on stage. Even if they believed Escott was deceased they would be more likely to remember a familiar face. Cutting his hair and shaving off Escott's beard had helped alleviate that to some degree but it was still a danger. His face might be less familiar to the Scots, but the men he was tracking were from London. He wanted to travel light. He could fit a change of clothing, a few caps, and a couple of scarves in a satchel. The proper attitude would supply the rest.

He asked the cabby to drop him at the British Museum and he walked to the back entrance of the flats. As he was packing, Mrs Denton tapped on his door.

"Is there anything you will be needing, Mr Sherlock?"

"No, thank you. I will be doing some travelling myself," he said.

"And where are you going?"

"It is confidential."

"How long will you be gone?"

"I really can't say."

"Such mysterious gentlemen I keep house for!"

"While I am gone—"

"Yes, I know. If anyone calls looking for a detective get their name and where they can be reached."

"Yes, thank you, Mrs Denton."

He left dressed in a pair of brown trousers, a shabby brown jacket and a flat cap. The strap of a satchel crossed his chest. He could be a labourer seeking work or a common man on holiday. He walked back to the museum where there were often crowds and plenty of cabs. He found one to take him to Euston Station. He gave him no special instructions and paid the standard rate, nothing to remember him by. He purchased his ticket at the window and leaned against a wall until the train was ready to board. It was initially beneficial to play the role of a working man on holiday for it gave him an excuse for buying travel guides and maps *en route*. He studied them and he studied the documents Abrahams had given him, including the article in *The Sport* newspaper and Abraham's summary of the case. He made his own notes on the summary. He had plenty of time as the trip took over eight hours to complete.

Edinburgh was well endowed with pubs, inns, and hotels. That was beneficial to a man seeking accommodations, but presented challenges to a man hunting a man. The night was cold and there was a light drizzle as Holmes stepped from the train carriage. He paused on the platform in a sheltered spot. He sat the satchel upon the ground and used both hands to light his pipe. He drew upon it strong and puffed out clouds of smoke. He knew it would not stay lit long.

The train rattled off into the night as he drew upon the pipe twice more. Then he began to climb the stairs up from the Waverley Railway Station to the North Bridge which connected Old Town Edinburgh to New Town and spanned the railroad tracks.

Once on North Bridge, he pocketed his pipe that had gone out already and turned north toward Princes Street. Ahead he could see the equestrian statue of the Duke of Wellington, glossy with rain, sitting before the dark registry office. On the east and west corners facing the registry building were the Waverley Hotel and the post office. Few lights were on in the post office where a single clerk sat at the telegraph desk. The hotel was more brightly lit. Holmes stepped into the Waverley Hotel and asked the desk clerk if Druscovich was registered there.

He did not know enough Scots to pretend to be a native, but he could convincingly present himself as a Yorkie come north seeking a friend, taking a holiday, or looking for work, as the need arose. He spoke as little as possible in any case which fit the character of a Yorkshireman as well.

"No," said the man at the desk after consulting the registry.

A second, older man stepped up as he responded.

"Tha Scootland Yaird 'spector?"

"Tha'd be 'im," Sherlock Holmes said.

It did not seem logical to deny what Druscovich was if they already knew. If they ask why he wanted to find him, he would improvise.

"He was 'ere in the mornin' wi' Detective Linton o' the local police asking aboot three fellas. They'd bin an' gone again."

"I was hopin' to catch him, but I doon't know where 'e's stoppin'. Thank'ee. I'll ask doon the street."

According to the travel guides, there were several other hotels half a mile west on Princes Street as well as some east towards Arthur's Seat and a few behind the registry office. He turned west and walked. A cab rattled up and he waved it off. Speed was not going to benefit to him now. If Druscovich was still here, it was likely he was either at one of the pubs or had settled into a hotel room for the night. He wanted to find him without Druscovich knowing he had. A short walk would allow him to think and get his bearings.

Few were out this late in the rain. Most of the buildings across the street were dark. From the looks of them, they were offices and shops. Ahead, something like a spire loomed up through the mist and vanished in fog. As he drew closer it became clearer and he saw a statue of man on a chair below the spire. It was the monument to Sir Walter Scott, who was much revered in this town. The railway station and the hotel had been named after Scott's Waverley novels. Holmes passed the Princes Street Gardens, which were not much to see in the dark, in the rain, in November. Below them lay the tracks the trains ran on. Ahead a church chimed the half hour.

He could now see lights from windows ahead, blurry through the rain. Those were likely pubs and inns. As he walked past the St John's Church, he saw that the road split three ways directly ahead with the Rutland Hotel in the fork. He went in a tavern nearby. There were a few patrons. They looked up when he entered and then dismissed him. The walk in the rain and his now unshaven face had helped to achieve the look he sought: unremarkable.

He lifted the satchel strap from across his chest and sat it on the floor at his feet. He ordered a pint and lit his pipe. The proprietor offered him pie and he accepted it, digging a fork into the crust and spicy mutton filling. It had been more than twelve hours since he had last eaten. Over the pie and the pint he scanned the patrons for any resemblance to Druscovich and found none. He decided not to enquire after him here. He could do so later if he did not find him at the hotels.

The patrons were a lively group of friends, perhaps from childhood, meeting here to tell stories and jokes. They were loud enough for him to hear but he didn't know the language. He caught the gist more from the intonation and the response. Occasionally there was a word in common with Broad Yorkshire or borrowed from English. Amidst a roar of laughter he felt more than heard a train rumble into town just as he finished the pie. He stowed his pipe in his pocket, then picked up his satchel, slung it across his shoulder and ambled out the door as the church began to ring the hour of ten.

The cab he had refused earlier discharged a tall passenger as Holmes gained the street. He noticed another man waited before the Rutland Hotel. They approached each other. Words were exchanged. They were too far for him to hear. The two men walked towards the Rutland Hotel. As they reached the light from the hotel, he could see that the tall man from the cab had black hair and a heavy moustache like the description of Druscovich.

Sherlock followed, moving from shadow to shadow to avoid their attention. If the man was Druscovich, it was a bit of luck that would save him from making further enquiries.

Who was the other man with him? Could it be the local policeman, Linton, they had mentioned at the Waverley? If not, who?

He was tall and broad like the unknown man mentioned by the landlords in London.

The Rutland Hotel lobby was well lit and a fire roared in the hearth chasing away the damp of the rain outside. The two men had taken some chairs not far from the fire but not in front of it. Sherlock approached the fire directly, as if employed to tend it. He kept his back to them. He poked at the fire, rearranging and banking the coals.

"I suppose you are going to the Bridge of Allan?" the unknown man asked.

"Yas," the man with the heavy moustache responded.

"If you don't go to the Bridge of Allan, I will give you a thousand pounds."

"I moost go."

"If you go making enquiries, you will settle Meiklejohn. He introduced Yonge to a bank manager there."

"I cennot halp it. I moost go."

Holmes had no doubt now this was Druscovich. The tight treatment of the vowels and the heavy enunciation of the trailing t's pointed to eastern Europe. A Romanian man his family met in Greece a few years back had a similar accent. There was also something of the policeman in how he spoke, the habit of authority and duty. Yet there was an unsteadiness to it now.

The other must be Kurr, the man mentioned by the editor. The accent was the northern London suburbs. He was from Holloway or

Islington, perhaps. Holmes had caught a brief sideways glance at the man. He was definitely a big man with a ruddy, round face. He was attempting to assert dominion over Druscovich, but the policeman was resisting.

They spoke of Yonge which was one of the names associated with the fraudulent bookmaker Francis. Meiklejohn was another Scotland Yarder. Abrahams had not mentioned him as being involved with this case.

"You will find a letter at Queens Hotel from Palmer. Don't give that up," Kurr said.

There was an Inspector Palmer at Scotland Yard. Could he be involved as well or was this a different Palmer?

"Vhy do you not go to the Brridge of Allan, and git the letters away first?" Druscovich asked. "I vill keep to the hind part of the train, and you go near the engine."

"Not good enough," Kurr said. "If I go, I'll be seen by McNab, the cabman from Glascow."

"I vill telegraph them to send McNab to Edinburgh on the firstt train tomorrrow," Inspector Druscovich said checking his watch. "Come, I vill send it. Then I moost to catch the next trrain. I moost be therre tonight."

They walked out to the street again. Neither seemed content. Neither trusted the other. They were going separate ways. One of the difficulties of working alone in a case like this was deciding which to follow when they parted. Holmes made his decision quickly.

The cab had stayed at the curb, whether because Druscovich had paid him to wait or because the driver suspected it was a more likely spot for another fare. Druscovich and Kurr climbed aboard and instructed the driver to take them to the post office.

Sherlock Holmes had stowed his satchel in a shadow outside the Rutland and he fetched it as he as he followed them out. He grabbed on to the back of the cab as it started off through the rainy night. In a few minutes it pulled up before the post office on North Bridge. He hopped off and melted into the shadows again. He pulled a red scarf from his satchel and wrapped it around his throat and chin, and pulled his collar up against the rain that fell more vigorously now.

The mud that had splashed on him from the carriage wheels had not improved the look of his attire. Regardless, he walked boldly into the post office and commandeered a telegram form, seemingly ignorant of the other two customers composing their own wires. He dug in his satchel as if looking for the address and glance at them as he unbent. Druscovich and Kurr were ignoring him.

"Zee?" Inspector Druscovich said, "Thatt vill do it."

Kurr read it silently and nodded. He had finished one of his own. They handed their forms to the clerk, paid the fees, and left. Holmes handed his own telegraph form to the clerk. The message might have surprised them if they had seen it.

D met K in Edin. Imp Letters Queens Hotel Bridge of Allan. Staying with K. Michael John, Palmer involved? SH

Sherlock Holmes trusted that Abrahams or his clerk was intelligent enough to decipher his abbreviations. Palmer was a common enough name. He had broken Meiklejohn in two because it was an unusual spelling. He didn't entirely trust telegraph clerks. Some were too talkative, a trait he hoped to use.

As he paid the clerk, he said, returning this time to a standard southern English accent, "One of those men looked like someone I've seen in the newspapers. Would you know by any chance?"

The clerk leaned towards him.

"He's fae Scootlund Yaird. Williamson was th' name he wrote. Don't ken aboot th' other fellow. He just signed Jackson.'"

Charles Jackson was one of the aliases associated with the turf fraud. Now he knew Jackson was Kurr.

Through the windows he could see that the men spoke a few words then Druscovich headed towards the stairs down to the trains. Kurr climbed into the cab. Holmes left the post office and grasped onto the four-wheeled cab before it headed back down Princes Street to the Rutland. At the hotel, Kurr told the driver to wait once again and Holmes stayed in the shadows. He heard the rumble of another train arriving and departing.

Soon Kurr returned with luggage and directed the cabby back down Princes Street again. Sherlock left the cab before it reached North Bridge. He descended to the station by another staircase and hid near the ticket window.

There he heard Kurr purchase a ticket for Carlisle and purchased his own ticket after Kurr walked away. Holmes followed Kurr to Carlisle and then on to Leeds. He catnapped in the long stretch through northern Yorkshire. He took care not to sleep when the train was approaching a station for fear Kurr would shake him. He did not have the impression that Kurr knew he was being tailed but he did not want to be caught off guard.

Holmes changed his look several times along the way, brushing the mud off his trousers as it dried, changing scarves and caps. Sometime after sunrise he took advantage of a smooth bit of track to shave and change to a coat and hat. The out-of-work labourer was gone.

In Leeds, Kurr sent a wire and waited for a response. Holmes stopped in a café for coffee, some newspapers, and a bit of toast. Kurr entered before he was finished. He had left his luggage at the station, a sign that it was likely he was going to take another train. Holmes concentrated on reading the news. At a shop just opening he purchased a mackintosh and another hat. He folded the raincoat over the satchel. He found a bench within earshot but not view of the ticket office.

Finally he heard the voice he was listening for purchase a ticket to Derby. Holmes consulted the schedule and purchased a ticket for the stop after Derby.

It was mid-morning on a Sunday by the time they arrived in Derby, and Kurr had his luggage loaded on a cab. The sun was shining and people were returning from church. He could not hop on the back of the cabs as he had done in the dark in Edinburgh. He did make sure to note the address Kurr gave the driver.

He found a café near the railway station. As a grey-haired woman poured coffee for him, he asked if she knew most of the people in town.

"Loikely, was born an' bred 'ere."

"I met a couple once who lived in Derby," he said mentioning the address he had heard Kurr give. "Would you know if they are still there?"

"The Coopers? No, they sold the house. Superintendent Meiklejohn's there now. He's a Sooper of the Detective Department with the Midland Railway. Just took the position. Connect'd with Yard in Lonnon, too, was towd. Don't know 'ow that works. Seems to be allays comin' an' goin'."

"Does he?"

"Yes. Ee's 'ome this morning though an' 'as some guests."

"Does he have guests often?"

"Hard to say. He's lived 'ere such a short time. Perraps they're friends come t' see his new house."

That was an interesting development. He walked back to the station and sent another wire to Abrahams.

K and M at Derby. Possibly others. Awaiting developments. SH

It was indeed an impatient wait. Four hours later Kurr returned with luggage and all in a cart. Holmes quickly stepped to the ticket window while Kurr directed the luggage.

"What is the next train coming in?" he asked

"The southbound to St Pancras, London, sir."

"Of course. Sell me a first class ticket, please."

At St Pancras Station, Holmes only stayed close enough to Kurr to get the address, then he went to the telegraph office.

K 29 Marquess Rd Canonb Isl London SH

With that sent he found an unengaged hansom and instructed the cabby on to Marquess Road in Canonbury. Canonbury was a northern suburb of London in the borough of Islington. The horse clopped along Pentonville Road to Islington High Street then through Upper Street to Essex Road past trees, patches of lawn, and borders of flowerless gardens. It was the domain of accountants and middle managers, where they raised their families away from the smoke and the bustle of the city. They turned left on Canonbury Street and shortly right at the Marquess Tavern. Here the cabby paused his horse.

"We're here, sir. Which number should I set you at?"

"Just drive on down the street, taking a look at the neighbourhood."

The road was filled with detached and semi-detached villas so lauded by the advertisements: 'A bit of country so convenient to the City.' Number 29 was a few houses down from the tavern on the left near where Ashby Street branched on the right. There were narrow passages behind the tavern, and further down near where Clephane Street crossed, that reached to the backs and might lead to a mews or two. On the right side near the corner with Ashby he had seen a house that seemed empty with a potting shed to the side. At the end of Marquess Road was St Paul's church. There he told the cabby to drive to Mary-le-Bow Church on Cheapside.

Holmes donned the Macintosh and walked the short distance to come around to the rear entrance to the solicitor's office. He was intercepted by a young man coming out.

"Is your father in his office?" Holmes asked.

The man cocked his head to one side.

"Are we acquainted?" the young man asked.

"We have not been introduced, but you favour your father."

"May I ask who you are?"

"Sherlock Holmes."

"Oh, Mr Holmes! I am glad to meet you. I am Frederic Abrahams. Your telegrams have been most interesting. I was just on my way to take a look at the house on Marquess Road."

"I went there myself. I think he has settled at least for a few hours."

"Come along," Frederic said waving him in the door. "We enquired and it seems William Kurr and his wife have lived in that house for three years. They have a seven-year lease."

"Father, Mr Holmes is here," Frederic called as he knocked at the office door.

"Mr Holmes," Mr Abrahams said rising and shaking Sherlock Holmes' hand. "Please be seated. It seems your tour of Scotland was very brief."

"Yes, and very wet. You will have to pardon me for a bit of mud since I have not been home to change my shoes yet."

"No pardon needed. You have delivered a treasure trove in few words in less than two days. Tell me, if you can, what is Druscovich doing?"

"He is attempting to satisfy both ends. He is laying a trail to make it seem as if he is doing his job of detecting the criminals at the same time he is covering for them. He can't seem to bring himself to make a clean break with them and tell all to the Yard, or throw the law over entirely and run. He is frustrated with Kurr and Kurr does not trust him. Kurr, by the way, sent a telegram from Edinburgh under the name of Jackson, so now we can connect him to one of the aliases."

"Ah, good. Things begin to fit."

"I do not know Druscovich's relationship with the other Scotland Yard detectives, but it seems like he is willing to sacrifice them before himself. Yet he will protect them if he thinks he can without being caught. It is a frightful balance to try to maintain. Druscovich is close to breaking under the strain."

"I sent him a wire telling him to pick up the letters at the Queens Hotel in Bridge of Allan," the solicitor said.

"He must wonder where you obtained that information."

"He already knew we were doing our own investigations. It could have come from someone at the hotel."

"True."

"Superintendent Williamson would be surprised to learn that I saw Druscovich send a telegram in his name."

"That is stepping over the line," Abrahams said. "What did it say?"

"The gist was that the Glasgow police should bring a cab driver witness to Edinburgh. He wanted that witnesses out of Bridge of Allen so Kurr could get the letters. Kurr didn't want to do it. Instead he met with Mieklejohn in Derby and came back to London."

"What did you hear about Palmer and Mieklejohn? I confess your spelling of Mieklejohn stumped us for a few minutes. It was my son here who realized it was one name."

"Kurr said that the letters at the Queens Hotel implicated Palmer and that Mieklejohn had introduced Yonge to a banker in Alloa. Kurr was at Mieklejohn's house in Derby this morning for a four hours so there is no doubt there is a relationship there. I was told there were other guests, but I did not want to press enquiries in that direction for fear of making Mieklejohn or Kurr suspicious."

"You made the right decision to follow him. It was pretty brazen of Kurr to return to London."

"There are some men who feel invincible on their home turf even when all the world is against them, and I believe Mr Kurr is among them. In my spare hours riding trains I have been attempting to work out his brain for I believe that will be essential to catching him."

"You have exceeded my expectations thus far, Mr Holmes. What are your plans?"

"Home to change then back to Marquess Road."

"I am off to Marquess Road now," Frederic said.

"Do not approach the house too closely and do not be too obvious," Holmes said.

"I believe I can handle myself," the younger Abrahams said.

"You would not expect Mr Holmes to advise you on writing a brief, would you, Fred?" his father asked.

"No," he replied.

"Then take his advice in his area of expertise. What would you have him do, Mr Holmes?"

"The Marquess Tavern is at the end of the road just a few houses away," Holmes said. "Wait outside there. Read a newspaper. Act like you are waiting to meet someone. Avoid staring at the house. When I arrive to take up surveillance again, leave."

"Yes, yes, alright," he agreed.

Fred Abrahams left.

"Do not mind him, Mr Holmes. He has done good work on this case. He is excited that you found Kurr, who seems to be the elusive ringleader."

"We need to avoid scaring Kurr off or scattering the other members of the gang before we can locate them," Holmes said.

"Yes, of course."

"We still have not found Yonge or Francis. I believe that Kurr will lead me to him. I don't know when or how that will be."

He said good day to the solicitor and took a hansom to the British Museum. Once again he approached the flat on Montague Street from the back entrance, letting himself in with his latch key. His inclination would have been to ask Mrs Denton for some hot water and apologize for the state of the laundry. However, it was Sunday, her day off. So he made his way to the kitchen himself and set the water on the stove. He found some bread and some cold beef and ate while the water heated.

He washed and changed, this time in layers like they sometimes did in the theatre when a quick costume change was required. The outer costume was as a bent over old woman with grey hair and a wrinkled face. He packed the satchel with essentials in case he needed to follow Kurr over long distances again. He placed the satchel in a cloth sack slightly larger than it. He walked over to the British Museum as the old woman and took a hansom to St Paul's church in Canonbury. He walked Marquess Road to Clephane Road. Near there, the old woman, seeming lost, wandered down the alley and back again to Marquess Road. There was a bit of a mews but there was a curve to it and he could not tell if it continued to number 29. The old lady was becoming footsore and limped a bit. She stopped at number 28 and rang. There was no answer. This was the house that had drawn his attention when he had driven through the area earlier. The old lady enquired at the next house for a niece she was attempting to locate and had been given that address. She was told that the family was away and the house closed up for the winter. The neighbour was not familiar with the name of the niece.

"Perhaps the address was wrong," the neighbour suggested. "I don't know of another Marquess Road. There is a Market Street in East Ham, but that's near ten miles from here."

The footsore old woman hobbled down to the Marquess Tavern and asked for a glass of beer. She spoke briefly to a young man reading a newspaper who looked startled and left a few minutes later. The old woman then went down Quadrant Road and disappeared. She disappeared because Sherlock Holmes found an alleyway there which reached behind number 28. He dove behind a fence and quickly shed the skirts, shawl, and grey wig which disappeared into a bundle, revealing his black hair, a workman's shirt, waistcoat, and canvas breeches. He pulled on a cap and made his way to the potting shed he had spied next to the vacant house.

There was a grimy window which provided an excellent view of number 29. He had seen it from the other side. He didn't expect Kurr to leave that night but he was prepared to watch all night in case he did, or if he had visitors. Evening was already settling in with a bit of fog. He arranged the old woman's costume in the cloth sack in case he needed it again. His wrinkles had merely been a few thin vermillion lines accentuated by facial expression. They worked as well for a craggy-faced workman and could be smudged to make a grimy beggar if he chose. A hunk of bread and a slice of cheese made for his evening meal. After he finished that off, he lit his pipe, covering the match and initial glow by turning his back to the window.

It was a particularly uneventful night. The lamps were lit and the curtains were drawn in the houses including the one across the way. Sometimes he could see the shadows of the man himself, his wife, and a young girl. The maid and the cook seem to come days, and they left after supper was over. After a few hours the lamps were extinguished as the family went to bed. It could have been any Sunday night at any suburban home.

Holmes supposed Kurr had told his wife that he had been away on business. She may have no idea of the nature of his business or the criminal activities which financed her home.

Would he be attending to business in the morning? It seemed not. At the usual hour Monday morning the neighbours set off to the city in their carriages or on foot to meet omnibuses or find cabs, but nothing stirred at the house of Kurr.

Chapter 4

Irregularities

"We are, as usual, the irregulars, and we must take our own line of action."
Sherlock Holmes, "Disappearance of Lady Frances Carfax"

However, late in the morning something did stir in Holmes' observation post. He heard a small noise. It could have been an animal. He slipped into a shadow, keeping the door in sight. Soon there popped out a small head. It was a boy with tangled hair and a smudged face. The boy crept around the shed keeping low. Neither of them was visible to the house. As the boy came closer, Sherlock Holmes reached out and grabbed him, placing one hand over his mouth and the other arm across his chest to prevent him from leaving. He drew the wiggling child into the shadow with him.

"Be still. I'm not going to harm you," Holmes whispered.

He glanced up at the house again. No one had come out. A hawker was crying a few houses away.

"Will you be quiet if I remove my hand?"

The lad nodded.

"What are you doing here?" he asked.

"Could ask the same o' you, guv'nor."

Holmes chuckled silently.

"Perhaps I'm a robber or an assassin?" Holmes suggested.

"Nah. More loike a peeler."

"No."

"Then why you watching the 'ouse?"

"To see if the man leaves."

"Same as me."

"Why do you want to see when the man leaves?"

"On account o' the pie in oven. Could Auntie it. Babblin' will gimme a slice if he's not around."

It took some quick thinking to keep up with the boy's rhyming slang. Auntie was short for Auntie Nell for "smell" and Babblin' was Babbling Brook for "cook."

"Do you do a lot of cadging?" Holmes asked.

"When I've a mind to."

"Ever run into any trouble?"

"With peelers? Nah. I know how stay outta their way and avoid onyone who would complain. Most babblin's are kind. Not that one down there," he said pointing to one house. "She gives me the broom." He pointed another direction. "The one at the end gives me sum o' what's left from luncheon. That one over there gives me sweet cakes and biscuits. They 'ave fruit trees down there."

"You know where the best meals are to be had."

"I do."

With that the boy's countenance changed. His eyes were now wide and pleading. He'd sucked in his cheeks to make them seem hollow. It was a pitiful aspect of a starving child, likely to take in a tenderhearted woman. Then that melted into an angelic look of innocence. The boy had more than one trick in his bag. Sherlock Holmes shook his head. This explained how well fed the little street urchin was.

"You are not from around here."

"Who says?"

The boy was undoubtedly Cockney. His family could have moved to the suburbs recently. He seemed streetwise and yet his clothes, while worn, fit him and were not in need of mending.

"Where do you live?"

"None o' your bizness."

Holmes had not been quite that small when he had been sneaking out to explore London, but he understood that giving an address meant possibly being hauled back home in shame.

"What is your name?"

"Wiggins."

"Well, Wiggins, tell me what you have seen at the house of pie."

"There's a man, a missus, and the bricks, Alice. Mary, the maid, Mrs Cranston the babblin'.

Bricks from 'bricks and mortar' meant Alice was the name of the daughter.

"Oh, and Zak, he fixes things and drives when they need it," Wiggins continued.

"Do they have a horse and carriage?"

"A dabble and gig."

"Does master of the house work?"

"For a few months 'e was going to City regular every day, then 'e was away on bizness."

"Does he get many visitors at home?"

"A few sometimes."

"Anything you noticed about the visitors?"

"Nah."

"Was there a man who had trouble walking?"

Wiggins looked thoughtful then shook his head.

"Nah, but I'm not always round here. Bizness to attend to, y'know."

Perhaps Kurr had kept his partners in crime away from home? Might that be why he felt secure in his suburban refuge?

A bicycle bell trilled just out of sight. Then a uniformed telegraph boy appeared on his bicycle.

"You may get your pie yet. Could you get close enough to hear the destination if they bring the carriage around?"

"For a consid'ration."

"I'll give you a shilling if you get the address and give it to the old lady you will find near the pub."

"Deal."

Wiggins vanished. Holmes was content that he did not see him reappear. The boy had talent for this type of work. Holmes watched the telegraph boy depart on his bicycle. He expected Kurr would be travelling again, but when, where, or for how long he could not predict. It could be a warning that he had been traced. It could be an appointment to meet at a specified time and place. Holmes reset the wig and donned the skirts again. With the shawl up over his head he made his way to Canonbury Street where he started looking for a passing cab. He was beginning despair of finding one when Wiggins appeared. The boy gave him a quizzical look.

"Come, lad, tell me what you know," Holmes whispered in a high pitched scratchy voice.

"St Pancras to catch 2.30 to Leicester."

"Well, done, m'lad. Worth two shillings," the old woman said digging the coins out of some hidden pocket in her skirts and dropping them into the boy's cupped hands.

Just then a cab appeared down the street with the slow walk of one looking for a fare. The old lady lifted her bag and waved her free hand and the driver pulled towards her.

"Enjoy your pie!" she said to the boy as she mounted the cab.

Holmes knew he was putting a lot of faith in a child in order to anticipate Kurr's next move. If Kurr did not arrive at the station or took another train, he would know he had erred. That could mean that either Kurr or Wiggins had played him. He had weighed the probabilities and had been satisfied enough to take the risk.

Yet in the time Holmes spent waiting at the station in the guise of a bent old woman grasping her ticket waiting for Kurr to arrive, he began to doubt and re-evaluate.

How did he know that the boy wasn't Kurr's ally?

The sight of Kurr arriving not long before the scheduled time of the train reassured him. The fact that Kurr carried no luggage suggested this was to be a short trip. Or did it? As the old woman boarded the train, Holmes speculated. Another possible, though he felt, not probable, explanation was that Kurr was so spooked that he was going to run without telling his wife he was going or giving any followers any clues either. Holmes filed the alternative away and held on to his first theory.

The train was a local, making more than a dozen stops between London and Leicester. This made for a slower, more tedious journey than the previous ones to Scotland and back, but Holmes knew he had to remain alert in case Kurr bolted at any of the stops. When they arrived that evening at the station in Leicester, Inspector Meiklejohn was waiting on the platform. The old lady walked past him as he greeted Kurr.

"Benson's at the Bull Inn, a short walk from here," Meiklejohn said.

They started walking south along the old London Road. Following them there in the guise of the old woman would be treacherous. Holmes found a dark alley and ditched the old woman. The skirts, wig, shawl, and cloth bag folded into the satchel. The shirt, waistcoat and trousers he had on underneath were chilly in the November night but there was no rain. Meiklejohn and Kurr had vanished when he returned to the road. He continued along it and found the Bull Inn. It looked to be an old coaching inn that had seen better days. It had a bar. He entered.

Meiklejohn and Kurr were at a table with a third man. A quick but incisive glance revealed a small man with a slightly darker cast to his skin with a large nose and large ears. There was something almost elf-like about the man. His delicate fingers played a tune soundlessly on the table top.

A musician?

He was expensively dressed with a diamond stud on a cravat at his throat.

This must be Francis/Yonge – now Benson.

He seemed troubled.

There was an empty table not far from them and he took it with his back to them. He ordered a pint. The men were being served their drinks.

"What's this about a telegram?" Kurr asked after the bar maid moved off.

"Here," Meiklejohn said handing the telegram to him. "He wanted me to meet him in Edinburgh tonight."

"You didn't," Kurr said.

"No, I telegraphed back that I couldn't come tonight."

"What does he mean by 'your knowledge as to three persons who have been staying here'," Kurr asked.

"I think he's heard of our meeting in Bridge of Allan and the dinner at Dumblane," Meiklejohn said.

"How did he do that?"

"In small towns they report all visitors in the newspaper. They've nae much else t' report. The dinner was even reported in the *Evening Citizen*, a Glasgow paper on the 8th," Meiklejohn said.

"Vhat is he going to say about the men menshonned?" Benson asked.

Ah, the hint of French accent there.

"He could say the description of Yonge did not match the man he was looking for, but Wilson and Gollan were there as well. They might contradict him. He's rather stuck," Meiklejohn replied.

"You mean you are rather stuck," Kurr said.

Not much honour among thieves, Holmes thought.

"We are all in this," Meiklejohn insisted.

"They know you by name and profession. They don't know me as anything but Gifford," Kurr said.

"Druscovich does, and I do," Meiklejohn said. "I can take care of myself as long as you two keep your mouths shut."

The threat was more than implied.

"You should go to New York," Kurr said.

"Vhy?" Benson asked.

"Palmer wants you out of the way. You are too easy to identify."

"Vhat are you and Murrray doing with zhe money?"

Ah, Benson was feeling the others were trying to cut him out.

"All will be set right," Kurr said.

"Vell for you to say. I have no English money. I had to leave £3000 in zhe bank in Scotland."

"I sent Murray to the bank at Alloa with two cheques in favour of Mr Carson. One of these was drawn by Henry Yonge for £3000 and the other by William Gifford for £500. I have no doubt he will get the money and then we will share it."

"If you will give me some English bank notes, I'll go to Dublin and await instructions."

"Here," Kurr said. "Take these and go tonight."

"Then gentlemen, I must leave you to prrepare for my departurre."

Benson rose somewhat painfully and slowly left. He was not using sticks to assist him but it was easy to imagine he had not long ago.

"In the circumstances, I don't think I should telegraph any more to your office," Kurr said to Meiklejohn.

"Telegraph to Thompson at the Railway Hotel or the Midland Hotel, Derby. Where shall I telegraph to you?"

"To Matthews, at the Mitre, Kingsgate Street, Holborn."

"You are going back to London?"

"Yes. You take care of Druscovich. I'll talk to Palmer."

Sherlock Holmes was nearly finished his pint. He rose to leave.

As he did he heard Kurr tell Meiklejohn, "Benson might be clever with written words but I'm afraid he'll talk if they catch him. We need to get him out of the country."

Holmes returned to the railway station and sent a telegram:

K, M, Y in Leic. P connected. B to Dublin. K to London. Murray at bank at Alloa with notes. Read Glasgow Evening Citizen Dumblane dinner. SH

Holmes took the next train south without waiting for Kurr. He arrived in London before dawn. The streets were empty. The air was damp yet warm for November. He entered by the front of the flat at Montague Street. He was confident by now that no one was following him or knew of his involvement in this case. On the table in the sitting room was a telegram. It was from Abrahams dated the evening before. He presumed his later telegram had answered the question. He stripped off the worker's clothes and pulled the old lady's costume from the satchel. Those would no doubt puzzle Mrs Denton. The other clothing he had left on Sunday night had been laundered and returned without a note. He lay down and slept in his own bed.

He was smoking a pipe in his dressing gown a few hours later when there was a tap on the door. Then it tentatively opened.

"Come in, Mrs Denton," he called.

"I was not sure you were home, Mr Sherlock."

"I will be off again soon."

"Would you like some coffee and toast before you go?"

"Yes, thank you, Mrs Denton."

"I'll be back with it directly."

A couple of hours later he was back in Canonbury. He came from the other end of the street, past the stables where Kurr kept his carriage, past the back of 29, Marquess Road, then around the other side, where he made his way through a broken bit of fence to the garden shed.

"He's back," Wiggins said from the shadows.

"I know," Holmes responded quietly.

Holmes found a place to sit on a potting bench where he could see through the window. He took out his pipe and lit it. The boy came out of the shadows and sat opposite. They shared the watch for a few hours, mostly in silence. No one came or went from the house across the way. As the churches were ringing noon, Sherlock Holmes extracted a brown paper parcel from his satchel. Mrs Denton had insisted on preparing a lunch.

"I'm afraid I don't have pie," he said ripping the sandwich in half and holding one half out.

"Ha!" the boy exclaimed and took it.

The hours ticked away.

"I wonder if your friend the cook could tell you if the master plans to be home for supper."

Wiggins said nothing but vanished. Holmes saw him briefly as he approached the side door of number 29. He reappeared in the shed a few minutes later.

"Says t' master 'spects supper at eight o'clock."

Then he dug into a pocket.

"She gave me some biscoots."

He held one out.

Sherlock Holmes shook his head.

"You keep it."

Holmes took up his satchel.

"I need to go somewhere."

He walked several streets away and caught a cab to the City.

Abrahams was glad to see him.

"Mr Holmes, look here," Abrahams said.

He handed him a piece of newspaper folded over with an article circled. It described a dinner of some distinguished visitors at the Stirling Arms at Dumblane. They included Superintendent Meiklejohn of the Detective Department of the Midland Railway, Derby, who was visiting his father at Green Loaming, Inspector William Wilson of the Glasgow police and Detective Gollan of the sheriff's department Edinburgh. The other gentlemen dining with these police detectives were a Mr Gifford, a large, full-blooded man about twenty-five and a Mr Yonge, a small, lame man, walking with two sticks, of about thirty-five years of age.

"This is the Glasgow *Evening Citizen*?" Holmes asked.

"Yes, but I have received word that it will be all over the Scottish papers tomorrow."

"That will not please Scotland Yard."

"No, it won't."

Holmes recounted for the solicitor what he had heard in Leicester.

"It is remarkable that Kurr and Meiklejohn seem so secure," Abrahams said.

"I believe they will all turn on each other when they are rounded up. There is no loyalty. Each is guarding his own interest."

"Their financial interest at least. A man going by the name of Carson did attempt to negotiate two cheques at the Clydesdale Bank of Alloa, one from Henry Yonge for £3000 and another from William Gifford for £500 at the Clydesdale Bank of Alloa. He was detained but released because they had no proof that he had known the funds were obtained illegally. The cheques were kept by the bank."

"That might make them desperate enough to attempt to negotiate the missing bank notes."

"We have warned banks all over to watch for them. The Scottish police think 'Carson' went south. He could come up to London."

"I suppose Benson reached Dublin?"

"As best I can tell. I am attempting to get the Metropolitan Police to ask the Dublin police to look for him. They want to know where I obtained my information."

"Kurr is the most dangerous of the gang."

"Yet the one we have the least evidence against."

"Yes, not by accident, I believe. He looks like a thug but that man has a first rate brain. I don't want him to get away."

"On the other hand Benson is the one that the police have the most evidence against. If they would catch him he might turn on Kurr."

"Even Kurr recognizes that."

"Are you on watch at Marquess Road today?"

"Yes, he is not leaving before supper."

"How can we get a message to you if we need to?"

"Send your son to the Marquess Tavern where he watched before. I will contact him."

Holmes returned to the observation post in Marquess Road. The boy was gone. The lamps were lit in 29. He struck a match and held it to his pipe and settled in for the long night.

Early the next morning a hansom cab clopped up to the door of number 29. A young man jumped out and went to the door. Holmes saw a maid answer and take him inside. The cabby waited by the curb and soon the man came out again and it drove off.

Was this the man named Murray, mentioned in Leicester, who was presumably the same man who presented himself at the bank in Scotland as Carson?

Holmes considered attempting to send a message to Abrahams that Murray may be in London. However, the possibility of the account of the dinner at Dumblane coming out in other newspapers in Scotland and perhaps even repeated in the English papers kept him at his watch. The news would expose Meiklejohn and the Scottish policemen, who, if innocent, were likely to provide additional information about Yonge and Gifford, if only to clear themselves. Kurr might run.

Holmes waited and gave it some thought. Finally he decided to try his luck spotting a telegram boy along Essex Road. He managed to intercept one and supply him with the form he had written out in the potting shed. He made his way back to the potting shed by a different route through Ashby Street. Kurr did not seem to have done anything extraordinary in his absence.

The presumptive Murray returned in the evening. This would make sense if his mission was to convert more of the banknotes to a more usable form. He would either be handing over the proceeds or reporting his failure. He stayed longer this time so it was possible additional planning was discussed. After he left, the Kurr household settled into the usual domestic tranquillity and the master of the house showed no sign of bolting. Holmes himself settled in for a long winter's night with only his pipe as company.

The traffic along Marquess Road the next few days was the usual round of milkmen and postmen, men off to work in the morning, children to school, women to the market, and all returning later in the day. Their comings and goings were familiar by now. Would it surprise any of them that amidst all this domesticity sat a wanted criminal?

Murray came on Saturday and there was a flurry of telegraph boys coming and going in the afternoon. Clearly some type of long distance communication was taking place, but who was he communicating with? Kurr had told Meiklejohn to wire him at a different location and Meiklejohn would be unwise to be wiring to him under his current state of suspicion. Could it be Benson once again stressed for funds or some other member of the gang?

It was late in the afternoon that another character entered the pantomime that caused Sherlock Holmes to leave his blind. This was a man walking up and down next to the tavern, checking his watch and looking extremely impatient. It was a role that Frederic Abrahams played well because he was an impatient person. Undoubtedly he carried a message from his father.

Holmes left the potting shed and made his way unseen through the backs between Ashby Road and Quadrant Road and then out and around to the Marquess Tavern. He greeted the young solicitor with a slap on the shoulder and with a few words ushered him into the tavern itself. They found a corner with a view of Marquess Road and ordered a couple of pints, bread, and cheese. The tavern contained a number of patrons talking, laughing, and drinking. Once their needs had been supplied Holmes asked Frederic what he had come for.

"And don't look around. It makes you look suspicious. No one present has been near Kurr's house."

"The news was all over the newspapers in Scotland on Wednesday with the London papers picking it up by the afternoon editions. Word got to the Commissioner, who demanded an explanation from Superintendent Williamson, who in turn wrote to Meiklejohn demanding an explanation. Williamson is also unhappy with my father's claim that Druscovich and Palmer are shielding the criminals as well, but we believe he has thus far withheld that from the Commissioner. An investigation into the dinner and the men present is likely to be opened in Scotland on Friday.

"Inspector Druscovich returned to London this morning with the letters," Frederick continued. He and Williamson brought them to my father's office and opened them there. Then Williamson said 'These are in Palmer's handwriting.'"

"How did Druscovich react?"

"He seemed to be in shock. He could not seem to say anything. No, he did say one thing which is why I am here. He is sending plain-clothed detectives to watch Kurr's house starting tonight."

"We shall see how well they do."

"You aren't concerned about running afoul of them?"

Holmes chuckled.

"No."

Frederic looked puzzled.

"Why not?"

"They won't spot me any more than you did. Have you had any luck intercepting Murray?"

"We are talking with the money changers again."

"Excellent. Now drink your pint, look jolly, and leave with me. Pretend we are old friends. We will part on Canonbury Road. Walk down the road a bit before you hail a cab."

Frederic Abrahams played the role as directed and Holmes returned to the potting shed.

Holmes saw a policeman appear shortly thereafter. He was not one Holmes knew, but his surveillance methods were clumsy enough for Kurr to notice. After having spied the man from his window, Kurr decided to take a walk and he addressed the man by name as he passed him. How Kurr knew the man's name was an interesting question.

On Sunday the flurry of telegrams continued. Murray also visited a few times, and the clumsy police detective left and was not replaced. Had a telegram in the midst of that flood gone to Druscovich telling him to call his dogs off?

Whether it was the telegrams or the visits by Murray, something was upsetting the domestic tranquillity of the Kurr household. Holmes saw at least one scene through the open curtains that seemed to be a disagreement between Kurr and his wife.

Was she asking what was happening or was he saying he needed to go away? Or was it about an unrelated matter?

Early Monday morning the gig was brought around. Holmes

rushed out to Quadrant Road and thus to Canonbury Street where he was fortunate to snag a hansom quickly. He jumped in and spoke to the driver.

"There will be a dappled grey horse and gig coming out from Marquess Road shortly. Follow it. Don't be too obvious about it but go where it is going. If I am correct it is going to Paddington Station."

"I might be long in the tooth, but I am still sharp in the eyes. I could follow a dapple anywhere."

He was good to his word, always keeping the dappled grey horse in sight but not following too close. At Paddington he pulled up a few down the line of cabs. Holmes flipped him a sovereign and made for the ticket window quickly. He stayed back in the crowd close enough to hear Kurr's destination and then a few ticket buyers later he bought one as well. They were heading to Reading.

The ride there was uneventful and Holmes dozed when he could. As the train approached the station at Reading, he saw Benson on the platform. He seemed paler than before, but perhaps that was merely the frosty atmosphere. Kurr was far from frosty. He was more ruddy than ever and obviously angry. The sight of the large red-faced man looming over the small pale man and tossing harsh words his way was attracting attention. It was curious how unmoved the smaller man was by the sound and fury. However, Benson's lack of reaction seemed to infuriate Kurr more, Holmes began to fear that the fraud investigation was going to end in a homicide. There was no doubt that the two men were under stress with warrants out for their arrest, and their police protectors under investigation. Cooler heads eventually prevailed and they retired to a nearby café where Holmes managed to follow them unseen. They spoke in soft tones yet Holmes was able to make out the words. The conversation was enlightening. Benson was concerned about funds. He had a lifestyle to maintain, he said. He had done all his work quite admirably, etc. He felt Kurr was keeping his share. Kurr denied this and tried to explain the difficulties Murray was encountering.

"They took the drafts from him in Alloa. They arrested him, but he was able to convince them that he knew nothing about the account holders. He tried to convert some of the bank notes in London, but the Venable exchange house held them. Murray went to a solicitor named Froggatt for some assistance getting them released. Froggatt said he had some other changers who might not ask any questions, at a premium. They've been able to get very little. Here. Have all of it but you need to leave the country. Fred and Bale have already gone."

"Is it safe? Are they watching the docks? I am afraid they are going to arrest me if I attempt to board a ship."

"Come up to London then and I will check with Palmer and put you on a boat myself."

So it was decided. Benson already had a first class carriage reserved for the next train to London which was what had prompted Kurr to intercept him before he went knocking about London exposed. Sherlock Holmes was certain that it was not Kurr's concern for Benson that spurred him, but rather because he considered Benson a danger to himself as long as he was in England.

The train arrived at Paddington close to 10 o'clock. As Benson and Kurr descended from the train at Paddington they were greeted by a third man that Holmes did not recognize yet both Benson and Kurr did. They called him "Street." Holmes was uncertain if that was a surname or a nickname. Street had already reserved a growler large enough to accommodate the three men and Benson's luggage. Holmes considered his options as they were arranging the luggage. Then he saw his driver of the morning. The man winked at him. He walked over to the cab and the driver said in a low tone:

"Need someone followed again?" the cabby asked.

"I do indeed. The one with the quantity of luggage."

"Weighed down like that it will take an effort for me to stay behind them. Climb in."

"I don't want them to know they are followed."

"Then you're in luck. The fog is going to help with that."

He was right. There was fog rolling into the station.

They followed the four-wheeler as it lumbered past Hyde Park, through Piccadilly, by Buckingham Palace, across Westminster Bridge over the Thames to the less fashionable district of Lambeth and stopped in the street. The fog had increased as they neared the river. The hansom driver stopped his horse at a distance from the four-wheeler and doused the lights. Holmes watched Kurr and Street climb down from the four wheeled cab and walk to a house on a side street.

"What street is this?" Sherlock Holmes asked the driver.

"Kennington Road."

"And that one?"

"Methley Street, number 38, I believe,"

The address meant nothing to Holmes. The wait was long, cold, and damp. Holmes extracted the mackintosh from the satchel. It was past midnight by the time the men returned to their cab, to much grumbling by both Benson and the driver. Then cab took off, slowly, for the fog was getting very thick. The hansom driver followed their lights.

After about a mile the driver knocked on the trap and opened it.

"This is Southwark Bridge Road. I'll wager they're going to St Katharine Docks."

This fit with the conversation Holmes had heard earlier in the day. Kurr didn't want Benson even spending the night in London. It was unfortunate that Holmes was working in opposition to the police rather than in conjunction with them for if he had a Scotland Yard detective with him now they could arrest them both.

The journey was slow despite the lack of the traffic because the fog grew even thicker as they crossed the Thames again. By the time they pulled up to St Katharine Docks, Holmes could hardly see beyond the length of his arm. He dismissed the cabby to his bed with a generous tip, but asked a final favour of him.

"If you find a telegraph office open, send this," he said giving him a yellow telegraph form.

"I will, sir. Thank you. Name's Blake if you need to find me again. Don't fall in."

Sherlock Holmes chuckled at the ironic warning. The driver did not know that he had plunged into the Thames under dramatic circumstances twice in his life already.

The fog here made it easier to approach the four wheeler cab. They were unloading the luggage onto the quay. He had sent the driver off with a telegram to Abrahams. While the solicitor had promised to have someone available at his office at all hours he did not have high hopes that the solicitor would be able to drag someone from Scotland Yard to the docks past 1 o'clock in the morning, especially in a fog like this. He had urged Abrahams to insist Scotland Yard alert foreign police agencies.

The four-wheeler pulled away after being relieved of its burdens. Kurr and Street stayed with Benson. They huddled about a barrel of fire for warmth. The stevedores loaded the luggage. It seemed Kurr and Street were anxious enough to get Benson out of the country that they chose the first steamship with space available. Benson grumbled about having to travel 2nd class and Street laughed that he was lucky not to be stuffed in steerage. The ship was headed to Boulogne.

More people began gathering at the dock despite the fog. The ship was destined to sail with the tide in the early hours. Kurr and Street watched until Benson boarded and the ship left the dock before they found a cab and headed off with Holmes upon their tail quite literally, for he used the dense fog to hide him as he clung to the back of their cab as it crossed London.

Morning brought another surprise at the Kurr residence. Murray came as usual but after he had gone, a four wheeler drove up to 29, Marquess, and a man stepped out that was about the same height and weight as Kurr. He seemed to be moving in.

Holmes walked around to Quadrant Road and out to Essex Road, and up to the northeast end of Marquess Road, and walked down it. He had a note pad and a pencil. He knocked on the front door of each house in turn asking them about their gas service. When he reached Clephane Road he went up and down each side and explored into the mews to the northwest. He saw the stable where Kurr kept his horse and gig. He saw similar facilities of other residents. There was also a stable for hire which was probably mostly used by neighbours. He came back around on Marquess Road and knocked on number 29. He told the maid he was there to check the gas.

"No need to bother the master. Just show me t' the pipes and I'll be done in a jiffy."

Sound travels along pipes, but sometimes too much of it does, resulting in overlapping conversations from different rooms. It was not reliable. There was also the cup on the wall method of eavesdropping or the classical method of just getting near enough to hear what you want to hear without getting caught. He used combinations of all the above, sometimes singly or in couples to listen in on Kurr, Stenning, and various other members of the household. He heard a great deal that was not pertinent to his investigation, including some small talk and reminiscing between Kurr and Stenning. Nonetheless he did obtain enough information to make the subterfuge worth the gamble. He was correct that Stenning was moving in at least temporarily and the similarity to Kurr was very much part of Kurr's plan.

Stenning laughed.

"You want me to dress in your clothes and go for a ride in your gig and pretend to be you?" he asked.

"Yes."

"Wait, you are not the target of an assassin, are you?"

"Not that I am aware of," Kurr responded.

"So what is the purpose?"

"To show those officers a good time."

Stenning laughed again.

"Is there an arrest warrant out on you?"

"Come now, Stenning, if there was would I be sitting here enjoying a cigar with you?"

"You might at that. What if they arrest me thinking I'm you?"

"Then you just prove you are you and they will release you."

"I'm a decoy."

"You are a guest," Kurr said. "I'm just asking you to play this little game with me."

"What if they want to arrest me as an accessory?"

"To what?"

"I have no idea."

"Then how can you be an accessory? You are my guest. You will have good food and drink, fresh air, some games of whist, good companionship. Think of it as a holiday. Then in a few days I will be able to give you the loan you have been seeking."

It was time to go to avoid overstaying his welcome.

Holmes followed up on the rest of the nearby houses before

stepping into the tavern and asking about their gas. He worked his way down Quandrant Road and into his hideaway again.

"Nice lil show there," a voice said.

"An elementary ruse."

"Loike the old lady?" Wiggins asked.

"Yes."

"You were on stage in trooff?"

"I was for nearly two years."

"You ain't no more?"

"There were better uses of my talents."

"Watching blokes from a potting shed?" Wiggins said with a grin.

"Not precisely."

"Did you get in?"

"Yes."

"Who is the bloke who moved in?"

"Name of Stenning. Kurr wants him to act as a double to fool people watching him."

"Loike the peelers at ends o' street or one around the corner?"

"Yes."

"Are they going to arrest him?"

"Not yet."

"He doesn't know about you?

"I don't think so."

"Do they?"

"Unlikely."

"Are you a foreign spy?"

"No."

Holmes wondered where Wiggins had been the days he was gone. He doubted the boy would tell him if he asked. Beyond his name, Wiggins had kept his personal life close to his vest. They shared the watch for a few hours. Wiggins left in the twilight. He did not return the following day.

Kurr and his associates continued their costume play through to Wednesday, even to the point of strolling down the street and wishing the plainclothes officers a good day. When Murray arrived in

Wednesday evening he had shaved his whiskers and beard off.

As clumsy as some of the plain clothes detectives were in their surveillance, it did take some pressure off Sherlock Holmes for there were more than one of them and if Kurr did something dramatic they were likely to follow. He was not at all fooled by the antics of Kurr and Stenning changing clothes. They did not stand or walk the same way. It was simple to tell them apart. He didn't think even the Scotland Yarders would be duped.

That was one factor in his decision to return to Montague Street. However, the primary one was that he was out of tobacco. He could tolerate the shortage of sleep and food, but the want of tobacco was irritating. So after the lamps were extinguished on the night of November 22nd he walked to Essex Road and flagged a cab home.

Other than the stack of mail on the table and a few notes from Mrs Denton wondering if he was still alive, nothing had changed. He left her a note asking to wake him for breakfast. Then he peeled off his clothes and fell into bed.

The next thing he knew there was a tap on the door to his bedroom. He grabbed his dressing gown, ran his fingers through his hair and was met by the smell of coffee as he opened the door. He picked up a pipe as he passed the mantel on his way to the table. Mrs Denton was pouring a cup. There were eggs, rashers, toast and jam arranged upon the table.

"You are psychic, Mrs Denton. I am starving."

"You look awful. When was the last time you slept?"

"About two minutes ago."

"I meant before that."

"I napped some on trains to and from Reading a day ago."

"Hmmph. If you get killed, your brother will never forgive me."

"I have not been in any real danger. Tracking some cheats, is all," he said.

He set the cup down and snatched up a pencil and a telegraph form. He wrote a few words and handed it to her.

"Could you see that this gets sent? There will likely be one in return."

"Yes. And I will get the laundry out to the washer woman. You have been leaving some peculiar laundry recently. If I hadn't known you had been an actor, I would have wondered...."

Sherlock Holmes laughed. There it was.

"You eat all that. You are skin and bones," she said.

He swallowed a bit of toast before replying.

"I will indeed. I think I could eat an elephant at the moment. Thank you."

After devouring the food on the table and downing three cups of coffee, he poked through the mail and began going through the accumulated newspapers.

Mrs Denton reappeared with a telegram and a tray to remove the dishes. He ripped open the telegram as she piled dishes on the tray.

Mr Sherlock Holmes
Please step around this morning when you can.
Michael Abrahams, Esq.

It was what he had expected.

"Mrs Denton—"

"The water is on the stove. I will bring it directly."

"Thank you, Mrs Denton."

Washed, rested, fed, in starched collars and cuffs, shined boots, and top hat, Sherlock Holmes descended from the cab in Old Jewry. He was soon led to Mr Abrahams' office by his clerk where his son Frederic was already in attendance.

"So, Mr Holmes, is this another of your disguises?" asked Frederic Abrahams with a smile.

"Merely the first time I've had time to dress properly before arriving."

"You are confident that Mr Kurr will not leave in your absence?"

"Mr Kurr is enjoying being watched by Scotland Yard too much to bring it to an end prematurely."

"He must be very confident that the police can't hold him."

"Yes. We must allow him to rest in the glow of that confidence until we extinguish the light. Have you had any luck tracing Murray?"

"We have had reports of places he may have been. For example, three £100 Clydesdale notes were changed recently at Kulb's and Burt's but since they have no serial numbers we cannot know for certain that they were those same Clydesdale notes. Another exchange house by the name of Messrs. Venables had someone bring in several Clydesdale notes. He was unable to give a satisfactory account as to how he had obtained them. So Mr Venables detained the notes but not the man. We have amplified the message that it is essential for them to contact us or Scotland Yard when the notes are presented and to give some excuse to delay the exchange so we can assemble."

"What of Benson? It was impossible for me to prevent him boarding that ship. There was no constable to be seen and if I had raised the hue and cry, Kurr and Street would have escaped in the fog."

"I understand your position," Abrahams said. "Superintendent Williamson did send out warnings to all the agencies at foreign ports including France, Belgium, Netherlands, Norway, Sweden, Spain, and the United States. He included the descriptions we had of Benson, Bale, and Frederic Kurr plus known aliases. There has been no response."

"We need to isolate Kurr from the others, including Druscovich, Mieklejohn, and Palmer," Holmes said.

"Mieklejohn came up to London on the 18th and reported to Williamson. He claimed to have been unaware that Yonge and Gifford were the men wanted for defrauding the Comtesse. Yet we know that that Mieklejohn patrolled the racetracks where Kurr/Gifford was a regular. His explanation made no sense. He has called in sick since then. So has Palmer."

"Speaking of Palmer, his house is on Methley Street," Frederic said.

"So it is possible that was who Kurr and Street were meeting with," Holmes said.

"Yes. I suppose they were consulting with him as to which of the docks was the least likely to be well patrolled," Frederic agreed.

"If that was the case, he was well advised. Where is Druscovich?" Holmes responded.

"Still going about his duties, but he knows he is suspected and Williamson is keeping an eye on him."

"Not close enough, I'll wager. There was at least one undercover policeman assigned to watch Kurr on the 18th, but he left with no relief. Either Druscovich called them off or one of more of the junior detectives was remiss in his duties. If I had not been there to follow Kurr we might have never known of the meeting with Benson and placing him on the steam ship."

"Or the meeting with Palmer," Frederic said.

"Druscovich still seems to be in a position to protect Kurr here in London. Druscovich needs to be gotten out of the country. Perhaps the superintendent could send him to Boulogne to assist the police there in looking for Benson."

"I can suggest it to him," Abrahams said, "but he might be hesitant to allow him out of his sight."

"Druscovich has already done too much right under his nose," Holmes insisted.

"Murray is the most exposed at this time. If Murray was arrested, and Druscovich sent out of the country we might have a chance of arresting Kurr."

"Arresting Murray will cut off Kurr's funds," Abrahams said, "but it is unlikely to send Kurr to prison. Benson is the one we must catch to convict Kurr."

"First we must find him."

"Yes."

Mr Abrahams held out a piece of paper.

"Well, Mr Holmes I was remiss in not giving this to you a few days ago but here is your draft for the second week. Are you in need of any additional funds for expenses?"

"No," he said taking the draft. "If we can move the other chess pieces out of the way, I believe we can take the king without further travel. He is in check, but not quite checkmate."

Holmes stood.

"Unless you gentlemen have further need of me, I shall be returning home. You can reach me there if a need arises."

They stood and shook his hand.

On Saturday November 25th, Holmes received a letter from Abrahams to the effect that Edwin Murray had approached an acquaintance named John Lindsay Savory with £10 000 in £100 Clydesdale notes that he needed cashed. Savory offered to do it for a commission. He went with him to a money changer's opposite Charing Cross Station and spoke to them while Murray waited in the street. When he came out he told Murray he could not get it done that day and made an appointment with him on the Monday the 27th at St Martin's Church, Trafalgar Square. Savory then went immediately to Scotland Yard and spoke with Chief Inspector Clark, who took him to Superintendent Williamson, who later relayed the information to Abrahams. Superintendent Williamson assured Abrahams that Druscovich was not in the office at the time and not expected to be in until Monday, and the information was being very tightly controlled. Abrahams also wrote that Williamson had taken over personal supervision of the surveillance of Kurr's home.

A short telegram arrived on Monday.

Murray in custody

Holmes waited and read the papers. The London papers reported on the Habrons' trial for the murder of PC Cock in Sheffield on November 27th. That was the murder mentioned in the clippings Jonathan had sent. Even by that date there was something rather suspect about the charges. The police believed there was another accomplice but had been unable to produce one. The jury split, convicting one of the brothers, and acquitting the other.

Another telegram arrived from Abrahams on Tuesday.

Detective Sergeant Littlechild now in charge of surveillance in Marquess Street. Kurr visited a solicitor named Froggatt.

The newspapers reported that two nights after the trial of the Habrons, a man named Arthur Dyson was shot dead in the passageway next to his house at Banner Cross Ecclesall Road near Sheffield. The perpetrator was thought to be a man named Charles Peace, a picture framer, who had quarrelled with Dyson over his wife. There was a manhunt out for him and a reward of hundred pounds. Peace was described as a "wiry, insignificant-looking individual" fifty to sixty years of age, five feet four or five inches in height, with a grey or grey-white full beard and moustache. Another paper reported that Inspector Bradbury of the Highland Division described Peace as having "longish whiskers, of the variety known as a peg top." He was also described as missing fingers from his left hand but that was not unusual among the labouring classes. So many men could fit those descriptions that Holmes doubted anyone would know him if he stood before them. The newspapers reported an increasing number of burglaries in Hull and Nottingham.

Four days later, Holmes received another telegram from Abrahams: *Three men arrested in Rotterdam believed to be Benson, Bale, and Frederick Kurr. Kurr and Stenning leading police around London.*

Holmes' return wire: *Is Druscovich still in London?*

And the response: *Yes. Pressuring W to send him to Rotterdam.*

Another telegram came the next day: *Druscovich ordered to go to Rotterdam on Friday.*

Sherlock Holmes jumped up and pulled on his frock-coat, hat, and overcoat.

Mr Abrahams welcomed him when he arrived. After the usually preliminaries, Holmes got to the matter which had brought him.

"Are they going to arrest Kurr?"

"The magistrate won't issue a warrant unless someone will identify him as Charlie Jackson or one of the other aliases related to the matter."

"Murray won't?"

"Murray says he knows nothing about that matter."

Holmes tapped his fingers on Abraham's desk.

"Then I shall have to find someone who will identify him."

"How can we support you in this effort, Mr Holmes?"

"Kurr must not be allowed to escape. The detectives watching must be diligent."

"I will speak to Superintendent Williamson again and we shall add more of our own agents."

Holmes pulled out the papers Abrahams had first given him. They listed the locations connected to the fraud. They all had been searched previously, but how carefully had the landlords and the neighbours been questioned when the case was under Inspector Druscovich? Holmes took it upon himself to question them. He quickly confirmed his initial impression that the aliases were not used consistently by one person. Lodgings at 11, King Street, St James' were let by one man giving his name as Andrew Montgomery which did not fit the description of either Benson or William Kurr, but rather his brother Frederick Kurr. The Comtesse, on the other hand, was of the understanding that 11, King Street was the residence of Thomas Ellerton. Neither Mrs Ireland, the landlady at the lodging at King Street, nor her servant, Laura Salter, had ever seen anyone fitting the description of William Kurr. Ellerton's business address at Agar Chambers, Agar Street, did not exist and had never existed.

The two other bookmakers, Jacob Francis and Charles Jackson, lived at 2, Cleveland Row, St James' and 12, St James' Place respectively. William Woodward, the landlord at 2, Cleveland Row said the room was let by a person fitting Frederick Kurr's description for a friend whose name was Jacob Francis. He only saw Jacob Francis once and he fit the description of Benson. He had never seen someone who fit William Kurr's description. Frederick Deane was the landlord at the St James Place address. He, too, described Frederick Kurr as the man who took the rooms under the name of Andrew Montgomery. Letters came addressed to both Andrew Montgomery and Charles Jackson. The description of Jackson did not fit William Kurr but rather the third man arrested in Rotterdam, Charles Bale. So the pattern continued through the majority of the locations.

Rather than attempt to create consistent identities for any of the aliases, the operational theory of the gang seemed to be to sow as much confusion as possible to delay investigators who might come after them. The difficulty with such a plan is that once suspicion develops, as it had in this case, the tangle of identities increases suspicion rather than alleviating it. Even the police were likely to dig further... unless they already knew the answer.

The interviews consumed days until all that remained was the offices at 8, Northumberland Street next to the Northumberland Hotel. The landlord's name was George Flintoff. At Holmes' first enquiry, Flintoff's wife had said he was out of town. Holmes' attempts to question her were resisted.

"No, no, I wouldn't know anything about it. I brought some towels up a few times but I wouldn't recognize anyone. My eyesight is very poor these days. All I can do to avoid bumping into things. I concentrate on that. No, you come back when my husband is here."

Holmes determined that there weren't any clerks or servants at 8, Northumberland Street to be interviewed and thus he had to wait for George Flintoff. The man was an engineer as well as the holder of the primary lease on the property. He did much consulting and speaking on his craft. Unfortunately, his wife did not know the exact day or hour of his return. It was thus with biblical anticipation that Sherlock Holmes staked out a spot at the window of the bar at the Northumberland Hotel.

Abrahams knew where Holmes was and occasionally sent him telegrams. Druscovich was by this time in Rotterdam, though reportedly not happy about it. Benson, Bale, and Frederick Kurr were not willing to snitch on Bill Kurr. Stenning was still living in Kurr's house. Two other men believed to be Street and Walters, both with previous entanglements with Kurr and the men arrested, also visited Kurr. Detective Sergeant Littlechild was still overseeing the surveillance of Kurr, with strict orders to report to no one but Williamson. Holmes was disturbed when Abrahams reported that Druscovich had come back to London on December 24th without Williamson's consent. Holmes watched for the Scotland Yarder in case he was trying to influence Flintoff. However, two days later Williamson sent Druscovich back to Rotterdam.

The noose was tightening about Kurr but he still had allies. George Flintoff, engineer and landlord at 8, Northumberland Street, seemed to be their last best hope to bring him up on charges whenever Flintoff returned home.

The accommodations for surveillance at the Northumberland Hotel were far better than those of the potting shed. He took advantage of his many hours there to interview every employee of the hotel as well. The most useful was George Hall, the foreman at the Northumberland Hotel. He told Holmes that he took refreshments to No. 8 occasionally and saw people whose descriptions matched Benson, William Kurr, and Frederick Kurr. He had seen them coming in and out of No. 8 and the Northumberland Hotel. However, he didn't know any names or whether they were the owners of the business or customers. Sherlock Holmes reported this information to Abrahams who feared it was too thin to satisfy the magistrate. So Holmes waited with his pipe, a glass, and a newspaper. Abraham's clerk also spelled him in the evenings so he could return to his own bed. It was an easier, yet more frustrating surveillance than that at Marquess Street.

On December 29th a cab pulled up before 8, Northumberland Street and a bent over man with a shock of grey hair stepped down. Holmes was out on the pavement within seconds, helping him with his luggage, and carrying it in the door held open by his wife. Rather than take his leave once the luggage was inside, he turned to George Flintoff.

"Mr Flintoff, I have a very urgent matter to discuss with you."

"He has been haunting the door practically since you were gone," his wife said as she took his coat.

"Yes, sir, but is an urgent matter," Sherlock Holmes interjected. "I suppose you have read of the men who were arrested in Rotterdam regarding the fraud of the Comtesse de Goncourt?"

"Terrible thing. People stealing other people's money. Happened to me before. Try to make an honest living and people take advantage. Disgusting," Flintoff grumbled lowering himself into a chair.

"Those were the men who were renting your rooms upstairs."

"Indeed? The police searched months ago and never told me that. Bring me some tea, my dear," he said to his wife.

"Was one a small, dapper gentleman, who walked with crutches or canes?"

"Yes, yes, what was it he called himself? Brooks! Yes. Of Brooks and Co., of Glasgow, advertising agents. He was a fancy dresser, always wearing jewellery, too much for my taste. Arthur Chapman first approached us, but Brooks was often there. I supposed that made sense with his name of the door, so to speak. They never really put their name on the door. I don't see how they expected to make a go of advertising when they didn't even advertise themselves."

"The men who called themselves Brooks and Chapman were arrested in Rotterdam under other aliases. They tried to use one of the notes received with the Comtesse' money"

"Ah."

"Was there a very big man, tall and barrel-chested with a round face who worked with them?"

"Oh, yes, Kurr. Couldn't mistake him."

Holmes' pulse was racing. He had been hoping Flintoff recognized the description of Kurr and would be able to tie him to Benson as a business partner. He had not expected Flintoff to know Kurr by name.

"You knew him by that name?"

"He was never introduced to me. I only knew his name because I heard it used by the boy who drove him in a horse and trap every morning to the office."

"You heard his driver call him Mr Kurr?"

"Oh, yes, a number of times."

"Did you tell this to the police when they came?"

"They didn't ask."

Holmes resisted a laugh. He merely smiled. His eyes twinkled.

"Kurr worked with the man you knew as Brooks?"

"Oh, yes. Brooks or whatever his name was generally came in a brougham, about half past nine each morning, and left again about 5 o'clock in the afternoon. Kurr would drive up in a horse and gig each morning, or nearly every morning, and was frequently fetched away by the same horse and gig in the afternoon. He would come somewhere about from 9 to 10 o'clock in the morning, and he would leave at all kinds of times in the afternoon, generally from 4 to 6 o'clock. The other two, Chapman and Bale, were in and out of the office continually during each day. The impression on my mind being that they were servants of the other two, Brooks and Kurr."

"Mr Flintoff, you are needed to identify Kurr as being involved in this enterprise."

"I'll do my duty as long as I get my expenses covered. It is a hard thing these days to pay the rates."

"You will need to take that up with the solicitor who is handling the prosecution, Mr Michael Abrahams. He or his clerk will call upon you soon. Good day to you, sir."

Holmes walked to the nearest telegraph office and sent a wire notifying Abrahams that Mr Flintoff could identify Kurr by name and description as one of the controlling partners of Brooks and Co. He waited for a response, but instead Michael Abrahams himself stepped out of a hansom.

"Thank you, Mr Holmes. Why had he never come out with this before?"

"No one asked," Holmes replied and this time he allowed himself to laugh.

Michael Abrahams shook his head.

"It is going to be a very long time before the Yard lives down this case," he said.

"I think you will find that Mr Flintoff has a lot to say about his former tenants once you ask the right questions."

Michael Abrahams pulled another draft out of his pocket and held it out.

"Here is your final pay with a well-deserved bonus. Introduce me to Mr Flintoff and we will take the case from there."

The following morning Flintoff went to Scotland Yard to report that he could identify William Kurr, Benson, Bale, and Frederick Kurr as the men who rented his rooms where they produced the mailings for their gambling swindle. From there he was taken to the Marlborough Street Courthouse where he testified before a magistrate under oath and a warrant was issued for the arrest of William Kurr.

The arrest warrant for William Kurr was handed to Detective Sergeant Littlechild on December 31st. The exact timing of the arrest was at his discretion. He hesitated to crash into the house and arrest the man before his wife and child. Kurr had been in the habit recently of walking out to greet the officers and demonstrate that he knew they were there. Such would be a perfect opportunity. Kurr, however, seemed to forgo his walk this day. Littlechild was becoming uneasy by the time Kurr appeared. He was also uneasy about the other men who were watching especially the one near the tavern. Who was he and why was he watching? He had considered confronting him but feared that was the type of distraction Kurr was seeking. They would stay at their posts.

The sun had set. It was quite dark and frosty. The three policemen had been there all day. Detective sergeants Littlechild and Manton were watching from Marquess Road a house over. Roots was in Ashby Road when four men exited number 29. Kurr and one of his companions started walking down Ashby Road toward Essex Road. When they reached Essex Road they turned west until they reached Canonbury Road, and then turned south. Littlechild and Manton followed about 200 yards behind. As the policemen were gaining on them they increased their speed and then one of them suddenly yelled "Now, run" loudly. Kurr began to run, and Littlechild began to follow, but the second man caught him under the armpits and stuck his leg out to trip him up. Littlechild threw him off, and pursued Kurr. When Littlechild caught up with him, Kurr wheeled around in a threatening manner.

"I am an officer of the police. You are under arrest him on a charge of defrauding the Comtesse de Goncourt."

Kurr attempted to pull something out of this pocket.

"Don't be foolish, come quietly," Littlechild said.

"I will," Kurr said.

Littlechild placed Kurr in a cab with Manton. He looked around. There was a crowd growing. They might mostly be curious onlookers. However, he saw the man who had assaulted him and the mysterious man near the tavern. He did not know if the latter was friend or foe. There were only three of them and he had strict instructions not to allow Kurr to escape. The second man would have to wait.

"Move along," Roots was saying in an attempted to disperse the crowd, "Nothing to see here."

"Roots, you return to the house and secure it," Littlechild said.

As he did, the second man was standing at the cab door trying to speak to the prisoner. Littlechild nodded his direction.

"See that fellow does not do any mischief."

Then he signalled the driver to take them to the Islington police station.

As the cab pulled away the crowd separated into smaller groups. Many were curious neighbours who now returned to their homes to wonder what the man had done and supposing they would read about it in the newspapers. Some were Abraham's agents sent merely to assure Kurr did not escape the police. Some glanced at the mysterious bystander that no one had seen before and wondered who he was. Was he another police man? Stenning, the man who had assaulted Littlechild, ran off to find a cab himself. The mysterious well-dressed man that no one recognized was enjoying the fact that no one could place him even though he had spent weeks in the neighbourhood, no one, save a small boy who shortly appeared at his elbow as he walked up the street.

"So peelers got him," the boy said.

"Yes, they did," he said.

"And you 'elped?"

"In ways they may never know," he said.

They reached the corner with Essex Road, and the man waved at a cabby who was pulling over.

"You ne'er told me your name," Wiggins said.

The man pulled a card from his pocket and squatted down to the boy's height.

"My name is Sherlock Holmes, and if you ever need any help, you can reach me here," he said and handed the boy the card before stepping into the hansom and disappearing into the night.

94

Chapter 5

The Long Wait

Sherlock Holmes began the new year of 1877 feeling especially pleased with himself. His advertisements had attracted a client within days of his having begun them. He was confident that they would continue to do so. The fact that no other clients had come calling in the weeks since could be attributed to the holiday season and the abominable weather. At least that's what he told himself.

While that sole case had not been intellectually challenging, having been more leg work than brain work, he had contributed substantially to the arrest of several criminals who had the protection of Scotland Yard detectives. His work could result in members of Scotland Yard losing their positions and possibly facing charges. Yet he was quite certain no one there knew of his involvement. Michael Abrahams had told him that he thought it best to keep his name and work confidential unless absolutely necessary to reveal it. He might have a need in the future of an agent who was not well-known to most at Scotland Yard, though Abrahams confessed he expected that special status would not last long.

Holmes had been unable to resist making an appearance when Kurr was arrested. He wanted to see the final act, and yet being the mysterious observer who no one knew except the boy Wiggins, rather than an active participant in the arrest, suited his sense of drama. It seemed both finale and prologue.

This meant, of course, that he had received no public credit in either of the cases he had been involved with since his return to England. His work on the Turf Fraud case, as the newspapers had called it, had also forced him to miss the coroner's inquest into Sassanof's death.

Now that he had the time and the intent to resume his work on his own criminal records, he spent his days before the fire with his pipe, newspapers, and commonplace books.

The weather had been a major concern in the newspapers recently. Violent winds and severe storms along the coasts, and to a lesser extent, in the interior of the British Isles, had characterized the close of the old year and the beginning of the new one. While there were some short breaks in some regions, the unsettled weather was showing no sign of general abatement. As the days passed, the newspapers continued to report rainstorms, snowstorms, gales, and flooding throughout Britain and Ireland. There was extensive flooding in the Thames River valley.

Queen Victoria was proclaimed Empress of India at Delhi on New Year's Day. The Viceroy presided over some sort of spectacle with ruling chiefs and Indian nobles and other persons of distinction, Holmes surmised from a scan of the accounts. Back in England, the proclamation had been overwhelmed by the news of shipwrecks and flooding. On the south coast, and both sides of the Irish Sea, piers and sea walls were destroyed, vessels wrecked, and houses flooded.

For that first week of January Sherlock Holmes enjoyed the warmth of the fire as he scanned each new edition. What he did not see was much in the way of crime. There had been some burglaries in Nottingham and Hull in December. The police speculated that they were the work of a gang. That brought to mind the burglaries near Manchester in the clippings related to the murder of Constable Cock. He reviewed those pieces but the details were so scarce that it was impossible to see any relation. Not that there was any shortage of burglars in England, though as the year began there were few in London.

That could be set down to the weather. Flooding in Lambeth, Hammersmith. Rotherhithe, Woolwich, and Shadwell rather complicated robberies, and other villainous plots, or perhaps the discovery of them. The London & SW Railway flooded. Lewisham was a sheet of water. There was a soil slip at Harbury onto the Great Western Railway line, and heavy snowfall at Sheffield. The Midland Railway line to Scotland was blocked. Each time he reviewed a new paper he tossed it aside and went back to organizing and pasting clippings.

On the 6th, a determined messenger made his way through the weather to the door and knocked. He handed Sherlock Holmes a small packet labelled with nothing other than his name. That, however, was written in Mycroft's distinctive hand. As Sherlock took it to the couch to investigate, he wondered if it had travelled to England in a diplomatic pouch. Inside was a brief note from his brother:

Dear Sherlock,

Please accept the enclosed with my wishes for a happy birthday and a prosperous new year. I thought you might find the book interesting. It was just published recently and has not yet been translated into English. It is somewhat controversial and I am certain you will have you own opinion of it, assuming your Italian is up to the task.

Mycroft

Mycroft had always been more diligent at observing Sherlock's birthday than he had been himself. The book was entitled *L'uomo delinquent.* He knew enough Italian to translate that into *The Criminal Man.*

The method of delivery had maintained the mystery surrounding Mycroft's current location. Sherlock had not failed to notice the mentions of meetings in Berlin, leading up to a conference on January 1st in Constantinople. According to the newspapers, the British Empire was attempting to protect its interests related to the Ottoman Empire against Russian aggression. It was just the type of thing he expected would call his brother out of the country.

On the 13th the papers reported that Inspector Druscovich had returned from Rotterdam with Henry Benson as well as Bale and Frederick Kurr who had been minor players in the drama. Druscovich had things to answer for himself.

A letter addressed to Mr Sherlock Holmes with a London postmark arrived the following week. He tore it open quickly hoping it was from a potential client. It was instead a note from Henry Irving.

Dear Mr Holmes:

I have a box reserved in your name at the Lyceum for our first night of Richard III on January 29. Will you not come and see if I do him justice?

Yours Truly,

Henry Irving

The international news reported that the conference in Constantinople was not proceeding as well as had been hoped. After proposals presented by the British ministers were rejected by ministers of the Ottoman Empire, the conference was rather unceremoniously declared to have reached its end on the 20th.

Mycroft returned unannounced late on January 28th. He said little before heading to his bed. But the following evening the brothers were able to belatedly celebrate Sherlock's birthday at the Lyceum as they had two years before.

"I appreciate the chance to enjoy some entertainment after weeks of the most gruelling and disappointing work," Mycroft said as they took their places in the box. "Which I am not at liberty to discuss," he said, foreclosing Sherlock's questions, "and wouldn't especially care to if I could. I fear there will be long lasting repercussions of the stances taken during that conference, but I am helpless to avert them. It is aggravating when you are dragged away from home for the purpose of providing advice and expertise, and both are roundly ignored. In any case, I am quite glad to be back in my own accommodations."

The curtain was rising so they turned their attention to the stage. In the moment before Irving as the hunchback began to speak, Sherlock clearly recalled the sensation of being in that exact position on a stage in a theatre since reduced to cinders and demolished. It seemed like a very long time ago now.

"Perhaps," said Mycroft over dinner afterward, "I am in an especially critical mood, or perhaps it is merely familial bias. However, I think you did a better job of it than Irving."

Sherlock chuckled.

"Well, thank you, brother. If I were to construct a theory concerning that, I'd say Irving has to imagine what evil is like, while I know it. I can see it."

"How is it that you can see it, as you say?"

"I have learned to see the criminal type. Not merely the thug or the ruffian. Sometimes a hard man can be gentler at heart than his looks suggest. It is the smiling and charming villain who deceives the average man."

Mycroft looked thoughtfully at Sherlock wondering if there was an archetype in his brother's mind. That was not the question he asked, however.

"Do you believe there are many such men in our society?"

"I have not done an exact census but based on my limited experience there are far too many. Dowson was one such. I believe that if I had actually interacted with him while I was with the Corycian Company, I would have seen the truth much earlier. Knowing such a man is involved makes me enquire further, beyond appearances. That's how I suddenly understood the significance of the sawdust. I had observed it, but not intellectually challenged its presence."

"Yet you merely saw him for an instant in a crowd."

"True, but that's not when I recognized his character. That was merely when I recognized his face as that of a man I had studied years ago when he had been on trial for another matter. He was a cheat, a confidence man, and yet he had potential to go beyond mere financial schemes, as he proved. If I had not had that prior experience to call upon, that brief glance of his face would have told me much, but not enough to determine the matter."

"Is that why you are constructing these records of crimes and criminals?"

"In part. As you know I have been collecting the articles for a few years now. It is about time I organized them."

"Yes."

"These books will help me remember details about specific criminals and their *modus operandi*, but also prior crimes can be templates for future ones. It is rare that something new is invented by the criminal mind. Most are variations on a theme."

Thus went the conversation of the evening. Mycroft was able to escape from the absorption with the Eastern Question, and because Mycroft did not enquire, Sherlock was able to escape from the nagging annoyance of the lack of clientele. Yet he spoke of crime in the general sense and made some comments on parts of the book Mycroft had sent to him that he had so far deciphered.

February was not pleasant for either of the brothers. Tensions were continuing to mount in relation to the Ottoman Empire, and no clients came calling at Montague Street for a detective. Sherlock Holmes became increasingly agitated. His commonplace books were arranged, indexed, and annotated, and although he added to them daily, the work was no longer as engaging as it had been in the early stages. Even the new cases about London had little interest: the occasional pickpocket, the smash and grab from a store front, and portico thieves in Lambeth. He sorely missed his violin which had been destroyed aboard the steamship returning to England.

"Baron" Dowson's trial convened the first Tuesday morning in March in the Central Criminal Court, commonly known as the Old Bailey for it sat at the prior location of the "bailee" defences outside the western wall of the old fortified city. The wall was gone and the defences rested now with the judge and jury rather than the sword and spear.

The building was also sometimes referred to as the Sessions House. It was an elaborate stone edifice that paled in the shadow of St Paul's Cathedral, yet stood tall next to the remains of the old Newgate prison.

Sherlock Holmes arrived quite early, but a number of people were already waiting in the bail dock, the courtyard in front of the Old Bailey. The bail dock was separated from the street by a semi-circular wall. He made his way towards the door as more of the curious public began to gather in the street. He doubted they were there as friends and followers of Sassanof's or merely friends of justice. The demise of the theatre had been dramatic enough to ignite public curiosity. They were the audience come to see a drama. He hoped that his lack of beard and shorter hair was enough not to call to mind the supposedly deceased William Escott to any who may have been patrons of the Corycian. In the months since his return to London only the dowager duchess had identified him as Escott and that had not concerned him. Nor had he heard any mention of the actor. Were those performances so easily forgotten? Was the applause merely part of the show? Or was it merely loudest on the stage as the buzz is loudest in the bee hive?

As the doors opened and people began to file in, there was a whiff of old smoke from the interior, for the Old Bailey itself had suffered a fire in the dining room on the upper floor a few weeks prior and some of the smell still clung to the building. It seemed a fitting atmosphere in which to review the inferno from which Sassanof's body had been extracted. Holmes could not say that he was fond of the deceased, even after working with him nearly two years, but he was reminded of the sensation he had felt before when he had personally known a homicide victim. Merely variables in an equation, he told himself, yet it was different when you knew the factors in life.

The courtroom was a square hall lit by three large windows in the wall opposite the door. Holmes could see the top of Newgate prison looming beyond those windows. Beneath the windows was the jury box and behind that the gallery where spectators such as himself were hunting for seats. The bench was to the right from the entrance or to the left from his seat in the gallery. It extended the whole length of the wall, with tall seats and desks for the judges.

The dock for prisoners was to his right now, elevated from the floor. Between the dock and the gallery was the circular witness-box. The centre of the floor was occupied by a large mahogany table with a row of law books down its middle. The table was surrounded by robed and be-wigged barristers for the prosecution and the defence, as well as clerks and stenographers.

The witnesses were not there. They were held in a separate room until they were called. The fourteen jurors and alternates now filed into their places and Dowson was brought to the dock from the holding cells by the staircase directly below the dock itself. Then all rose as the judges entered. After everyone was seated again, the clerk read the charge.

The prosecutor stood to present his case. This was why Holmes was there. While he had spoken to Inspector Gregson about the case a number of times, he had never spoken to the prosecuting attorney. For the first time he was going to observe how well the prosecution would handle a case he had solved. The prosecuting barrister called the first witness, Lord Cecil Hamley.

In deference to the occasion, Lord Cecil's attire was more subdued than usual, yet the black frock-coat with silver buttons and charcoal grey slacks accentuated his pale features and strawberry blond hair. He had a starring role in the drama as the last person who had seen Michael Sassanof alive, with the exception of the murderer himself. Holmes wondered how many in those observing the inquest might have recognize him as the actor Langdale Pike. The newspapers made no mention of it. Lord Cecil knew so many members of the press personally such restraint was as likely a personal favour as much as deference to class.

"When did you last see the deceased?" the prosecutor asked.

"On November 6th of last year we arrived at the Criterion Bar about half past seven. We departed about an hour later in separate cabs. I returned to my club in St James Street. I never saw him again after we parted in front of the Criterion Bar."

The prosecutor did not asked if anyone else was present at the meeting or what was discussed, so the question of the demise of William Escott never came up, which pleased Holmes. It would have merely clouded the matter in any case, and the prosecutor did not wish any clouds on the horizon.

"Did the deceased say where he was going?"

"No."

"Did the deceased have a valise or any other bag with him when he arrived?"

"No."

"When he left?"

"No."

"Had you known the deceased ever to have a valise?"

"Yes, he had a black valise with chrome hinges and corners when we disembarked from a ship that had brought us back from the United States that morning. It contained money the Corycian Company had earned in the States."

"Do you know the exact amount of money it contained?"

"I do not. However, he was always very nervous about it so I assumed it was a considerable sum."

"Do you know the defendant, Mr Reginald Dowson?"

"He was introduced to me as Baron von Marienburg. I was led to believe he was a member of foreign nobility. I now understand that was false."

"In what capacity was he acting under the name of Baron von Marienburg?"

"He was Mr Sassanof's business partner. He found investors for the theatrical company and arranged for work on the theatre. He may have participated in the company in other ways."

The defence had no questions for him.

"Thank you for your assistance, Lord Cecil," the judge said. "You may step down."

The next witness sworn in was Patrick O'Reilly, a husky broad-shouldered man with a shock of red hair.

"What is your occupation, Mr O'Reilly?"

"I'm a member o' de London Fire Brigade."

"You were on duty on the night of November 6th when the brigade was called to a fire at the Criterion Theatre?"

"I was."

"It is my understanding that you found the body of the deceased. Is that correct?"

"Yes."

"Please tell us when and how you found the deceased."

"We arrived at the scene o' the fire at the Corycian Theatre shortly after 10 o'clock. The theatre was not yet fully engulfed in flames. While other members o' the brigade prepared the 'oses and pumps, I searched the building for occupants. I entered through the stage door to the south. I found no one in the dressing rooms. I went up some stairs to an office. The fire was continuing to spread. In the office I found the deceased slumped in a chair wit his 'ead and 'ands on a desk before the body. De body did not seem to be breathin' at the time. There was blood on the 'ead and the desk. There were papers in the room that were on fire and part o' de desk was burnin'. I lifted de body and carried it out the way I 'ad come."

"Did you look for anyone else in the building?"

"By de time I was clear o' the building wit dee deceased's body, it was not possible to return and look for anyone else."

"You said there was blood on the deceased's head?"

"Yes."

"Was there anything on, or near the body, that could have caused the injury?"

"Nothin' that I noticed."

"Were there any signs of a struggle?"

"It is not possible for me to say. The room was burnin' on all sides. I did not wait to do an examination."

Defence counsel had a single question for him

"Did you see anyone else in the burning theatre or leaving it?"

"No, sir."

After a short recess, the police surgeon was sworn in. He was a tall slim man with grey hair and beard. Spectacles perched on his nose.

"You performed the post-mortem examination on the deceased?"

"I did."

"Tell us your findings."

"I performed the examination at 11.45 p.m. on November 6th, 1876. The deceased was a male in his mid-sixties approximately 5 foot 6 in height and 15 stone in weight. The state of *rigor mortis* at the time of the post-mortem indicated—allowing for the effect of the heat of the fire—that the deceased had been dead two to three hours."

"You are saying that he died sometime between 9 o'clock and 10 o'clock in the evening."

"Yes."

The prosecutor looked at the jury box.

"That is consistent with the time frame given to us by the previous witness," he said and then turned back to the witness. "How would the heat affect *rigor mortis*?"

"It would accelerate the process. In this case rigor was more advanced on his upper back and arms that were more exposed to the fire and less so in his legs, torso and face. The difference in the state of rigor in the hands versus the feet suggests about a half hour to hour acceleration in rigor. I included that in my calculation."

"Tell us more about those burns." the coroner said.

"There were third- and fourth- degree burns on the hands, the outer forearms, and the back. There were few burns on the face and front upper torso."

"What does that tell you about the position of the body after death?"

"It suggests it was in a sitting position with head and hands on a table or desk. The parts facing the table or desk would be shielded initially. The lack of *livor mortis* or discolouration on the face and torso and *gluteus maximus* suggested that the body had been in that position less than an hour after death before it was moved."

The prosecutor once again gave the jurors a knowing look as if he was sure they were in on the secret that he was about the reveal since the police surgeon had not heard the prior testimony.

"A member of the fire brigade testified earlier that he found the body in just such a position."

Then the prosecutor returned to the time of death.

"So your examination of the body suggests the time of the death was between 9 and 10 o'clock?"

"Yes."

"Were the burns the cause of death or perhaps the smoke?"

"No. He was dead before the fire."

"How do you know this?"

"There was no smoke in the lungs or burning in the nasal passages."

With those issues dispatched, the prosecutor turned to the heart of the matter.

"What was the cause of death?"

"The deceased had a wound approximately four inches in diameter that fractured the left lower parietal bone between the squamous and lambdoid sutures – behind the ear – which had forced fragments of the skull into the occipital and parietal lobes of the brain. Death would have followed rapidly."

"What could have caused such a wound?"

"A blunt instrument of some kind. It must have been a few inches in diameter and must have either been heavy or swung with substantial force to create such a wound. It is possible it was caused by more than one blow. The damage is so pronounced it is difficult to determine if it was made by one powerful blow or several."

"Could it have been caused by something falling on the deceased?"

"Not if he was sitting or standing. Then the blow would have struck near the coronal suture where the frontal bone and the parietal bone meet."

"What if his head was lying on the desk before the blow was

struck?"

"If his head had been on the desk at the time the blow was struck you would expect some kind of damage on the opposite side of the head due to the impact with the desk when the blow was struck. There was none."

"So you are saying he must have been standing or sitting at the time the blow was struck?"

"Correct."

"Was the blow struck from behind?"

"It could have been struck from behind or from the side."

"Could you determine if it was done by a right-handed person or a left-handed person?"

"Either could have done it depending on whether it was from behind or from the side. If the scene could be examined for blood spatter we might have a better idea."

"However, since the scene was consumed in the fire, we have no other evidence related to that."

"Correct."

"Were there any other wounds? Any sign of a fight?"

"The hands and arms were too badly burned to show bruises or cuts. There were no wounds on the face."

The next witness was a Mrs Hayworth, Sassanof's landlady. She was a petite, elderly lady.

"When did you last see the deceased?"

"Not countin' when police asked me to identify?"

"Excluding that, yes."

"Was t' mornin' of November 6th. 'Ee arrived in a cab with his luggage lil after nine o'clock. 'Ee'd just come back from 'is voyage to the States."

"Did you see a black valise with chrome hinges and corners?"

"Don't recall seeing anythin' like that."

"Do you know the defendant, Mr Dowson?"

Her eyes narrowed.

"Yes. 'Ee'd come by offen when they were workin' together. Dinnot much care for 'is flashy ways."

"Did you see Mr Dowson that day?"

"No."

"Are you certain?"

"My sittin' room is near the front so I see if onnyone comes or goes. Mr Sassanof was in and out durin' the day so 'ee could have met with that man but I dinnot see 'im. That evenin' the 'andsome young man with the blond hair—"

"Lord Cecil?"

"Yes. 'Ee came in a cab after seven an' spoke to Mr Sassanof briefly an' they both left in the cab. I never saw Mr Sassanof alive again."

The next witness was a stiff, young clerk from Sassanof's usual bank who testified that Sassanof had not made a deposit in their bank on November 6th.

Court recessed for lunch. The crowd was buzzing as they filed out of the building. Runners shot off towards Fleet Street or the nearest telegraph office. A well-known newspaper editor snagged Lord Cecil as he exited and pulled him aside. The police surgeon had been wise enough to use a back exit and kind enough to take the landlady with him, leaving the member of the fire brigade to the vultures of the press.

Holmes ducked through the crush and evaded the boys offering extras filled with things he already knew. At a newsstand he bought several newspapers. He leaned against a post, lit his pipe, and skimmed through the crime news. A burglary, domestic assaults, a tavern brawl. As time neared he headed back to the Old Bailey.

Lionel Palgrave was sworn in next. He had attempted to tame his wild reddish brown hair but he still had a leonine look to him.

"How did you know the deceased?"

"He was one of the partners in the Corycian Company. I was hired to renovate the theatre for the company by his partner who introduced himself to me as Baron von Marienburg, though I have recently learned his name was Reginald Dowson."

"Did you have a congenial relationship with the partners?"

"At the beginning, yes. It was a beautiful theatre and they seemed happy with the work. They asked that I add a few people to the crew. They seemed to work well enough so that was not a problem.

Then after the renovations were complete most of my men moved on to other projects I had going, but a few were going to stay with the theatre. Sassanof wanted me to oversee some of the larger set pieces, especially Juliet's balcony. I agreed to for a small fee with the understanding that I would be inspecting the plans and the final work but not be supervising daily."

"That relationship changed?"

"Many people will remember the failure of the balcony because it was all over the newspapers. That's when the silly rumours started of a curse on the theatre. I had reviewed the plans and inspected the finished construction of the balcony. It looked lovely, but more than that it was strong. It was sturdy. It should have been able to hold ten men. And there was no sawdust. That might seem trivial, but a good carpenter cleans away the sawdust before the painting begins. I know there was none. However, I happened to be at the theatre the day of the collapse. There was sawdust on top of the paint. There were signs that someone had used a saw to weaken the structure. To me it looked like sabotage. I tried to warn Sassanof but he dismissed it."

"Did you speak to Mr Dowson about it?"

"I did not."

"In December of 1875 the stage collapsed, did it not?"

The witness's face flushed at the question.

"A portion of it did, yes," Palgrave said tersely as if restraining himself.

"What happened at that time?"

"A four foot wide hole opened in the stage during a performance."

"Were you present at the time?"

"No."

"What did you personally see?"

"I was called to the theatre. Sassanof and the Baron, or Dowson rather, were there and a few of the cast and crew. Dowson blamed me for the collapse of the floor. He claimed I failed to notice a weakness in the stage floor when my firm was restoring the theatre. He threatened me with lawsuits. I know the stage floor had been sound. I wanted to inspect the floor from below. He refused to allow it. He had me escorted from the building and threatened to call the police."

"He dismissed you as chief carpenter?"

"Yes."

"Were there any lawsuits?"

"No. I never heard from his solicitors. I considered a defamation suit, but my solicitors did not think the case was strong enough."

"After the fire, you went with Inspector Gregson and Captain Shaw of the London Fire Brigade to inspect the stage floor?"

"Yes."

"What did you see?"

"The heavy oak beams of the stage floor were intact. They had even survived the collapse of the upper floors on top of it."

"Was there a hole or any sign that a hole in the stage floor had been repaired?"

"There was a hole in the stage and no sign that there had been any attempt to repair it. Debris from the fire had fallen through the hole. Captain Shaw and I inspected the edges of the hole. It was clear that the wood had been sawed partially through a number of months before and splintered the rest of the way under the weight of the actors."

"It was not caused by the fire?"

"No. There was no charring in that area."

Next the fire chief was brought to the stand. Captain Shaw's scraggly moustache waggled as he elaborated on the fire itself and what they had found below the stage of the theatre. His testimony corroborated that of the chief carpenter.

"Was any weapon found?"

"Based on the building plan, the area which had been the office had been completely destroyed and fallen into the lower level by the time we were able to examine it after the fire was extinguished. Nothing significant was found."

"Not the valise the police were looking for?"

"No."

"Could it have been consumed in the fire?"

"I don't know its composition so I can't say for certain, but that area was subject to extremely high heat even before the chemicals in the paint room began exploding. Wood, leather, even some metals could be completely consumed. The front of the theatre was subject to much lower temperatures, yet stonework was cracked in some places."

John Travis was brought from prison to testify concerning his knowledge of the scheme to defraud investors. He also said he had known Dowson as the Baron von Marienburg. He said that the Baron had hired him to keep the plays from being too successful. This part of the plan was waylaid when Sassanof fired him and hired another actor named Escott. Dowson then convinced him get his revenge. He was arrested and convicted for assaulting Escott.

"My time is up in a few months," he said.

Travis was led away and the last witness took the stand.

"State your name and occupation."

"Detective-Inspector Tobias Gregson of the Metropolitan Police."

"Inspector Gregson, you had charge of this case?"

"Yes, I was called when the body was found."

"What do you know about Mr Dowson?"

"I reviewed his record in the Habitual Criminal Registry. He has a long list of prior convictions for theft, fraud, and confidence games. His record indicated that he often pretended to be a foreign aristocrat or royalty. One of his nicknames is Royal Reggie."

"Can you explain to the court the nature of the confidence scheme Mr Dowson is alleged to have been perpetrating in relation to the Corycian theatre?"

"From my investigations—"

Sherlock Holmes chuckled, to the surprise of those sitting near him.

"It seems Dowson, under the name of Baron von Marienburg, was skimming funds from the investors in the theatrical company with the hope that the company would fail and he would merely tell the investors that there was no money left. Unfortunately for him, the company had some successful runs which would have left the investors expecting a return. That's when the accidents started happening. They disrupted the income and gave Mr Dowson an excuse to return to investors for additional contributions."

"Why wouldn't he merely allow the company to make a profit and pay the investors a dividend?"

"Unfortunately what records there may have been were destroyed in the fire or by Mr Dowson. However, based what we have been told by the investors we have been able to track down, we think he sold more than a hundred percent of the company, which would make it impossible to satisfy the investors even if he had not been skimming off the funds."

"Why resort to murder?"

"He was a desperate man. His partner Mr Sassanof had just returned and would soon discover that he drained the funds meant to repair the stage floor. He intended to set fire to the theatre to cover the fact that the repairs had not been made to the stage."

"Why wait until his partner returned?"

"That is a puzzle. I think that Mr Sassanof had been sending him updates from the States about how well the theatrical company had been doing there and the fact that he would be returning with the profits. In my mind I think Mr Dowson thought he could kill two birds with one fire, so to speak, and asked Mr Sassanof to meet him at the theatre. When Sassanof did, he killed him, took the valise of money, and set fire to the theatre."

"So you think the evidence points to premeditation?"

"It does to me," Inspector Gregson said

"Has the valise of money been found?"

"No. He could have hidden it somewhere after leaving the theatre or it may have been consumed in the fire."

"Mr Dowson was seen near the theatre when it was burning?"

"Yes, I saw him myself," the inspector said.

"Quite a coincidence, isn't it?"

"Yes."

The defence had asked little of the prior witnesses but the defence barrister had some questions for the Inspector.

"Has Mr Dowson ever been convicted of assault or attempted murder?"

"There was no record of such a conviction in the Registry."

"Armed robbery?"

"No."

"Arson?"

"No."

"So there is no evidence that my client was ever a violent man?"

"No."

"Yet, you now accuse him of murder and arson?"

"Yes."

It was a weak defence, but the defence barrister milked it for all he could in his final statement.

The judge summarized the evidence presented for the jury and sent them off to deliberate. They were back 15 minutes later with a verdict of guilty on all counts.

The prosecution had not told the whole story, but they had told enough to convince the jury of the scam without exposing the dower duchesses and other investors to the public. That was as much a political tactic as an evidentiary one.

When Dowson was asked if he would like to make a statement, he declined. He seemed both puzzled and angry as if he could not understand how his luck had finally given out when he had pushed it too far.

The judge donned his black cap and sentenced the prisoner at the bar to be taken from that place and, at the appointed time, hanged by the neck until he was dead.

Sherlock Holmes filed out of the courtroom with the crowd. He pulled his overcoat close. The air was chilly. The sun was low in the sky, though not quite set. The buildings cast long shadows and the lamplighters had begun their work.

He decided to walk, not just to preserve his declining funds, but because he was in no hurry to return home. His brother Mycroft had been in the foulest mood in the weeks since he had returned to London. It was uncharacteristic of Mycroft, but he refused to be drawn out as to the cause. That reticence was characteristic. Sherlock believed it was related to the "Eastern Question" that had kept him away for months. Even the newspapers were speculating that war was likely. A Russian diplomat was expected in London the following week to attempt to settle the matter but the newspapers held out little hope. The few comments Mycroft had made suggested he felt his advice was being ignored. In any case it seemed best to leave Mycroft his evenings in peace.

Sherlock himself had been rather melancholy of late. Despite advertisements and direct enquiries, no new clients had made an appearance. Mrs Dalton knew where he was, and he had left strict instructions to send a message if clients had appeared. He was not surprised that no messenger had come.

He should perhaps feel some sense of triumph at the verdict for he had given Gregson the clues to solve it. But that was months ago. The thrill of the chase was long gone and the trial had not revived it. He was curious about a few things, however, and decided to visit the prisoner before the execution.

As it came about, it was the night before the execution before arrangements could be made. Dowson seemed willing to see him.

"Come in, come in," the condemned man said as if inviting someone to his parlour rather than a prison cell.

Despite his aristocratic manner, Dowson bore no resemblance to a baron. Gone were the jewels and elegant clothes. He'd lost weight due to the diet and regimen of prison life and the flesh on his face now sagged in folds. Yet those folds smiled in a more pleasant manner than one would expect from someone soon to meet the gallows.

"Thank you for seeing me," Sherlock Holmes said.

"Oh, I hold no ill will towards you for tackling me in the street. I was a bit warm about it, but you can understand."

"Yes."

"I've been told that Escott is not your name. I shouldn't have been surprised. I would be more surprised that anyone involved with Corycian was there under their real name."

"Sassanof was," Holmes said.

"Well, I suppose," Dowson said with a wave of his hand and rapidly changed the subject. "I don't understand your role in this business, Mr—"

"Holmes, Sherlock Holmes. I put you here," he said with a sweep of his hand to the surroundings. "I pieced together your scam and told Scotland Yard that you had killed Sassanof."

Dowson was surprised and a bit miffed.

"So I have more to thank you for than some scrapes and bruises. That seems something of a mental feat for an actor, though I admit you were a rare one. A bit too good, perhaps."

"I have left the stage and become a detective."

"Well, what the law has gained the stage has lost. What can I do for you, Mr Holmes? My time is, thanks to you, limited."

"Blanchard attempted to kill Sassanof, Devigne, and myself on the ship returning to England. I presume that was on your orders."

"You presume too much. His assignment was merely to keep the company from returning intact. How he did it was up to him."

"Even though you intended to set fire to the theatre?"

"Sassanof would have gone on tour again. The man was insufferably good at turning misfortune around. The next act needed to cut to the heart of the company itself. If not Sassanof, then his headliners. Of course, I had no idea you were planning on leaving the stage."

"It was Blanchard's attack that made up my mind," Holmes said.

"Then I suppose he did you a favour."

"Sassanof would have still been a problem for you."

He frowned and shrugged. He now looked like an old wrinkled man.

The warder was at the door.

Sherlock Holmes stood and walked towards the door. He looked back before he reached it.

"Did you take the money? Or was it destroyed by the fire?"

There was an instant of silence, then Dowson threw back his head and laughed. Somehow mirth fleshed the man out again. He was once more the merry Falstaff.

"I'll just leave that a mystery," he said and laughed again.

Holmes left him laughing. He did not return the next day to see the hanging but he heard tales later that the "Baron" Dowson had laughed his way to the gallows and only stopped when the trap fell..

Chapter 6

Trials of Spring

*"I had rooms in Montague Street, just round the corner from the
British Museum, and there I waited, filling in my too abundant leisure time."*
Sherlock Holmes, "The Musgrave Ritual"

In April of 1877, Sherlock Holmes' detective practice still seemed in danger of being nipped off in its budding. On the 4th the newspapers reported a "daring burglary"—though Fleet Street seemed to identify most burglaries as "daring"—at the mansion of a Mr Cameron in Sevenoaks in Kent. A pane had been removed from a window and over £350 of plate had been stolen. No immediate suspects, nor any response from Mr Cameron to Holmes' offer to investigate. Such solicitation seemed somewhat humiliating yet nothing else was working. On the 8th there was a report of an inquest of the death by poison of a colour sergeant of the Royal Marines and a mysterious note found in his pocket stating his life was in jeopardy. The man had been an orphan with no siblings. Holmes did not know the detective in charge of the case and offers to assist were ignored.

The following day there were reports from the police courts of a woman arrested for passing forged cheques and a man smuggling tobacco into the city to avoid the tax. A burglar was caught after the police traced a dropped fish-and-chips paper and watched the place for known second story men.

The Turf Fraud case, as the newspapers were calling it, was coming up for trial on April 12th. Sherlock Holmes had spent time watching trials at the Old Bailey the first summer he had resolved to become a detective. That had been when he had come upon the broadsheet about Dowson in the first place. If the crime at the bar was not worth studying then the people attending the trial almost certainly were. Sherlock Holmes knew from his involvement in the Turf Fraud case that there were people worth studying on both sides of the case. So having nothing at hand he decided to observe.

The clerk read the charges against brothers William and Frederick Kurr, Harry Benson, Charles Bale, and Edwin Murray for "feloniously forging a warrant or order for the payment of £10 000, with intent to defraud" and utterance of the forged document (the latter posed some legal jurisdiction difficulties that were unfamiliar to Holmes.)

The first witness was a printer in Edinburgh. His testimony was not of much interest to Holmes, but it immediately underlined that the difference between the trial of Dowson and this one was that it had not been necessary to prove all the elements of Dowson's fraudulent scheme because they were merely being used to demonstrate his motive for the greater crimes of murder and arson. Perhaps that is why the prosecutors in the Turf Fraud case chose to limit the indictment to the forgery rather than include the numerous other petty offenses the defendants committed along the way to acquiring the funds, converting them to usable currency, and attempting to escape the law.

The Solicitor General was prosecuting the case with barristers Bowen and McConnell. Solicitor Michael Abrahams was present below as prosecuting solicitor to represent the interests of his client, the Comtesse de Goncourt.

The printer was followed by landlords and owners of tobacco shops, every one of them being a place the prisoners had lodged or collected letters. Then the postmaster on the Isle of Wight was followed by Mr Flintoff, the civil engineer at 8, Northumberland Street, who Holmes had ambushed at his door after a long wait. Flintoff had rented office space to the defendants and he had quite a bit to say about the four of them. He connected their faces to several of the aliases they had used. Next was the Comtesse herself who described through an interpreter how she was drawn into their fraudulent betting scheme.

The Scotland Yard detectives Holmes had followed appeared on the witness stand to testify against brothers William and Frederick Kurr, as well as Benson, Bale and Murray. Holmes wondered if the positions would eventually be reversed or if the police would conceal the participation of their own detectives. There was no mention during this trial of charges of corruption or bribery of police officers.

The trial was long, running ten days excluding Sundays. He had plenty of time to observe the prisoners on the dock. The round, ruddy face of William Kurr seemed undaunted by the prosecution. He smirked as if he held a secret. The elf-like Benson was nervous and impatient. He did not take well to prison and would do anything to get out.

Holmes scanned the newspapers in between sessions. There was the report of another "daring burglary" of a baker of Deptford-Bridge while the man was at church with his wife. The burglar turned out drawers and took valuables including a watch and chain. An assistant was in bed and called out when someone passed his door. The thief then scampered down the stairs and the assistant in night shirt ran after him but lost him. The police suspected a gang from London, though Holmes thought they might want to question the assistant more carefully. In any case he found no toehold there, nor any aspect that was particularly interesting. A few days later the newspapers reported a burglary near Greenwich and Holmes wondered if the police were correct in their theory that a gang was responsible.

Baron Huddleston, the presiding judge, in his summing up of the Turf Fraud case said that the governor of Newgate prison, having reason to suspect that an attempt had been made to corrupt the officials of the gaol, caused Benson to be searched and found documents which disclosed a scheme for an escape. It was also established that Benson had found a person willing to help him communicate with others outside the prison. Despite those efforts the jury found Benson guilty of forgery; William Kurr, Frederick Kurr, and Bale guilty on some of the counts, and Murray an accessory after the fact. Benson was sentenced to fifteen years of penal servitude; William Kurr, Frederick Kurr, and Charles Bale each to received ten years penal servitude; and Edwin Murray eighteen months' hard labour.

The next day the newspapers were full of Russia's declaration of war against the Ottoman Empire. In the days that followed reports came of the progress of Russian troops across Romania and the abandonment of Turkish posts to the Russian army. On May 1st the Queen issued a proclamation enjoining her subjects to maintain strict neutrality. With each day came new reports of the advance of the Russian army and clashes with the Turks and Kurds. Sherlock expected a further decline in his brother's spirits but instead sensed a kind of resignation. It was as if once Mycroft's prediction had come to fruition it relieved the strain of attempting to avoid it.

On the 7th of May Sherlock received a note from his brother at mid-day:

I have tickets for the Royal Albert Hall this evening. Wagner is conducting. Will you join me?

Thus evening wear was prepared and the brothers arrived at the Royal Albert Hall in due time. While it was advertised that Wagner was to conduct the first half of each evening of the London Wagner Festival, and the rehearsal conductor, Hans Richter, was to conduct the second half, in practice Richter conducted the majority of the program which included selections from *Der Ring des Nibelungen, Tannhäuser, Der Fliegende Holländer, Lohengrin,* and *Die Meistersinger.*

After the program the Holmes brothers made their way to a restaurant where their places had been reserved and the menu set by Mycroft earlier in the day. As they settled in with a glass of wine and some oysters, Mycroft asked his younger brother what he thought of the concert.

"I enjoyed it very much," Sherlock said. "It is a rare opportunity to see Wagner conduct his own music. I am not sure the music was improved by it."

"There did seem to be some friction between the conductors," Mycroft observed.

"And between Wagner and the orchestra," Sherlock agreed. "Yet, Wagner's prowess as a composer is undeniable. He does not merely make pleasant sounds with music. He paints with it. His canvas is the human mind. His tints are the instruments and the musicians are his brushes. He creates not merely a static painting, but one that mutates, intuitively telling a story that you cannot completely comprehend until the final note. Perhaps it is the complexity of his own nature that causes the creative tension in his music that also gives rise to the tension with other musicians."

"Perhaps so. As the musician in the family, what is your opinion of the acoustics of the Royal Albert Hall?"

"They are a bit off. I do hope they work on that because otherwise it is a magnificent hall."

"I thought so. Now brother Sherlock, I must apologize. I realize I've been a bit neglectful of you these last few months since my return."

"I understood you had much on your mind."

"While true, that does not excuse my behaviour. The highly confidential nature of the work combined with the frustrations it has entailed—You know that I am not normally an emotional person."

"No."

"But the recent work had strained my equilibrium."

"How so?"

"Well, without violating any confidences or state secrets I can say that I overestimated the willingness of certain members of the current government to put any credence in the opinion of a mere clerk, no matter how strenuously they are advised to."

"I think I have some understanding of the matter."

"As far as they have been illuminated in the newspapers, I am sure you do, but there are other things that have occurred behind the scenes, so to speak. I could foresee outcomes that were literally laughed at before they came to pass and viewed as anomalies after they did. Thus no effort was made to avoid the harsher consequences, some of which are still in the offing. I can work with people of lower intelligence, but not a fool."

He shook his massive head.

"Mark me: we have some difficult years ahead. Ah, there I have said too much."

"Given that I have only the vaguest idea what that prognostication refers to I don't think any harm has been done."

"In any case I am helpless to prevent it. That realization allowed me to find my balance and request that the exclusivity with the foreign office be terminated, which it was, much to the delight of other, more appreciative, offices. So now I am free to make myself useful."

There was a pause as the wait staff brought the next course.

"Now, how has your practice been progressing?"

Sherlock sighed.

"It has not."

"Not at all?"

"Well, I had one case while you were out of the country but none since."

"I've noticed you've been out a great deal. I hope that was not on my account."

"Not entirely. I've been at the Old Bailey watching trials."

"Ah. They convicted those fellows involved in the betting scheme a couple of weeks ago, didn't they?"

"Yes. I watched that one," Sherlock said.

"Well, I can say that Treasury is completely unnerved about that one. There's more to it that the public knows."

"Indeed."

"There is a lot of argument about how it should be dealt with. It may be some time before it is decided. It is not something one dives into without due consideration."

"You can't tell me any more?" Sherlock asked.

"No."

"Interesting. I will keep an eye out for developments."

"No cases, eh?"

"No cases."

"I guess that explains why you've seemed a bit downtrodden."

"Yes. I've tried everything I can think of. I run advertisements. I've sent direct solicitations to people involved in unsolved cases I've read about in the newspaper. I have even resorted to responding to agony column advertisements seeking persons or lost articles, offering my services. I have received no responses."

"I suspect they receive many such offers. They don't know your name from any of the others."

"It is ironic that I achieved unwelcome notoriety under a stage name, but am unknown under my own. I am at a loss as to what else I can do to find paying clients. While I am perfectly willing to apply my talents without remuneration, I do need a method of support, other than the largesse of my brothers."

Mycroft closed his eyes, twisted his lips a bit, ran his finger in a circle on the edge of his plate and then opened his eyes again.

"Perhaps you should write to your fellow students at college announcing your new career."

"Yes, a note from the infamous dynamiter of Sydney Sussex College is bound to draw attention," Sherlock said sarcastically.

"Come now, you said that your fellow students were generally supportive, even admiring, of your early efforts."

"Yes," Sherlock admitted.

"And many of them are quite well off," Mycroft reminded him. "Even if they are not in need themselves, they might refer a friend or relative who has a problem you could resolve."

"Yes, yes, you are right, Mycroft. It is a good idea. I should not allow my scepticism make me pass up such a potential opportunity. I will make a list tomorrow and get on with it."

With that resolution their dinner conversation turned to more trivial things.

The following morning Sherlock Holmes busied himself with compiling a list of names and addresses of his former fellow-students, writing and posting letters to them. With the exception of himself, Lord Cecil, and Victor Trevor, the men of his year at Sydney Sussex had taken their degrees while he was acting at the Corycian Theatre under the stage name of William Escott. It was doubtful any of them knew what had become of him the past two years.

Victor Trevor had occasionally posted a letter from the tea plantings in India where he seemed to be getting on well enough. He was unlikely to be in need of a detective in London. Nevertheless Holmes wrote a letter to Victor telling him that he had finally taken the step Victor's father had suggested and begun his career as a detective.

When Sherlock looked up Reginald Musgrave he found there was some talk of him standing as member of his district. Holmes sent him a letter inviting him to contact him, if he should find himself coming up to London. From there he segued into a brief mention of opening his detective practice.

Matthew Simons had taken Holy Orders and obtained a living in Leicestershire. In what spare time his flock left him he had written a couple of obscure religious pamphlets. A short greeting and announcement was not inappropriate, though Holmes felt it was unlikely that he would see business from that direction.

Wickery had indeed gone into politics. He had thrown his lot in with the Liberal Party and was supporting efforts to restore Gladstone to the premiership. The sporting men, Blankton, Slackmire, and Hackstead had gone into business together, likely financed by their fathers. B, S & H, Ltd had opened a factory in Manchester that was manufacturing kits for the British Army, and jerseys and knickers for footballers, ruggers, and cricketers.

Mickleby had earned a fellowship and was continuing his scientific studies, and most likely his practical jokes. Ericcson was teaching Classics at a small private school in Norfolk. Tom Holmes had also taken Holy Orders and recently taken on the position of Vice-Principal of the Wells Theological College in Somerset. Holmes wrote them each a friendly note.

In addition to the men of his year, there was Mortimer Maberley, the 3rd year at Sydney Sussex who had suggested that he join the other fencers at Cambridge. Sherlock had fenced with Drake and George Rowland of Trinity College, and Buckley and Darnell who had both been a year ahead of him at Sidney. Darnell had introduced him to the climbers Bensen and Vaughn from Jesus College, and Walters, the Kingsman. He found their addresses as well and wrote to them, thanking his governesses and tutors throughout his childhood for teaching him the art of writing friendly, banal letters into which he slipped the information that he was now working as a private detective in London. He posted the lot of them, uncertain anything would come of it.

Holmes continued his frequent perusal of the newspapers and added interesting clippings to his scrapbooks. He also continued his direct solicitations in response to agony columns and crime news. To stave off his mounting frustration he scanned other parts of the newspaper that might lead him to some opportunity. He noticed a new column called "Prattlings" written by Langdale Pike, and knew that Lord Cecil had found himself a new occupation, one he was eminently suited for. He could rattle off a column of gossip a day with no effort. No doubt he did so without even leaving his club. He skirted writing about actual scandal which showed he remembered the lessons of their college days, though Sherlock Holmes had no doubt that if he ever needed to know the latest scandal that was the quarter to apply.

However, his concentration now was not in finding scandals, but cases, and for that he was not going to apply to Lord Cecil. Lord Cecil had found him the position as an actor and remunerated him for his first case of his detective career. That clearly absolved any debt that he may have owed from the doings at college. Sherlock Holmes knew he needed to find his own clients somehow. He continued to read the newspapers.

The epidemic of burglaries had shifted westward from Greenwich and Deptford to Peckham and Camberwell. On May 14th, the Globe reported a burglary at Earl of Kilmorey's residence Gordon House, Isleworth. The body of an elderly man of respectable appearance was discovered Saturday in a suburb of Dublin hanging from a rope passed over a stone in a ruin at the seashore. The hands were bound together with a handkerchief which made a verdict of suicide difficult. On the 19th, the Police News wrote that Church of St Mary the Virgin Greenhithe had been robbed on 11th. The thieves stole altar vases, broke an altar cross, and destroyed a stained glass window. That seemed more like anti-papist vandalism that a robbery, or perhaps that's what the robbers wished the police to think. Seven of her majesty's ships had arrived at Port Said to guard the entrance of the Suez Canal during the conflict between Russia and the Ottoman Empire.

Essex police were investigating a suspicious death. The body of a man about 50 years old with dark hair and a beard wearing clothing of superior make but no identification (*No laundry mark?* wondered Holmes) was discovered in Wandstead Common. He had been dead for hours and his face and neck were covered in blood which seemed to have flowed from his mouth and nose. No signs of struggle. *An aneurism?*

An inquest was held at Ilfracombe, Devonshire about a strange series of events. A seaman was confined for violence towards his captain. When he was released he rushed at another seaman who stabbed him with a knife and killed him. The captain went ashore to make a deposition about the incidents. Afterwards he was seized by a fit and died an hour later. Thomas Jones who had been nursing the captain was also seized with sickness and died the same day. Some form of poison that induces madness and violence in small doses and seizure and death in large doses, Holmes speculated. It would be a fascinating case to investigate but he had no connection to do so. On May 23, 1877, he read an article about tobacco smuggling on the Thames, and considering the low state of his supply of tobacco, he favoured the smugglers.

It was a blustery day in London on the last day of May. The barometer was dropping, but Sherlock Holmes' temper was up. He was pacing the floor of the sitting room in Montague Street.

"Sit down, Sherlock," Mycroft said without looking up *The Times*. "You are making me dizzy."

He sat down.

"How could my pacing be making you dizzy when you weren't even looking at me?" Sherlock asked his brother.

"The sound of your footsteps was tiring," Mycroft countered.

"You are changing the facts. A sound alone cannot make you dizzy," Sherlock scoffed.

"I will concede the point. But don't you have something better to do than wear out the rug?" Mycroft asked.

"I wish I could say I did. This city is full of crimes I could solve if given the chance," Sherlock said.

"No clients this week?"

"None."

"No responses to your letters?" Mycroft asked while turning a page of *The Times*.

"None bringing me any work to do," Sherlock said impatiently as he jumped up and resumed his pacing, mumbling more to himself than to his brother as he did.

"No interesting cases at the Old Bailey?"

"No. There are plenty of crimes and criminals, but does anyone have the presence of mind to look at advertisements in the newspaper when faced with trouble?" Sherlock ranted. "Perhaps not. But perhaps a friend may see it and recommend that they call? I have to reach them somehow. I know I can help if they would just let me.

"There are numerous disappearances that have never been solved. For example, on December 12, 1829, John Ten Eyck Lansing,

Jr., a prominent American politician and previously Chancellor of New York, the highest judicial officer in the state, left his Manhattan hotel to mail a letter at a New York City post office and was never seen again," he continued.

"Less than four years ago on September 3, 1873, James Burne Worson bet his friends that he could run from Leamington to Coventry. The friends followed him in a cart. They told the police that a few miles along the road Worson stumbled and disappeared while they were watching, an absurd claim. Yet the case remains unsolved. There are many more such unsolved disappearances because no competent detective was called in."

Sherlock picked up a section of the *Daily Telegraph* from the floor. He jabbed his finger at it as he continued talking and pacing from the fireplace and back.

"For example, this case has been haunting the newspapers for three days. A young woman, Claire Newhall, is said to have vanished from her home sometime Sunday night or early Monday morning. The police initially had but one idea: an elopement. After querying nearly every young man for a mile around her home they have dismissed it as merely an unfathomable woman's whim. The newspapers report her mother does not think they are looking any more. After three days they have given up!"

Sherlock sat down, dropped the newspaper, and buried his head in his hands.

"Sherlock," Mycroft said.

Silence.

"Sherlock. Stop. Either solve the case or stop following it before it tears you apart."

Without a word Sherlock Holmes pulled in his boots, tossed aside his dressing gown, grabbed his hat and coat, and left. He passed the housekeeper at the door as he went out.

"Well, where is he off to in such a rush?" Mrs Denton asked.

"To find a young woman, I suppose."

"About time. You should find one for yourself."

Mycroft laughed, but didn't bother to correct her.

"But for now all you have is me. Would you like your tea, Mr

Mycroft?"

Claire Newhall lived with her mother in some rooms at Furnival Inn, Holborn. The building had once been one of the Inns of Court. It had been sold and converted to flats decades ago while retaining "inn" in the name. It was said that Charles Dickens had lived there in his bachelor days. It was but a short walk from Montague Street.

As Sherlock Holmes approached the building he noticed a number of loungers about, members of the press most likely. A bobby stood at the entrance. Holmes paused, took out his pocket book, tore a page out, and wrote a note. He approached the entrance.

"Just move along," the bobby said.

"Good day, constable," Holmes said tipping his hat. "You mistake me for a member of the press. I merely seek to deliver this note to Mrs Newhall. I am a detective and I think I can assist her. Here is my card."

He held out the note and his card.

"Whot's this?" the man said taking them from his hands.

"You are welcome to read them."

He squinted at them both and back at Sherlock Holmes.

"Aw right, go ahead," the constable said handing them back. "Y'know the number?"

Holmes said he did. He proceeded to it and knocked on the door. A small grey-haired woman opened the door. She looked hopefully up at him with red-rimmed eyes.

"Pardon me, madam. My name is Sherlock Holmes. I come in the hopes that I might be a service. I have written down some of my accomplishments in similar matters by way of introduction."

She took the note and his card.

"You did these things that you wrote?" she asked after a moment.

"I did indeed, ma'am. You may check with Inspector Gregson."

"Come in then and have a seat, young man."

He followed her inside and sat.

"Mrs Newhall, I would like to find your daughter. I have read what the papers say but they leave many questions. May I ask you?"

"I will tell you everything I know."

"Do you think anyone would kidnap your daughter for ransom?

"Good heavens, no. I don't have any money."

"No wealthy relatives?"

"No."

"Have you had any disagreements with her recently?"

"Not really."

"You hesitate. Tell me."

"Well, I felt she should find herself a husband. There were several eligible men about. We live so close to the Inns that there are a number of barristers and solicitors to be seen in the neighbourhood. She said they were all too old. So I arranged an introduction to the son of a barrister, nephew of a friend of mine. We had him over to tea once. He is studying at the University of London, a very nice young man. She was not interested. There are also medical students hereabouts studying at that University of London and at St Bartholomew's Hospital. I even suggested the greengrocer's son."

"She was not interested in any of them?"

"No. I am afraid I might have upset her by urging them on her."

"Do you think she ran away because she was angry with you?"

"That would not be like Claire at all. I don't think she was really angry. I think she just felt pestered."

"May I see her room?"

"Of course, if you think it might be helpful."

Claire's room was sparsely decorated. There was a photograph of a man in uniform.

"That is her father," Mrs Newhall said. "He's been gone many years."

There were a few photographs of girls with nuns.

"Where were these taken?" Holmes asked.

"The convent school of St Etheldreda in Ely Place."

"In Holburn?"

"Yes. Not far from here."

"Which one is your daughter?"

"That's her," she said pointing to one of the girls. "That was taken about five years ago."

"Do you have a recent picture of Claire?"

"Yes. I will get one for you."

When she left the room, Holmes looked about it. Once again he noticed how sparse it was. There was a small writing desk with some paper and pens and the photographs. He picked up a piece of writing paper and held it up to the light. He could not see any impressions. There was a book about the history of Norfolk and a few religious tracts stacked neatly. It was all so orderly, except the bed. The counterpane and blankets were in a heap. He examined the window. It was latched. The outer sill was a mere three inches. The inner and outer sills were clean.

Claire's mother returned.

"Here. This was a taken a few months ago."

Sherlock Holmes took the photograph and placed it in his pocket book.

"Is the bed the way you found it?"

"Yes, and that is highly unusual. She always made her bed when she rose."

"But nothing was knocked about in here?"

"No. The door was open and the front door of the flat was standing open."

"So it is like she sat up in bed, walked out the door, and disappeared."

"Yes."

"Are her shoes all here?"

"I hadn't thought of that and the police didn't ask."

She looked in the closet.

"Yes. How strange."

"And her slippers?"

"Yes. They are here, too. How very, very strange that she would walk out in her bare feet. Mr Holmes, I think you are making the mystery darker rather than lighter!"

"Mrs Newhall, you have told me of the young men Claire was not interested in, what of those she was interested in?"

"There weren't any to my knowledge."

"Are you certain there weren't any secret admirers?"

"Well, no, I am not certain. Mr Holmes, my greatest fear is that she has run off with some soldier."

"Why would you fear that if you desired her to marry?"

"My husband was an officer with the East India Company stationed at Meerut when the Indian Mutiny broke out. We were preparing to attend church when the Sepoys broke into the civilian quarters and the officer quarters. Claire doesn't remember it, but I do. They set some buildings on fire. There was gunfire and swords everywhere. I held her close to me and ran. It was later they told me that Philip had been killed. We came back to England after that. We've lived a retiring life. Claire was educated at the convent school of St Etheldreda in Ely Place. I want the best for her. I want her to marry a husband who can provide for her. I don't want her to marry a soldier who will die and leave her alone the way I was."

Ah, mother confesses, Holmes thought.

"Did you tell this to the police?"

"No. They just assumed she eloped with some local young man. Why would she do that when she knew I would be happy for her to marry?"

"Anyone but a soldier."

"I never told her that."

"Do you think she knew it?"

"Well, no."

"Perhaps, she sensed it?"

"Perhaps, but there are not many opportunities to meet soldiers around here."

Why would she elope in her bare feet? he thought.

"Does your daughter still communicate with the young women she went to school with?"

"Yes. They visit each other and exchange letters."

Perhaps that was where she could have met someone, he thought.

"Does she keep the letters?"

"Yes. In a box in this closet."

Sherlock Holmes skimmed through the most recent letters. Her former classmates were talking about their children, the gardens, and reminiscing about school days. All innocuous topics. No mention of young men.

"Could she have gone to visit any of them?"

"The police enquired about that. She is not at any of their homes."

"Was she closer to any one of them than others?"

"Sally Worth, I think."

"Is this her address?"

"Yes."

"Now I am going to look around outside."

"Do you think there might be a clue outside?"

"There might be one or more if the police and the press have not trampled them all."

Sherlock Holmes greeted the bobby who had allowed him to pass and began his examination of the ground from the front step to the street, to the amusement of the lounging journalists before him and the policeman behind. But Holmes was used to working with an audience and not shy about it. He made an elaborate show of taking out a magnifying glass and working forward on hands and knees. There were snickers and outright laughter. As expected he found only a few fragments of bare footprints. Most had been obliterated by many other prints. He stood up at the edge of the street to sarcastic applause to which he smiled and bowed. He looked across the street and right and left. There was nothing near to hold a print.

He turned back towards the building and walked around it. He found the window to Claire Newhall's room. There was gravel next the building but there had been none on the sill. No dings in the glass or on the stonework as sign of an errant shot. No cigarette or cigar butts. If there had been any shoe prints leading away from the gravel they were gone. He returned to Mrs Newhall.

"Mrs Newhall, I have some further investigations to do but I hope to bring you word about your daughter soon," he said before leaving.

Hope. It was essential. He wasn't going to take that from her as it had been—

He said good day to the policeman at the door and the waiting members of the press. One very young scribbler ran up and asked for his name and he rewarded him with a card. Perhaps he would see a paragraph about himself in the evening papers. Surely they had nothing better to write about if they were spending their time waiting for Mrs Newhall to come out.

He walked down the street thinking. There had been no indication in her room or in the hall or on the street that Claire Newhall had been forced to leave. There was no sign that she was frightened or in a hurry. Yet there was also no sign that her departure had been planned in advance.

Even if it was a sudden inspiration why had she not put on her shoes?

Holmes still had a number of theories to explain the disappearance but none that explained that.

He visited Sally Worth. She said she did not know where Claire was.

"Did she ever speak of going away?"

"No."

"Did she ever speak of a soldier or sailor?"

"No, she never seemed interested in men."

"Did she seem unhappy?"

"Not at all. She is always a cheerful person."

"Was she angry with her mother?"

"She mentioned that her mother was urging her to marry but she just laughed about it."

It was raining when he left Sally Worth's house. Holmes hardly noticed. He was sifting through the data in his mind as he walked down the street. Thus far every question he had asked had eliminated possibilities. There seemed to be little left, which suggested he was missing something. The "inscrutability of women" was merely an excuse, not a rational explanation. There must be some reason why she left as she did—

That thought again linked in his mind to the old insolvable puzzle: the one that drove him to be a detective, to work on this case, and yet which he could not permit himself to think about. He stopped and broke off that thought. He looked about, for he had not been paying attention to the direction of his walk. There was a café on the next corner. He could dry off and light his pipe.

There was a fire lit in the café even though it was the last day of May. It expelled the damp. He sat at a table near the fire and wrapped his long fingers around the coffee cup that was brought to him. For a moment he merely felt the warmth and banished all thoughts to clear his head. After he finished the coffee, he filled his pipe and lit it.

It was a small place. It was filling as the sun sank low in the sky. The customers seemed mostly to be writers and artists discussing their art and the politics of the day. Their voices merged into a general hum that filled the room. He wondered how many came here every day to do the same thing.

He turned his thoughts back to the case and examined each piece of evidence individually from every angle. A newsboy, himself seeking a spot out of the rain, came in hawking newspapers. Holmes bought one. He leafed through the pages. There was a three-inch column on the case that offered nothing new. He went back to his examination of the facts. A young woman had walked out of her home in the night in her bare feet and disappeared.

Why? Where was she?

While the first question might resolve the second one, it was the second question that was most important. He did not know the answer to either.

It was dark out now and the rain had stopped. The buzz of conversations was becoming more of an irritant. He left the café and headed to the streets again. He had no desire to return to Montague Street. He wanted to be alone with his thoughts. He wouldn't sleep until he solved this puzzle.

While the rain had stopped, the streets were still wet. This brought to mind a new question.

What had the weather been like the night Claire Newhall had disappeared?

He was near Kings Cross station. He asked at the ticket window if the man remembered what the weather had been like Sunday night.

"Shore, do. Twas clear and warm. Few clouds now and then across the full moon but not much to speak of."

"The moon was full?"

"Yes, sir."

"Thank you very much."

The weather was clear and the moon was full. Was that significant? Claire's window faced west. Did that matter?

He stopped under a gaslight to light his pipe again. He walked, and smoked and thought. Now and then a bobby gave him a curious look but did not approach because he seemed harmless enough.

It was after three in the morning near the steps of St Paul's Cathedral when he grasped the missing clue. It was nothing or nearly so. He had taken his mind back to his tour of Claire Newhall's room. It was sparsely furnished, sparsely decorated, like a cell. Not a gaol cell, but a monk's cell or a nun's.

The eastern sky was already starting to lighten with the approaching dawn. The rain from the night before had turned to fog. He made his way through that fog back to Holburn to Ely Place to the Roman Catholic Church of St Etheldreda. As he approached he heard voices celebrating the Matins. He waited outside. As the nuns and novitiates filed past him he softly called out her name and Claire Newhall turned and looked at him. He did not approach her and she continued on. He knew now the where, if not the why.

Sherlock Holmes spoke to the parish priest and then the Mother Superior at the convent. He explained to them that Claire had been missing since Monday morning and her mother was worried about her. They would not tell him how she came there, but they spoke to Claire and she agreed to an interview with him in their presence.

He stood and introduced himself when she entered. There was an ethereal quality about her that made one wonder that her feet touched the ground. It would be advantageous if they did not since they were still bare.

"Miss Newhall, I am glad to see that you are safe. Your mother has been worried about you."

"She need not worry," she said with a ghostly smile.

"You have been missing for five days and the police have been looking for you."

"Has it been that long? I have been so full of the Spirit that I little noticed the passage of time."

"Would you mind telling me how you came to be here?"

"Not at all. I was asleep in my room and then I was surrounded by a bright light. The next morning they found me kneeling in the church."

"She came to us in the throes of religious ecstasy," the Mother Superior said. "The Holy Spirit brought her to us and it was our duty to shelter her. Our sister Claire has always been a dear child but this is a sign that God has greater plans for her."

"You do not remember walking here?" he asked Claire.

"No. Next I knew I was kneeling in the church and I felt great peace."

"You do not intend to return to your mother?"

"No. This is my place. God has called me here."

"She has joined us as an initiate. She is free to leave if she wishes. Her mother may visit. However, now, Mr Holmes, we have our duties to attend."

He left Ely Place mulling over the results of his investigation. He had read of lights or sounds falling upon someone sleeping causing somnambulism in someone susceptible. The light of the setting full moon had flooded Claire's bedroom before dawn on Monday morning. She had risen without covering her nightgown or her feet and walked the short distance between her home and St Etheldreda's, a route she knew well and a place where she had attended school and had happy memories. She awoke there and interpreted the phenomena as a religious experience.

Who was he to say it was not to her, no matter what the scientific explanation?

It was still quite early when he approached Mrs Newhall's door with the news her daughter had been found. Holmes decided to simply tell her where Claire was and leave the explanations to Claire. Then he walked back to Montague Street.

When he arrived he found his brother at the breakfast table reading the morning papers over the remains of his breakfast. Sherlock sat down, charged his pipe, and lit it. He smoked in silence.

After a few minutes Mycroft folded up his newspaper and said, "Well?"

"I found her," Sherlock said.

Mycroft fixed his brother with a piercing gaze and waited a few more minutes.

"Yet you failed to enter triumphantly proclaiming success. That leads me to believe that those three words must be qualified in some way. Is she alive?"

"Yes."

"Has she been reunited with her mother?"

"She does not want to come home."

"This interrogation is becoming painful for at least one of us," Mycroft said. "Why did she not want to come home? Had she eloped with a lover?"

"No, she joined a convent."

"Well, there certainly might be worse alternatives."

"I suppose."

"I don't think you are thinking about Claire Newhall and the convent."

"No. It is just not something I had thought of before, that someone might disappear because they did not want to be found, and not because they were wanted by the law. Do you think—"

"Sherlock, do not do this—"

Sherlock shook his head.

"No. The horse returned."

"Yes."

His pipe had gone out. Sherlock set it down and rubbed his head with his hands.

"Have the headaches come back?" Mycroft asked.

"Yes. A few weeks ago."

"It has been a long time."

"Yes. Since the play in Cambridge."

"You need to keep busy."

"I know. I thought this case would help. I was culpably slow."

"You were faster than the police."

Sherlock snorted.

"It took you less than a day!" Mycroft insisted.

"I should have seen it all when I walked into her room. All the clues were there."

"You were not thinking solely of the case."

Sherlock sighed.

"That is true. I found parallels when there really were none. My thoughts kept straying."

"You know what happens if you go on this way. You must find something to keep your mind busy. If the cases are not coming, then find something else to do."

Sherlock Holmes could not deny the truth of brother Mycroft's advice. It was a conclusion he had come to himself some time ago. Yet he needed reminding. Shakespeare's words came to him: *What fates impose, that men must needs abide; It boots not to resist both wind and tide.*

Chapter 7

The Tobacconist

"When you pass Bradley's, would you ask him to
send up a pound of the strongest shag tobacco?"
Sherlock Holmes, *The Hound of the Baskervilles*

There was another factor that Sherlock Holmes had not confessed to his brother, for he knew what his brother's solution would be. Despite practicing severe economy, he was nearly out of funds. The generous payments for his services he had received from Lord Cecil and the solicitor Abrahams were nearly gone, as was all he had earned as an actor. Mrs Newhall had offered to pay him, but he knew she was not a wealthy woman. Finally she had pressed a single sovereign upon him and he had kept it. In a few more weeks he would not have enough to continue the advertisements.

Thus the problem before him was not merely to occupy his mind to keep it from tearing itself apart, but to do it in such a way as to improve the flow of funds until his detective practice was paying more regularly.

With this in mind Sherlock was out early Monday morning as the shops were opening. He walked west towards Tottenham Court Road then south to Oxford Street. He bought a newspaper, leafed through it, found nothing of interest pertaining to crime or otherwise, and tucked the newspaper under his arm. He knew from his previous experience that applying to random positions listed in the newspaper was hardly of any use, for there would be a hundred other applicants including some with clearer references.

He was hoping he could find a position that had not been advertised. He passed the post office, a greengrocer's, a butcher shop, a chemist's shop—something perhaps he could learn with his knowledge of chemistry—but they were not hiring. A locksmith—he had never tried his hand at making or repairing locks but he knew how to open quite a few. His reference? How would he explain that a retired second story man had taught him what he knew of locks? Next was a barbershop—not a likely prospect. A bookstore? Perhaps. Past Regents Street he saw a tobacco shop. He looked longingly at it because he was perilously low on tobacco. As he looked his luck improved. The tobacconist was placing a sign in the front window seeking an assistant. Holmes crossed the street.

It was a narrow building which seemed all the narrower by being wedged between two taller and broader ones. The shop windows were plastered with placards advertising tobacco brands. Below there were tobacco jars and stacks of tobacco tins. Above the door were faded gold letters painted over green that said "Bradley's."

Sherlock Holmes entered. It was a very small shop with the counter not much more than a dozen feet from the door. He suspected the back was taken up by storerooms and workshops. The walls to the right and left of the entry were densely covered with nautical décor, paintings of ships, floats, nets, small wooden models of various types of sailboats and steamships.

Behind the counter were shelves up to the ceiling. The shelves were packed with boxes of cigars and cigarettes and jars and tins of tobacco. There was a ladder to one side that would allow access to the higher shelves. On the counter were two showcases full of pipes, cigarette cases, pouches, cigars, and cigarettes of every kind. On the counter top between them was a tobacco-cutter and a pair of scales. There was a space enough at one end of the counter for a person to walk behind it or to access to a door next to the shelves.

The smell of tobacco pervaded the place. It was not the smell of one brand or type or fresh or smoked, but rather all of them in an olfactory chorus. Holmes had been in tobacco shops before, but none quite as intense as this.

The grey-haired man whom he had seen at the window had turned from it and was now lighting a cigar.

"Good morning!" he said brightly.

"Mr Bradley?" Holmes said addressing him by the name out front.

"That's me. What can I do for you?" he replied.

"I saw your sign," Sherlock said. "I'm looking for work."

Mr Bradley looked him over.

"Well, you seem an able young man. It would not be a full

week's work. I'm looking for someone who can help me run the shop two or three days a week."

"That would suit me quite fine," Sherlock said. "I am looking to supplement my own business."

"And what might that be?"

"I'm a detective."

"What kinds of things do you detect?" Mr Bradley asked with a smile.

"Anything. Crime mostly."

"How do you do that?"

"I have my methods. For example," Holmes said, with an introspective look. "You have been a seaman, but not military, merchant marine, I'd wager, and a man of authority, but not a captain, first mate, perhaps. You left the sea for medical reasons. You began acquiring your expertise by sampling tobacco at different ports. When you retired from the sea you considered the wholesale tobacco trade but you are too social to be content with figures and warehouses. So you came up to London instead and opened this shop. You have been married a long time, at least 30 years. You have no children. Your wife thinks you should be retiring but you don't know what you would do with yourself if you did."

Mr Bradley seemed somewhat taken aback.

"Good heavens. How long have your been investigating me?"

"I assure you, I knew nothing about you before I walked in your shop."

"Then how do you know these things?"

"Your bowlegged walk is like that of a man accustomed to navigating a heaving deck. You carry a folding knife in your pocket as every good sailor would. You have a demeanour demanding respect yet are not as stiff as a navy man. You obviously retired from the sea because you are here running a tobacco shop and have been for decades. Yet you surround yourself with reminders. That suggests that you miss it and did not leave voluntarily. It seemed most probable that there was a physical reason."

"All true. I hit my head during a storm at sea. I could not maintain my balance on the ship afterwards. Doctor said it messed up something in my inner ear. And my marriage? How do you know about that?"

"The age of your ring and how far it has embedded itself into your finger. I suspect you can't take it off very easily."

"True. I haven't tried in a decade. What about my wife wanting me to retire?"

"Your age, and the fact that you are hiring an assistant. I wager you compromised by saying you would hire an assistant so you would have more free time."

Bradley shook his head.

"Well, well, that's very interesting, my boy. You obviously are quite bright. Let me show you what needs to be done around here and if you are interested I'll put you right to work. Are you a smoker yourself?"

"I smoke a pipe."

"What – No, allow me to turn about on you. You are a young man, obviously with some education. I would say that you took up the pipe at university and smoke whatever is strong and cheap."

Sherlock Holmes chuckled.

"Correct."

"Well, we shall see if we can't broaden your horizons a bit in that regard. Here, try this cigar. I just received them and I can't make up my mind about them."

Holmes took the cigar and Bradley lit it for him.

"I'm thinking they are a bit too sweet," Bradley said. "That's alright if you like that kind of thing. I prefer something a bit more robust. You just think on it while I show you around. There is some tedious work to be done such as sweeping the floors. I like to have that done once a day to keep the place respectable. The stock must be kept up here in front and inventory maintained in back. We must place orders when we are running low, though the salesmen often drop around and say 'Mr Bradley, you must be running low on this or that, and would you please try this new mixture?' I've known most of them for decades and they know where my interests are and what my customers like. However, sometimes they want me to try something new, like these cigars."

Bradley took him into the back. To the right here was a large room with a door opposite that must lead the back alley. The room was piled high with crates stamped from locations around the globe. Next to crates were boxes, many opened. To the left of the hall were smaller rooms with tables for rolling cigarettes and other tasks.

"I've rolled my own cigarettes for decades," Bradley said. "It is a specialty of the shop. I'll teach you how to do it."

One door was locked with a sign warning not to open it without permission.

"I have recently taken up photography as a hobby. My wife doesn't like the chemicals around the house. But here, the tobacco overwhelms them."

The bell over the front door rang.

"A customer. Come along—Blow me over, I haven't even asked your name."

Holmes chuckled and told him. They went to the front counter where a customer was waiting. Holmes watched as Bradley interacted with the customer and complied when he was asked to mount the ladder and retrieve a ceramic jar containing a certain mixture of tobacco. Another customer came in before that one left. The flow continued off and on for the rest of the day. Between customers Bradley showed Holmes the ledgers, how to record a sale, and how to look up past purchases. Bradley paid him at the end of the day and told him to come back on Wednesday.

Sherlock Holmes soon learned that his employer not only sold tobacco, but was a great enthusiast for it. Bradley sometimes would have long discussions with the customers about the merits of the different types of tobacco, but he always respected a customer's preference.

"It is a personal thing, choice of tobacco, like whether you want cream and sugar in your tea. No man can tell your taste is wrong even if they disagree."

Bradley's knowledge was not merely retail, for he gave Holmes lectures on the different species of the plant, the best growing conditions, and the methods of curing the leaves.

"There are over forty different species of the tobacco plant,"

Mr Bradley said as they were reviewing inventory one day, "but most products sold are combinations of just a few: Bright, Burley, Corojo, Criollo, Turkish, and Perique. Bright leaf and Burley are both light coloured plants grown in the United States. Unfortunately an attack of flea beetles last year destroyed half the tobacco crop in United States. I hope they are having better luck with this year's crop or Bright leaf tobacco could become in short supply. Burley is also grown in South America and is less likely to be effected. Burley is used in chewing tobacco, American blend pipe tobacco, and American-style cigarettes.

"Turkish tobacco, sometimes called Oriental tobacco, is the next most commonly used. It is a highly aromatic, small-leafed variety grown in Greece, Bulgaria, and the Ottoman Empire. The current war between Russia and the Ottomans could lead to a shortage of that. It is important for a shopkeeper to keep an eye on affairs that might affect the supply.

"And here we have perique, the strongest of all tobaccos, except the legendary 'wild tobacco.' Perique is grown in Louisiana, one of the southernmost of the States. It is too strong to be smoked alone, but a little adds zest to any blend. Corojo and Criollo are grown in the Caribbean and are primarily used in cigars."

"This little box here contains Dokha tobacco grown around the Persian Gulf. It is not cured like other tobacco. The green leaves are dried and shredded into flakes and smoked with a special pipe. I have one gentleman who comes in for it occasionally.

"I mentioned curing," Bradley continued. "There are several methods of curing tobacco and the method used has a substantial effect on the flavour. Tobacco is air-cured by being hung in well ventilated barns for four to eight weeks. Air-cured tobacco has a light, mild flavour, yet is high in nicotine. Burley and most cigar tobaccos are air-cured.

"Fire-cured tobacco is hung in large barns where hardwood fires smoulder over three to ten days. Some types of pipe tobacco, chewing tobacco, and snuff are fire-cured. Twenty years ago most of the tobacco grown in the States was dark-leafed and fire-cured, before the movement to the bright and burley variants.

"Latakia is a fire-cured tobacco produced from Oriental varieties grown in Cyprus and Syria. They add aromatic shrubs to the curing fires which results in a very distinctive aroma. It is used in some Balkan and English-style pipe tobacco blends.

"Bright leaf tobacco is flue-cured. The curing barns are heated by external fire boxes. That reduces the amount of smoke the leaves are exposed to. The result is a sweeter tobacco with a lower range of nicotine which is favoured among many cigarette smokers. Turkish tobacco is hung outside to cure in the sun. The result is a tobacco with a much lower level of nicotine. It is used in blends of pipe tobacco and cigarettes.

"Perique and some other tobaccos are fermented. Cavendish tobacco found in some pipe and cigar blends, can be made by fermenting any tobacco type. English Cavendish uses a dark flue or fire-cured Bright leaf tobacco, which is steamed and then stored under pressure for several days or weeks to permit it to cure and ferment."

"I suppose you have an interest in poisons?" Bradley asked.

Holmes confirmed he did.

"Do you know that tobacco is in the genus *Nicotiana* which is in the family *Solanaceae* with deadly nightshade?"

"I do. I also know tobacco has been used as a poison. There was a case in Belgium in 1851 where a count was executed for poisoning the countess' brother with liquid nicotine distilled from tobacco leaves. In 1858 here in London a man committed suicide by drinking nicotine."

"I think we will just keep that information to ourselves," Bradley said with a wink. "Don't want to give the customers dangerous ideas."

In his second week of working at the tobacco shop, Bradley introduced Holmes to individual cigars and cigarettes, pipe tobacco blends, and ropes of chewing tobacco. Bradley had him retrieve them from the shelves and examine them on the counter so he could become familiar with their size, shape, colour, and smell. Occasionally, Holmes had a chance to sample the merchandise. He learned to differentiate an Indian lunkah from a Trichinopoly from a Cassandra or Bahadur Burma Cheroot. He could tell a Villar-y-Villar cigar from a Corona and many others. There were more blends of pipe tobacco than he imagined. Bird's-eye, Player's Navy Cut, Lone Jack, Cameroon, the Stage-Coach Mixture, Royal Indian Wood, Briarbrae Purely Naval and Majordomo's Royal Tan Blend were among them. There were many different brands of cigarettes and long plugs of chewing tobacco. He learned to measure and cut a plug, and to weigh the loose tobacco.

The customers of the tobacco shop were interesting, too. They came from all classes of society and all walks of life. Wealthy customers sent a servant around to pick up an order. Most people came themselves. Many had been coming to the shop for years and Bradley knew exactly what they wanted. Bradley told Holmes about them and he learned quickly. While there was a ledger that recorded the purchases of customers, he understood that it would be an asset to remember a customer's usual brand when they entered the store.

It was Holmes' habit to tie that bit of information to what he quickly deduced about them in the few minutes they were in the store. The tall, balding gentleman by the name of Smith with the taste for Cabañas, who addressed himself broadly and loudly to Mr Bradley and Mr Holmes—after introducing himself—and the stool and various jars and bits of decor, was undoubtedly a barrister who practiced at the Old Bailey (though not one Holmes had seen at work), accustomed to addressing and appeasing juries, mostly on behalf of criminal defendants.

"You are on the mark there, Sherlock," Bradley said.

The bell rang. A short man entered with thin legs but an ample belly. His suits were fresh, well-cut of expensive stuff and well-tailored. His hat was the latest fashion. His hair was dark, with bit of grey on the side. He sported a great nose, reigned over by piercing eyes with ample wrinkles and a pair of bushy eyebrows. His chin was prominent, his smile warm.

"Oh, Bradley, I have another fête coming up. All the best laddies and ladies attending, you know. I want to refresh my stock of cigars, cigarettes, and pipe tobacco for my guests. You know what I like. Package it up and send it over, ol' chap."

With a wave of his hand, he was out the door again before Bradley could even respond.

"That, Sherlock, is Mr Habbernathy. What do you think of him?" Bradley said as he began to gather the order.

Holmes leaned upon the broom and gave it a moment's consideration.

"He was once a billiard shark," he said, "then a wine-merchant, which may be when you first met him. Since then he's trafficked in army commissions, and become a successful bill discounter. He still has a large army connection, and can tell off the encumbrances on most of the large landed estates of Great Britain and Ireland. He has a fine cellar of old wines and a collection of old masters, neither of which he paid the retail price for. He has a large house and gives fabulous parties which many young men of first families find it worthwhile to attend to keep in his good graces. Three balls do not hang over his door, yet he is a broker of sorts."

"Heavens, you are a dangerous man," Bradley said as he was writing down the address. "Now, you just get underway and deliver this to his house and you can see how far that goes towards the truth."

Holmes chuckled as he put the broom away and took up the stack Bradley had prepared and headed out to find a cab. He found nothing at Mr Habbernathy's house that surprised him.

One day half dozen young men entered the shop in very high spirits. Their method of placing an order resembled a theatrical ensemble.

"We are most desperate you see," one began.

"Not quite desperate, you ninny," said another.

"It is a most serious case," said the third.

"There was an echo in the can," replied the first.

"As empty as my belly," said another.

"Just get done with it."

"We need a tin of the Arcadian Mixture."

"Make it two."

"Two?!"

"We'll all pitch in."

"We can't have this happening again."

"No, of course, not. Yes, make it two."

The tins were brought forth and wrapped up, the price stated and crowns and shillings were heaped upon the counter from pockets and pocketbooks until the total was reached, and then they swarmed out with their prize, talking amongst themselves as they did.

"Do you think Watson is in?" one asked his fellow.

"He was hard at the books when I left."

"We'll need to put an end to that."

The door closed behind them with a clink of the bell.

"Go on," Bradley said.

"Medical students, University of London, I fancy, rather than Bart's. Mostly well-to-do parents, though not gentry. A few need to pinch their pennies. Some are very serious about their studies and some are very ambitious. A couple are neither."

It wasn't quite two weeks that Holmes had been working there when Bradley looked up from the newspaper he was reading.

"Now you see, Sherlock, I could never be a politician."

"Why not?" Holmes asked because he knew that was what Bradley wanted him to ask.

"See here, the Duke of Argyll asks what is going on in Afghanistan and the Marquis of Salisbury politely replies that the Ameer of Afghanistan had refused to receive a British resident at his court, but that the assemblage of troops on the north-west frontier had no reference to the negotiations going on at Peshawar, and that our relations with the Ameer had undergone no material change. If I was Argyll, I would have asked if the Viceroy of India was trying to start a war in Afghanistan, and if I was Salisbury I'd have frankly replied that I thought the Ameer was treating with the Rooshians and that hurt our pride even more than our foreign policy, and people were likely to get killed over it. Then at least people would understand what was going on."

"You are too honest to be a politician," Holmes agreed.

He suspected that his brother Mycroft was of the same opinion as the tobacco merchant.

"I'm going to take the afternoon off and take my wife for a ride in the park," Bradley said. "I think you've learned enough to handle the shop for a few hours."

So it progressed that sometimes Sherlock Holmes had the shop to himself. At first it was for a few hours at a time and then whole days. Eventually Bradley gave Holmes a key so he could open in the morning and close in the evenings on days Bradley was not coming in. Sometimes the shop was busy and he had enough to do to keep up with the customers. When they were gone there was cleaning and inventory to do. There were, however, times when Holmes sat behind the counter smoking—which was, of course, permitted—reading the newspapers. The newsboys knew the shop was a good place to sell a few and often stopped in for that purpose.

There was one old sailor named Sam who frequented the tobacco shop, perhaps more to talk than anything else. He bought chewing tobacco. He never bought in quantity, but rather came by nearly every day for a little more. One day he rolled in the door with the clatter of the bell and Holmes set down his newspaper. It had been a slow day.

"Mr Bradley tells me you are starting out as a detective," Sam said.

"Yes."

"Well, there are a lot of queer things that I could tell you about. There's a lot of goings on the police never see. Things change when a peeler comes in sight."

"I suppose they do," Holmes answered.

He wanted to ask what kind of things, but just then the bell rang and he had to attend to another customer and some others followed. By the time Sherlock had a spare moment, the old sailor was gone. But the sailor's comment left him thinking.

The following morning after his brother had left for Whitehall, Sherlock dug his make-up kit out of his trunk. He had played characters older than himself, so creating wrinkles was not something new to him. He knew it needed to be more subtle than it would be for the stage, but the principles were the same. He had some bits of wig and whiskers in his kit and he knew where to purchase more. It was a more elaborate method of disguise than he had used following Kurr and Druscovich, but then he had used what he could carry and be able to change rapidly. He was now considering establishing complete identities so he could see London through the eyes of others.

He began walking as an old man with no particular destination in mind. One of the first things that he noticed was how differently an old frail man was treated that a young vigorous man. The old man was treated with much kindness. He was offered assistance crossing roads and offered a seat on omnibuses.

However, especially in some parts of London, gangs of young boys sometimes stalked him intent on robbing him. Sometimes he could avoid the confrontation by entering a pub or catching up with a group of other people. On his third day out he had found himself in the lower quarter of Lambeth, not far from the Thames. Turning a corner, he saw such a gang stalking a man. To a casual observer they may have seemed to be merely walking down the street laughing and joking. But he could see the looks and signals they exchanged and how they manoeuvred towards him. The man they were stalking was an older man, though not as old as he himself seemed to be. His hair was grey and he wore blue-tinted glasses. He was lanky and stooped over the packages he carried. Holmes quietly followed the gang, trying not to attract their attention. As he drew close one of them struck the other man with a stick across the ankles. As he lost his balance another of the gang shoved him from behind. His packages flew from his arms and his spectacles clattered to the ground. As he groped for them, a third gang member waved a knife in his face.

"Just give us your purse, old man, and you won't be hurt."

Sherlock Holmes could see the fear in the man's eyes. He struck the knife with his cane. It flew off and the knife-wielder recoiled, howling with pain. The first gang member started to dart forward, but the rap of the cane struck him in the collarbone and he drew back. The old man caught up his spectacles and looked up at the man standing over him. What he did not see beneath the fake whiskers was the surprise Holmes felt. When their eyes met he realized he knew this man, or had known him a long time ago. The reunion would have to wait.

Holmes was now leaning on the cane which had proved to be such a formidable weapon. The knife was under his foot and one hand held a police whistle.

"Be gone or ah'll blow this whistle an' bring the constable from the next road," he growled in a scratchy voice.

The gang members darted off.

"Cowards," Holmes as the old man, grumbled.

Slowly he bent down and retrieved the knife and tucked it away in some inner pocket of his old coat. The other man stood up.

"Thank you, sir," the man said holding out his hand.

The older man scowled and ignored it. Holmes knew that looking and sounding like an old man was easier than replicating the feel of an old man's hand.

Somewhat embarrassed the man withdrew his hand and began to gather up his packages.

"You deserve some reward for the service you have done me," he said reaching for his purse.

The decrepit old man merely snorted and shook his head. So he put his purse away and took up his packages.

"Well, honour me by joining me for tea."

Holmes said nothing, but shuffled along behind as the man made his way down Pinchin Lane. The man stopped at the third house on the right-hand side and fumbled for his keys. There was a stuffed weasel holding a young rabbit in the window and a sign: "Hans Sherman - Birds Stuffed - Trophies - Live animals."

"That you?" Holmes growled.

"Yes, yes, that is me. Welcome to my shop," Sherman said pushing open the door.

Holmes entered and was struck with a wave of memories a decade old at the odd cries and barking that greeted them. He allowed a small smile creep onto the craggy, disguised face. A curly haired dog rushed forward and nosed at the men. Holmes caught his breath for the spaniel resembled his own dog, Sandy, gone many years now.

"Don't worry about Lulu," Sherman said, "She's gettin' on in years. She's most likely to love you to death."

Holmes reached out a hand and stroked the dog's head and sighed. Lulu followed them.

Sherman offered the old man a chair, but he took a stool by the kitchen instead. The stool hadn't been used much lately. Sherman didn't find it comfortable. Ah, but the lad had liked it. Lulu sat at the foot of the stool and the old man reached down to scratch her head.

Attempts at conversation seemed futile so Sherman said nothing as he put his packages away. As Sherman put the kettle on, he felt the silence was thick and uncomfortable—if silence of any kind was to be had in the shop, so he said, "I didn't catch your name, sir."

But instead of the crackly voice of the old man, a young man's voice responded, "Do you remember me, Sherman?"

The voice was somewhat familiar though much changed. Sherman turned. There on the stool where he had left the decrepit old man, sat a tall, slim young man.

Sherman blinked. The young man seemed vaguely familiar. He was definitely much taller and perhaps a bit thinner, if that was possible, and the chin and nose had developed a bit these past 13 years, but there was no mistaking those eyes. Those piercing grey eyes now twinkled and sparked as the young man chuckled to himself.

"Mr Sherlock? Is it really you, lad?" Sherman asked.

"Yes, Sherman, it is I!"

"Oh, but you aren't a lad now. You're a grown man!" Sherman said as he clapped his hands on the younger man's shoulders and gave them a squeeze.

"Well, Mr Sherlock, I'm glad to see you," Sherman cried. "I thought to never see you again since you'd gone back to Yorkshire. I had no notion what had become of you."

"So you were the old man?" Sherman asked.

"'Twas I," Sherlock responded holding up the cane and a wig as testimony. "I had no idea it was you the gang was attacking until you looked up at me."

Sherman shook his head.

"You played it well," he said, and fetched a pair of cups from the cupboard and poured tea.

"So what is Mr Sherlock Holmes doing parading about the streets of Lambeth dressed as an old man? Have you taken up actin' now?" Sherman asked.

"After a fashion," Holmes replied, taking the cup Sherman proffered. "In truth, my days on the stage are behind me. I spent two years trodding the boards with a theatrical company. I gave it up when I decided that it was time I was about my proper business."

"Which is?" Sherman asked.

Holmes looked at his old friend over his teacup.

"I am a detective," Sherlock Holmes said.

"Were you followin' someone in that guise?" Sherman asked.

"Oh, no. I was merely observing people. Research, you may call it."

Lulu nudged him and Sherlock scratched her head.

"Was Lulu in the same litter as Sandy?" he asked.

"She was. How is old Sandy?"

"She died a few years ago."

"Life and death. Tis the way of the world. Always fightin' for one or t'other."

Sherlock Holmes set his cup down and stared at it.

"Come along, then, Mr Sherlock. Time to feed the animals."

They moved among the maze of rooms and cages. It had changed little. They were greeted by bright eyes and enthusiastic voices. Some of the animals like Lulu ran free; others were confined. Birds flitted about in the rafters.

"How many animals do you have, Sherman?" Sherlock asked.

Sherman laughed.

"I have no idea."

"I've been thinking, Sherman," Sherlock said as they returned to the kitchen. "It might be useful to me to have some places to stash costumes about London so I can make a quick change. Would you allow me to keep some things here?"

"Certainly, lad. Even have a spare cot if you need it, though you might have to evict a few critters."

"Excellent, Sherman!"

That evening over supper, Sherlock excitedly told his brother Mycroft of his reunion with Sherman. Mycroft noted his brother's enthusiasm. He also noted that these long walks improved Sherlock's appetite which often was hardly enough to keep a bird alive.

"The idea came to me while I was there at Sherman's that there would be an advantage to having refuges about London where I could change my identity rapidly. Sherman's in Lambeth would be an ideal place. I will need to find others."

"What about Bradley's?"

"Perhaps. I think it is too early to ask that now. I've only been working there a short time."

Though clients and cases still evaded him, Holmes' days were fuller now. He worked three days a week at Bradley's. He spent some days and evenings walking the streets in disguise, observing people, listening to them. The remaining days were spent reading newspapers, adding information to his reference books and planning—for he was optimistic of the growth of his clientele in those days. His advertisements for detective services continued to run and he remained hopeful that new clients would come his way. His earnings from the tobacco shop were enough to cover the cost and a little over. He was not flush. He walked whenever possible and took omnibuses rather than cabs when necessary.

One day in early July, Sherlock Holmes, in the guise of the old man, headed east towards Smithfield Market shuffling past the stalls then northward to St Pancras—Kings Cross Station where he found a seat and watched the trains and listened to the drama of people coming and going, many on holiday.

He rapped the knuckles of one pick-pocket and sent him off, knowing full well he would return later. After a time he walked again. He turned westward and made his way along Euston Road to the station of the same name. It was there he picked up unwanted company who merely saw an old man to rob. He crossed Euston Road and turned into Tottenham Court Road. He hobbled up the steps of a pawnshop. It was a dirty-looking shop and even the items on display in the front window were covered with dust and cobwebs. He had been past it many times before but never entered. Now his purpose was to discourage the pair of ruffians who were following him. Holmes had no doubt he could best the two of them, but he did not want an altercation that might expose his disguise. So he had entered the pawnshop. The proprietor came out from somewhere squinting and blinking like a mole at the extraordinary sight of a customer.

"Do for you?" the pawnbroker mumbled.

Holmes, disguised as the old man, grumbled something which seemed to satisfy him since he scurried off to a stool behind the counter. Holmes pretended to look at some articles in the front window. The ruffians were still waiting out there. He wandered towards a corner of the shop and gazed around at the dust-covered merchandise, odd items pawned and never redeemed. The owner must make more on interest if it was not a front for some other business, for no effort was made to make the abandoned property look attractive for sale.

Then he saw it. Just the neck was visible until he moved a hat out of the way. There between a meat grinder and a pile of cracked books sat a violin. It was missing two strings and the bridge was askew. It was so dirty that it was difficult to tell much about it. He reached out and touched it. The wood seemed firm but a greasy substance and a thick layer of dust coated the instrument. On closer inspection he could see that it was actually sitting in a case that was thrown open on the table and half buried as well. The outer part of the case might be in fine condition but the inner lining was grimy and moth-eaten. There was nothing at all attractive about the violin or its case, yet somehow it cried out like an abandoned child to his musician's soul.

He wanted it.

The proprietor shuffled up.

"How much for the old violin?" Holmes asked.

"Three quid," the man said much to Holmes' surprise.

Perhaps it was in worse condition than it looked. It didn't matter. Holmes had made up his mind. If he had that much on him, he would take it now. He dug into the pockets of his costume and drew out his hand with all the silver he had. There was the sovereign Mrs Newhall had given to him, which he had clung to as the most recent payment from an actual client, a florin, two crown, twelve shillings and two sixpence: fifty-five shillings all told.

The pawnbroker took the money from his hand.

"Yours."

Then he pushed everything else aside and unceremoniously slammed the case, closed the clasps, and picked it up. He carried it to the counter mumbling something. He wrote out a receipt for the purchase and handed it to Holmes, then wrapped the case in brown paper and tied it with string. As he was wrapping it, Holmes turned back to the front window. The boys were still out there. As he took the package he asked the broker if there was a back door.

"There are some rough fellows in the street. I fear they would rob me," he said.

The pawnbroker did not seem surprised by the request and led him to a door that opened into to an alley. Holmes thanked him, followed the alley to some mews to another street and then walked swiftly home bearing his treasure.

Once in the safety of the sitting room at Montague Street, before removing his disguise, Sherlock cut the string and peeled back the brown paper. The case was not in any better condition on the outside than it was on the inside. The act of flipping the clasps strained its integrity. This did not concern him as he still possessed the case and bow from his prior violin—which now lay in pieces on the floor of the Atlantic Ocean. He opened the lid. In the brighter light of the sitting room this violin was even less attractive than it had been in the dark pawnshop. He lifted it from the case and set it on the brown paper. Something rattled inside as he did.

He examined it carefully. Rubbing at the furry outer coating rolled up pills but did not effectively remove the grime. The f-holes on the front of the violin were clogged with it. He blew into them sending up clouds of dust that blinded him and set him coughing. He squinted inside and blew again. He was peering in one of the f-holes with his magnifying glass when his brother Mycroft returned.

Mycroft chuckled at the old man bending over the table.

"I am never quite sure who I will find here. What have you there?" Mycroft asked.

"Possibly a violin. Possibly a very valuable violin. Look," Sherlock said proffering his lens.

Mycroft took the lens from Sherlock and leaned over the table with great care not to associate with any of the grime.

"Right here on the slip inside: *Antonious Stradivarius fabricus 1732.*"

"Are you certain it is genuine?"

"No, I'm not. I have just begun my examination. It would be marvellous, if true!"

"Especially if it can be restored. How did you come by it?"

"I paid fifty-five shillings for it at a pawnshop."

Mycroft laughed.

"That would be a handsome return. A Stradivarius violin must be worth two hundred times that."

"At least," Sherlock responded.

Sherlock examined the violin thoroughly with the lens. The outer layer seemed to be ordinary household dust. The dust was adhered to it with a thick coating of grease. He sniffed at it.

"Cooking grease. In fact a bit fishy. Fond of their fish and chips? But not very careful of their instruments. Perhaps it was stored in a kitchen or its owner only had one room."

Sherlock turned the violin over. The post rattled inside. He had seen that it was down when he had looked through the f-holes.

The varnish on the back of the violin was clear and the stripped pattern of the wood was bright. He gently tapped on the back. The sound was muffled but not bad. He looked at the inside of the case. He could see the outline of the violin in the bottom of the case.

"Clearly the violin sat in the open case exposed to the grease and dust and was rarely ever taken out of the case. Why abandon it so?" he said aloud.

"Ah, you have a mystery!" Mycroft said over his newspaper. "Perhaps a string broke and they could not afford a new one? Perhaps the musician in the family fell ill and could no longer play it."

But then the housekeeper appeared with their supper and Sherlock Holmes removed the violin to his room and changed.

The next day he worked at the tobacco shop, but the following he spent some time at the British Museum. He discovered it was quite common for violinmakers to create replicas of different models of Stradivarius' violins and label them the same way as the originals. There were differences: subtle variations in the f-holes, the quality of the wood and how long it was aged and differences in contraction. There was no single and easily recognizable determinant. It took an expert eye. He took the violin to a luthier who said it was a fake, but was willing to take it off his hands for five pounds. A shop that sold musical instruments also proclaimed it was merely a replica, but offered him several pounds more than he had paid. These offers did not entice him but rather made him suspicious. He was far from ready to give up on it. It might not be a Stradivarius but if it could be restored to playing condition he would be satisfied. He returned to the museum to read more books about violins. There he met a violinist with whom he shared the story of buying a violin at a pawnshop which might be a Stradivarius.

"You should speak to John Thompson. He lives in Peckham. I was at a party at his house recently. He owns a number of violins by Stradivarius. He seems to know all about them."

The violinist dug a card out of his pocket book.

"Here's his address: 5, East Terrace, Evelina Road, Peckham."

Sherlock Holmes wrote down the address and thanked him. He returned home and wrote a letter to Thompson asking if he could bring it over for his inspection. By return post he received an invitation to visit the following afternoon.

Holmes replaced the violin in its tattered case and rewrapped it in the paper and set off for Peckham. He found the house at 5, East Terrace, Evelina Road was an ordinary two story suburban villa. There was garden at the back with a stable and a lane that ran down to the Chatham and Dover railway line. He was led to a drawing room with a bow window overlooking the street. It was a large room with walnut furnishings, a Turkish carpet and magnificent mirrors. It featured a piano upon which lay a Spanish guitar. Wooden cases with glass fronts displaying violins and other musical instruments lined one wall.

The man himself was remarkable. He was at least eight inches shorter than Holmes with a wizened, tanned face, and a limp. He was sombrely dress in black, but had a gentle manner.

"Hello, Mr Holmes, I was very glad to receive your letter. I am always happy to meet a fellow musician. Let's see what you have here."

Holmes unwrapped the violin and drew it from the case. Thompson took it reverently and examined it closely.

"Interesting, very interesting. Would you consider selling it?"

"No. Regardless of its value."

Thompson handed the violin back to Holmes who sat it upon the table. Thompson drew out a ring of keys upon a chain and approached the display cases.

"I must be careful. There have been a number of robberies in the area," he said.

Thompson brought out two other Stradivarii that he had from the 1730s and several replicas.

"See here, the gracefulness of the curve? The curve in this replica seems forced, artificial, but this one was divinely inspired."

Thompson handed Holmes a magnifying lens and pulled the lamp closer.

"Now look inside. See the sound post? Notice how these replicas have larger ones?

"Yes."

"Pull it up next to the lamp. Look as best you can at the sound post and the interior joints. Notice the tiny nicks here and there."

"Tool marks."

"Yes. Compare the different ones."

"I do see some subtle differences."

Then Thompson began rapping each of the instruments with his fingers.

"Listen. No two violins sound exactly the same. But you can hear similarities between these two as opposed to the replicas."

Thompson lifted one of the Stradivarius violins to his chin and applied bow to strings. Despite missing a finger on his left hand he played very well. Then he handed the violin and bow to Holmes. It had been months since he had tossed the remains of his violin overboard. He let the music now flow.

Thompson applauded when he finished.

"You do it justice!" the gnome of a man cried. "You truly do it justice. Now try the others."

Holmes did and he soon understood what Thompson was saying about the similarities between the Stradivarius violins and the differences between them and the replicas.

"You see? They can replicate the overall look, even to the neck replacements, but the craftsmanship and the sound; that they cannot replicate."

"And this one?" Holmes asked.

"I am sure you know by now. Yours is in no condition to play.

Yet the craftsmanship all argues that it is a true Stradivarius," Thompson said.

"Can it be restored?" he asked.

Thompson picked up the dirty violin.

"It is possible that this ugly coating may have protected the violin from fluctuations in humidity that might have cracked it. As you can see from the back it is not cracked. It also might have preserved the finish and kept it from chipping, or worse yet, mould. Mould can be a problem here in London and it can eat right into the wood. It is rare for a Stradivarius to get mouldy, but I've seen it. The fact that the finish is intact on the back is a good sign that the finish may still be intact under this coating. You want to remove it very carefully to avoid saturating the wood inviting mould.

"I recommend using a borax solution of one part borax to three parts water and a soft cloth. Do not soak the wood. Wet the cloth and rub gently. Take your time. Work on a square inch at a time and allow it to dry before you do another area. You will probably need a soft brush to reach into some parts. Let it dry and then wipe it down again with a damp cloth. When it has all been cleaned let it dry for several days then bring it back and we will take a look at the finish and see if there are any parts that need refinishing before you restring it."

"Thank you, sir. I will do as you say. Thank you very much," Holmes said shaking Thompson's hand before repackaging the violin.

He returned to Montague Street in the best of spirits.

Chapter 8

Ashes, Ashes

"I have made a special study of cigar ashes—
in fact, I have written a monograph upon the subject."
Sherlock Holmes, *A Study in Scarlet*

Sherlock Holmes spent the rest of the summer of 1877 dividing his time between the tobacco shop, walking the streets of London in disguise, and the painstaking cleaning of the Stradivarius violin. He left the two strings attached to hold the bridge and tailpiece in place and to keep the instrument from flexing too much during the cleaning process. It was slow, but it was a labour of love. He began with the ribs and was pleased as each inch of varnished wood was revealed.

He did not begrudge the time he spent at the tobacco shop, for income from the shop had partially paid for the violin itself and paid for the advertisements for his detective services which he continued to run in several newspapers. He learned much from his time at the shop as well. There were interesting customers. Holmes was especially fascinated by Sam, the old sailor. On days when he was alone in the shop and no customers were around, he drew Sam out to tell him more about these "queer things" he spoke of.

"Know what a coal torpedo is, laddie?" Sam asked one day leaning upon the counter.

Holmes said he did not.

"Tis a little box as looks like a lump o' coal but its hollow inside. Usually has a spring or slide t'open it. A cove insures his ship for more than its value. He makes one o' those an' fills it with dynamite or some such. Drops it among t'other coals when the vessel is filling 'er coal bunkers, an' in time box is shovelled into the furnaces an' BOOM! The whole ship blows sky high. Many a good ship an' crew gone t' bottom like that. If they're alone at sea they vanish an' no one knows what becoom o' 'em."

Holmes filed that information away in case he ever had a case involving a ship that disappeared at sea. In return he asked the sailor if he'd ever known anyone who had been shanghaied, and related his adventure in San Francisco saving two of his fellow actors from such a fate. Then Sam told him another story as well. But Holmes wanted more than tales. As they spoke Holmes studied the look and the mannerisms of the old sailor.

Sam's face was thin and dark with many lines upon it. It was difficult to determine his age, so weathered was he. He had a perpetual squint as if from too many days staring into the sun. His teeth were brownish yellow and crooked and his hands were bent and arthritic. He wore an old cap and grizzled hair stuck out like wires around the edges. He walked with his legs spread and bowed at the knee and he rocked side-to-side as if to an invisible sea.

The next time Holmes was out walking as the old man, he visited the dockyards and found a second-hand clothing store nearby. He invested in a pea jacket, striped shirt, dungaree trousers, coarse red scarf, cap, and a pair of old boots. That evening as he was cautiously cleaning another small section of the violin he thought about the look of this new character he was creating. While Sam was his inspiration, he wanted to establish a new persona at the docks with his own look and story. He spent a few days working on the makeup and rehearsing the speech, the mannerisms, and the walk. One morning when he was ready he opened up his bedroom door and rolled into the sitting room. His brother Mycroft looked up as he entered. He raised his eyebrows and chuckled.

"Bravo, Sherlock. That's quite good. There are one or two subtle indications, but other than that even I would have difficulty telling you from an old salt."

"If ya did I'd show ya twern't good for ya,"

"So where are you off to?" Mycroft asked.

'Jus' wanderin' 'round t'docks. Nobody pays no mind t'an old drunken sailor an' there's queer things t' be seen."

Over time Holmes developed a number of different characters which he used throughout London. They were to serve him well, especially as he became more well-known and his likeness was published. The old sailor he first created in July of 1877 became one of his favourite impersonations which he returned to many times during his career.

One role that Holmes did not have to impersonate was that of a tobacco merchant's assistant, for he lived it for a number of months. That role was to benefit his detective career in ways he had not imagined when he first sought it out to supplement his income. It would heighten his profile in the world of crime detection and introduce him to a person with whom he would work closely for decades to come. It was while he was tending Bradley's tobacco shop that he first learned of major events that would change Scotland Yard forever.

On the 12th of July Holmes was perched on the stool behind the counter of the tobacco shop just lighting his pipe when a newsboy came in with an extra and he bought one. "Detectives arrested" the headline said. Scotland Yard Inspectors Mieklejohn, Druscovich, and Palmer, together with the solicitor Froggatt had been arrested, and were going before the magistrate at Bow Street on charges of conspiring with William Kurr and Harry Benson, who had been convicted in the Turf Fraud trial earlier in the year.

Holmes had no doubt that Druscovich, and Mieklejohn were guilty, for he had heard them conspiring with William Kurr and Harry Benson himself. He had only heard about Palmer's involvement second-hand and did not know the solicitor Froggatt. In the months that had passed since the trial and sentencing of Kurr, Benson, and the rest of the gang, he had begun to despair that the Home Office would hide the criminal behaviour of the detectives which he himself had uncovered. As long as they remained at Scotland Yard it was difficult to know how far the corruption went and who was enforcing the law rather than breaking it. That could be hazardous for someone such as himself to work with the Yard. He was glad to see some attempt was being made to clean house no matter how scandalous the revelations might be.

The hearings at the Bow Street Magistrate's Court lasted 28 days. He followed the reports in the papers with interest. On September 8th the newspapers reported that Chief Inspector Clarke had been arrested and added to the Bow Street hearings. On September 22nd, the Magistrate bound them all over for trial to commence the following month. It was the talk of all London, including Bradley's tobacco shop.

While talking of the news of the day was common enough at

the shop, serving the customers, maintaining the ledgers, and cleaning the shop were part of the daily routine. As tedious as cleaning the tobacco shop was, Holmes became fascinated by the ashes in the sweepings and those that accumulated in the ashtray upon the counter. His restless brain studied those ashes as well.

"What are you looking at, Sherlock?" Bradley asked as Holmes was leaning on the counter examining the ashtray one day.

"Looking at the different types of ash in here," he replied poking at them with his finger.

"Oh, yes, my boy, different tobaccos, different curing rates. It is even more distinct than that. The ash from a cigarette smoked by a man who draws hard upon it will be different from that of a man who is more casual about it."

"Like bellows on a furnace," Holmes said, "drawing harder makes it burn hotter and the combustion is more complete," Holmes observed.

"I suppose that is it."

"Someone should write a treatise upon the subject."

Bradley laughed.

"Why would anyone want to read a treatise on tobacco ash?"

"It would be extremely important to the detection of criminals," Holmes responded. "If you can say definitely, for example, that some murder had been done by a man who was smoking an uncommon type of cigarette, it narrows your field of search."

"Then you are the very man to write it, Mr Detective!"

"I've hardly studied the subject at all."

"You'll have time and material enough here between customers."

"You would allow it? I would need to pick your brain and do some experiments."

"Studying tobacco has been my life's work. Consider this a tobacco laboratory. It could make your name, my boy, and wouldn't hurt the reputation of the shop none."

"I suppose that is true."

"And as a bonus—well, come along—" Bradley said waving his hand at him.

Bradley led Sherlock Holmes into the back to the door with the warning. He unlocked it and pushed the door open. Photographs of a woman, a house and garden were clipped to a piece of string hung across one wall. A table held several trays and jars of chemicals, including silver nitrate and potassium cyanide. Atop a cabinet was a box of glass plates. In a corner stood a camera on a tripod.

"The first step is to create the negative on the plates. It is important to get the light and exposure correct. It becomes second nature after a bit of practice. After exposure the image is fixed on the plate with potassium cyanide—another reason for keeping this room locked. Tobacco isn't the only poison kept in this shop," Bradley said with a laugh.

"The print process is much easier than many people realize. I buy albumenized paper for consistency but it can be made at home with egg whites. When you are ready to make prints you float the albumenized paper in the silver nitrate solution."

"Creating silver chloride which is unstable in light."

"Correct. Then you allow it to dry in the dark. When it is dry you place it in a frame next to the plate negative and expose the frame to sunlight until the image develops on the paper. When you have the image you desire, you bathe the paper in a solution of hyposulphite of soda to remove the remaining silver chloride. Really very simple and available right here in the shop."

"We can photograph the ash!" Holmes exclaimed, suddenly understanding Bradley's intent.

"Yes. We could provide the publisher with photographs that they could include as plates in the book."

"That would improve the book's utility immensely!" Holmes said.

Thus the study of tobacco ash became a project for his spare time at the tobacco shop, whether when he was there alone or assisting Bradley. In truth, Bradley himself became very excited about the project, sometimes explaining it to select customers. He taught Holmes how to operate the camera, how to develop the plates, and make prints. Being a chemist—if one of a notorious reputation unknown to Bradley—Holmes learned the process quickly.

Holmes took meticulous notes about each type of tobacco in the store plus a few samples that salesmen brought in. He noted the name, the blend, the curing process, the use (pipe, cigar, or cigarette), the colour and texture prior to consumption and the colour and texture of the ash. Among the pipe tobaccos there was a range of colours to the ash, from the dark brown of the Royal Indian Wood, the blue-grey of the Briarbrae Pure Naval. Texture also varied. Some created ash that was fluffy and smooth, others course and rough or flaky. He experimented with different smoking rates and how that affected the look and feel of the ash.

Holmes became curious as to why some tobaccos burned as they did. While Bradley's knowledge of the breeding and curing of the various tobacco products was extremely useful, Holmes wondered what effect the breeding and curing might have on the chemical composition of the tobacco leaves and the final product. The composition was likely responsible for the variations in the colour and cohesiveness of the ash. That kind of study was beyond the resources of the tobacco shop.

Sherlock Holmes wished now he had access to the laboratory at St Bartholomew's Hospital again. He had stayed away from Bart's for years for fear they might have heard of the explosion at Cambridge and would ban him. Perhaps that had been forgotten? Perhaps he should make some enquiries? Was Stamford still there?

There was also the trial of the Scotland Yard detectives at the Old Bailey. Detective Inspector John Mieklejohn, Detective Chief Inspectors Nathaniel Druscovich, William Palmer, and George Clarke, and solicitor Edward Froggatt were charged with conspiring with William Kurr, Harry Benson, and others to obstruct, defeat, and pervert the due course of public justice.

Holmes had more interest in this trial than he had in the trial of Kurr and Benson in the spring. He knew Kurr and Benson were scoundrels, but the detectives had betrayed the public trust. Since he was not called to give evidence, he assumed it was the convicts themselves who would testify against the policemen. He wondered how truthful they would be.

The trial opened at the Central Criminal Court at the Old Bailey on the 24th October and continued for three weeks. The Attorney General's opening statement occupied the first day. William Kurr was called as the first witness on the second day and his testimony lasted through the 29th of October. He was followed on the stand by Harry Benson. As Holmes was minding the tobacco shop three days of the six days each of those weeks, he could not watch every day of the trial. He was able to see a portion of each of Kurr and Benson's testimony. Newspapers followed the trial closely and he read their reports on days he could not attend.

Benson and Kurr were both quite loose with the facts, especially in relation with Chief Inspector Clarke. Holmes did not know Clarke and had heard only that Superintendent Williamson had left him in charge while he was absent. He had not heard his name mentioned by Benson or Kurr during his own investigation. However, at the trial Kurr claimed to have met with Clarke at times when Holmes knew he had not because he had been watching Kurr during those times. Fortunately, Clarke's barrister was aware of at least some of those discrepancies. He challenged Kurr and introduced witnesses who testified that they were with Clarke at different places when Kurr claimed he was meeting with him. Kurr maintained his smug self-assurance even at such times.

The prisoners in the dock were far from smug or self-assured. Froggatt, the solicitor, seemed annoyed. Clarke looked uncomfortable. Palmer was very unhappy. Mieklejohn was defiant and Druscovich had the look of a broken man.

Superintendent Williamson followed Benson on the stand and then the convicted co-conspirators Frederick Kurr and Edwin Murray. Next was a seemingly endless array of clerks, bank cashiers, housekeepers, valets, waiters, and hotel managers. These were the nails that held the case together. The convicts may have a motivation to lie, but all these different people did not. It was this testimony that assured Holmes that the Home Office was serious about this prosecution. These witnesses corroborated many of the details of the accusations against four of the defendants, but not Clarke. Clarke's barrister poked holes in the prosecution's case against his client. Baron Pollock, in summing up, recommended the jury to consider the case of each prisoner separately. The jury found Clarke not guilty, and the other prisoners guilty. His Lordship sentenced each of the guilty parties to two years imprisonment with hard labour.

It was, however, remarkable how much Fleet Street had changed its tune. Not too many years before the press had condemned plainclothed policemen as spies on the public. Yet now when a golden opportunity to condemn the detective branch presented itself there was nearly a universal call for improvement of the detective system rather than its abolition. The *Pall Mall Gazette* praised the government for prosecuting the detectives publicly instead of trying to hush the matter up. *The Morning Post* held out hope that "the Detective Service be so organized that it shall not be possible for those who are engaged in it to betray their trust." *The Times* insisted that "A detective department is a necessary adjunct to every modern police system."

Whether in response to, or in concurrence with the opinions of the public press, the Home Office convened a Departmental Commission to investigate the detective system of the Metropolitan Police. Sherlock Holmes, like other residents of London, turned to other matters.

The process of cleaning the Stradivarius took not weeks, but months. Holmes heeded Thompson's advice not to hurry. After he believed he had removed all the grease and dust, he examined every nook and cranny of the instrument with his magnifying lens to find more and remove it. He forced a clean dry cloth through one f-hole, pushed it around inside and pulled it out the other. The cloth brought with it a little dust, but nothing else.

John Thompson had written to him periodically asking of his progress, and he had responded with the latest news. Now in mid-December he wrote that he thought the violin was ready for inspection. Thompson wrote back inviting him down that very afternoon. Sherlock Holmes packed the Stradivarius in the case that had once held his prior violin, along with his bow and a new set of strings, and hailed a hansom to Peckham.

"Come in, come in," Mr Thompson greeted him warmly. "Let's see what you have accomplished."

Holmes set the case down on the table, released the clasps, and drew the Stradivarius out.

"You have done well," Thompson said reaching for it.

He held the violin under the light and examined it. He tapped it with his fingers.

"You have done very well indeed. It is looking very good. The finish seems to have survived the neglect and abuse. Next we must reset the post."

Thompson retrieved an odd looking tool from a drawer. It had pincers like a lobster. He reached into one of the f-holes and managed to capture the little wooden post. He set it upright and wedged it between the back and the front of the violin.

"Now it is ready to string," he said handing the violin back to Holmes.

Holmes attached strings to the tail where two were missing and then wound them around their respective posts and tighten them. He then removed the two old strings one at a time and replaced them. Now with four new strings in place he began to tune the violin. When the strings were in tune, he lifted the violin to his chin and took up the bow. He drew it across the strings and the instrument sang. He closed his eyes and began to play. When he stopped he sighed.

It was worth the fifty-five shillings many times over. It was worth the months of patient work. He had enjoyed playing his prior violin. At times he had needed to play it, and he had sorely felt its loss over the past year. Playing the Stradivarius was different. He could not have explained the difference if he had been asked. Thompson did not ask. He seemed to know.

"It is beautiful and you play well. I believe that violin was always meant to be yours. Scoff if you like. I'm a man of science myself, an inventor. Yet I believe there are some things beyond what science can understand. One of them was the look I saw on your face while you were playing."

"Thank you for your assistance," Holmes said. "How may I repay you?"

"May I play it?" Thompson said.

Sherlock Holmes handed his Stradivarius and bow to John Thompson who tucked it under his chin and played Paganini's "Caprice #13" twice through with precision. It was not a long piece but it was very complex. Once again Holmes was impressed that the lack of a finger on Thompson's left hand did not interfere with his playing. The little gnome of a man was very talented. He seemed most alive when he was playing a violin. He almost looked like a different person.

"It has a lovely tone," Thompson said as he handed back the Stradivarius.

A maid came in to light the gas for the December sun was dropping low in the sky. She was followed by Mrs Thompson.

"Oh, Susan, dear, this is Mr Sherlock Holmes," Mr Thompson said taking his wife's hand.

"Pleased to meet you, Mr Holmes. Will you be joining us for dinner?"

"I should be off," Holmes said as he packed the violin and the bow in the case.

"We will be having a few guests over for music afterwards," she said.

"Thank you, but I really must be going."

"Well, at least you must meet my daughter and her fiancé," Thompson said. "They are visiting us for the festive season. Jane Ann, this is Mr Sherlock Holmes. Mr Holmes, Mr William Bolsover."

The pleasantries dispensed with, Holmes made his escape.

"Take good care of the Stradivarius, and yourself, of course," Thompson said as they saw him to the door.

"Have a Happy Christmas," Susan Thompson said.

"Happy Christmas," the friendly foursome echoed.

Another week passed. It was the 22nd day of December and the weather had been chill and gloomy. No clients had come calling. Yet with his newly restored violin in hand, Sherlock's mood was light and he was exploring some tunes he had not played for many years.

The night was rather advanced when he was interrupted by a vigorous knock on the door. He had no expectations of guests. His brother was out and Mrs Denton was long gone for the day, so it fell to him to answer it.

He laid the Stradivarius gingerly upon the table and the bow beside it before opening the door. As he did so, in whooshed Lord Cecil bundled in a fur overcoat against the weather and his strawberry blond hair glistening with the mist peeping out around the edges of his silk top hat. He was carrying a bottle, some glasses, and a small box tied with string.

"I see your festive decorations are limited to the exterior," the estranged scion of a duke said as Holmes closed the door behind him.

"The housekeeper's contribution," Holmes said.

"Ah, but did I not hear some strains of a French carol through the door of—Oh, that is a beauty," his lordship said espying the gleaming violin as he set his bundles upon the table.

Holmes gathered up the violin before Lord Cecil could touch it.

"It is a Stradivarius," Holmes said with a touch of pride.

"How did you come by it? They are fairly rare, aren't they?" Lord Cecil asked as he hung his fur overcoat and hat upon the rack. Underneath the fur coat, he was dressed in a suit of green and gold fitting for the season though somewhat garish.

Holmes chuckled.

"That's a tale," he said.

Holmes put the violin and bow away in their case while Lord Cecil opened the box he had brought, extracted a small plum pudding, and poured liquid into glasses.

"Good. Then we both have tales to tell, and I have brought some festive brandy and pudding here to accompany them. Is your brother here?"

"No, he is away at a reception at the Foreign Office."

They took up chairs before the fire with their glasses.

"What has it been? A year?"

"Slightly more, though I saw you testify at the trial," Holmes said.

"Yes, nasty business. You are looking well. The detective trade must agree with you."

"There has been little enough of that."

"There was the miracle in June."

"Yes."

"Fear not! The winds brought me more details than were print-ed. I quickly decided it was best the girl be left alone. I learned such discretion from you! However, a little birdie also told me there was some private agent behind much of the revelations in the Scotland Yard scandal and coincidently you utterly vanished after the Corycian business. Not a hint?"

"What tale do you bring?" Holmes asked, unwilling to be drawn out about the cases.

"No, yours first, my dear boy, mine's a bit of a mystery and I think you are going to want to savour it and I shan't get you back to your tale afterwards. I remember that your previous violin was de-stroyed on the voyage back across the Atlantic. Now tell me how you came by that magnificent instrument."

"It may help you to understand the circumstances to know that I've made it a habit to walk about London in various disguises."

"Oh, fascinating! I predicted your time on the stage would teach you some useful skills."

"It did indeed," Holmes agreed.

"What is your purpose in these perambulations incognito?" the young lord asked.

"To learn how people act when they don't believe they are be-ing watched and how they interact with the different characters I play. It also tests my skills at disguise in close proximity, which you must admit is far more of a challenge than from the stage."

"Indeed."

Holmes proceeded to tell the story of finding the Stradivarius.

"Over six months' time I cleaned it inch by inch. Just weeks ago Mr Thompson declared the restoration complete and the violin fit to be strung."

"As close as you permitted me to it, it seems you did a fine job of the restoration."

"Thank you. I am a bit leery of letting anyone near it."

"Like a young woman with her jewels," Lord Cecil said.

"I did allow Mr Thompson to play it," Holmes said, "for that was all the compensation he desired for his invaluable assistance."

"Oh, that is a fabulous little tale! Disguised as an old man you bought a Stradivarius for fifty-five shillings! I wonder if the result would have been the same if you had appeared in your own person. We shall never know. But here, let us not allow this plum pudding to go to waste," the young lord said approaching the table.

"Are you stalling, Cecil?" Holmes asked

"Oh, not at all, but this tale involves punch, puddings, raisins, almonds, flaming brandy, and all the other trappings of a grand holiday party, so this is the perfect accompaniment to it," he said as he cut Holmes a piece and refilled his glass. "We shall see, Mr Detective, if you can solve this case from your armchair despite those at the scene having failed."

"I accept the challenge," Holmes said also accepting glass and pudding.

"I was attending a house party this evening," Lord Cecil said reclaiming his seat.

"So I gathered," Holmes said.

"Oh, so you didn't think my attire was for your benefit?"

"No."

"Correct as usual. After what happened, the lady I was escorting wished to return home. That having been completed, I realized it was too early to retire and the events too fresh in my mind for sleep in any case. I can't really tell it at my club yet without a satisfactory conclusion. So I thought why not to bring it to you."

"You are telling the tale hindmost forward."

"So I am. A bit of suspense always heightens the thrill," Lord Cecil said with a twinkle in his eye.

If Lord Cecil made his living these days—in addition the allowance his father provided as assurance that he would never set eyes on him again—it was as a collector and dispenser of gossip, a raconteur, a teller of tales. He regaled audiences at his club and at parties, and sold columns under the pen name of Langdale Pike to newspapers. A simple statement of fact was too much to expect from him.

"'An honest tale speeds best being plainly told,'" Holmes said.

Lord Cecil chuckled.

"Touché. You score a point for invoking the Bard in favour of your argument. As I said, I was at a house party not far from St James

Park. I shall keep this as anonymous as possible, at least for now. The house was festooned with holly, ivy, evergreen, and ribbons of red and gold. It was lit with hundreds of candles. The guests were forty to fifty young people all dressed gaily, the women flaunting their jewels and other assets. Everything was sparkling and flickering. There were trays of puddings, cakes, biscuits and canapés, flutes of champagne and bowls of punch. There was music, dancing, and games. One pretty miss—Let's call her Agnes, though, of course, that is not her real name."

"Of course not," Holmes said setting aside his empty glass and picking up his pipe from the mantel.

"You aren't going to smoke that thing?"

"Yes."

Lord Cecil frowned.

Holmes waved his hand towards the door.

"Ha," Lord Cecil laughed, "you shan't be rid of me that easily."

"Pray continue then," Holmes said as he struck a match.

"This Agnes had recently returned from a tour of the Mediterranean and was showing off an unusual necklace she had brought back from Rome."

Holmes tossed a few more coals upon the fire before retaking his seat with his pipe. He leaned back, closing his eyes. The smoke encircling his head showed he was still alert.

"It was very different from the necklaces of gemstones or pearls worn by the other ladies. The stones were somewhat in an oval shape, each about a half inch long with some carvings. At first glance they appeared to be a warm brown colour but they flashed gold and red streaks in the candlelight. She told me they were sardonyx. It was an unconventional choice but the stones complemented Agnes' fair skin and chestnut hair. Such novelty did not detract from her desirability. She arrived on the arm of one young man, but danced with many others."

"Including you?"

"Of course. That's when I had the best look at the necklace and she told me about it."

"I suppose the necklace was stolen?" Holmes asked.

"Who is now jumping to the end? Patience, my dear fellow! If you want details, you must allow me to set the scene. The front door to this house opens on to a great hall. Just inside the door were servants taking coats and wraps. Beyond that to the right was the punch bowl and attendants pouring champagne and a table laden with sweets. At the far end of the hall were the musicians, and dancing couples filled the intervening space. Lady May—also a pseudonym, you understand—and I took a few turns on the dance floor, together, and with other partners. Then we went to explore the game rooms set up on either side of the great hall. Each room had a game master who would occasionally change the game being played but they had a list so they never intruded on the games played in other rooms.

The first room we entered had some chairs arranged in circles with space in the middle for the person who was it. We began with a rather sedate game of The Minister's Cat followed by Charades with some very literate and enthusiastic guests. Then Lady May and I moved to another room for Reverend Crawley's Game. Chairs had been removed from this room to allow space for more vigorous games. I believe they also played Blind Man's Bluff in that room. We had our game of Reverend Crawley's and left as they were about to start another round. Agnes and her beau were just entering for the new round as we left. I am certain she was still wearing the necklace then. I suspected that room first when the necklace was not found in the parlour. A light fingered thief could pocket the crown jewels during that game. Are you familiar with it?

"Enlighten me."

"In Reverend Crawley's Game the players stand in a circle. Then each takes the hands of two other people but they cannot be the hands of the people next to them. By the time everyone has hold of two hands the players are tangled in a very large knot. The goal is to entangle the knot without letting go of anyone's hands. It requires a lot of twisting and ducking under arms and stepping over people. Sometimes the tangle gets worse before it gets better."

"What time was it when you saw her then?"

"I know it was before 10 o'clock because I had promised the hostess to be in the parlour to tell a ghost story at ten and I left the game room and headed to the parlour with Lady May on my arm shortly after the clock chimed the third quarter."

"Another guest was just finishing his tale as I entered the parlour. There were four wingback chairs before the fireplace. Between them and around them were various settees and small chairs. Some of the audience sat and some stood. The previous storyteller introduced me and we swapped places."

"The room was dimly lit by the fire alone—for atmosphere, you see. There were about a dozen people listening to my tale, some sitting and some standing. A few more came into the room and joined us after I began telling my story. About halfway through, Agnes and her beau entered the room. They did not come toward the fire and sit down. They were standing near the table. Perhaps they were waiting for the snapdragon bowl. I just caught a glimpse of them from across the room. I could not tell if she was still wearing the necklace.

"After the chilling conclusion of my story, as guests were standing, a servant brought in the snapdragon bowl and lit it. Everyone gathered around the table to test their skill. I stood with Lady May for a few minutes watching from near the fireplace before we rounded the table. From the other side of the table I noticed there was something different about Agnes's appearance, but at first I could not make out what it was. Then it hit me like a stroke of lightning: the sardonyx necklace was missing from around her neck. I thought perhaps she had removed it to play the game.

"There was a lot of laughter and shouting as people challenged the blue flames. I am a bit of a coward at playing games of fire so I did not participate. When Lady May tired of it after a few minutes we rounded the table again. I did not see the necklace on the table next to Agnes but perhaps she had it in a pocket. I was curious. As we passed her, I leaned over her shoulder and asked what had become of her lovely necklace. She immediately grasped her hand to her throat with a look of horror. She nearly toppled me as she jumped up from her chair.

"Immediately everyone began searching for the necklace. We looked under the table and the chairs. The search began in the parlour and spread to the halls and to the other rooms. The gas was turned up; lamps were brought in to aid the search. Eventually the police were called when it became clear that the necklace had not merely broken its clasp and fallen somewhere but must have been stolen. A thorough search was done of every surface and in everything of every room of the house. The servants were searched as well. Though highly unusual with such an esteemed company, all the guests agreed to be searched before departing. The holiday mood had been destroyed. Yet no sign of the necklace was found."

"No one left the house without being searched?"

"Correct."

"You said that a snapdragon was brought in after you finished the story?"

"Yes."

"Who brought it in?"

"One of the servants. He was a short, stocky fellow with dark hair. I believe his name is Jacob."

"Describe what he brought in."

"He carried a large tray. It contained a wide bowl. The bowl was perhaps 20 inches across. In the centre of the bowl was a plum pudding—a round one slightly larger than this. The remainder of the bowl was filled with raisins and almonds. There was also decanter of brandy and some other items on the tray. After setting the bowl in the middle of the table, Jacob poured brandy over the pudding and the fruit and nuts and lit the brandy with a match. A blue flame raced across the brandy in the bowl and over the pudding. The guests gasped with delight.

"Do you know how snapdragon is played?" Lord Cecil asked.

"Yes. The object is to snatch the burning raisins and nuts from the bowl and eat them."

"Without burning yourself, yes."

"It seems strange to call it a game," Holmes said.

"Yes. Jacob explained the object and warned of the dangers as he poured the brandy and lit it. In fact, I heard him specifically warn Agnes not to lean too close to the bowl or she might catch her hair on fire."

"Was she already sitting at the table at the time?"

"She had just sat down."

"Where was she in relation to this servant?"

"She sat down right next to him. He blew out the match and looked over at her and said 'Take care, milady, that the fire not light your hair,' he said as he stood up."

"Did he touch her in any way?" Holmes asked

"He may have brushed against her hair or her shoulder as he said it, but there was much movement at the table and jostling as people sat down and began snatching at the almonds and raisins and others gathered about to watch. It is just as likely she brushed against him as the other way round. He used a large wooden spoon to push some of the fruits and nuts back from the edge of the bowl. Then he gathered up the decanter and the box of matches and withdrew from the table."

"Where were you when this happened?"

"I was behind them about perhaps six feet away. Shortly after that Lady May pulled me around to the other side of the table when a seat became vacant. She wanted to play. I stood behind her and cheered her on."

"And the room was still dimly lit?"

"Yes, just the fireplace and the snapdragon threw any light in the room."

"Did Jacob leave the room?"

"He moved back to a corner. He was still there when the alarm was raised."

"What of the snapdragon?"

"What of it?"

"What became of it?"

"It was abandoned in the search for the necklace. The brandy burned off. The last I saw it there was nothing but the charred remains in the bowl."

"It was still in the parlour?"

"When I last saw it, yes. Why?"

"Because that's where the sardonyx stones are hidden – or were, for they may have been moved by now. It was the perfect hiding place for the necklace."

"But how could they have gotten there?"

"Jacob likely unclasped necklace while warning her and palmed it. He is the light-fingered chap you were concerned about in the other room. I am certain he will be found to have a history as a pickpocket. This was a perfect opportunity for him. It was a dark room with people jostling about the table. Then he pushed the necklace under the raisins and almonds when you saw him moving them with the spoon. The sardonyx stones would be indistinguishable amidst the almonds and raisins except to a sharp eye. By leaving it there until later he avoided the risk of it being found on his person if the loss was discovered. He could claim it later under the guise of cleaning away the remains of the snapdragon."

"Good heavens! I must see if they have emptied the bowl yet!"

Lord Cecil bounced up, grabbed his fur coat, and fled.

Holmes chuckled. Now he had solved a grand total of two cases in 1877. He set his pipe aside and took up his Stradivarius again.

178

Chapter 9

We All Fall Down

*"He sprang from his chair and paced about the room in
uncontrollable agitation, with a flush upon his sallow cheeks."*
Dr John H. Watson, "The Adventure of the Five Orange Pips"

It had been Mycroft's habit, when they both were in London, to treat his younger brother to a night at the theatre and a sumptuous dinner on Twelfth Night which coincided with Sherlock's birthday, and this tradition, while interrupted at the commencement of 1877, was resumed on the occasion of Sherlock's 24th birthday in 1878. However, the 6th being a Sunday when many theatres closed they decided to celebrate on Saturday the 5th instead.

After they had begun their wine and oysters, Mycroft presented his brother with a small package which again contained a book. This one was in English, if the American distortions could still claim to be English. It was *The Mollie Maguires and the Detectives* by the famous American detective Allan Pinkerton.

"I thought perhaps you might enjoy a little lighter reading." Mycroft said.

"Ah, interesting," Sherlock Holmes said, "The Molly Maguires were being tried while I was in the States. The news reports were rather sensational and not very informative. Perhaps this will provide a clearer account. I've regretted that I was unable to meet with Mr Pinkerton while I was in Chicago but since his stroke a decade ago he has not been receiving visitors."

"I also have bit of news," Mycroft said. "Some of us in the government offices have decided to form a club."

"A club?" Sherlock exclaimed with a laugh. "Surely the world has gone mad! Why Mycroft, I thought you were one of the most unclubable men! Have you suddenly developed a craving for witty conversation?"

Mycroft smiled.

"Actually it is intended to be a club for the unclubable."

"How would that work?" Sherlock asked.

"It will be entirely silent."

"Indeed?" Sherlock replied with a raise of his eyebrows.

"And no member is allowed to take notice of any other."

"That is rather anti-social."

"With one exception: there will be a Stranger's Room, where conversation will be allowed."

"That does sound unique. What will you call this club?"

"The Diogenes Club."

"At least there is a bit of humour in the name."

"We've pooled funds and taken a lease on a building in Whitehall. It is being renovated and furnished to our specifications. It will feature a dining room with a highly rated chef, parlours with comfortable chairs, newspapers, magazines, books, a fully stocked wine cellar and liquor cabinet, and complete silence. It is expected to open in April. Once it does I will be taking many of my meals there."

"Keep me apprised as to how this experiment progresses."

Still no clients came knocking on Sherlock Holmes' door through the winter and early spring of 1878. He was, however, busy at Bradley's tobacco shop, working on his notes on tobacco ash between serving customers, wandering the docklands as an old sailor, and playing his Stradivarius.

The Departmental Commission studying the detective division of the Metropolitan Police reported in early 1878 that it had determined that the most significant issues contributing to corruption included insufficient pay, lack of centralization, and secrecy. It recommended that detectives be given an increase in pay to reward performance and to avoid temptation. The committee also advised that all detectives, even those who worked out of the divisions should be controlled from headquarters. Detectives should also be prohibited from accepting outside positions while employed by Scotland Yard.

It was not immediately clear what the Home Office intended to do in response to the report, but on April 6th, 1878 it became so. On that date the Home Office created the Criminal Investigation Department of the Metropolitan Police. This new department assumed control of the detectives serving at Scotland Yard headquarters as well as all detectives stationed in the divisions previously under the command of the Divisional Superintendents. Additional detectives were to be promoted up from the ranks to increase the number of detective inspectors both at headquarters and in the divisions.

Superintendent Williamson, who somehow had survived the scandal, was made chief superintendent of the new department, commanding three chief inspectors and twenty inspectors, and an office staff of six sergeants and constables. Williamson reported to the new Director of Criminal Investigation, Howard Vincent. Vincent answered directly to the Home Secretary.

Howard Vincent's background was not that of a policeman. He was educated at Sandhurst and had purchased a commission with the 23rd Foot, been promoted to lieutenant, and served as a correspondent with the *Daily Telegraph* while stationed abroad. After resigning his commission with the 23rd Foot, he served with the Royal Berkshire Militia and Middlesex Rifle Volunteer Corps. In May 1873, he enrolled as a pupil barrister at the Inner Temple and was called to the bar in January 1876, although he never really devoted himself to the practice of law. In 1877, Vincent enrolled as a student at the *Faculté de Droit* of the University of Paris and investigated the Parisian police organisation. Later that year he was asked by the London Metropolitan Police to report on the Paris detective system. His report impressed the Home Secretary and led to his appointment as Director of the Criminal Investigation Division.

Naturally some members of the CID were initially suspicious of a director who had not come up through the ranks, though others argued that a fresh point of view was exactly what was needed. Good relations between Director Vincent and Chief Superintendent Williamson, who was highly respected by the detectives, did much to alleviate their concerns.

By April 1878, Sherlock Holmes had recorded observations and taken photographs of over 100 types of tobacco. Sometimes in their enthusiasm for the project, Holmes and Bradley allowed the time to get away from them and closed the shop late. This did not usually cause any difficulty (except perhaps with Bradley's wife). If a customer came in after the usual hour of closing they simply fulfilled the customer's needs. However, one evening as Holmes carried the camera back to the dark room after a photography session, he heard the bell on the front door ring. He thought nothing of it at first but then he heard Bradley speaking in a tone he had never heard.

"I'll give it to you. Don't do anything with that," Bradley said.

Holmes turned and ran down the hall. As he reached the doorway to the front of the shop, he saw a man leaning over the counter grab money from Bradley's hand. The man held a gun in the other. Before he reached the counter the gun fired and Bradley slumped to the floor. Holmes grabbed the robber by the shirt with his left hand and hit him hard in the face with his right fist. The gun flew across the room and the robber fell to the floor.

Holmes ran to Bradley's side. He was bleeding badly. Holmes ran out to the street and shouted for someone to get a doctor and the police. He heard police whistles shrill. He ran back in again and knelt by Bradley's side. His eyes flickered open. He looked at Holmes, and said, "Don't forget to lock up" and died.

A crowd gathered outside the shop. Constables came running in, followed by a man with a black bag. Holmes looked up at him hopefully but he merely shook his head. A constable pulled Holmes through the door to the back and sat him at a table in one of the workrooms. There Holmes sat for some time ignoring them all until a familiar voice caught his attention.

"Mr Lestrade, how is this matter proceeding?" the voice said.

"Trying to get this young man's statement," was the response.

"Ha!" the voice said recognizing the witness at the table, "He's always been talkative enough with me. Mr Holmes, we meet again."

Sherlock Holmes looked up at Detective Inspector Gregson.

"Mr Sherlock Holmes, Detective Inspector Lestrade," Gregson said.

Lestrade was lean, ferret-like fellow with dark eyes. Those dark eyes narrowed.

"You know this fellow?" Lestrade asked.

"I do indeed," Gregson said.

"Arrested him before?"

"Oh, no, though I can't say the idea hasn't cross my mind once or twice. However, he seems to be more useful in the outside."

"Useful? A snitch?"

"Oh, no, he imagines himself something of a detective."

"Not with the Yard?" Lestrade stated.

"Entirely private, something of an amateur. He has a good idea now and then," Gregson admitted.

If Sherlock Holmes had been in a better mood he might have enjoyed listening to this discussion, or at least contributed to it, perhaps even defending his record. However, he could not see the humour in it, or even the purpose, while Bradley's corpse lay in the other room. He was angry. He wanted to be alone with the man he was angry with. That wasn't the man he had knocked unconscious. It was himself. Duelling with Scotland Yard detectives was not going to get him what he wanted. So he was silent.

A constable appeared.

"They're ready to take away the body."

"You know any reason we shouldn't, Mr Holmes?" Inspector Gregson asked.

"No."

"I'll take another look," Lestrade said and left the room.

"Don't mind him, Holmes," Inspector Gregson said. "Just promoted up from the ranks. He's a bit of a doer. Set on making an impression. We have a lot of them in this new 'Criminal Investigation Department,' as they call it. To me the work's the same: keep your nose to the grindstone and don't get cosy with the criminals. Now tell me how you came to be here, Mr Holmes, and what happened."

"I was working as Bradley's assistant," Holmes said.

"Detective business not working out for you?" Gregson said with a grin.

"Clients are a bit scarce at the moment."

"Cases are thick enough for the official police."

"I am sure you would find it so," Holmes snapped. "I've been working here a few days a week."

"Shop was open a bit late."

"We were working on a book."

"A book?"

"On tobacco ash. It will be very useful for detecting criminals. We were photographing some ash. The time got away from us. I was putting the camera away in the dark room. That man came in and he shot Bradley as I returned to the counter. I knocked him out."

"You walloped him one good," said Inspector Lestrade, who had returned to the room and been taking notes. "He's just starting to come around. Just in time to be hauled off to gaol."

"I've done some boxing," Holmes said.

"Ah, that explains it. Weren't you afraid that he'd shoot you, too?" Lestrade asked.

"I didn't want him to get away," Holmes responded.

He could have said that he had not been concerned about being shot.

"Well, it was a brave thing you did there but leave catching criminals to the professionals. You might get yourself killed," Lestrade said. "Did you recognize the man? Was he a regular customer?"

"No."

"I have your address in case we have any further questions," Gregson said, "But for now you should get yourself cleaned up."

Cleaned up? Holmes thought.

He looked down. There was blood on the knees of his trousers. There was blood drying on his hands. He stared at them. It wasn't all Bradley's blood either. He'd skinned three of his own knuckles when he'd hit the robber. He washed his hands in the darkroom. He met the inspectors at the front door.

"He told me to lock up the shop before he died," Holmes said "so if you are done here."

They looked at each other.

"I think we have seen all there is to see," Gregson said.

"He has a wife," Holmes said.

"Do you know her address?"

He told them her name and address.

Holmes locked the shop and began walking home. He climbed the steps to the flat at Montague Street, unlatched the door, and closed it behind him.

"Mrs Denton left you—" Mycroft began as he looked up.

Then he stood up, quickly. Mycroft never stood up quickly, but the sight of the blood soaked trousers had him on his feet.

"Are you injured?"

"No," Sherlock said shaking his head. "Bradley's dead. Killed by a robber. I need to change my trousers."

Sherlock was gone for a few minutes and returned to the room wearing clean trousers and holding a revolver, not by the grip, but with the cylinder lying across his palm. While the sight was not enough to bring Mycroft out of his chair again, he did find it disturbing.

"I did not know you had a gun," Mycroft said.

"I brought it back from the States."

"Is it loaded?"

"No," he said. "I unloaded it shortly after I received it. I've never loaded it since."

Holding it in both hands now, Sherlock push out the cylinder and spun it.

Mycroft was relieved to see the chambers were empty. It was not that he feared for his own safety. He was confident his brother would not harm him. He was more concerned about the volatility of Sherlock's passions at the moment. He knew the direction they tended to turn when they were aroused. He knew nothing else of what had happened at Bradley's other than Sherlock's cursory summary. Yet it was obvious to him that Sherlock was barely containing his temper. That could bode ill for someone.

Sherlock turned the gun over in his hands. It seemed more than a weapon in his hands. It seemed like a token, a reminder of something else.

"Have you fired it?" Mycroft asked.

"Yes, twice. I hit a fence the first time, and a wall of a railway carriage the second. The first was a miss, and the second a hit, though a wall is rather difficult to miss."

There was a sardonic smile on Sherlock's face. It wasn't a pleasant thing. It faded when he shook his head.

"We hear stories of the American West. I saw the reality. A boy dreamed of being a gunfighter until he fired a foolish shot at an amateur train robber who fired back in fear. The boy died. I was inches away from the boy. I've never spoken about it to anyone but I always felt—"

He squeezed the gun in his hand, the cold steel resisting, and the effort making his knuckles white. He slammed the pistol on to the table and left it there.

"If I had reacted sooner I could have stopped the boy from firing. If I had reacted faster this evening when I heard the shop bell, Bradley might be alive. And if—"

Mycroft cut him off.

"Sherlock, you can't predict the future. You can't always know what people will do."

"Why not? If we can reason backwards to determine who committed a crime, and how and why, why can't we synthesize a probable future course of action?

"The synthesis is possible," Mycroft replied, "but the results are only probable and there are likely to be various solutions with varying probabilities. Humans are not very tractable. They don't like to conform to mathematics. I have encountered that far too many times recently in foreign affairs."

"In that case you are dealing with the whims of countless humans rather than a select few. What good is it to solve crime if I cannot prevent it?"

"I think you are expecting too much of yourself," Mycroft said.

"Bah!" Sherlock cried, stormed off to his room and slammed the door.

Mycroft heard no more from him the rest of the evening. After a few hours he lifted the pistol from the table and placed in a drawer so Mrs Denton would not be alarmed by it. Then he went to bed. In the morning the door to Sherlock's bedroom was slightly ajar. He was gone. Mycroft opened the bureau drawer. The revolver was still there. Mycroft set about his morning routine. When Mrs Denton enquired if Sherlock was joining him for breakfast he merely said he had already gone out. Then Mycroft hailed a cab as usual for the drive to Whitehall.

Mycroft never forgot for an instant that his brother had disappeared without a word. That itself was not unusual. However, the mood he had been in was treacherous. Yet Sherlock was not a boy. He was a man and that great tragedy that still haunted the darkest corners of his mind was more than six years in the past. He must find his own way to cope with this new shock.

What Mycroft had not known was that when his brother left at dawn that morning he had not left as himself, but rather disguised as the old man. He needed to work and right now his work was to study the people of London. In addition, for now, he needed to be someone other than Sherlock Holmes. He went to Lambeth and after some surveillance, paid a visit to Sherman and the cacophony of his animals. He arrived back at Montague Street at dinner time and startled Mrs Denton as she was serving.

"Sir, you just can't walk in here!"

Mycroft chuckled.

"Begging your pardon, Mr Mycroft, what is so funny?"

"You've just complemented Sherlock on his acting skills again."

Sherlock bowed and pulled off the grey wig.

"Such nonsense," Mrs Denton grumbled and left.

Dinner was on the table, but Sherlock ignored it as he removed the rest of his costume.

"You received a letter," Mycroft said indicating where it lay.

Sherlock picked it up. The return address showed it was from Bradley's widow. However, it was not written in her hand. Perhaps a neighbour had written it for her.

Dear Mr Holmes,

The police told me that you were with my husband when he was murdered and apprehended his killer. I thank you for that. However, I now have a great favour to ask of you. The shop is my only source of income. My husband was the member of a burial club so those expenses are covered. He left a little savings but I fear they will be quickly drained. Could you continue the shop? You are the only person he ever trained and he praised your knowledge and intelligence. I will be at home to you tomorrow afternoon if you wish to discuss the matter.

Mrs Belle Bradley

He tapped the folded letter on the table, set it down, and then lit his pipe. He sat and thought for a while. His inclination would be to avoid the place and not have to think of it again. Yet he felt he owed it to Bradley to see his widow was taken care of. He would pay his respects on the morrow. He set his pipe aside and went into his room where the Stradivarius gleamed in its open case. He picked it up and tuned it. He sat cross-legged on his bed and played. The first few minutes consisted of odd snatches and raw strokes until he settled on Bach's Violin Sonata no. 3 in C major. He played it through before lying back and falling asleep with the Stradivarius at his side.

Holmes arrived at the Bradley residence at one o'clock in the afternoon. He had never been there before but he recognized it from the photographs he had seen in the darkroom at the tobacco shop. He met with Mrs Bradley in the drawing room and expressed his condolences. She was a pleasantly plump woman with silver hair escaping from a bun behind her head. Her eyes were rimmed with red.

"Regarding the favour you asked of me, I am sorry to say that I cannot oblige you," he said.

"I understand, Mr Holmes. I was asking too much," she said.

"I am willing keep the shop open for a while until you find someone else to run the business."

"Thank you. That is very kind. Lincoln Bradley, my husband's nephew, might be interested. He lives in Great Grimsby on the Humber. I will write to him. I am sure that even if he is willing it will take some time to get his affairs in order. Could you stay on for a few months until he can come and you could train him?"

He agreed. Through the late spring and early summer of 1878 Holmes worked full days at the shop, first awaiting Lincoln Bradley's arrival and then training him, broken only by his testimony at the inquest and trial of the man who had murdered Lincoln's uncle

During that time he completed his monograph *Upon the Distinction between the Ashes of the Various Tobaccoes* and found a publisher for it. He dedicated the work to Bradley and shared the proceeds with his widow. At the end of that time he handed the keys of the shop over to Lincoln Bradley with his assurance that he would remain a frequent customer.

Chapter 10

Crime & Crutches

"Now and again cases came in my way, principally
through the introduction of old fellow-students."
Sherlock Holmes, "The Musgrave Ritual"

While preparing Lincoln Bradley to take over the tobacco shop had consumed much of Sherlock Holmes' time for a couple of months, it had not taken all of it and he continued to take steps to be a better detective. He finally admitted to himself that being a detective was not entirely cerebral. In some cases he was likely to find himself in dangerous situations. He needed to be able to defend himself and others. He took the Colt revolver to Henry Stanton Morley's Gun Shop and Shooting Range at 92, Tottenham Court Road. Morley taught him to disassemble it, clean it, and reassemble it. Morley also explained the legal requirements for Holmes to own and carry a gun in London and Holmes took the required actions. Holmes practiced once or twice a week through the spring and summer to improve his skills with the pistol.

He also gave some consideration to other weapons and tactics. He had boxed as a youngster. It had been a good many years since he had been in the ring. He found a boxing gym where he could go rounds with other amateurs and improve his skills. He even participated in some contests for prize money.

The additional work at the tobacco shop combined with the small income from the sales of the tobacco ash monograph had given him a financial cushion which would last for a few months at least. The publisher was encouraging him to write other works, which he was seriously considering. There were a number of topics related to the science of detection which were not adequately covered in the current literature, and the thought of increasing that stream of income was attractive. He still was far from independent of his brother, not that Mycroft complained.

He saw less of Mycroft these days. Sherlock suspected that the Foreign Office was once again monopolizing Mycroft's attention. He did know that Mycroft was out of the country at the same time the newspapers were talking about a large international conference in Berlin.

In addition, the Diogenes Club had opened the first week of April and Mycroft spent much of his spare time there. Sherlock had visited the club as Mycroft's guest. The interior of the club was as sumptuous as any gentlemen's club he had seen, though quiet as a tomb. No gossip, no arguments over art, religion, or politics—and that he supposed was precisely the point. This was a refuge for those who lived within the political sphere from all talk of it, either professional or amateur.

After Sherlock Holmes left the tobacco shop he continued his study of the streets of London and the people who filled them. As he had previously arranged, he stocked a small room at Sherman's menagerie in Lambeth with costumes, false hair, and make-up. Sherman provided him with a key to a backdoor so he could come and go as he pleased. That summer he was still building his character as the old sailor. He was not only practicing his performance, but establishing this old sailor as a familiar sight at the docks and the pubs. He added a thick oaken cudgel to the sailor's outfit, both as a support for the old sailor's weak knees and bent back, but as a weapon should he need it.

He would ride a cab south from Bloomsbury in his own person, cross Vauxhall Bridge, and set down a few streets over from Sherman's. At Sherman's he would transform into the old sailor, cross the bridge on foot, and walk north past Lambeth Bridge, Westminster Bridge and Waterloo Bridge and then eastward toward Southwark Bridge.

He had done this several times and noticed each time a crooked man with grey hair and beard with a pair of spectacles was standing at the Middlesex end of Vauxhall Bridge with a big leather bag in his hand. The third time Holmes saw him he had his driver turn around and drive back over the bridge. This time he saw a growler pick up the man. It was approximately 10 o'clock in the morning. The following morning he had his driver set him down on the Middlesex side of the bridge at a quarter to 10. He watched as the man walked to the same spot with his large bag and was picked up by the same four-wheeler.

There was nothing illegal about a man making an arrangement with a cabby to pick him up at a designated place and time, but there were several things that piqued Holmes' curiosity. One was that he was certain the man was not as old as he was trying to appear. His stance, his walk, and his ability to carry that large bag with ease, all argued that this was a man in the prime of his life. Another was that the man always closed all the windows after he entered the cab despite the warm weather.

Holmes continued on to Sherman's and transformed into the old sailor whom he was certain was more convincing from a distance—or up close—than that man was. Then he walked back over the Vauxhall Bridge to the Middlesex side and waited. His patience was rewarded three hours later when the cab returned; the man stepped down, paid his fare and walked away with his big leather bag. Holmes followed at a distance until the man disappeared into a dead-end alley from which a dozen different little shacks opened. He returned to the bridge but saw no more of the man that day.

That afternoon in his own person, Holmes rode to Paddington station. After dismissing the hansom that brought him north, he found the cabby named Blake he had worked with before and made his own arrangements. The next morning when the man with the grey hair and beard and the large leather bag was picked up by the cabby, Holmes was in a cab behind them and his driver had instructions to follow. The two cabs made a grand tour of Metropolitan London for three hours and returned to the Middlesex side of Vauxhall Bridge. Holmes laughed and told his driver to take him home.

Back in the rooms in Montague Street he lit his pipe.

That man was not going anywhere. What was he doing?

After several hours and a pound of shag (which remained his refuge despite Bradley's efforts to convert him to another type of tobacco), Holmes jumped up and ran out to hail a cab to Scotland Yard. Notwithstanding the reorganization he found Inspector Gregson's office in the same place, but Gregson was out and not returning for a week. While wondering what to do next he saw that new inspector, Lestrade, walking down the hall.

"Inspector Lestrade!"

"Mr Holmes, is it?"

"Yes. I have some information for you."

"If you want to file a police report—"

"Inspector, if you will just give me a few minutes to explain."

Inspector Lestrade lead the young detective to his office.

"Five minutes is all I can spare," Lestrade said.

"Have any men been released from prison in the last few months who are experienced at forging banknotes?" Holmes asked.

Lestrade squinted at him. He rubbed his chin.

"There was John Malone."

"Is he about five feet ten inches with a narrow build?"

"Something like."

"What if I could tell you where to pick him up tomorrow with proof of recent work right in his hand?"

"I would wonder where you came by this information."

"Observation and deduction."

"Observation of what?"

"Each morning a cabby picks up a crooked man with grey hair and a grey beard and a pair of spectacles with a big leather bag and a few hours later he brings him back."

"So he's a salesman making his rounds with his sample bag," Lestrade said.

"They don't go anywhere. The cabby just slowly drives around London for three hours without stopping and then brings the man back."

"Just going for some air."

"With the windows closed in the summer?" Holmes asked.

"That is odd," Lestrade conceded. "But John Malone isn't an old man."

"It's a disguise," Holmes said.

"I see," Lestrade said.

"It would be a feather in your cap."

"Or a waste of my time," the inspector said sceptically.

"It won't take an hour. I am certain he has the whole note printing plant in that bag. You can take that out of circulation as well. I'll tell you when and where to meet them as they are coming back."

"I'll give you your hour," Lestrade said, "but if you are wrong, Mr Holmes, you just might be warming a cell instead."

"I am willing to take that chance," Sherlock Holmes said.

At one o'clock the following afternoon the growler with the window coverings down passed a tall, thin young man as it approached the Middlesex end of Vauxhall Bridge. Beyond him was a ferret-faced man looking very serious. Just before the bridge stood two constables looking attentive. It stopped and a crooked man with grey hair and beard jumped out with a large bag in hand. The constables surrounded him and the serious man approached and took the bag. He looked inside it.

"I arrest you, John Malone," Inspector Lestrade said.

"On what charge?" the man asked.

"On the charge of forging Bank of England notes," answered Lestrade.

"The game is up, Malone!" said Holmes coming up to him.

He reached out and pulled off the grey wig, showing chestnut brown hair underneath.

"I suppose it is," Malone said.

"Cuff him!" Inspector Lestrade told one of the constables.

"Good-bye, cabby," Malone cried, as the two constables led him off between two of them.

"No, you don't," Inspector Lestrade said to the cabby. "You are coming with us to headquarters to make a statement."

Holmes and Lestrade jumped on board. Lestrade sat Malone's bag in his lap.

"This kit alone would be worth many hours. He hid it when he was arrested last time so he could start up again when he got out. He would not reveal the hiding place even with the offer of a shorter sentence."

They sat down with the driver at Scotland Yard. He was a old veteran, with a weather-beaten face and white side whiskers.

"How did you get involved with that man?"

"One morning I was driving across Vauxhall Bridge when he hailed me right there where you arrested him. He said 'Drive anywhere you like,' he said; 'only don't drive fast for I'm getting old, and it shakes me to pieces.' He jumped in, and shut himself up, closing the windows, and I trotted about with him for three hours, before he let me know that he'd had enough. When I stopped, out he hopped with his big bag in his hand."

"'I say cabbie!' he said, after he had paid his fare.

"'Yes, sir,' said I, touching my hat.

"'You seem to be a decent sort of fellow, and you don't go in the break-neck way of some of your kind. I don't mind giving you the same job every day. The doctors recommend gentle exercise of the sort, and you may as well drive me as another. Just pick me up at the same place tomorrow.'"

"I'd find the little man in his place every morning, always with his black bag, and for nigh on to four months never a day passed without his having his three hours' drive."

"Did you swallow the story of the doctors having recommended him on a hot day to go about in a growler with both windows up?"

"Not altogether, sir. However, it's a bad thing in this world to be too knowing, so though I own I felt a bit curious at times, I never put myself out o' the way to find out what the little game was. I couldn't see how it could be anything illegal."

They took the driver's cab number and his address and told him they would call on him if they needed more.

"Alright, Mr Holmes, Malone is reserving his defence. He'll say no more. We've examined the kit and it is what you predicted. Looks like it is all there. I am, however, puzzled about why he took the cab."

"My theory was that he was afraid he would be interrupted at home and someone would notice what he was doing and tell."

"I suppose it will do. Criminals come up with queer ideas, sometimes. Thank you, Mr Holmes, for doing your duty and reporting your observation," Inspector Lestrade said.

Over his second cup of coffee the following morning, Holmes was reading the how the counterfeiter John Malone had been arrested through the brilliant work of Inspector Lestrade, when an extraordinary thing happened: a client knocked on his door. Mrs Denton, who was gathering the breakfast things, opened it.

"I'm Mortimer Maberley," the man at the door said. "Is Mr Sherlock Holmes in? He knows me. We were in college together," he told her.

"Come in, Maberley, and join me in a cup of coffee," Holmes called.

"Thank you, yes," he said sitting down and accepting a cup. "I'm sorry, Holmes, to drop in without warning but I saw your advertisement in the paper. It reminded me of the letter you sent last year and all the remarkable things you did in college. Once the idea struck me to consult you, I had to come at once."

"What do you wish to consult me about?" Holmes asked.

"The short of it is this: my father's clock is killing him!"

"Indeed?"

"At least he thinks it is."

"If I had a possession that I thought was killing me, I would get rid of it. Case closed," Holmes said.

"He won't part with the thing."

"Tell me more about this clock."

"It is one of those longcase clocks. The kind they call 'grandfather clocks.' I believe his father received it as a gift or some such. It is quite handsome to look at but that's all it has been all my life. My father claims it stopped working when he was born. I once offered to bring in a clockmaker to restore it, but he would not have it. He has this idea that if it starts running again, he would die soon after. It was merely a peculiar superstition until a few months ago when the clock suddenly chimed. I ran into the hall where it stood and heard it tic-toc. It has continued to keep time since then and my father has gone into a decline. He has always been a strong active man, but now he is weak in the knees, has hardly any grip strength, and has pain in his joints."

"Is he bedridden?"

"Not yet, but it is becoming more difficult for me to get him up and around. The doctor says staying in bed will do him no good."

"How was his health before?'

"Quite good for his age. He's close on seventy now. He's forgetful sometimes, but that's a normal consequence of getting older, isn't it?"

"Tell me about the household. Have there been any changes to it recently?"

"Well, yes, there have been. My family has an estate in Kent. It brings in some rents, but the house itself is not large. We live quietly and don't do much entertaining. We don't keep a large staff, just a housekeeper and a gardener. We do the rest for ourselves. I've lived on the estate and helped manage it since I got my degree. The house-keeper, Mrs Cooper, has been with us forever and is utterly devoted to my father. However, father fired the gardener because he found he'd been drinking during the day and neglecting his duties. He hired a new gardener. Then there is my older brother Samson, half-brother really."

"From a prior marriage?"

"Yes. He is actually 16 years older. He was ten when his mother died. He and my father only had each other for six years until Father met my mother and married again. Then my mother died in child-birth. I think Samson always resented me and felt I had supplanted him in our father's affections."

"He lives on the estate?"

"He does now."

"Are you saying there was a time when he did not?" Holmes asked.

"Samson and my father had a bit of a row some years back be-fore I went to Cambridge and had been estranged. He reappeared six months ago and did the whole prodigal son thing. My father did not quite kill the fatted calf, but they reconciled."

"You are not quite convinced?"

"Sam has always had an angle. So I expect one in this. He's done nothing to make me suspicious but that just makes me more nervous."

"If your brother was estranged for a number of years, how was he making a living?"

"I know he was involved with an investment in developing alu-minium manufacturing. I don't know the details. I know he was always talking about 'silver from clay.' Sounds like alchemy to me."

"Not at all," Holmes said. "I think there are great possibilities in aluminium. There is a large display of items made from aluminium at the *L'Exposition Universelle de Paris* continuing through to November."

"In any case he was very enthusiastic about it," Mortimer said, "However, I have heard no mention of it since he has been back."

"As the older brother is he due to inherit the estate?"

"That may have been the case at the time they became estranged, but it is not now. Since I have been managing the estate these past few years, my father's will currently leaves the estate to me."

"Does your brother know this?"

"I believe so."

"Does Samson have any prospects under your father's will?"

"Yes. Five hundred pounds from my father's shares and other investments, assuming...."

"Assuming what?"

"Assuming that the money is still there."

"Why shouldn't it be?"

"I have long suspected that Samson has tried to influence my father into investing in some of the projects he was involved with."

"Could that be what your father and brother argued about?"

"I do not know the details. I believe it had something to do with money. I was just a boy at the time. There is also another factor."

"What is that?"

"I am engaged to be married in the autumn. I would like very much to solve this before then."

"I am confident that I will be able to do so. Is it possible that Samson sees your impending marriage as another threat to displace him?"

"Possibly, though I don't know how this could have anything to do with the clock."

"Just a few more questions. The gardener who was fired? What was his name?"

"Tom Nicholson."

"And the new one?

"James Lankley."

"Does the gardener live on the estate?"

"No. The gardener and the housekeeper come for days only.

I've even suggested that we could economize by doing the gardening ourselves."

"Is there some time when I can be alone in the house without the family or the servants? At least an hour. Two would be better."

"Sunday afternoon is the gardener's and the housekeeper's half day and we usually take my father for a ride. Doctor says the air will do him good."

"Could you be certain your brother is along for the ride?"

"He rarely leaves my father's side these days."

"And the gardener must be away."

"I will see to it. Is there anything else you need from me?"

"I need a letter of introduction to your father's doctor. I need him to speak frankly with me."

"Of course. Could you join us for supper? Or would that interfere?"

"I think that would be an excellent idea."

"How shall I introduce you?"

"The truth will serve," Holmes said.

"I'd rather not mention that I'd consulted you."

"Not initially, but there might be an appropriate time. Just introduce me as someone you met at university."

"All right, Holmes. I'll trust you. We usually have supper at 7 o'clock."

Holmes made some enquiries in London before heading to the estate in Kent.

Saturday afternoon he took the train southwest to Folkstone and hired a driver to take him to Hythe. The winds off the channel were cool and damp in contrast to the stifling heat in London and the reek of the Thames. Hythe had once been a prosperous port city until its harbour silted up. In 1400 a fire raced through Hythe destroying over two hundred buildings including two of its churches. There was talk of abandoning the location and rebuilding elsewhere but many of the residents stayed and rebuilt. By 1878 Hythe survived as a small town of stone and red brick buildings overlooking the Channel. A beach walk framed the southern edge of Hythe and a canal from Romney Marsh snaked through the town.

Holmes quickly found the residence and consulting room of Dr Kissell. He rang the bell and was escorted before the doctor. He was a short man with a shiny dome on the top of his head and fringe around the back.

"Please be seated. How may I help you?"

"Dr Kissell, my name is Sherlock Holmes. Mortimer Maberley has consulted with me about his father," Holmes said presenting the letter Mortimer had given him. "I need some information from you."

Dr Kissell read the letter, folded it, and set it on his desk.

"How can I help?"

"Have you examined the elder Mr Maberley recently?" Holmes asked

"I have."

"What is your diagnosis?"

"My diagnosis? He has some vague symptoms: confusion, muscle weakness, pain in the joints. I would say time ails him," the doctor said.

"Time?"

"Time, manifested in growing older, and time, embodied by that damn clock."

"So you do see a connection with the clock?"

"Oh, yes, and that worries me more than anything else. If a man thinks he is going to die he is likely to will himself into his grave."

"Thank you," Holmes said. "That's all the information I need at this time."

He spent the night in Hythe at the Bell Inn, an old brick building with an even older portion in back with cobblestone walls that might have survive that ancient fire. On Sunday he walked out to the Maberley estate. It was a nice country walk of a few miles. The sun was shining, the birds in the trees were singing and a fresh breeze was blowing inland from the Channel.

It was a large, half-timbered house with a roof of red tiles surrounded by ancient cedars. Despite what difficulties they may have had with the gardeners, the hedges were neatly trimmed and the borders alive with blossoms. It seemed a cheery place on a summer's day. A long curving drive led up to the front of house. Holmes bypassed it and watched the Maberleys leave from the distance.

Holmes unlocked the front door with Mortimer's latchkey and walked in. There was no difficulty finding the longcase clock for it drew attention even from the doorway. It had a handsome walnut case and a brass face with black Roman numerals. He could hear its gentle tic-toc as he stood before it. Holmes examined the floor, the exterior of the clock, and the wall behind, to which it was anchored. The housekeeper was not negligent at her task and few indications of tampering remained on the outside. While Holmes made no claims to be a horologist he had done some research at the British Museum on clocks of this type and familiarized himself with their inner workings. He opened the case and looked inside. The first thing that caught his attention was a grey powder on the floor of the case. He removed the pendulum and looked at the inner works above it. One thing immediately stood out: While most of the clockworks were brass one piece was not. It was a shaft ending in a fork that had surrounded the pendulum rod. At the upper end it was attached to the anchor escape mechanism. He gently removed that part, and when he had he noticed grey powder on his hands. He also noticed pitting on the end that had been attached to the brass anchor mechanism and some in the fork. He examined the pendulum rod and found some pits in the brass as well. He wrapped the grey piece in his handkerchief. He scraped some of the powder from the bottom of the case into a small vial. Then he rehung the pendulum straight without imparting any motion to it, and closed the case.

Holmes made his way to the kitchen and found a porcelain teacup. He placed a small amount of water in it and then dropped a tiny amount of the powder in the water. The powder did nothing but sink to the bottom. It did not dissolve. He stirred it slightly. No change. He rinsed off the saucer and spoon, dried them, and put them back where he had found them.

He searched each of the bedrooms and the gardener's shed. In Samson's bedroom he found a small bottle of powder. It seemed to match the powder found in the clock.

He returned to the village and spoke to the doctor again.

"Dr Kissell, I am sorry to disturb you on your Sunday. I have just a few more questions. Based on your examination of Mr Maberley do you think he could be anaemic?"

"That is possible, though he eats a good diet from what I have seen."

"However, sometimes something else can interfere with the blood?"

"Certainly."

"In such a case would you recommend a change of scenery perhaps?"

"Certainly. Remove him from the cause and build up his constitution."

"Perhaps a visit to Tunbridge Wells where he could take the waters at the Chalybeate Spring?" Holmes suggested.

"If he was truly anaemic that would be an excellent choice."

"Then I suggest you prescribe that to Mr Maberley. I'll put a bug in Mortimer's ear and perhaps we can find some more time for his father. Good day, Dr Kissell."

Holmes walked to the village green and found a spot under a tree and lit his pipe. He had no doubts about the facts. He needed to think how best to handle the persons involved.

He presented himself at the Maberley house shortly before 7 o'clock. He was greeted by Mortimer and was introduced to his father and his brother Samson as a fellow undergraduate at Cambridge. Over supper Mortimer asked if he still fenced and Holmes responded that he had not done so in a few years, though he had recently taken up boxing again. It seemed the elder Maberley had also boxed in his youth. The conversation wandered in a number of directions including techniques, the Marquess de Queensberry rules, and famous boxers. Holmes observed Mortimer's father and brother during supper. Samson seemed agitated though mostly silent. The father seemed somewhat weak but hardly on his deathbed.

"Well, Mr Holmes," Mr Maberley said rising from the table, "I am glad to make your acquaintance. I seldom have an opportunity to meet Mortimer's friends from Cambridge. Now if you will excuse me I think I am going to rest a bit."

Samson offered his arm. Holmes saw the elder Maberley reach

out and pat the silent clock in the hall as he walked past it. Samson frowned. Mortimer drew Holmes into the study.

"Your father does not seem to be at death's door," Holmes said.

"He perked up considerably when we returned and found the clock had stopped again. Was that your work?"

"Yes, I removed this from its inner workings," Holmes said pulling the grey object wrapped in his handkerchief from his pocket and showing it to him.

It was several inches long with a bend and a fork at one end.

"What is it?" Mortimer asked.

"It is called a crutch. It transfers motion from the pendulum to the anchor mechanism which is what creates the tic-toc sound and moves the hands of the clock. There are several remarkable things about this crutch. What do you think it is made of?"

Holmes handed the handkerchief and crutch to him.

"Is it pewter?" Mortimer asked hefting it in his hand. "No, it is too light to be pewter. Yet it is duller than silver."

"It is actually aluminium. That means several things," Holmes said pausing to light his pipe. "The first is that it was obviously not part of the original works. The original crutch may have bent or broken causing the clock to stop. I saw no other reason for it having stopped and no other part had been recently replaced. Aluminium parts such as this are fairly rare and hard to find unless someone happened to work in the aluminium industry and had it specially made or made it himself."

"Ah," Mortimer said.

"Note the corrosion at the top and in the fork. It tells another story. It demonstrates that the person who placed it either was not familiar with chemistry, or was very familiar with it and only needed the clock to work for a short time. You see, the workings of that clock, like many clocks, are brass. If you place aluminium and brass in contact in damp sea air as you have here in Hythe, a weak electrical charge is created as aluminium cations move towards the brass. That causes the corrosion. You can see that it is worse at the spots where the aluminium came into contact with the brass. In a few more months it would have corroded through and fallen and the clock would have stopped again."

"Someone did this intentionally?"

"Yes. The intent was to take advantage of your father's superstition. I believe other actions were taken as well. However, it is difficult to determine how effective they were."

Just then the door open and Samson entered.

"Who is this man really?" he demanded.

"I told you we met in college," Mortimer responded.

Samson's eye fell upon the aluminium crutch in Mortimer's hand.

"What is that? Where did you get it?" he asked.

"You know perfectly well what it is," Holmes said. "It is the aluminium crutch you placed in the clock to make it run again. You are correct, however, that your brother did not tell you everything about me. We did meet at university. However, I am now a detective. I made some enquiries about you. You did invest in an aluminium fabrication business but it is failing and you are heavily in debt. But rather than ask your father for assistance, you decided to drive him to his grave and collect your share of the inheritance. You remembered your father's superstition. You had a bit of engineering knowledge and skill and thought you could fix the clock. You opened it, found the broken clutch and removed it to use as a model for a new one you fashioned from a scrap of aluminium.

"You weren't content with that. I also found this," Holmes said drawing a small bottle of grey powder from his pocket. "A preliminary analysis suggests it is aluminium oxide that you have been feeding to your father. I will have to do further analysis to confirm it."

"It is all a lie and you can't prove any of it," Samson cried and stormed out.

"Is all that true?" Mortimer asked Sherlock Holmes.

"Yes, and he proved it so by his reaction. Yet what court would convict him? For what? Repairing a clock with poorly chosen piece of metal? Feeding your father mineral supplements that have not been proven to be harmful? Even if we could prove he did it, proving he intended harm, or caused any harm would be very difficult. The symptoms could be a result of ingesting the aluminium compound, or they could be a physical manifestation of his superstition."

"What effect would the aluminium compound have?"

"That is difficult to say. There has been no medical research on that question. However, based purely on biochemistry it is possible that it was causing anaemia which would account for his weakness, soreness of joints, and other symptoms. I suggested to the doctor that your father spend some time at Chalybeate Spring at Tunbridge Wells and he seemed to think it was a good idea. The iron rich waters, the walks along the Pantiles, perhaps even a friendly game of bowls, in addition to the termination of the tic-toc of the clock maybe precisely what your father needs."

"Sounds like a fine idea."

"However, allowing Samson to believe you could prove a case against him might keep him at bay. I will put these in a safe place," Holmes said taking back the crutch and placing it and the bottle of powder in his pocket, "in case you might need them in the future."

Just then Mortimer's father entered the room.

"Where is Samson off to?"

"I don't know," Mortimer said honestly. "But let's have some brandy and cigars and talk a bit more before Holmes must leave us."

"Surely, your friend could stay the night and return to London in the morning?"

"What of it, Holmes? Will you?"

Holmes assented.

Chapter 11

The Blackheath Burglar

"Burglary! This is more interesting. Let me hear the details."
Sherlock Holmes, "The Adventure of the Six Napoleons"

In August 1878, driven once again by the lack of cases and the need to keep himself busy, Sherlock Holmes decided to introduce the sailor to the foreshore and meet more of the people on the Surrey shore. He began at Sherman's in Lambeth and wandered north as the old sailor with the weak legs and cough. It was low tide as he cautiously descended the water stairs west of Westminster Bridge to the foreshore. He found beneath his feet silt, sand, and stones of all sizes. Around, about, and in-between were all mixture of flotsam and jetsam.

He moved slowly in character, picking his way carefully along, breathing heavily. Sometimes he stopped and looked up at the warehouses extending over the foreshore on sticks which would be underwater at high tide. Green slime lined the yellow brick where the river rose. He passed one empty spot where a warehouse had burned a few years back and never been rebuilt. He had been there at the time and jumped from the burning warehouse into the Thames at high tide. The window through which he had made his exit and the wall surrounding it had collapsed into the river. It all seemed a very long time ago.

Continuing along eastward he passed Waterloo Bridge. St Paul's Cathedral loomed in the distance across the river. He saw barges and ferries on the river. Lightermen were directing their small craft close to shore. In Bermondsey, he paused to watch an old woman. Her hair was bound in a scarf. She had over-sized boots on her feet and her skirts were tied up to her knees. She was bent double poking in the mud along the shoreline. Sometimes she would pull something out and place it in a bag next to her. The bag was swollen with her treasures and caked with drying silt.

The old sailor with the craggy face and white tuffs of hair was leaning on his oaken cudgel and making no effort to conceal himself.

In time she noticed him.

"Whatcha lookin' at?" she said with a scowl at him as she slowly unbent herself as much as age and habitual assumption of the stooped position now allowed.

"Nowt," he said.

She began to make her way up the shore toward him.

"Nothin' better t' do than stare?"

"Waitin'"

"For a mark? Or a lay? No sense beggin' from me. Ah make an honest livin', but have none t' spare. An' never sold m' body an' ne'er will. Would sooner jump off one o' them bridges."

"For a ship to sign on," he wheezed.

"Like that is it?" she said as she passed him moving to the east. "Don't look loike much t' sign."

He turned and followed her.

"What do ya do wi' them things?" he asked.

"Ah sells 'em. Unless its coins, then Ah spend them. Ah do find coins now an' then. Not today, mind you. No silver on me. Not a tuppence. Mostly find old clay pipes, buttons, scraps o' metal, little trinkets. Sometimes fancy stuff. Some's been down there long time. Some fell yesterday. Found a dead man once. Just left 'im there. Wasn't goin' t' matter t' him if 'e lay a bit. Ah didn't 'ave time to waste wi' peelers."

"'Twas a jumper?"

"Loikely. Dinna stop to ask. Just moved down the foreshore an' went aboot my business. Constables came later an' took 'im away."

She moved again. From her looks at him and efforts to put more distance between them, he could see his presence was giving her nerves. So he walked on, slowly. The sun was high now and the heat of the day brought out the reek of rotting wood, drying algae, and sewage in the river. A breeze from the east brought a hint of fresh sawn lumber, new ropes, and sweat. A turn of the wind brought more savoury smell of stew and ale. Ahead was The Angel, a pub against the wall marking the boundary between Bermondsey and Rotherhithe. The Rotherhithe stairs led up to the entrance. He climbed them as the old sailor would and found a seat among the tables. He was brought crusty bread and stew and ale. He exchanged a few words with the landlord of the place.

"Light custom today?"

"Usual for this early. The lumpers come in after work an' fill up the place, especially on pay day!"

"So once a week?"

"Naw, three times. They are paid Tuesday, Thursday, and Saturday and the place is rollin' then!"

"Perraps, ah'll come around sometime. If I'm still here."

"Ain't seen you around before."

"Spend most o' m' time at sea. Lookin' for a new berth."

"Ah. There might be some ships in the docks looking for hands. Best o' luck to you."

He stayed for a while studying the patrons, their speech, and their habits. Then he headed out again and made his way down the King's Stairs east of The Angel and walked along the foreshore again. The tide was coming in. The lapping waters left less of the foreshore visible. He soon found the source of the smell of lumber and much of The Angel's patronage: Timber yards, cooperages, shipyards. He passed more warehouses storing paper and canned goods, and granaries. St Katharine Docks, Wapping, and the London Docks lay across the river and the traffic on the river was increasing.

A bit further on he climbed some stairs again. Above he was passed by deal porters carrying huge baulks of deal timber across their shoulders. There were many ships here about the wharfs and pools. Goods were being loaded and unloaded. He wandered about the Surrey Commercial Docks enquiring about a position. He had to seem enough in earnest to establish the character without actually taking another man's berth. Someone hearing the cough of the old man suggested St Mary's Workhouse.

"It's not far, just off Deptford Lower Road. They have a new infirmary—St Olav's infirmary. Could 'elp with that cough."

"Ain't goin' near no workhouse, ever again," the old sailor said, waving away the suggestion and leaving. He went on to another place to enquire.

As the sun descended lower in the sky he turned southward toward Downtown Rotherhithe, so named merely because it was the part of town south of the docks as opposed to the Village of Rotherhithe to the northwest. Twilight lingered in the late summer, but there were some streets of Downtown Rotherhithe the twilight did not reach and no street lamps lit the way. He continued on until it was full dark. He was contemplating turning back when he met another white-haired old man struggling with a handcart. The cart was piled high with rags. One wheel had fallen into a pothole.

"Ahoy! Can ya use a hand?" he said as he hobbled up leaning harder on his stick.

The old man stopped his efforts and looked up.

Holmes' old sailor coughed to maintain his character.

"Seen better days myself, but between us..." he wheezed.

"Be obliged," the ragman gasped.

Holmes could have easily lifted the wheel out of the hole and pushed it on, but the old sailor would not. Instead he found a flat scrap of wood that he wedged under the wheel. The two of them pushing and pulling used it as a ramp and rolled the cart up and out.

"Thank you," the man said. "The name's Ned."

"Basil."

Ned pressed a hand to his heaving chest as if to still the pounding of his heart.

"Where ya off to?" Holmes asked.

"Going home t' my tea and then t' sort."

"Sort?"

"The rags," he said pointing to the pile on the cart. The man was still breathing heavily and each breath came with a wheeze. "A good load today. But I have t' sort 'em an' dry them t'night before I take them t' the dealer tomorrow."

"Do they pay well?"

"Depends on the size and colour. They pays 2-3 quid a pound of clean white cotton or linen. Colours are less. Wool is less."

"Why so much for white?"

"They make it into paper, fine white paper for the lawyers in the City. The colours are made into wrapping paper and cardboard. Wool is felted for cheap clothes they sell to the likes of us. And bones. Haven't the foggiest what they do with them. Don't get many of them."

Ned stopped to cough into a kerchief that was not white linen, then took up the handles of the cart again.

"Don't know how much longer I can do this. I take the load to the dealer each morning then head out to collect more. I collect some on the streets of Rotherhithe, but the best white linens are found in Blackheath and Greenwich among the fine houses. Some of house-keepers will set out a bundle to be collected but other places I have to rummage through the bins. The gents and ladies really don't like to see you on their streets so most of the collecting has to be done after dark. The hours are long. I don't have the strength I used to."

He began pushing the cart still breathing heavily.

"Could you use some help?" the old sailor asked. "I've few days before my next ship comes in. Wouldn't mind making a few pennies."

"Would make sortin' faster tonight. Perhaps I can get some rest and feel stronger tomorrow."

The ragman led Holmes to the tiny shack he called home. There was a worn mattress on the floor, a candle, and a spirit lamp for boiling the water for tea and space to sort the rags. He offered Holmes a crust of bread and then showed him how to sort the rags. They made quick work of it between them. Holmes parted with a promise to be back the next morning to go with him to the dealer.

In the morning Ned seemed weaker yet and Holmes pushed the cart to the dealer's at his direction. The dealer made a quick assess-ment and handed over some coins. There was no dickering. Then they were in the streets again. Holmes accepted a tuppence for his share but spent it on some rolls for their mid-day.

"Rags and bones!" Ned cried hoarsely as he pushed the cart, followed by a fit of coughing. "Rags and bones!"

Children followed them through the streets, but few people of-fered rags. Through Rotherhithe the work was nasty, digging rags from drains and bins. Ned directed him to the likely spots and leaned against the cart gasping as Holmes collected them.

As the sun set they headed into Blackheath. As Ned had said, some bundles had been left out for collection. That was the easiest work and probably the most lucrative for there were worn but clean white cotton and linen shirts in those bundles. Ned also showed him where the bins were. Some yielded nothing for them.

Around them fine ladies and gentlemen passed in their carriages going to the opera or charity balls, or a simple dinner with friends. They paid little heed to the wheezy old man or the decrepit sailor with him. Once or twice a servant shooed them away when they were looking in the bins, thinking they were beggars.

"Imagine confusing us with beggars?" Ned said. "We put in an honest day's work!"

"Good thing you are not a burglar, you must know all these houses," Holmes said.

"It is," Ned agreed, "If I were a younger man, I might be tempted."

"Have you seen anything of the Blackheath Burglar the newspapers have been talking about?" Holmes asked.

"Don't know anything about it. I don't have time to read newspapers. Sometimes I see some coppers at a house, but I steer clear and go about my business."

By the time they turned about towards Ned's shack, his wheezing was worse and he was dragging his feet. The following morning he could hardly walk. Holmes insisted on taking him to the infirmary and with some effort he found a cab who would take them.

A nurse spoke of consumption.

"There is a great deal of it about."

"Here," said Ned, brandishing the latchkey to the shed. "You lock it up, then take the load to the dealer."

Holmes promised he would.

After leaving Ned at Olav's infirmary, Holmes returned to Ned's shed and took the load of rags to the dealer as he had promised. The trip to the infirmary and back had eaten into the day. He locked the cart in the shed and returned to Montague Street.

In his own person back in his sitting room, Holmes thumbed through the newspaper clippings. He made a list of the burglaries over the past two years. As the newspapers contended, it was Blackheath where the majority of the burglaries were occurring most recently. But that was a change. He unfolded a large map of London on the table and marked where the burglaries had taken had taken place since January 1877. Obviously there were some in other places, but the clusters were intriguing. It was improbable that there would be successive waves of burglaries in different parts of London by sheer coincidence. If they were the work of different gangs or individual burglars, the dispersal would be more random, at least among the more affluent neighbourhoods.

He was staring at the map when Mrs Denton brought supper and he had to whisk it away and fold it. He ate without paying much attention to what he ate.

The following morning he dressed as the old sailor again and made his way directly to the infirmary. There he was told Ned had died in the night.

"Consumption, was it?" he asked.

"Oh, no, it was his heart."

They gave him a note addressed to Basil that one of the nurses had written at Ned's direction.

"Keep the shed and the cart," it read and was signed with an X witnessed by the nurse who wrote it. It was, perhaps, the simplest will a man had written.

He left the infirmary and walked to the shed. He had hardly known Ned, and Ned certainly had not known who Holmes really was. But Holmes knew immediately that this would become another of his hideouts. The door to it was down a short, dark passage. It would be easy to enter and leave without be noticed, especially at night. The Rotherhithe he had seen was full of hard working Irish immigrants and descendants of the same. Poverty loomed in some alleyways among the old and infirm. Downtown was itself a den of crime, but the shed was conveniently located not far from more affluent neighbour-hoods.

But there was more to think about. He would need to stock it with costumes and other useful items. He opened his notebook and made a list of things he needed to bring to the shed. He thought about Ned and decided that perhaps a middle aged rag-picker would be a good character to develop for this area, someone who took over Ned's route. Of course, he would not be able to do it all the time and others would encroach on Ned's former route. That was the nature of the business. In the late afternoon he put the notebook away, locked the shed, and headed southeast.

He had not yet introduced the sailor to Greenwich and now was as good a time as any. He might need both of the characters in this investigation. He spent some time over a pint in a pub in King Street and headed out again with the loose kneed stagger of the drunken sailor. He ducked into a shadow as a constable appeared around a corner. He had no desire to add a night in a cell for the development of the sailor character. The constable passed. Holmes had begun making his way down the street when a sound from behind caught his attention. He turned in the direction the constable had gone with a bit more haste than he usually moved in that disguise. He heard voices in Stillwell Street. He melted into the shadows as he turned into it and crept near a pair of men surrounding the constable. The constable had his whistle to his lips, but one of the men had an arm around the constable's chest and a gun to his head. Next to them a jeweller's shop window was smashed in. One fellow was holding a bag and loading things into it through the window.

"One sound from ye an' they'll be wiping ya brains off t' street," the man with the gun said.

Moving swiftly from shadow to shadow Holmes was on them before they noticed, twisting the muzzle of the gun around.

"Well, matey, looks like ye axiden'lly got tha gun pointed at your own 'ead," the sailor said. "I suggest y' drop it an' let go o' the constable 'fore it goes off by axident."

The man at the window took off down the street as the constable was released and blew the whistle. Holmes held the other man in an iron grip.

"Here, clap the derbies o' him and take custody o' him before ye fellows show up," he said as he turned his prisoner around. "No word o' me in this."

The constable did as he suggested. A second constable arrived. Others appeared shortly with the other thief in tow. When the first constable turned around the old sailor was gone.

"What's this, Robinson?" his fellow asked.

"Caught 'em robbing the store, Geordie. What does it look

like?"

"Alright. You take them in and I'll watch the window."

Holmes followed the constables in the shadows, more for the sport of it than anything else. As they hauled the miscreants up the stairs of the station at Blackheath Road he spied a pub called the White Swan two doors down and had an idea.

He backed into an alley nearby, stretched to his full height, pulled the scarf from his neck and used it to wipe the make-up from his face. He removed the side whiskers and tucked them and the cap in a pocket. Transformed, he entered the White Swan as himself and nursed the landlord's ordinary in a corner. Not thirty minutes had gone by when he saw the constable enter out of uniform, down one quickly, and request a second.

The constable was on alert since the robber had the drop on him. He looked up quickly at the young man who took the stool next to him and signalled the barkeep to bring him another.

"If you don't mind me saying so, Constable Robinson, you look a bit shaken," the young man said.

"How'd you know my name and that I'm a constable?" he asked suspiciously.

"Oh, this close to the station house half the gents in here are police out of uniform," the man said. "Besides, I've seen you on the streets and heard one of your fellows call you by name."

Robinson grunted. It sounded reasonable enough.

"I'm sorry. I'm a bit jumpy. Had some fellow get the drop on me this evening and nearly blow my brains out," Constable Robinson said.

He looked down at his pint.

"If it hadn't been for some sailor coming by—and I didn't even get a chance to thank him," Robinson said.

"'Twas nothin', matey," came the sailor's voice from beside him.

Startled, the constable looked up and then right and left. There was only the young man and no sign of the sailor.

"It was you?" Robinson whispered in disbelief.

"Aye?" the young man said in the sailor's voice.

Robinson grabbed the young man's sleeve and pulled him over

to a quiet table in the corner.

"Who are you?" Robinson said. "I'd like to know the name of the man I have to thank."

"My name is Sherlock Holmes. I am happy to have been of assistance, Constable Robinson."

"I'm not sure I could have done what you done in cold blood. I'd have been terrified the gun would go off in the middle of things. Then you just run off like that leaving me to take the credit. You could have had your name splashed all over the papers," Robinson said.

"At the discredit of yours and the loss of one of my most useful disguises," Holmes said.

"The way you left, it certainly did me good. I appreciate it," Robinson said.

Then he squinted at Sherlock Holmes.

"Now about that disguise. What was that about?"

"Research," Holmes said. "I walk the streets in a variety of different disguises observing people."

"What for?" Robinson asked again.

"It is my business to know about people, especially the criminal classes," Holmes said.

"What kind of business is that?"

"I am a consulting detective. People bring me problems and I solve them," Holmes said.

"Then I don't see why you wouldn't want to show up the police and have your name in the papers," Robinson said.

"It doesn't benefit me to discredit the police," Holmes said. "I need to work with them sometimes."

"How so?"

"If during an investigation I encounter an actual crime, it is useful to know who I can trust to report it to."

"I see. The detective scandal didn't help. Most of us on the street are on the up and up. Just a few of them at Scotland Yard were on the take."

"Good to know."

They chatted a bit more and parted. It had been a sudden inspiration to reveal himself to this constable. It could be useful in his current project.

He returned to Montague Street where his crime records still lay scattered about the sitting room. He looked at them again. He had noted the waves of burglaries, as had the police, but he had been unable conjure up a paying client for whom to apply his special knowledge and skills. So now, for neither the first, nor the last time, he was going to use them to assist the police in catching a criminal.

He spread out the map again. As he had noted before, the pattern of the burglaries was not random, nor was it linear. If there is a pattern, it was not a simple one.

Was it based on opportunity? Was there an inside confederate who was shifting from house to house? Was there an outside informant?

Such thoughts raced through his mind as he lay down upon his bed. Sleep came eventually.

The next day he purchased another jacket that had seen much use, a floppy hat, felted wool trousers, and some old boots. He also purchased additional hair pieces and make-up. He bundled these up and took them to the shed that evening. Then he made his way to the White Swan, sat at the bar, and ordered a pint.

Constable Robinson entered after his shift and greeted him straight away.

"So what does a consulting detective do? Is it like a private inquiry agent following husbands around to see if they are unfaithful to their wives?"

"No, I don't do that sort of thing. I recently found a young woman who was missing."

"How did you do that?"

"I looked around her home, spoke to her mother and a friend of hers, and smoked a lot of tobacco."

Robinson laughed.

"Then you walked right up to where she was."

"Precisely."

"No."

"Yes, indeed."

"How?"

"I sorted through all the facts I had and arrived at a logical solution."

"Catch any murderers that way?"

"Yes, one was hanged last year."

"So how come I've never heard of you?"

"Most of my work for clients is confidential. When I have worked with the police I have not taken credit."

"Like last night."

"Yes. These Blackheath burglaries. That's your division, isn't it?"

"Yes. He is causing us no end of trouble."

"He? Do you think it is a single man?"

"It could be, though many think one man couldn't do this."

"How so?"

Robinson pulled him over to a table in the corner.

"I really shouldn't be telling you this. But this isn't an ordinary burglar. He seems to know the house plan and the inhabitants like his own family. He knows when they go to bed and when they rise in the morning—their entire schedule. He knows who sleeps in each bedroom and he screws the doors shut before he begins his work."

"Could it be a gang of servants?"

"That was investigated. There were no servants in common. None fired by one and then hired by another. No servants who had any connections by family or friends."

"What of tradesmen?"

Constable Robinson shook his head.

"Eliminated."

"Then it must be a guest or a friend of the family"

"You believe a person of their own station, who may have dined at their table, would rob them?"

"I follow where the facts lead."

"You tell me if you find him."

"I will."

"That would show the Yard, if the constables on the beat find him after all their investigations."

The interview with Robinson had helped eliminate several possibilities but there was still much he did not know. He decided the new ragman would begin making rounds the following evening.

His surveillance of Kurr and the Scotland Yard detectives had had a much narrower focus, even if it had required him to travel many miles following them. In this case he had a wide area to cover and no idea who he was looking for.

In the Rotherhithe shed the following afternoon, he began the development of the ragman character. He was not as old as the sailor, but he had had a hard life. He was burnt by the sun and the wind during his rounds. Holmes darkened his skin and added some lines. He decided to forgo any whiskers or hair pieces. He ruffled up his own hair and pulled the floppy hat down over it so it rested at eye level. The jacket was large for him, the trousers baggy and the boots much scraped.

He started out with Ned's handcart, but he skipped the rounds of Rotherhithe and headed directly to the more affluent neighbourhoods of Lewiston, Blackheath, and Greenwich. He followed Ned's route when it overlapped with his plans, picking up bundles Ned had shown him and delving into likely dust bins. He was less thorough than Ned because he was less concerned with the resulting remuneration of the night's work than with observing the neighbourhoods he passed through.

It soon became clear to Holmes that the houses that had been skipped over by the burglars were not those of people who never went out of an evening, but those who did not entertain in their home. This reinforced his theory that the burglar, or one of them, if it was a gang, was a house guest at the burgled houses. Perhaps it was a minor celebrity like an artist, author, sportsman, or musician. If he had a client, or had been working with the police, he could have interviewed the owners of the burgled houses and ask them who they had recently entertained. He had no such advantage.

Instead he decided to mark their carriages with clay so he could see which carriages might reappear. As he passed them with his cart he smeared a bit of damp Claygate clay on the backs of each carriage in a small circle. It was darker than the London clay they might encounter in this area which both made it less noticeable and unmistakable to him. If they did see it then it would likely pass as something thrown up on a drive to those who had less knowledge of the clays of England. He realized he ran the risk of discerning instead whose servants were more or less diligent at cleaning their carriages, but it was a necessary risk.

Some carriages belonging to people who lived in the local area appeared multiple times during his study. This did not mean they were the portico thief, but rather that they were popular dinner guests. He gave them a second mark. Not long into his study he noticed that so many of the carriages had multiple marks that he began to doubt the marks were of any use at all. But it was that very night that he saw it.

After all the carriages had gone on their way and he had moved on to retrieve some bundles of rags down the street, he saw a carriage approaching without its lanterns lit. It was moving slowing and quietly down the street. He pushed the cart behind a hedge and ducked down beside it. The carriage passed him and stopped further down the road, though still at a distance from the house that had been entertaining. He watched as a figure descended from the carriage and move away from it. The figure was short and stooped, whether by nature or stealth. He walked in a crab-like manner. As the figure approached the house, Holmes crept up to the carriage and confirmed his marks. He withdrew.

The figure circled the house and disappeared near a balcony. Holmes was considering whether he should alert the household when the figure reappeared and returned to the carriage and moved on as silently as before. He was not carrying anything.

Holmes abandoned the handcart and tried to follow the carriage in the dark on foot. This was made easier because the carriage drove slowly and silently to another house not far off. Again the man— for it seemed to be a man—descended from the carriage, circled the house, and disappeared inside only to reappear a few minutes later. This explained one aspect of the pattern. He was scouting multiple houses at once, testing his ability to enter and exit quickly without being seen.

Holmes was now certain this was the man the newspapers were calling the Blackheath Burglar. When the carriage stopped at a third house, Holmes approached the carriage stealthily and applied a different mark to the back of the carriage. This was a thin crescent. Twice more the carriage stopped and the figure repeated the ritual. Holmes managed to keep up with it. But after the fifth, the driver drove with a bit more determination, though just as silently as before. He was still trending in a westerly direction. Despite his efforts, Holmes lost it. He made a few attempts to pick up the trail again. Eventually he gave up and returned to the handcart and moved on rag-picking, eventually arriving at to Ned's shed.

Holmes had not been as diligent as Ned at sorting and selling the rags collected during his surveillance. So he had accumulated a substantial amount in the shack. He sat himself down and sorted them as much to think as to discourage a rat infestation.

His work that night had substantially narrowed the field of sus-pects. The crab-walking man had visited five houses since he started following him. One of those five was likely to be his next target.

Was there another determining factor such as weather or phase of the moon? How did he choose which of his targets to rob first?

In his mind he ran through many possibilities as he separated white rags from coloured rags. It was well past dawn when he finished his mental and physical sorting and had the rags piled on the cart once more. He took them to the dealer, accepted the silver offered and re-turned the cart to the shed. Then he walked north towards the river in search of a cab. Back in the sitting room at Montague Street he rifled through almanacs and newspaper clippings and added data to his list.

Holmes returned to rag-picking that night and the next, stay-ing closer to the five houses. Nothing happened. He had begun to doubt his conclusions. Then on the third night one of the five houses was holding a dinner party. Carriages began to arrive. Many of them still held the small clay circles. Only one also had a crescent. He found a shadow to hide in near that carriage and waited.

It was a cool night, but it must have been warm inside the house for the windows were open. Holmes heard the hum of conversation and laughter. Then violin music wafted towards him. Applause fol-lowed. Once more the violin sang and the hairs stood up on the back of his neck. The music was faint from where he sat but it was unmistak-able. It was Paganini's "13th Caprice," called the "Devil's Laughter." He remembered when he had last heard it. He remembered who had played it.

Was it possible?

He thought of the physique of the man and the fine house and the cases of expensive violins. There was more applause from the house.

Holmes considered moving closer to the house to get a look at the player but he feared being discovered and tipping his hand. There would not be a second chance. He stayed, waiting for his quarry.

In time the guests began to file out. He watched as the curious man approached so close he could have reached out and touched him. Holmes watched as the man helped his wife into the carriage—the very woman he had introduced to him nine months before. The blood pounded in Holmes' ears, but he was as silent and immovable as a stone. John Thompson took the reins and pointed the horse's head home.

Holmes did not move. He had no need to follow him. He knew where the carriage was going. When the guests had all left and he was no longer at risk of exposure, he took off quickly towards Peckham. When he arrived at 5, East Terrace, Evelina Street he found the carriage with the markings sitting in front of the house. It had not yet been put away. He knew that the driver planned to do his rounds. Holmes returned to Blackheath and watched the man who had helped him restore his Stradivarius make his rounds of the five houses. After Thompson left for home, Holmes retrieved the rag cart and returned to Rotherhithe picking up a few rags on the way. He stowed the cart and removed his costume and makeup. Then he set out for the White Swan. Constable Robinson was there before him.

"Holmes! Haven't seen you for a while."

Holmes signalled for him to join him at a corner table.

"Pleasant weather," Holmes said.

"Not from where I've been. Cloudy and bit chilly walkin' the rounds," Robinson responded.

"The newspapers say it will be clear tomorrow night."

"And rain on Thursday. Surely you did not come to discuss the weather?"

"Do you still want to catch the Blackheath Burglar?" Holmes asked.

"Point me to him!"

"He will rob one of five houses in Blackheath tomorrow night."

"How do you know that?"

"It would take too long to explain," Holmes said. "Tomorrow night by 11 o'clock be near the corner of Shooters Hill Road and Van Brugh Terrace.

"I'll bring my sergeant and another constable."

"All well and good, but don't be too obvious about it. They need to be out of sight."

"Okay."

"There will be a ragman with a cart—"

"I can warn him off."

"Don't. He will tell you which house it is and when the man is inside."

"Is he a confederate of yours?"

Holmes smiled

"Oh, I see how it is," Robinson said.

The next night the ragman pushed his cart down the street. He stopped at the corner.

A pair of constables approached.

"Two streets over, 2, St Johns Park. He's inside," the ragman whispered to them.

Then the rag-picker continued on past them.

The two constables turned and walked towards the house he had indicated. When they arrived at it they noticed a faint light where it shouldn't be a light at this hour.

"Evans, you fetch Sergeant Girling," Robinson whispered to the other. "I'll wait here."

When the sergeant arrived, the three policemen conferred.

"No sign of him yet," Robinson said.

"How sure are you of your informant?" the rotund sergeant asked.

"Very," Robinson said.

Sergeant Girling was more sceptical. The night was also cold and damp and it was after midnight.

"Do we know whether the owner is home?" he asked.

"No," the two constables said.

"Well, I'm going to ring the bell," the sergeant said and headed towards the front of the house.

As they heard the faint ring of the bell in the quiet of the night, Robinson saw a man come out of the dining room window and start limping down the path.

"Just a moment!" shouted Constable Robinson as he took off after him.

The man turned and shouted, "Keep back, or I'll shoot you!"

When the unarmed constable continued to follow, the thief fired three shots. Each passed close to Robinson's head. Still Robinson stayed after him. He was certain Holmes was correct now and he was intent on catching this man. Another shot rang out clipping Robinson along the side of his head. Robinson fell, stunned. He was afraid the burglar would escape, but the man tripped in the dark and Robinson leaped on him before he could rise.

"I'll settle with you this time!" his captive cried out and fired at him at close range as they struggled. The bullet went through Robinson's arm just above the elbow and he lost his grip. But then the ragman appeared and struck the thief a heavy blow full in the face. Robinson wrestled the gun out of the man's hand and hit him on the head with it.

"Thank you," Constable Robinson said to the ragman as he sat down upon his prisoner and blew his whistle.

The ragman melted into the night as Sergeant Girling and Constable Evans caught up to Robinson. The three policemen handcuffed the thief and searched him. Besides the gun, they found a leather case, a crowbar, a gimlet, a centre-bit, a hand-vice, two chisels, and a pocket-knife. They searched the garden and found a bag of booty that the thief had dropped in his flight. They hauled their prisoner off to the station house.

When they saw their prisoner in the light at the station house he wasn't a very assuming fellow. He was short and thin with grey hair and bent over like an ape. His left hand was twisted and his left leg gimpy.

Early the next morning Robinson rang the bell at Montague Street. His arm was in a sling and there was a bandage on his head but he wore his bandages proudly as he was shown into the sitting room.

Sherlock Holmes was in his dressing gown devouring his breakfast. The night's activities had given him a rare appetite. He invited Robinson to join him.

"No, no, couldn't touch a thing," he said. "I'm too excited about all this. The sun's hardly up and it's all over the papers! They are calling me a hero!" he said tossing a stack of them on the table.

"Constable Nabs Blackheath Burglar!" the top one read.

"Excellent," Holmes said between bites.

"I've come to thank you. Not only did you help me to this fellow, but last night you saved my life again. There was one last bullet in his gun when we took it from him. If you hadn't helped me subdue him, that might have been the bullet that did me."

Holmes waved it off.

"What can I do to repay you?" Robinson asked.

"You can get me in to see the prisoner," Holmes said.

"I can probably do that. You know, he had no identification on him and won't give his name."

"He won't?" Holmes said looking startled.

"No, so they put him down as John Ward," Robinson mused.

But Holmes was agitated.

"The police haven't searched the house in Peckham?" Holmes asked.

"What house in Peckham?"

Holmes tossed off his dressing gown and grabbing his hat and coat.

"Come quick, we must go to the station house. I'll identify him. His name is John Thompson. I've been to his house. Here's his card," he said snapping it up.

Sherlock Holmes went to the Division R station house with Constable Robinson. When he told them he could identify their prisoner if he was allowed to see him for a few minutes, they lead him straight to the cell.

Thompson seemed shrunken by the cell. Never a large man, he now seemed much smaller. His face was blackened and swollen where Holmes had hit him as he was struggling with Robinson. He was a woeful looking creature and Holmes was almost tempted to apologise for the blow. Yet he knew if he had not hit him Thompson would likely have killed the constable. He and Robinson were in agreement on that.

Thompson seemed surprised to see him. Then he brightened with a thought.

"Halo, Mr Holmes. Have you come to free me?"

"No."

"This is all a mistake."

"I think not," Holmes replied.

"I was just in the neighbourhood and they have mistaken me for a burglar. A silly idea—"

"Mr Thompson, I am the one who discovered you. I was surprised when I recognized you, but I confirmed it before calling in the police."

"You are mistaken. I forgive you. Just tell them it is a mistake."

"I shall sign a statement identifying you, and they will get a warrant to search the house in Peckham."

Thompson startled.

"Oh, such a disruption to my wife, my household, why would you do such a thing?" he whined. "I never harmed you. I only helped you with your violin."

He seemed like such a miserable little man.

Holmes shook his head.

"I didn't know who you were then."

Thompson smiled. His face brightened. His eyes twinkled. He laughed.

"Do you know me now?" he asked.

Holmes shook his head again and left the cell.

'O villain, villain, smiling, damned villain!' he thought.

Holmes signed the statement identifying the man they had arrested as John Thompson. He stated that he had met Thompson for advice on a violin he had purchased and he had been to the man's house which contained many valuable items.

Then the wheels of justice began to grind to get a search warrant issued for the house in Peckham. Holmes caught a hansom directly there. As a private individual and someone known to the household, there was nothing to stop him. But the women were up and nearly done packing. A four-wheeler stood at the door. Bags and boxes were being loaded. He told his cabby to wait and attempted to speak to Mrs Thompson as she came out the front door with another woman and a child.

"I'm sorry, Mr Holmes. Something terrible has happened. We must go," she said boarding the four-wheeler with the others.

"But where are you going?" he asked.

"Driver, please go," she said.

The cab started off, leaving Sherlock Holmes with nothing but its number. His hansom driver attempted to follow but lost thefour-wheeler in the crush of traffic crossing the Thames. Holmes instructed the driver to take him to Montague Street instead.

The vision of Thompson's smile and the sound of his laughter still troubled Holmes. Less than a year before he had told his brother Mycroft that he could recognize criminals. John Thompson had made a liar of him. From scholarly man to thief to potential killer, his estimation of John Thompson had evolved rapidly and Holmes had been surprised at each turn.

Thompson had asked, "Do you know me now?"

He seemed to be—No, there was no doubt.—Thompson had been laughing at him, the devil.

The Devil's Laughter—Paginini.

A memory clicked. He had seen it nearly two years before he had first met this devil. Holmes jumped from the cab on Montague Street and threw the fare to the driver. The commonplace books were stacked in the sitting room. He began digging through them.

He found the article about the murder of Arthur Dyson in Sheffield dated November 29, 1876. He remembered the case because he had been paying attention to northern cases after Jonathan had drawn his attention to the murder of Constable Cock. Dyson had been murdered the day after the Hebrons' trial.

He paged through the articles about the Dyson murder. The suspect was a friend or former neighbour of the victim named Charlie Peace. He had attempted to seduce the wife of the deceased and killed him when he intervened. Peace had previously served time for burglaries near Manchester and had been known to live in Liverpool and Hull where there had been a spate of burglaries in 1876 and early 1877.

There were several different descriptions of Peace. Holmes remembered thinking at the time that the contradictions in the descriptions made identification difficult. This one said he was 'a wiry, insignificant-looking individual about 50 years of age, with grey hair and full grey beard and moustache.' Another said he was thin and slightly built, 46 years of age but looked older, 5 foot 4 or 5, grey hair and beard, long or short. Seems a kindly man.' A third said 'He is a man about 55 to 60 years of age, five feet four inches in height; thin, grey hair and longish whiskers, of the variety known as a peg top. He had three fingers off his left hand.' Another reported 'He had lost one or two fingers on the left hand. Had cut marks on hands and forehead, walks with legs wide apart, talks funny and boasts a lot.'

Here it was: December 4, 1876, a police notice with an amended description was posted, but it was the headline Holmes was looking for: Charlie Peace, alias George Parker, alias Alexander Mann, alias Paganini.

Why Paganini?

The notice did not mention any musical connection. Neither did any of the newspapers. The description could be a bad description of Thompson or a better one of any number of other people.

Holmes scribbled notes from the articles in his notepad. He checked Bradshaw, and stuffed the newspapers Robinson had given him in a satchel. Then another thought struck him and he paused.

What of the killing of Constable Cock in a suburb of Manchester in the summer of '76?

That was the case in the newspaper clippings Jonathan had sent. That case had always seemed off to him. One of the Hebrons was still serving time for it. Holmes flipped the pages of the commonplace book and there was his note that he would have looked into the burglaries and stabbings of the constables in Manchester. Manchester, where Peace had been convicted before. Too much of a coincidence. He wrote a note and left it on the table:

Gone north on a case. Not certain where it will take me or when I shall return. Sherlock

As his cab pulled up to the stand near St Pancras Station, he saw the same four-wheeler he had seen in Peckham. With a suitable financial incentive he convinced the man to tell him that the ladies were heading to Nottingham. He considered for a moment. It was likely they were heading away from areas they might be recognized and associated with Thompson. On the other hand, he was investigating whether Thompson was Charlie Peace, the killer of Dyson in Sheffield. He boarded the train to Sheffield.

In Sheffield Holmes spoke to Chief Constable Jackson.

"They tell me that you might have some information concerning the location of Charlie Peace," Jackson said.

"In the notice of December 4th, 1876, one of his aliases is listed as Paganini. Was there any significance to that alias?" Holmes asked.

"Oh, there is a great deal of significance to that, young man. For a while he made his living as a strolling musician in these parts. He played in every tavern in Sheffield and the surrounding towns. Quite talented with the violin from what I've heard. Someone called him the Modern Paganini and it stuck. I am not familiar with violinists myself...."

"I am a violinist, Chief Constable. I know of a man who is fond of playing a particular piece by Paganini who has been arrested for burglary and attempted murder of a constable in Blackheath, London," Holmes said.

"Now you have my attention, Mr Holmes. Charlie Peace has twice served time for burglary. We would love to put a rope around his neck for the Dyson murder," the Chief Constable said.

"Here are reports of the arrest in the London papers," Holmes said handing him the newspapers.

The Chief Constable made some notes on a telegram form. He

stepped out of his office, handed the form off to someone with orders to send it right away, and called in a police constable.

"Mason, you know Charlie Peace by sight?"

"Indeed I do."

"Mr Holmes, here, believes Charlie may have been arrested today in London. I have just sent a telegram to the station where he is being held, notifying them that their prisoner maybe wanted for murder here. I want you to go up to London with Mr Holmes and see if they really have our Charlie."

Holmes and Constable Mason caught the next train to London.

In the meantime police in London had searched the house in Peckham and found numerous stolen articles, abandoned by the women in their flight, which connected Thompson with burglaries. The women had gone but the police had no interest in pursuing them. While they may have known how Thompson made his living there was no evidence that they were involved otherwise.

When Constable Mason and Sherlock Holmes arrived in London they immediately caught a cab to the Blackheath Station House.

"That's Peace," Mason said, "I'd know him anywhere."

Chapter 12

Corpses & Chemistry

*"Holmes is a little too scientific for my tastes
—it approaches to cold-bloodedness."*
Stamford, *A Study in Scarlet*

It was the weather that drove Sherlock Holmes off the streets, as it did many of those he had walked among in his disguises. The cold came in late October and brought early frosts and snow throughout the islands. It remained cold into November. On November 12th icy winds lashed those who ventured out and the snow piled up three feet high in some places. London came to a standstill and Holmes stayed before his fire pasting clippings in his commonplace books and indexing them. It was tedious work, but it was work that had born fruit in the case of Charlie Peace.

A week later temperatures grew milder, and winter let up on its ferocity. Holmes bundled up and ventured out to make his way to the Old Bailey where Charles Peace, aka John Thompson, aka John Ward, was being tried for burglary and the attempted murder of Police Constable Robinson. The testimony was uninteresting to Holmes. He spent most of his time watching the defendant. Peace on the dock bore little resemblance to the John Thompson he had known. Thompson had not been a handsome man, but he had seemed a gentleman and a scholar. His violin playing had been superb. On the dock Peace was again performing the role of a shrivelled, confused old man. Holmes had seen that performance in the Blackheath gaol. Peace would have fared better as an actor than a burglar, Holmes thought, then chuckled at the irony that it was a former actor—himself—who had undone Peace's career as a burglar.

This case had been a critical lesson for Holmes. Observation alone could be deceptive. Thompson had shown Holmes what he had wanted to see at the time: an expert on Stradivarius violins. What other signs had he missed? In the end Holmes had aided in the capture and conviction of Peace aka Thompson but that was because he had set himself on the track of the Blackheath Burglar. He had to admit to himself that it was entirely by accident that he had discovered the burglar was Thompson. Then vague memories of newspaper articles had lead him to connect Thompson with Peace. It was a lesson not to rely on his initial perceptions of individuals and to always follow the evidence.

Leaving the Old Bailey, Holmes passed the gate to St Bartholomew's Hospital. He looked up at it. Snow was piled high on the roofs and icicles hung from the eaves. Henry VIII stared arrogantly out from atop the gatehouse despite his frosty over-garments.

Holmes knew the break in the Winter Session was coming up in a few weeks, which would leave the chemical laboratory empty. That might provide him with the opportunity he was seeking. He entered through the gate and onto the grounds of the old hospital and went in search of Stamford.

He had met Charles Stamford five years before when he had taken a chemistry course at Bart's during his summer break at Cambridge. It had been a fateful summer because it was the summer he had decided to become a detective. Taking the class at Bart's had been part of his plan to change to the Natural Sciences Tripos at Cambridge and study topics more useful for the detection of crime. He had not known at the time that he would be sent down from Sydney Sussex College six months later after the accident in the laboratory.

Stamford had grown up within the community that was Bart's. His mother had been a charwoman who worked there and had taken him along as a small child when she worked. While his progress from child to medical student within the walls was unusual, it was not unique. Throughout its history, Bart's had been known for providing shelter and education to those who worked there and their families, as well former patients and their families. Stamford worked at the hospital and medical college to pay for his medical training. If Stamford was still there he must be close to getting his degree.

Stamford was unique in the manner in which he had adapted to his upbringing. Even in his teens he had become the font of all knowledge of the institution. He knew everyone and they knew him. If Holmes wanted to know if he was welcome within these walls, it was Stamford to whom he should apply.

He found Stamford in the post-mortem room going over a corpse with a group of students, most of whom were older than Stamford himself, though he was no longer a child. The air was heavy with the smells of formaldehyde and carbolic. The students were eager to impress one another at least as much as the long-time student who was assisting them.

Holmes entered quietly and observed.

"The notes the police provided to us," Stamford was saying, "indicate that about half-past one in the morning a cabby driving through St John's Wood was hailed by an stout, elderly lady and a young female companion with a veil over her face. Between them they were propping a man in evening dress against a lamp-post. They told the cabby that the man is the younger lady's husband worse for drink and they wanted to send him home in the cab. The cabby agreed. The two women bundled the man in the four-wheeler and gave the cabby a name and address in Clapham. The young lady paid the fare in advance and off the cabby went.

"When the cabman reached the address, he rang the bell, and rousted up a servant who said it couldn't be their master for he's away in India. The cabby and the servant tried to rouse the man in the cab to ask him for his name and address. After several shakes and other attempts, they decided that the man was dead and had been dead some time. Everything which might have identified him had been removed from his pockets. So the cabby dropped his passenger off at the nearest station house, and hence he came to us. No one has claimed him and there is no matching report of a missing person. The coroner will likely schedule an inquest soon. Let's see if we can't find something to help him."

The medical students looked for signs of struggle, broken bones, or abnormalities in the organs and found none. There was to be no cutting today so they were restricted to what their fingers and eyes could reveal.

Sherlock Holmes could tell from where he stood, as he saw how the body moved in respond to their efforts, that *rigor mortis* had slacked off some time before. It was a couple of days deceased.

"Cause of death?" Stamford asked them after a few minutes.

One student pulled up the eyelids to look at the eyes of the corpse.

"Asphyxiation probably, but not sure how," he said.

The other students gave similar responses.

"May I?" Sherlock Holmes asked coming forward.

Stamford looked at him, quizzically at first, and then with recognition.

"Mr Holmes, isn't it?"

"Yes."

"Please join us. We welcome any insight you may have," Stamford said.

The students made room for him at the examination table. Holmes carefully inspected the face, especially about the nose and mouth. Nothing unusual there. Then he studied the neck.

"Ah," Holmes said.

"Found something?" Stamford asked.

"Did you see these spots on the neck?"

"No. Show me."

"Right here," Sherlock said pointing to the left side of the neck. "There is one larger blue spot here, and three faint ones on the right side. That would be the thumb on the left and three of the fingers on the right."

"Yes, I see now," Stamford said.

Holmes spread out his hand to match the spread of the marks.

"It is too small for my hand or yours. I would say that he was strangled by a woman, either a very frightened or very angry woman."

"Why do you say that?" a student asked.

"Because she was obviously smaller than he was and it probably was not easy for her to strangle him. If it had not been in the heat of passion she probably would have found a simpler way to do it. Members of the fair sex are especially fond of poisons."

"Yes, that makes sense," Stamford said, urging the students each to take a close look at the marks upon the neck.

"Suggest to the coroner that he have a police surgeon take another look at the body tomorrow. The marks should be more prominent then," Holmes said to Stamford.

The mystery solved, the examination was soon at an end and the students drifted away to classes.

"Well, Mr Holmes, it has been a while. What brings you to Bart's these days?" Stamford asked.

"A few months ago I was doing a thought experiment on the galvanic corrosion of metals and was thinking it would be useful if I had access to a proper chemical laboratory again. I don't currently have the space for it at home. Do you think there is a possibility that I could make an arrangement to use the laboratory during the division as I did before?"

"Let's speak to Dr Russell about it," Stamford said and led him through the corridors.

Stamford made the introduction to Dr William Russell and Holmes presented his proposal. After a short, pleasant conversation, Sherlock Holmes was granted permission to use the chemical laboratory at Bart's between December 21th 1878 and January 5th 1879 while the students were gone for holiday. That permission came with two stipulations: Holmes must give way if any students or staff needed exclusive use the laboratory during that time and he must compensate Bart's for any materials he used or damaged. Holmes also agreed to make a donation to the hospital.

Holmes left Bart's relieved that the explosion at Sydney Sussex had not even been mentioned. Whether his association with it had never reached London, or whether the intervening years had faded the memory of it, was not something he was going to enquire into. In either case it was not now the barrier he had long feared.

The evening newspapers were all full of the trial of Charlie Peace. Yet it was soon drowned by the cry of war. The British army invaded Afghanistan on November 21st, and there were rumours of war with the Zulus in Africa, too.

Sherlock Holmes could only imagine what Mycroft's thoughts were on these matters. He could only imagine it, not only because Mycroft refused to discuss such matters of state with him, but because the brothers had not seen each other in weeks. During his recent week at home, Sherlock had learned from Mrs Denton that while he had been away for long hours and sometimes overnight for the previous few weeks, Mycroft had been away as well.

"He's at that club of his best I know. I don't think he likes my cooking any more. And my housekeeping—" she shrugged at the newspapers, commonplace books, maps, and almanacs which Sherlock had left about and she had not dared touch.

"I am certain he understands the fault there is mine, not yours," he said.

"Bachelors are always the hardest to keep house for. I shouldn't complain when they are not around!" she said with a chuckle.

Holmes was indeed interested in studying the corrosion of metals as he had told Dr Russell. At the time he had assisted Maberley he had neither the convenience of a laboratory nor the time. He had used his knowledge of chemistry to reconstruct in his mind what must have happened. During that analysis he had wondered how long it would have taken to corrode the aluminium crutch sufficiently to make it fall but he had discarded the question as its answer was unnecessary to accomplish the desired goal, which was to save Maberley's father's life.

His curiosity about the question had lingered. Such corrosion at the junction of two metals could be used to initiate a deadly mechanism or set off an explosion after an interval had passed. The delay could allow the villain to establish an unbreakable alibi.

In the weeks before the laboratory would be available to him he studied relevant books on chemistry and metallurgy at the British Museum around the corner from his rooms at Montague Street. He read the works of Louis Jacques Thénard, Alessandro Volta, Humphrey Davy, Michael Faraday, and James Clerk Maxwell. Davy's work with the Royal Navy to prevent corrosion of the copper sheeting of warships was closest to his current enquiry, while the others explained how galvanic corrosion worked, even though their interest was more related to the generation and use of electricity. These studies gave him ideas for variations on his experiment. He knew there were other books in the laboratory itself, but he also knew he would have plenty of time for reading while the experiments progressed.

While Holmes had been given permission to use the equipment available in the lab, he also brought in some items that he acquired on his own. He obtained a pound of sea salt and a number of metal samples. Small pieces of copper, brass, iron, silver, and even gold could be obtained easily in London. Aluminium was easy to find.

Stamford came by the chemistry laboratory as Holmes was setting up on December 20th.

"Do you know if Bart's has any aluminium?" Holmes asked.

"I think we do," Stamford said rummaging in the back of a drawer. "A salesman who was trying to convince the hospital that aluminium could be used to make medical equipment left some samples. It seemed impractical to me, but I don't make such decisions in any case. I believe they were tossed in this drawer with all the other miscellaneous objects. Ah, here they are."

He pulled out a few small pieces of grey metal. Some were half an inch thick and an inch long and others a few inches long and very thin. Those bent easily. They were all stamped with the name and address of the company that had manufactured them, which also provided Holmes with a source of more if he should need it.

"Capital!" Holmes cried taking them from Stamford. "Do you think anyone would mind if I used them in some corrosion experiments?"

"Not in the least. In fact your experiments might yield some useful information if the subject comes up again. In any case, I doubt anyone remembers they were here."

Holmes arranged a number of sealed glass containers. At the bottom of some he created a solution of sea salt and water to recreate a seaside atmosphere. Others had just the normal atmosphere of the room. Suspended above were pairs of dissimilar metals in direct contact with each other as the aluminium crutch had been in contact with the brass workings of the clock. He also had set up some containers in which metallic objects were lying in the brine in contact with each other.

These experiments were different from the one that had gotten him in trouble at Cambridge. That one required careful timing and reacted very quickly—too quickly. These were slow and once set up required little of his attention other than keeping records of the changes. So he spent his time reading.

Stamford, who lived in a cottage just outside the walls of Bart's, came by now and then to see how he was getting along.

"They don't seem to be changing much," Stamford said peering through the glass.

"It varies by the combination of metals, among other factors. It is early days. You have to look very closely. Look at the aluminium and brass in this jar. After only a few days, you can see pitting in the aluminium at the point of contact with the brass, yet no corrosion of the brass," Holmes said and then led Stamford to another glass container. "Over here where the aluminium and brass are laying in the electrolyte solution rather than merely suspended in an electrolytic atmosphere, you can already see fairly heavy corrosion and pitting of the aluminium but again no corruption of the brass. Some of the other metal pairs are progressing more slowly."

"Have you considered heating them?" Stamford asked.

"Since time is the variable I am attempting to determine, they must be allowed to progress naturally at room temperature or as much as is possible in the time allowed. However, speaking of time," Holmes said changing the subject, "have you ever considered how long after death bruises can be produced?"

"I can't say that I have."

"I've been rereading Taylor's *Principles and Practices of Forensic Medicine*, Holmes said pointing to the book on the table he had been reading when Stamford came in, "—which is where I learned to look for those marks on the man's neck a few weeks ago—Taylor states that bruises can be created by blows to the body up to two hours after death. He cites experiments by Robert Christison at the University of Edinburgh four decades ago when he was working with the William Burke prosecution."

"A rather notorious medico-legal case. Why would it matter if bruises can be created after death?" Stamford asked.

"Taylor suggests that police could confuse post-mortem bruises with peri-mortem bruising related to the cause of death and falsely accuse someone. There are other possibilities as well. What if someone wanted to hide the cause of death by creating what seemed to be evidence of a more obvious cause like a physical attack or a fall downstairs when in fact the victim was poisoned or smothered?"

Stamford looked thoughtful.

"Or perhaps the body was moved to another place," Holmes suggested.

"That would surely disarrange the post-mortem lividity," Stamford said.

"Quite right, depending on the timing. Timing is so important. Well, it is a question for another day, but if a fresh corpse comes in during the break perhaps we could explore the question."

"Perhaps," Stamford said.

Three days later Stamford once again found Holmes in the chemistry lab, studying scientific texts next to his galvanic corrosion experiments.

"We have one," Stamford said.

"One what?" Holmes asked extracting his brain from his reading.

"A fresh corpse has been delivered for dissection. I need to embalm it or it will be pretty rank by the time the students get back, but we can wait a day."

"Excellent," Holmes said picking up a metal rod as he followed Stamford from the room.

The body was of a young pickpocket who had slipped on some ice attempting to escape from a police constable and hit his head on a stone step. He was dead before the constable reached him. No known family. Known by the police to have been living on the streets for years. With the exception of the blow to the head and the usual ailments of the poor such as malnutrition, lice, and bad teeth, the body was in good health.

"Not long dead," Holmes said.

"No. Less than an hour I was told," Stamford agreed.

"And it is cold out."

"Yes, very well preserved."

"If we start now, we can determine whether bruises can be formed both before and after rigor. Taylor did not mention whether Christison had continued the experiment after rigor had slacked off."

"I'll just observe if it's the same to you," Stamford said.

"Have you become squeamish after all these years surrounded

by the sick and the dead?" Holmes asked.

"Not in the least, I dissect corpses regularly to educate new doctors and to advance medicine. I have less comprehension of the need for this type of experimental science."

Holmes began on the left arm, squeezing it tightly a little above the wrist, in a way that would leave a bruise on a live human. He penned a mark around the spot so he could be certain of it later. He made note of the time. He then used the rod he had brought to rap sharply on the corpse's upper arm. He intended to repeat both actions at regular intervals on different parts of the body. He turned to Stamford who had not said a thing, but had watched the proceedings somberly.

"If you could help me by holding his torso in a sitting position, there is one more experiment I want to do before rigor advances."

Stamford reluctantly agreed, but he jumped back and allowed the body to fall to the table when Holmes violently struck the torso with the metal rod twice in rapid succession.

"Good heavens, Holmes, what are you doing?" Stamford said.

"Testing different levels of violence," Holmes replied. "Some of Taylor's remarks suggest that heavier post-mortem blows created no greater discolouration than lighter ones, unlike pre-mortem ones.

"You could have warned me first!"

"I suppose now we will be able to examine the head and upper back for bruising though that is likely to be overwhelmed by the lividity."

"*Livor Mortis* should peak in about nine hours," Stamford said.

"Yes, and it will reach full rigor in a few hours after. No one will disturb the corpse here?" Holmes asked.

"No one else is in the building. Just you, me, and him," Stamford said hooking his thumb at the corpse. "All the sane people are sitting before their fires with a cup of steaming bishop, which is where I am going."

Holmes went back to the chemistry lab. There he obtained a wire and some string and returned to the corpse in the dissection room and performed a few tests of ligature marks that he suspected Stamford might have been disturbed by if he was shocked by beating dead bodies for the sake of science. Then Holmes resumed studying the books and taking observations of the slowly progressing corrosion experiments. At intervals Holmes visited the corpse and repeated the various experiments, except the body blows, on other portions of the body with appropriate annotations on the body and in his notebook. Once the body had stiffened in full *rigor mortis* he stopped and waited until it was half off before attempting any other experiments. It was an intriguing experiment to occupy him while he waited for the cations and the anions to work on the surface of the metals.

Bruises formed fairly quickly in the first hour on all areas he had performed the experiments on, but thereafter they were faint and none appeared from the blows post *rigor mortis*. The colour at the place of the severe blows on the torso was no different from the bruises at the places of the less severe strikes inflicted at the same time. The ligature marks on the neck, wrist, and ankle done within the first hour were similar to those expected if the binding had been done during life. One difference that he saw between these contusions and those on a live subject was that no swelling arose. Christison may have found other differences if he did subcutaneous examinations. However, he knew Stamford wanted to embalm the body before any cutting was done. Holmes left him a note on the corpse that he had completed his work with it and headed home in the early hours of Christmas morning.

The weather continued cold and snowy in January. On the 4th Sherlock Holmes was forced to disassemble his galvanic corrosion experiments. The metals lying in the brine had shown results within a few days. The aluminium had become pitted and the corrosion had increased over time. Some of pairs of metals suspended in the briny atmosphere had not reacted as quickly. He rinsed and dried most of the metal samples and boxed them for transport to Montague Street. Two of the experiments he decided to continue on a smaller scale. One was the aluminium on brass in the briny atmosphere which was the closest to the Maberley case. The other was a pile of different metals in the sea salt solution. He transferred them to smaller jars he had brought. Back at Montague Street he placed them in his bedroom and logged any changes each day.

Two days later he met with his brother Mycroft for dinner as was their habit on Sherlock's birthday. He told his brother of his investigations at Bart's as well as his adventures on the streets of London in disguise, and the capture and conviction of Charlie Peace.

"I did not see your name mentioned in any of the newspaper reports of his arrest and trial," Mycroft said.

"That was my doing," Sherlock said. "I need some dependable allies among the police, and not just with Scotland Yard. Constable Robinson seemed to be reliable. Giving him sole credit should help his career. Solving the case was my reward, though I was shocked when I discovered Thompson was both the Black Heath Burglar and the murderer Peace. That was an educational experience."

"What did you learn from it?"

"That I should be less cocky in relying on my impressions of people."

Mycroft chuckled.

The newspapers reported Charlie Peace was taken to Sheffield on the 17th of January for an appearance before a magistrate related to the Dyson case. There was a second hearing scheduled for the 22nd, but en route Peace attempted to escape by jumping from the train and was injured, delaying the hearing until the 30th. At that hearing he was committed to trial at the Leeds Assizes, which commenced the week following. Peace was taken to Wakefield Prison to await trial.

The trial of Charlie Peace for the murder of Dyson lasted only one day. According to the newspapers the first witness called by the prosecution was Mrs Dyson, the wife of the victim. She had no difficulty identifying the defendant as Charlie Peace. She described how on the night of November 29, 1876, Peace confronted her husband holding a revolver and how he said: "Speak, or I'll fire!" and Dyson fell, shot in the temple. Mrs Dyson admitted that in the spring of 1876 her husband had objected to her friendship with Peace.

The evidence of Mrs Dyson was followed by that of five persons who had either seen Peace in the neighbourhood of Banner Cross Terrace on the night of the murder, or heard the screams and shots that accompanied it. Evidence was then given as to threats uttered by Peace against the Dysons in July of 1876, and as to his arrest at Blackheath in the October of 1878.

The marks on the bullet extracted from Dyson's head were the same as those on the bullet fired from the revolver carried by Peace at the time of his capture 1878. To Sherlock Holmes that was the most interesting aspect of the trial. It was the first case to his knowledge in which the marks on a bullet had been used in a criminal trial. The jury retired at quarter past seven. Ten minutes later they returned with a verdict of guilty.

The death sentence having been issued, Sherlock Holmes turned to the clippings Jonathan Beckwith had sent him years ago and picked up his pen.

Jonathan,

It took over two years, but the murder of Constable Cock has been solved and William Habron has been released. Thank you for drawing the case to my attention. Without your assistance, I may not have seen the links from the Cock case to the Dyson case, and in turn to the Blackheath Burglar. With that information I was able to point the police in the right direction.

Someday, perhaps, I can tell you how Charlie Peace helped me restore a Stradivarius violin which has replaced my old violin. I used that friendly connection to write a letter to Peace urging him to confess to the murder of Constable Cock at Whalley Range and demonstrate the innocence of William Habron. Peace agreed to do so.

Yours truly,

Sherlock Holmes

The newspapers reported that Peace confessed to the governor of the prison. Initially the governor did not believe him until Peace drew a map of the place where Cock had been shot and told him details no one else would know. Then the bullets from the gun taken in the Blackheath case were compared to those in the case of Constable Cock as they had been in Dyson's case. They matched and William Habron was released.

If Peace had confessed in hopes of drawing more attention to himself rather benefiting Habron, then his hopes were likely dashed. For on the 12th of February word finally reached England of the awful destruction on January 22, 1879 of a British encampment in South Africa in which over a thousand British and colonial troops were killed.

The ensuing shock and horror among the public exceeded any reaction to anything that Charlie Peace had confessed to, or was likely to have done. In any case, Charlie Peace was hanged on a bitterly cold day in February and died instantly.

Chapter 13

Tiaras & Slippers

"I have heard of you from Mrs Farintosh,
whom you helped in the hour of her sore need."
Helen Stoner, "The Adventure of the Speckled Band"

The late winter and early spring of 1879 remained colder than usual. As a result Sherlock Holmes was not inspired to recommence his walks on the streets of London. He brought his commonplace books and their index—which he had neglected while he had been studying chemistry and corpses—up-to-date. He ruminated over his growing library of crime books. He recorded the progress of changes in the metals in the three jars in his room, and he played his Stradivarius.

In May, Sherlock Holmes was once again surprised to receive a response to one of his advertisements in the newspapers. On the 20th a letter came by the first post:

Dear Mr Holmes,

I have seen your advertisements in the newspapers and now find myself in sore need of your services. I wish to consult you at your earliest convenience, today if at all possible.

Mrs Farintosh

He immediately wrote back and invited her to consult with him at his rooms that afternoon. He took the time to tidy up the sitting room a bit before they came and warned his housekeeper that a request for tea was a possibility.

Mrs Farintosh arrived promptly upon the hour named with her daughter Mirabelle. The daughter dropped a glove as she entered behind her mother and lost her balance when she bent down to pick it up. Her face was tear-streaked and grim as Holmes helped her to her feet.

Holmes took their hats and coats, and offered them tea, which they declined. Then he invited them to make themselves comfortable upon the couch. He stood before the fireplace to better observe both of them.

243

"How may I help you, ladies?" Holmes asked.

The daughter giggled and then returned to looking miserable. The mother looked about the sitting room and then at Sherlock Holmes.

"You seem a bit young. Do you have much experience with this sort of thing?" Mrs Farintosh asked.

Holmes resisted the urge to roll his eyes.

"Do you mind if I smoke?" he said lifting his pipe from the mantel.

"Not at all, my husband always liked a good pipe."

He lit the pipe, and gave Mrs Farintosh and her daughter an unnecessarily thorough introspective look. It was unnecessary because he had seen all he needed when they entered. However, his years in the theatre had taught him the benefits of dramatic effect, especially in a case like this when a potential client was doubting his detective skills.

"I have sufficient experience to tell that you are a widow, madam. Your husband died about six years ago and you since have struggled to raise your daughter on your own, with some assistance from former associates of your husband."

"Yes, yes, they have been very kind," Mrs Farintosh affirmed.

"Miss Farintosh is somewhat absentminded and awkward, in part," he said to Mrs Farintosh and then turned his gaze directly at her daughter, "because you are more cerebral and fond of writing, and thus easily distracted from material things. Poetry is it?" he continued.

"Why yes!" Mirabelle cried out beaming.

"Now tell me ladies: what has been mislaid?" he asked them.

Suddenly there was fire in the young lady's eyes.

"I know I am forgetful, but I am certain it was stolen. It was there and then it was gone! I asked everyone!" Mirabelle Farintosh cried.

"What was gone?" Holmes asked.

"I guess we are going about this all backwards," Mrs Farintosh said.

"Then tell it to me forwards," Holmes said.

"As you said, my husband died a few years ago. Mirabelle is a debutante this year. It is essential that she find a good match. I've done the best I could. A friend, who travels in higher social circles than I, acted as her sponsor and Mirabelle was presented at court. Since then she has received some good invitations to balls, teas, and other entertainments, even a little lawn tennis. Mirabelle has met some very nice young men, but a match has not yet been made. However, we've had to make some economies, borrowing dresses and accessories from friends. That's the source of our problem, you see. We borrowed an opal tiara from a dear friend. I am sure it is priceless. It is quite impossible for us to replace."

"What mother is trying to say is that I wore it one evening," Mirabelle said.

"And you did look so lovely in it," her mother said.

"I took it off because it was giving me a headache," Mirabelle whined. "I sat it down on a small table then when I looked again it was gone."

"Will you help us, Mr Holmes?" Mrs Farintosh asked. "We simply do not know what to do."

"Oh, please, Mr Holmes!" Mirabelle begged.

Sherlock Holmes stared thoughtfully at the wall with his pipe clamped between his teeth and the smoke rising about his head. If the ladies could have read the young man's thoughts they might have been surprised, for Holmes was doubting his decision to become a detective. He had set his feet upon that path with grand ideas of solving mysteries and saving lives. Yet here he was reduced to finding trinkets that careless daughters had dropped behind the curtains or some such place.

However, he'd had no paying clients in months and six months had passed without bringing him any cases at all. There was always the possibility that Mrs Farintosh would recommend his services to her friends who might have more interesting problems, or at least more lucrative ones. He also could not think of a more polite way of removing the giggling, whining girl from his sitting room than taking the case. He took his pipe in hand and turned towards Mrs Farintosh.

"Yes, of course. I have a few questions," Holmes said.

"We will tell you anything we can."

"Have you gone to the police?"

"Oh, no, we wouldn't want to do that. The scandal and embarrassment for all would surely ruin Mirabelle's chance of finding a good husband. I don't care where it is or how it came there, we just need to get it back."

"So if I find it and return it, you won't ask any questions?"

"None at all," she affirmed.

Mirabelle shook her head as well.

"What type of an event was this?" he asked.

"It was a house party and dance. Whatever shortcomings she may have, Mirabelle is an excellent dancer. Dances allow her to put her best foot forward, so to speak, at least when someone is holding her hand."

"When was this party?"

"Last night."

"Good, the trail will be fresh. Where was it held?"

"Mrs Horace Bertram's home. It is on Wilton Crescent in Belgravia."

"How many people attended?"

"It was a small gathering. About 15 couples and chaperones."

"There were servants present, too?"

"Yes, of course," Mrs Farintosh affirmed.

"Regarding your fee, it might be necessary to pay it over time."

"Let's not worry about that at this time," he said, picking their things up from the coat rack.

"I shall make some enquiries," he said helping them into their coats and showing them out the door.

He closed the door firmly behind them and threw himself upon the sofa. He closed his eyes and savoured the silence. Then Mrs Denton knocked and asked if he would like his tea. He jumped up, grabbed his hat and coat, and told her he was going out. He had a growing appreciation for the concept of the Diogenes Club.

In any case, he had nothing to work with. He proceeded to the scene of the "crime" in hopes of finding something resembling a clue.

The address he had been directed to was in one of the most exclusive areas of London, less than a mile from Buckingham Palace. The Crescent held a mixture of detached mansions and attached town homes surrounding Wilton Crescent Park. Nearby streets held a number of embassies. These were the homes of the well-to-do and the well-connected. He told the cabby to let him down at the door and sent him off. He rang the bell and was greeted by a prim white-gloved butler who, at his request, enquired as to whether madam was at home, and led him to her sitting room.

Mrs Bertram was well-dressed, well-coiffed, and well-manicured. Combined with the house and the location, he surmised this was the wife of a man in the diplomatic corps.

"Mrs Bertram, thank you for seeing me. I am here on a very delicate matter. You see, one of your guests last night has misplaced an opal tiara that she wore. She removed it briefly and then was unable to find it. She has asked me to help her find it."

Mrs Bertram frowned.

"Is she accusing one of my servants of stealing it or one of my guests?"

"There are no accusations. If someone had admired it and merely borrowed it for a closer look, she completely understands and bears them no ill will if they return it. It is also highly possible that it was simply mislaid or it fell behind a piece of furniture. If I could take a look to eliminate that possibility and perhaps talk to some of your servants who were there that night then I might be able to establish where it has gone, and that will help me restore it to her. She would be extremely grateful if you could assist me in this matter."

"Oh, I certainly want to assist my guests in any way possible. I will ring for my housekeeper. She can show you the rooms where the guests were entertained and introduce you to those who were serving last night."

"Thank you, ma'am," he said.

The housekeeper, Mrs Burnsley, show him the rooms and he looked in every crack and crevasse, behind every piece of furniture, under carpets and on all sides of the curtains. He extended his search to window sills and balconies. There was not a thing out of place, not a speck of dust anywhere, not a bit of ash or a smudge of any kind. Housekeeping such as this could put detectives out of business. While he was making his examination Mrs Burnsley brought in the footman and the maids who had been serving the previous evening.

Holmes asked them about the guests.

"Do you remember Mirabelle Farintosh?"

They all nodded.

"Yes, sir."

"She was wearing an opal tiara when she arrived," he said.

Some of them nodded. One of the maids saw her wearing it when she arrived and another saw her wearing it later. The footman said he had not noticed.

"Was she wearing it when she left?" Holmes asked.

"No, sir. I was handing out the coats and I noticed she did not have it on," one of the maids said.

"Thank you—"

"Maizie, sir," she said.

"Thank you, Maizie. Now that we established that it was not on her head when she left, do any of you know what became of it?"

"I thought perhaps she put it in her pocket," Maizie said.

"None of you saw it sitting about on a table or on the floor?"

They all shook their heads.

"Tell me about the guests," he said.

They looked towards Mrs Burnsley. Holmes also looked towards her. He wished he had been able to interview the servants individually alone. They were more likely to be talkative that way.

"It is most essential and will be kept in strictest confidence, I assure you," he said.

Mrs Burnsley nodded.

"Who was here?"

Another maid, Rebecca began rattling off names. The young ladies and gentlemen were of the gentry and minor noble houses: Elizabeth Hawkworth, Simon Bradshaw, Ethan Langforth, Arden Winter, and others. The servants knew much about them, having seen them before.

"Then there was the foreigners," Maizie said. "Missus likes to invite some."

"Leopold Kulmer, the Austrian."

"Seemed a might shady to me," Maizie said.

"There was that French woman."

"Marie Oh'-something," Maizie said.

"Auclair," Rebecca corrected. "Very sophisticated."

"The American, Katherine Jenkins," Rebecca said. "She was enjoying herself. Pretty enough and wealthy. Wearing diamonds. Her father is in shipping, I heard."

"But she didn't know her forks," Maizie said.

The maids tittered and the housekeeper cleared her throat. They fell silent.

"The Italian woman, so lovely and refined, but she knew little English."

"Isabella Rossi," the housekeeper said.

"The German, Ilse Müller, was such a lovely dancer."

"And there was the Persian woman."

Heads nodded.

"So strange."

"How so?" Holmes asked.

"You might expect someone like that to not know our customs, but..."

"It was more than that. She was snobbish."

"Spoiled, I'd say."

"She got angry at me when I asked if she would like some punch. Said I was not supposed to speak unless spoken to."

"She didn't have a mother or aunt as chaperone. She had these two big male servants."

"They were dark skinned. Very dark. Much darker than she."

"They followed her everywhere."

"Her name?" Holmes asked.

"Azadeh Yazdani," the housekeeper said.

"Did any of these guests pay special attention to the opal tiara?"

"Katherine Jenkins was admiring it but I think her father would buy her ten if she asked."

"I heard some of her dance partners compliment it, but I think they were trying to make conversation."

"Did she fill her dance card?"

"Oh, yes, the missus always is careful that everyone gets a turn.

She prods the young men to pair up for every dance.”

"Thank you.”

"Now Mrs Burnsley, if we could have a word in private.”

The housekeeper dismissed the staff.

"Are any of the staff new?”

"No. They have all been with us for years.”

"All of good character?

"Impeccable.”

"None recently dismissed?”

"None, sir.”

"Thank you, Mrs Burnsley. I don't think I need to disturb your mistress again. Please thank her for me.”

Holmes returned home and reviewed his notes. While he had no basis for eliminating any of the guests, he thought the foreign ones might be worth investigating first. Members of London society were easy enough to trace. Experience had shown him that people claiming to be foreigners weren't always foreigners, but rather people trying to hide their true background. It was something a thief might do.

Sherlock Holmes had two primary sources of information about foreigners in London. One was, of course, his brother Mycroft whose contacts in the foreign office were likely to know about any foreigners visiting the city. On the other hand, if he wished to know intimate details of the lives of London society whether foreign or domestic, Lord Cecil Hamley, aka Langdale Pike, was the man to ask. He had no doubt where he could find him either. While he was out he had sent a wire to Lord Cecil's club. It was short:

Breakfast tomorrow?

SH

The response was waiting for him when he arrived home:

I would be delighted to have you join me at my club. 10 am?

LP

The following morning they exchanged greetings and sat down to breakfast. As usual Lord Cecil had already ordered.

"You are looking well. How is detecting?”

"A bit slow,” Holmes confessed after a sip of coffee. "However, I have some questions related to a current case.”

Lord Cecil leaned across the table with a twinkle in his eye.

"Is it a lurid murder or a sensational scandal?"

"I can't tell you what the case is about," Holmes said.

"You know I won't spill what you tell me," he said.

"Regardless of whether you would or you wouldn't, it is confidential," Holmes reminded him.

"Your questions?" Lord Cecil said making a circular figure with his hand.

"What do you know of Marie Auclair?"

"Lovely young woman. I've heard an engagement is in the offing," Cecil responded.

"Katherine Jenkins?"

"The American shipping heiress? Daddy has piles of money. He wants a title for his girl, but doesn't quite know how to get the right invitations. I hear she is a very nice young woman."

"Leopold Kulmer?"

"Young Austrian womanizer. His family has already had to pay off several young women but they can afford it. You would know that if you were reading my columns."

"His allowance is generous?"

"Very much so."

"Isabella Rossi?"

"Delightful woman. I met her once. Shy. She should find an English tutor if she wants to make headway in the London marriage market."

"Would she do anything illegal?"

"I think she would be horrified by the suggestion."

"Ilse Müller?"

"Fabulous dancer. A bit cold for my taste."

"Do you think she would do anything illegal?"

"She might stab a man who wronged her, but not any lesser thing of a criminal nature."

"Azadeh Yazdani?" Holmes asked.

Lord Cecil laughed, then leaned closer and whispered.

"If it has anything to do with her it must be sensational, even if a bit trivial. She is a spoiled child trapped in a young woman's body."

"That is your assessment?" Holmes asked.

"Most definitively," the young lord said.

"Do you think she would steal something?"

"If she wanted it, I have no doubt. However, she is more likely to ask one of her Abyssinia eunuchs to take it for her. They are utterly devoted to her and would do anything she asked. What did she steal?"

Holmes merely squinted at him and took a forkful of omelette. After he swallowed it he said, "Tell me more about her."

"She was born in the Oudlajan area of Tehran, Persia. He father is Ebrahim Yazdani. He is a merchant specializing in wholesale imports from Persia. Her mother died young and he never remarried, even though it is not unusual for a wealthy man such as himself to have a number of wives in his country. Azadeh is the apple of his eye. She grew tired of being left alone with servants in Tehran while he was here on business for months at a time. When she asked to go with him, he could not turn her down, but since they have been in London he has had to quash a series of scandals caused by her indiscretions. It is not entirely her fault. She wants to wear London fashions and go to society balls, but she has no training in what London society expects. She has no mother or governess to guide her. I feel rather sorry for her, which is why I have not written a word about her."

"Where is her father staying?"

"He is renting a townhouse at 139, Piccadilly, Mayfair."

"This is extreme useful," Holmes said.

"You won't tell me anything?"

"No. But I thank you for your information and for breakfast as well."

"I will be listening."

"I am sure you will," Holmes said as he took his leave.

After leaving the club, Holmes wrote a letter to Mr Ebrahim Yazdani requesting an audience with him. He quickly received a response including an invitation to call that afternoon.

While on the outside the house looked like any large house in Mayfair, inside was another world. Tapestries and paintings of exotic lands adorned the walls. Potted trees reached out from corners. Persian carpets covered the floors. A marble staircase wound up to a landing above.

A servant took Holmes' hat and coat and showed him to a room with an English desk and chairs; otherwise the décor was similar to what he had seen in the foyer. In a minute he was greeted by a tall slim man who was mostly bald and what little hair he had was trimmed close. His skin was swarthy and his face shaved clean. He wore a brocaded tunic and loose trousers.

"Mr Holmes, it is good to meet you," Mr Yazdani said. "Please have a seat. May I offer you a cup of tea?"

Mr Yazdani spoke English every well. There was a slight lyrical quality to his speech, but it was not as marked as he had heard from some people he had met who had come from India. Every indication was that Mr Yazdani had been trading in London for many years.

Holmes accepted his offer of tea. A servant placed a small table at his side and poured. Holmes sipped the fragrant tea.

"Now, Mr Holmes, what is it I can do you?"

"I hope, Mr Yazdani, you will not feel your hospitality is misplaced after I tell you why I have come. I am a detective."

Yazdani frowned and was about to speak, but Holmes held up a hand and interrupted him.

"I am not from the police. This is a private matter. Those I represent wish to avoid a scandal."

"As do I," Yazdani said. "I thank you for your consideration. What has she done now?"

Holmes explained about the missing opal tiara, and how he had come to believe that his daughter may know where it was.

"Please, wait here and finish your tea. I will speak to her," Yazdani said and left the room, closing the door behind him.

Whether it was due to the tapestries or the quality of the construction of the house, Holmes heard nothing over the next ten minutes as he drank the tea and observed the room.

After the passage of that time, Yazdani returned holding a bundle in one hand which looked to be something wrapped in a silk scarf. He offered it to Holmes, who took it, untied the scarf, and let the corners fall around his hand. There in his hand lay an opal tiara.

"I thank you, Mr Yazdani."

"Tell them also that the silk scarf is offered as some recompense for their inconvenience. And here," he said reaching into a ceramic jar on the desk and pulling out five gold sovereigns. "I hope these can compensate you for your time and expense."

Holmes accepted the gold coins with a slight bow and thanked Mr Yazdani again. He said good day and headed to the door which was opened by a servant, as another in the foyer offered him his hat and coat. As he was turning toward the front door, a beautiful young woman dressed in colourful brocades and silks appeared on the landing above. When she saw him she began vehemently shouting words in Persian and flung one of her slippers at him. Her father came out of his study and shouted something at her. She withdrew.

"My apologies again, Mr Holmes," Mr Yazdani said.

Holmes bowed and left by the door a servant was holding open.

As he reached the street, the other slipper sailed through an upper window and hit him on the back of the head! He laughed and picked it up as a trophy of his adventure. He returned home with a tiara in one pocket, five sovereigns and a slipper in the other, and a smile on his face.

Mrs Farintosh and her daughter were very happy to receive the opal tiara and the scarf, but even more pleased when Holmes told them that his fee had been paid.

Three weeks later a notice appeared in *The Times* announcing the betrothal of Azadeh Yazdani, daughter of Mr Ebrahim Yazdani, to Farhang Bahrami, the son of a merchant in Tehran, Persia, where they would be making their home.

The same paper announced that on the 26th of May a new Amir of Afghanistan, Yakub Khan, had signed the Treaty of Gandamak with the British government, ceding the Khyber Pass and the Kurram Valley, and setting up a British Residency in Kabul. The treaty had been ratified by Lord Edward Robert Bulwer-Lytton, Viceroy of India, on the 30th of May. The Second Afghan War was over.

Chapter 14

The Tarleton Murders

He was languidly interested by the papers in his hand, and page
after page was turned as he followed the argument of the lawyer.
Dr John H. Watson, "The Adventure of Charles Augustus Milverton"

The weather having improved and his coffers restored, Sherlock Holmes began to make the circuit of the London streets again. The previous year he had made an agreement with Lincoln Bradley for the use of a small store room at the back of the tobacco shop and stocked it with make-up, hair, and costumes. Lincoln also gave him a key to the back door that opened on the alley. Thus Holmes could enter the front door as a respectable young man and exit through the back alley as any number of people. He often posed as an old woman and explored north and east from the tobacco shop. He knew some of those streets already, but now they would know her.

Two days later he went south to Lambeth, greeted Sherman and his menagerie, and tended to his hideaway there. Then he once more walked as the sailor eastward along the foreshore of the Thames towards Rotherhithe, and on to dockyards of Greenwich and back. Another day he stopped in Rotherhithe and cleaned out Ned's old shack and took the rag cart south into Blackheath. As he had expected, he had competition along Ned's old rag-picking route and he skipped many of the more profitable bundles to leave those for the new ragman. It was his intent to keep these characters familiar to the local people, not to rob anyone of their meagre livelihood. He walked the streets two to three days a week through June, spending the remaining time at the ceaseless task of the upkeep of his criminal records and waiting for new mysteries to come to his door.

Early one morning as he set out from his flat towards Bradley's, he heard a young woman scream "Fire!" as she pushed open a door in a block of flats.

"'Elp! Fire!" she cried.

Holmes pulled out a police whistle which a constable had given him years before and blew several blasts. At the sound of her cries peo-

255

ple began running out of the building past her from surrounding flats, but she stayed at the entrance crying for help. Her red hair was tousled and her green eyes wild as Holmes ran up to her. She grabbed his arm.

"'Elp me, please, me parents! There is too much smoke," she said in a thick Irish brogue.

"Show me the way," he said.

Smoke continued to fill the hall. A young woman with a baby pushed past them as the young Irish woman pulled Holmes toward the stairs.

"At the top to the right" she said.

"Wait outside," he said pulling out his handkerchief and covering his nose and mouth.

The door to the flat was open, which accounted for the smoke in the hall. He ran in pulling the door closed behind him. The smoke stung his eyes, but once the draught from the door was stopped there seemed to be less of it. He saw no one at his first glance around. It was a sitting room much like that in the building where he lived. The source of the smoke was a fireplace choked with papers. He found a pitcher of water ready for washing and tossed the water upon the fire. The smoke declined. He looked in the second bedroom and saw two bodies on the floor. He knelt beside them and touched them.

They were dead, but it wasn't the smoke that killed them. There was blood. Lots of blood. The bodies were still warm, but the blood had already soaked the floor and the rug around them. He could see multiple slashes in the nightclothes. One was male and one was female. They seem to be in their early sixties. From their hands, he determined neither had seen much manual labour. The bare feet and rumpled bedclothes suggested they had been startled out of their bed, but had not gotten far before the assassin or assassins had attacked. A quick scan of the room revealed no weapon unless it was under the bodies. The amount of blood suggested a knife or knives.

Holmes backed out of the room and stood in the hall to the sitting room as a member of the fire brigade burst in and threw a bucket of water upon the smouldering papers in the fireplace. He was followed by another and they began poking at the papers and drawing them out looking for cinders. They searched other rooms. He could hear shouts of constables and other members of the brigade below. The smoke was dissipating.

The young woman appeared at the doorway to the flat. Holmes remained in the hall that led to bedrooms.

"Me parents? Where are they?"

He shook his head.

"No," she cried and tried to run past him.

He caught her.

"You don't want to go in there," Holmes said.

The smoke now was gone. Just the smell lingered. The men from the fire brigade left satisfied that the fire was out. A constable pushed past them at the door followed by a plain clothes detective; one Holmes had met before. The little ferret-faced Inspector Lestrade was unmistakable.

"Well, what do we have here? A bit of arson is it?" Lestrade said.

"No," Holmes said. "It's murder."

"Murder!" the woman gasped.

Lestrade turned around to look at him and said "Murder, is it? Where is the body?"

"There are two in there," Holmes said nodding towards the room behind him.

As Lestrade passed him, Holmes guided the young woman toward the door of the flat.

"Murder?" she said. "'Ow can that be? Why would—"

Once they were out in the hall he released her.

"You have no idea why anyone would do this?" he asked.

"No. This is 'orreble. I'd gone to get some buns for them to have with their breakfast tea. When I came back—I was afraid the fire had gotten out o' control and the smoke—."

"You lit the fire in the sitting room before you left?"

"Yes. There was a chill in de air. I'd boiled the water an' poured it on the tea in the pot and had gone—"

"And your parents were still in bed?"

"Yes."

"Did you see the papers in the fireplace just now?"

"Yes."

"What were they?"

They were interrupted by the constable passing them followed by the inspector.

"Well, Mr Holmes, amateur detective, we meet again," Lestrade said.

"Yes."

"Crime just seems to follow you around."

"Don't be absurd, Inspector. This young woman's parents have been murdered."

"Yes," Inspector Lestrade opening his notebook. "Your name, miss?"

"Tarleton, Charlotte Tarleton."

"Your parent's names?"

"Liam an' Brigid Tarleton."

"Tell me what happened," Lestrade said.

Miss Tarleton repeated what she had told Holmes. The Scotland Yarder's eyes narrowed at her Irish brogue.

"Is this your usual place of residence?"

"Well, no, we've only been here a few weeks. We lived in Killeigh, Ireland. But me father became obsessed wit 'is research. 'E said we 'ad to comb to England for it. He sold everything we owned. We travelled to Northumberland, crossed into Scotland, then to Lancashire and to Wales, then Liverpool again an' stayed there a few weeks and then 'ere."

"What kind of research was that?"

"I don't rightly know. Something about our family. 'E said he was gonna defend me rights but I'd no idea what 'e was talkin' about."

The constable had returned with some other men. Inspector Lestrade moved aside to let them through. When Sherlock Holmes attempted to follow, Lestrade blocked his path with his arm.

"You stay right here, Mr Holmes."

Another constable appeared behind them in the hall. The inspector caught his eye and said to him, "You keep these folks company."

The constable nodded.

Holmes pulled Miss Tarleton to one side and spoke to her softly. He dug a card out of his pocket and handed it to her.

"My name is Sherlock Holmes. My address is on this card. As Inspector Lestrade said, I am a detective, a private consulting detective. I solve crimes that the police cannot. If you tell the Inspector that you have hired me and insist that he let me inspect those papers in the fireplace, I can help you."

She bit her lip.

"I don't 'ave any money," she said.

"That's not important," he said.

"Do you think it is necessary?"

"Yes. You will see. The inspector will dismiss the importance of the papers. He will say your parents were killed by robbers or Fenians or some such, and they set the fire to cover the murder."

"You don't believe that?"

"No, I am convinced that your father's research is the key. I need to see his papers."

Four men pushed past them carrying stretchers. Lestrade came out in the hallway.

"I need to look at the papers in the fireplace," Holmes said.

"An' why would that be, Mr Holmes?" the inspector said with one quizzical eyebrow cocked.

"If my theory is correct—"

"Oh, you have a theory, do you?" the inspector said with a smile.

"Yes—"

"No room for theories here, Mr Holmes. It is all clear enough. They were tryin' to burn down the flat to hide the murders."

Holmes glanced sideways at Miss Tarleton.

"Who?" Miss Tarleton asked.

"The Fenians. It is clear that your parents were former members trying to escape their grasp and they kept moving to keep away from them."

"That's crazy, Inspector," she insisted. "Me parents were not Fenians. Ever. It is clear to me that this beyond you. I've 'ired Mr Holmes to investigate and find the real killers. He says 'e needs to see the papers."

Inspector Lestrade sighed.

"Miss, I know you are overwrought. Let's go to the Yard, have a nice cup of tea and we can get your statement in writing."

"First, I insist that you allow Mr Holmes to inspect me father's papers—or," she said with a tremble entering her voice, "what is left o' them."

Just then the men came to the door way with the two stretchers. Holmes took her arm and pulled her further down the hallway. Lestrade followed. Despite their attempt to block her line of sight, her eyes followed the covered stretchers until they passed from view. A tear rolled down her face. Then she set her jaw and turned to the Inspector.

"Well?"

"If it will make you happy, Miss. We have no use for them."

Without a word to the Inspector, Holmes passed around him, but was stopped by a constable at the door. He looked back at the Inspector who nodded to the constable.

"Let him in to inspect the papers near the fireplace. He's to touch nothing else."

The constable stepped aside and Holmes strode toward the fireplace. He set his top hat upon the ground beyond the spread of damp. He went down on his hands and knees to inspect the papers heaped before the fireplace. Some were nearly consumed; others were charred. All were soaking wet and many had pike holes piercing them. He carefully peeled them apart. He read through them quickly. He doubted the Inspector's tolerance would last long. He took notes. He estimated that there were over a hundred pages here. There were pedigree charts, and handwritten copies of deeds, records of births and deaths, newspaper clippings, letters or copies of letters, and court documents, many court documents. He made note of the names, dates, and places.

"Mr Holmes," came Lestrade's voice behind him.

He stood, brushed off his knees, and picked up his hat. He pocketed his notebook.

"I am finished, Inspector."

"Yes, you are. Now if you will come along with me, Miss."

She looked at Holmes who nodded to her and then she went

along with the inspector. Holmes followed them out of the building.

"I will be in touch, Miss Tarleton," he said tipping his hat before they parted on the pavement.

Holmes walked back to his flat in Montague Street and began reconstructing some of the documents he had seen from memory. Then he loaded his pipe and sat back, deep in thought. He snapped out of it to find a cloud of smoke in the room, and a commotion at the door. He opened it just as Miss Tarleton was asking his landlady if Mr Holmes lived there.

"Obviously, he does," Mrs Denton said looking about the room.

"Is there a fire?" Miss Tarleton asked somewhat taken aback

"No, he does that sometimes," Mrs Denton said and went around the flat throwing windows open.

"Come in, Miss Tarleton. I am sure the air will clear in a minute," Holmes said. "Mrs Denton, could you bring some tea? This young woman has had a very trying day."

"Back in a trice," she said and vanished.

"Mr Holmes, someone was following me!" Miss Tarleton cried.

"You are certain?" he asked.

"Yes, I think they would have assaulted me at your doorstep if your 'ousekeeper had not come up just then."

"Then it is fortuitous that she did. Have a seat. You are safe here."

Sherlock Holmes directed Charlotte Tarleton to the sofa.

"For certain?" she asked.

"One moment," he said, and disappeared into his bedroom. He returned rotating the cylinder of his revolver. He placed it on a small table next to one of the chairs across from the sofa and sat in the chair.

"Does that make you feel more secure?"

"Yes. Why would anyone follow me?"

"If we are going to get to the bottom of this I need you to put that out of your mind and tell me about your father's research. When did he start it?"

"When I was very small. I think after me grandfather died. Maybe it was something Daideó passed down to him. I knew it only as a 'obby 'e pursued in the evenings for many years. He would send away letters an' get letters in return. He wrote notes. I thought 'e was just studying our family tree like many people do. In the last few years he became obsessed. As I told the inspector, me father sold everything last year, our house, our furniture, everything. Then we started travelling."

"What did your mother think of this?"

"She—" Miss Tarleton began and paused.

"She loved my father dearly. She said she would go anywhere as long as she could spend the rest of her life with him. I suppose she did," she said and sobbed.

Holmes handed her his handkerchief. Fortuitously, Mrs Denton appeared at that moment holding the tray of tea things. She had managed to gather up some sandwiches and biscuits to accompany the tea. She saw Miss Tarleton's tears and gave Holmes a scolding look.

"Are you alright, my dear?" she asked.

"As best I can be," Miss Tarleton said as she wiped the tears away.

Miss Tarleton looked upon the tray ravenously.

"You haven't eaten?" Holmes asked.

"Not at all," she said.

"Poor dear. I can bring more," Mrs Denton.

"Will be plenty," Miss Tarleton said.

Mrs Denton poured them each a cup and left them alone.

Holmes stared into his cup.

"You said you went to Northumberland. Where in Northumberland?"

"A town called Unthank. Seemed a strange name to me."

"In Scotland?"

"That was a bit odd. Perhaps me father changed his mind because we stopped at a little place just o'er the border, and then we went on to Lancashire."

"Where in Lancashire?"

"A few places. That part o' our journeys was interesting. It was like he was giving us a tour. He told me mother and me 'This Tarleton ancestor lived in this hall here and this building is where this other Tarleton worked and this is the dock where their ships were loaded.

Some of the Tarletons were mayors of Liverpool and members of Parliament!"

"So you only visited Liverpool?"

"Liverpool and surrounding hamlets and estates. Places with names like Allerton, Toxteth Park, Garston, Aigburth, Speke, Otterpool and the Dingle. There were some really old buildings. I thought he was just connecting with the home of his ancestors, as perhaps an old man might, but there also seemed something bittersweet about it."

"Was your father unwell?"

"Not that I knew. It seemed like 'e was looking for something or someone and 'e expected it to be there. Then suddenly we went to Wales where 'e was checking census records and city directories, but they seemed to lead him back to Liverpool, and then to London.

"I am sorry, Mr Holmes. I don't know what it all means. I know where we went. I've seen the documents—"

"The documents that someone attempted to destroy. I think they heard you coming and dumped too many papers in the fire at once, partially smothering it and resulting in more smoke than fire."

"Then perhaps this why they were followin' me," she said, putting down a sandwich and picking up her bag.

She pulled out a package wrapped in brown paper and handed it to him. He unwrapped it. It was the papers, dry now, stacked out of order, but they looked to be all there.

"Since the inspector was certain that they were o' no use—mere tender for a fire meant to destroy the flat, I convinced him to allow me to bring them to you. I was not certain that de brief examination 'e permitted you would be adequate."

"Thank you, Miss Tarleton. These could turn out to be very useful."

She finished her sandwich and emptied her cup.

"Would you like another cup?" Holmes asked, offering to pour.

"Yes, please. I'd no idea how 'ungry I was."

Mrs Denton appeared as he was emptying the teapot.

"Here, I'll take the tray. I'll leave those biscuits behind in case you want to nibble."

While she was gathering the things on the tray, Holmes stood and picked up his pipe from the mantel.

"Did you ask Inspector Lestrade if you could remove some of your personal effects?" Holmes asked Miss Tarleton.

"He said I could take me clothes."

"You should do so. You can't stay there," Holmes said.

"But I've nowhere t' go."

"It isn't safe there."

He tapped his pipe against his cheek.

"Mrs Denton?"

"Yes, Mr Holmes?"

"Could you make my room presentable to a young lady?"

"Perhaps, Mr Holmes," she said.

"And after could you come along with us to Miss Tarleton's former residence and help her pack her things? You see, Mrs Denton, Miss Tarleton has been orphaned today and someone is stalking her, possibly with the intent of threatening her life."

"Good heavens, of course, I would! You poor dear!"

"What about you?" Miss Tarleton asked.

"I will make do on the couch," Holmes said.

"He's not likely to sleep in any case."

"Quite true."

"What about your brother?"

"He can keep his own room."

Mrs Denton chuckled.

"If he appears at all," she said.

"It is likely that Miss Tarleton and I will be taking a trip north early tomorrow morning."

Sherlock Holmes followed Mrs Denton into his bedroom. As she stripped the linens from the bed, he snapped the lid on the violin case closed and carried it into the sitting room.

Miss Tarleton looked up as he entered.

"Do you play?" she asked.

"Yes," he said as he set the case down upon the bureau.

"He plays quite well when he is in the mood," said Mrs Denton as she passed with an armful of linens.

"Your housekeeper is very outspoken," Miss Tarleton said to

Holmes. "I suppose it is not easy being the 'ousekeeper for bachelors, and one o' them bein' a detective. Is your brother a detective?"

"Oh, not at all. He audits government books. Very tedious, but mostly regular hours, though he has been spending most of them at his club recently. I, on the other hand, come and go at all hours, vanish for days, or sometimes don't move a muscle for weeks."

Mrs Denton came through again with clean linens, towels, and a duster.

"I sent cook out with a note to your brother apprising him of the situation."

"Thank you, Mrs Denton."

"I'll give you a fiver he spends the night at that club of his," Mrs Denton said as she passed.

"I'm not taking that bet, Mrs Denton."

She chuckled from the bedroom.

Five minutes later Mrs Denton appeared at the door of the bedroom.

"There. It is acceptable. I'll return directly, dear, to help you pack your things."

The flat where Miss Tarleton's parents had died was a short walk away. No one seemed to follow them on their way there or back, though Holmes was not entirely convinced they were not being watched.

The building still smelled of smoke when they reached it, but otherwise life had returned to normal, with an exception. One of the constables they had met earlier stood at the door to the flat. He allowed Mrs Denton to enter with Miss Tarleton to pack her clothes and necessities. Holmes waited at the door. His attempts to extract information from the constable concerning any steps Inspector Lestrade may be taking were unsuccessful. In a few minutes the ladies came out carrying some luggage and the three of them walked back around to Holmes' flat in Montague Street.

That task having been completed Holmes began spreading the water and fire damaged papers on the table and sorting them.

"I can 'elp with that," Miss Tarleton said.

They created piles of related documents. When they were done, Holmes picked up one pile of papers which appeared to be a transcription of a legal judgment in the case of Tarleton v. Liddell. He set another pile next to it related to the case of Tarleton v. Tarleton. Fraud. Bankruptcy. Estates in fee tail. Common recovery. They crossed from the familiar to legal obscurities. There were also marriage and birth records among the papers. The papers were sorted now, but what did they mean?

There was one very intriguing note that was more than half burnt away: "...told me his father came to visit about 1815 and tried to sweet talk his mother. She would have none of him after all these years.... were happy once....young and foolish...you broke your promise. Just another .... forced me to live in that monk's cellar with an infant. I thought we could be happy again after we moved.... but you were always....after John Ross died.... Leave and don't... lucky she was not a vengeful woman...."

Holmes asked Miss Tarleton what she made of it.

"That's me father's hand. John Ross was a brother of his father who died young. It must something his father told him about an argument between his parents. Perhaps it was something his father told him before he died."

Among the papers there was a pedigree chart that listed John Ross Tarleton and James Ross Tarleton as the sons of Mary (Ross) Tarleton and John Tarleton. L. R. Tarleton was the son of James Ross Tarleton.

Holmes consulted some reference books.

"John Tarleton was born in Liverpool in 1755, the third son of John Tarleton and Jane Parker. He entered the slave trade with his brothers Thomas and Clayton, and a third man named Daniel Backhouse. Married in 1790. 1792 MP for the borough of Seaford. In 1815 was declared bankrupt. He died in 1841 in London."

He now had a hypothesis, but he needed to know that the legal terminology was not obscuring something that contradicted his theory. He knew just the man. He stacked up the papers and put them in a satchel.

"Miss Tarleton, we are going to go visit a man who may be able to explain these papers. However, I ask that you do as I direct, but not speak during the journey. I would like to avoid leading your followers to his door."

"I could stay 'ere."

"No. I think it is important that you hear his explanation. He may have some questions for you. Also, is safer if you are with me."

"Who is this man?"

"He is a solicitor."

Holmes called upon his housekeeper once again.

"Could you create some combination of hat and scarf to cover Miss Tarleton's hair for our journey to the solicitor's office?"

"You don't like me hair?" Charlotte objected. "I came by it from me great grandmother Finola O'Brien who was a force o' nature."

"I'm sure she was," Holmes responded, "but it is a vivid signal to anyone who might be watching for an Irish young woman. I'd prefer that we lose your followers."

Mrs. Denton pinned up her red hair, encased it in a bit of lace, and topped that with her own hat.

"There. I'll get you a proper mourning hat and veil while you are out."

Sherlock Holmes walked the hatted and silent Miss Tarleton out the rear exit and towards the British Museum. There were always cabs there. He found one suitable.

"Paddington Station," he told the driver.

Miss Tarleton began to open her mouth to speak, but Holmes laid his fingers upon his lips and she remained silent.

At the station they descended and he paid the driver, then he walked her along the rank of cabs until they stood before another cab. The driver greeted Holmes familiarly.

"Someone to follow today?" Blake asked.

"Could you lose followers?"

"If I see 'em, I'll lose 'em."

"Take us to this address," Holmes said handing Blake a small piece of paper, "without anyone following us there. And don't lose the paper."

Blake took the paper, read it, and stuffed it in his pocket. Holmes offered his hand to Miss Tarleton to assist her in climbing into the cab. She was silent as he had asked, but her eyes asked questions. He said nothing more. A part of him was grateful that she had maintained her composure despite the recent loss of her parents. She was a client, a piece in a puzzle, nothing more. The satchel of papers sat between them as they rode.

The driver took them on an interesting drive through some of the more dense traffic in metropolitan London before cutting through a mews and driving another mile, declaring "all clear" and turning toward the City. At last they arrived at the address in Old Jewry. Holmes asked the driver to wait.

Inside the building he led Miss Tarleton through hallways until they reached a clerk's desk.

"Mr Holmes, what can I do for you?" asked Mr Abraham's clerk, James Midwinter, standing and shaking Holmes' hand.

Holmes held out a note folded in half.

"We were hoping to see Mr Abrahams. My apologies for arriving without prior arrangement but it was necessary in the circumstances. Any correspondence ran the risk of being intercepted. This note will explain the matter to Mr Abrahams."

"I'll take it to him. He's with a client right now so there may be a bit of a wait. You may sit over there."

Fifteen minutes later they were ushered into Michael Abrahams' office.

"Welcome, Mr Holmes, it is good to see you after all this time. Miss Tarleton, have a seat."

Charlotte Tarleton gave a questioning glance at Holmes, who nodded.

"How do you know me name?" she asked.

"It was in Mr Holmes' note."

"Oh, I see."

"It is a very interesting note. Of course, I am familiar with the Tarleton cases. They both made quite a stir in legal circles in their time. The attempted fraud on creditors by a common recovery was enough of a public scandal—not that John Tarleton was known as a man of high scruples. He was a slave trader after all, when the tide of public opinion had turned against the trafficking in other humans.

"But the attempt to reclaim the estate over twenty years later was quite sensational, if unsuccessful. It is rare that Fleet Street follows these types of legal cases, but that one was discussed widely in the press. I am not sure many of the public quite understood what it was about.

"That's why we are here. Can you explain to us in layman's terms exact what these cases meant?"

Mr Abrahams consulted a fat legal tome which lay open upon his desk.

"On September 30, 1790 it all began with the settlement signed before the marriage of the first John Tarleton to Isabella Collingwood. His future father-in-law, Alexander Collingwood, who had only daughters, settled the Collingwood Estates upon John Tarleton in consideration of a marriage.

"Translated into simple terms that means once John Tarleton married Isabella, he had a full use of the estates during his life, then his wife could use the land during her life, and after she died it descended to the oldest living male born of their marriage, and then to his oldest son and so on. The father-in-law retained a remainder. If John and his wife Isabella died without having a son, then daughters would share the estate. If there were no daughters, the estate would revert to Alexander Collingwood and his heirs. While this marriage settlement was more complicated than some, settlements of this type are fairly common among landed gentry.

"Twenty-five years later John Tarleton was insolvent, on the verge of bankruptcy. His business partnership was falling apart and his partners were demanding large payments from him. Perhaps it was because his wealth was dependent upon the slave trade which had been outlawed in 1807, though that law was not strictly enforced until 1811, or perhaps it was due to overall bad financial management. In 1815, shortly after his eldest son, John Collingwood Tarleton, turned twenty-one years old, but before his creditors seized his assets, John Tarleton attempted to remove some of his property from the reach of his creditors by a legal manoeuvre called a "common recovery." The process is complex and requires the adult male heir's cooperation. We don't know precisely what the father told the son, but the Chancery court was later convinced that son was not aware of the father's debts or the impending bankruptcy.

"Just a few months later John Tarleton was declared bankrupt and the assignees of the bankruptcy estate filed the first case here, Hornby v. Tarleton, claiming that the recovery was an attempt to defraud them, which it obviously was. After a trial, the court declared that the recovery was void against creditors and the assignees could seize the property. The son, John Collingwood Tarleton, eventually made a deal with the assignees to reacquire some of the land.

"After John Tarleton and his wife died, John Collingwood Tarleton sold the remains of the estate to Thomas Liddell for a large sum of money. It is this sale that John Collingwood's son, Banistre Tarleton—great nephew of the famous Sir Banistre Tarleton who fought in the American War of Independence, and who was brother to the John Tarleton who went bankrupt—was challenging in the lawsuit cited in some courts as Tarleton v. Liddell and others as Tarleton v. Tarleton.

"The court ruled that the 'common recovery' had broken the fee tail and John Collingwood Tarleton's interest in the land had become a fee simple—the standard interest in real property, and he was the sole owner. Therefore, JCT's deed to Thomas Liddell was valid and his son Banistre had no legal interest in the land.

"That's where things stood in 1851," the solicitor concluded.

"Give him the papers, Miss Tarleton," Holmes said.

She presented the stack of water-stained and fire damaged papers.

"These papers add to the story," Holmes said. "We have attempted to organize them."

He separated out two portions of the stack.

"These are the copies of court rulings related to the story you just told us. I think it is safe to say they can be set aside."

"These, however, are copies of census records, marriage records, birth and death records, and related documents."

Michael Abrahams quickly scanned through the documents with the skill of an experienced solicitor and got the gist of it. He had paused, as Holmes had, over Liam Tarleton's half burnt note.

"This is your father's research?" Abrahams asked Miss Tarleton.

"Yes."

"Your father wrote this note?"

"Yes."

Holmes stood up and picked up two of the papers on the desk.

"This chart," he said holding one up, "shows the descendants of Alexander Collingwood up to the present day, and this one," he said holding up the other, "shows the descendants of John Tarleton. In the middle it shows his marriage to Isabella Collingwood in 1790 and their descendants, but on the left side there is another marriage 14 years earlier to Mary Ross and two offspring from that relationship, though one died early. If this is true, and this first marriage was valid, and the first wife was still alive in 1790, wouldn't the marriage to Isabella be bigamous?"

"Yes."

"What effect would that have on the marriage settlement?" Holmes asked.

"The marriage settlement was contingent on John Tarleton marrying Isabella Collingwood. If John Tarleton was married to another woman at the time, then the marriage to Isabella would be void and the marriage settlement would fail. The estate would revert to the heirs of Alexander Collingwood. In addition John Collingwood Tarleton and his siblings would be bastards and unable to inherit from their parents."

"If I may," Abrahams said, reaching for the paper Holmes was holding up.

"If that is true, all of his descendants on this side of the chart lose not only their rights under the settlement, but also by intestacy. They lose not only the Collingwood Estate, but any rights to inherit any other property John Tarleton owned in Lancashire and other places, which was also considerable. The Collingwood Estate would have gone to Isabella's sister Margaret and her descendants, which are listed on that other chart."

Miss Tarleton had been silently listening to the discussion but now she interrupted.

"Me great grandmother was Margaret Collingwood."

The solicitor and the detective turned to the client.

Abrahams said, "Could you repeat that, Miss Tarleton?"

"Me great grandmother was Margaret Collingwood. Here," she held out her hand for the Collingwood chart Holmes still held. He handed it to her, and sat down looking at her attentively.

"See here she is: Margaret Collingwood married Charles Michell and they had a son named John Michell who had four children one of whom is listed here as B. C. M. Harris, Brigid Collingwood Michell Harris. Me mother had a previous marriage to a man named Harris so she was known as Brigid Harris when my father met her. Her first husband died at sea. They 'ad no children. She 'ad been widowed for years before me parents met. Me father's first wife had also died."

"And your father was a Tarleton," Holmes said.

"Sure as me name is Charlotte Collingwood Tarleton. There he is: Liam Ross Tarleton on that chart."

Abrahams found L. R. Tarleton on the side branch on the Tarleton chart. He was the grandchild of John Tarleton and his first wife Mary Ross.

"Good heavens," Abrahams said.

"It seems your father hid your parent's names on the pedigree charts," Holmes pointed out.

"Unless someone knew what to look for. The fact that those are the only entries using solely initials on both charts makes it clear it was intentional," the solicitor added.

"You are descended from Alexander Collingwood through his daughter Margaret and from John Tarleton through his first wife," Holmes said.

"Clear paths of inheritance from both Alexander Collingwood and John Tarleton not tainted by bigamy or consanguinity," the solicitor said.

"Yes, her parents weren't blood relations at all."

"The two o' you are looking at me like me father used to when he was working on his research," Miss Tarleton said.

"That's because you are the missing piece of the puzzle!" Holmes said. "That's what he meant when he said that he was going to protect your rights. He didn't have any expectations of an inheritance down the Tarleton line since John Tarleton went bankrupt and there wasn't enough to satisfy his creditors even with the Collingwood Estate. His elder brother Thomas had sons. No inheritance would flow from the direction.

"However, if your father could prove both his grandmother's prior marriage to John Tarleton and your mother's descent from Alexander Collingwood, the Collingwood estate would revert to the Collingwood family, and your mother, and now you, would be due a piece of it."

"That's what this is all about? Me parents were murdered over some possibility of inheritance? Some treasure hunt?" Charlotte Tarleton cried standing up.

Her face was red. Her green eyes flashed with anger and welled with tears. Here was the reaction Holmes had feared for hours. He did not dismiss it as hysteria, but he didn't know what to do with it. Solicitor Abrahams, with decades of experience with clients in a variety of emotional situations, spoke softly and firmly.

"I am afraid it is, Miss Tarleton. Unfortunately, none of us can change what happened to your parents. Now that you understand what your father was working on, you could decide to take it no further and forget about it."

"However," Holmes broke in, "I do believe your life is in danger. That danger is not going to go away that easily."

Miss Tarleton sighed and sat down.

"I understand," Miss Tarleton said. "What do we need to do to make the danger go away?"

"We need to determine who feels threatened enough to take these drastic steps."

"No one on the Collingwood side stands to lose anything. In fact, if Miss Tarleton makes her case they might gain from it. The gain would certainly offset the necessity of sharing it with her."

"So it falls to the descendants of John Collingwood Tarleton."

"His family would have benefited from the sale."

"True but obviously some of them were not happy about it. His eldest son, Banistre, was only five when the suit was brought to reclaim his rights which had been extinguished. Another stood in his place as 'next friend.'"

"Perhaps it was the mother, John Collingwood Tarleton's wife, who was not happy."

"Jane Turnbull Tarleton," Abrahams read from the chart.

"She's dead," Miss Tarleton said. "My father had been trying to find her address for years, but letters kept being returned. After we arrived in London he found a Cheshire address and wrote to her about his research. She never responded but the letter was not returned. He recently wrote to her again requesting an audience. In response he received a notice that she had died last year."

"Interesting," Holmes said.

"Do you think her death is significant?" Abrahams asked.

"No, but those letters may be," Sherlock Holmes said. "Suppose some other member of the family found Liam's initial letter to Jane after her death and felt threatened by his research and tried to confront him?"

"They wouldn't have found him home. We were travelling," Miss Tarleton said.

"So perhaps this threat has been following you longer than you realized, perhaps since the date of Jane Tarleton's death."

"They have three surviving sons Banistre James, Thomas Owen, and Turner Allister Tarleton," Abrahams said. "That's three suspects."

"Do not discount the daughters," Holmes said.

"Do you think a woman could have done it?"

"Everyone who could have benefited by hiding this information must be considered," Holmes replied.

"That burnt note suggests that John Tarleton thought his family would not approve of the marriage to Mary Ross and tried to keep it hidden from them."

"If this had happened ten years ago without all the intervening legal actions, it might be a simple case," Abrahams said. "But it happened nearly a hundred years ago, witnesses are deceased, and written records weren't kept as consistently then. Even if all the records are found, counsel on both sides would argue why the obvious result should not happen. The case could stretch on for decades."

"A *Bleak House* type of case," Holmes suggested.

Abrahams chuckled.

"Charles Dickens was not fond of lawyers, but yes. The legal fees and expenses would be enormous. I wouldn't recommend that a person in Miss Tarleton's circumstances gamble on a positive outcome."

"This legal talk is giving me a headache," Charlotte Tarleton said.

Michael Abrahams chuckled.

"Sometimes it does that to me, too," he said.

"What would you recommend?" Miss Tarleton asked.

"If you were to secure that evidence, I would recommend sitting down with the other parties involved and coming to a private settlement instead, perhaps an allowance."

"And what of the death of my parents?" she said.

"If you find who killed them, turn that matter over to the police. I would also like to make another recommendation, if I may?"

"Go on," Miss Tarleton replied.

"I recommend that you allow my firm to store the majority of these papers for safekeeping. We have a safe on the premises."

"Mr Holmes?" she asked.

"I will need to retain a few. Otherwise it is excellent advice."

Holmes extracted the papers he needed and they rose to leave.

"One last question, Mr Abrahams: If you were a young man in 1776 and wanted desperately to get married—legally, you understand—without your family knowing, where would you go?" Holmes asked.

"The toll house at Coldstream Bridge," the solicitor responded without hesitation.

"Then that is our destination tomorrow," Holmes said.

A hat box sat upon the table when they returned to Montague Street. It contained a black hat and veil as Mrs Denton had promised. The remainder of the day was spent consulting Bradshaw and making other preparations for the journey. Holmes had made arrangements for Blake's cab to pick them up the next morning. Mrs Denton prepared them a basket for the long train ride, and Holmes once again asked Miss Tarleton to remain silent until they had gained the railway carriage.

"Y'donna even trust your cabby friend?"

"I trust he will help us evade followers. I know nothing of what prejudices he may have. Let's not test them."

It was cool and raining as they set out but the driver did his job of discarding any followers and they were not accosted at the station. Once the train was pulling away, Miss Tarleton rolled the veil up to the rim of the black hat.

"Is it safe to speak now?" she asked.

"Yes."

"Mr Holmes, if I understand correctly you think that John Tarleton and Mary Ross were married in Scotland?"

"Yes.

"That's why my father took us across the border to Scotland and then turned around and came back to England?"

"Yes. He was probably on the same mission as we are now: to get proof that they married. I am hoping he was successful, but whatever documentation he may have gotten was either destroyed in the fire or was stolen.

"My theory is that John and Mary Ross wished to marry," he continued, "but he did not think his mother or uncles would approve. His father had died a few years prior according to your father's records. John might have feared they would not release the funds due him under his father's will when he came of age. It is a long journey for a mere dalliance. It seems probable that he had sincere feelings for her at the time."

"Why would he go to Scotland to get married?"

"The Clandestine Marriage Act of 1753 required banns of matrimony to be published in the parish church or a registered public chapel for three Sundays preceding a wedding ceremony. The other option was to obtain a special license from the Archbishop of Canterbury. The law in Scotland did not require such formalities. The Act was repealed in 1849."

"Could she have been with child?"

He looked out at the passing landscape.

"It is possible," he said, and began unfolding some newspapers he had picked up at the station.

Miss Tarleton gazed out at the English countryside. She had seen a lot of it this way in the past year: rain soaked and sliding by. She dozed off.

As usual, Holmes read through the crime news first. Miss Tarleton's parents' murder had a small mention in the newspapers. They had taken the Fenian story from Scotland Yard, but two inches in the bottom of the fourth column was all they gave it. Holmes doubted the police would give it more attention than that. He had neglected to mention to Miss Tarleton that Inspector Lestrade would be very annoyed when he discovered they had left London.

It was raining in Scotland when they arrived there, too. Holmes asked Miss Tarleton to lower her veil as they departed the train at the railway station in the English village of Cornhill-on-Tweed. They crossed the Coldstream Bridge over the river Tweed and found the Toll House on the Scottish side. Holmes explained to the clerk in charge of the record books that Miss Tarleton's father had died recently and she needed some records to settle his estate.

"He came here last year looking for his grandfather's marriage records from 1776. You were kind enough to find them for him but now they are missing and we need another copy for the lawyers," Miss Tarleton said.

The clerk remembered her father and quickly found the record of the marriage of John Tarleton and Mary Ross of Liverpool. The date they were married was June 15th, 1776. The clerk wrote out a certified copy of the record and Holmes paid him to write out a second.

"One for the lawyers," he said, "and one for Miss Tarleton."

With the certificates tucked away in an inner pocket, they returned to the train station and bought tickets for the next train to Liverpool. Holmes sent a telegram to Michael Abrahams requesting that he send a confidential messenger to meet that train on arrival in Liverpool to take one copy of the certificate to London.

As Holmes was helping Miss Tarleton down from the train at Liverpool, someone approached, calling her by name. She looked up thinking this was the messenger from the solicitor. As Holmes looked at him he knew it was not, because he saw Frederic Abrahams, the solicitor's son, in the background. Holmes stepped between Miss Tarleton and the stranger with his hat pulled low, and demanded to know who he was. The man bolted. Holmes called Fred over and asked him to stay with Miss Tarleton. He ran in the direction the stranger had taken, but saw no sign of him.

"He escaped," he told Miss Tarleton and Fred Abrahams as he re-joined them. "Miss Tarleton, this is Fred Abrahams. You spoke with his father in London. Fred is also a solicitor. Fred, this is Miss Charlotte Tarleton, our client."

"How do you do, Miss Tarleton? Every time I meet Mr Holmes it seems to be an adventure."

"Well, I hope your journey back to London is less of one. I was surprised you came rather than a clerk."

"I was on Liverpool on business already. It made the most sense for me to accept the commission and take the document to London with the other documents in my possession."

"Here is a certified copy by the clerk at Coldstream Bridge Toll House of the marriage details in their record books. We are handing it over to the custody of your firm. I have a second copy."

"Very good. I accept the document and will deliver it to our safe. Hope to see you both in London soon. Good day, Miss Tarleton," he said tipping his hat to her.

Holmes and Abrahams shook hands and parted.

"That proves someone knows you are back in Liverpool. I don't know if they somehow intercepted a message to Fred Abrahams, or if it was just a coincidence that they tried to seize you here. I am going to recommend that you keep your veil down."

They found a pair of rooms at a quiet little hotel with a small tea room. As they sat down for tea, Charlotte Tarleton asked, "Why are we here, Mr Holmes?"

"There are two reasons," he replied. "There first is that the danger to you seems to originate here. We must find the source to extinguish it. It might have been safer to leave you somewhere else, but you know where you father went and what he did, and retracing his steps might give us a clue.

"The second rests in a series of unknowns that make me doubt that finances are the sole motivation. The murder of your parents was an extreme act unlike the usual methods of the wealthy in this century, whether that involves wealth of landed gentry or of the merchant classes.

"I have considered whether it was intended to defend the honour of John Tarleton and his descendants, but he was not an honourable man. Even putting aside his abandonment of your great grandmother, we must consider that his wealth was largely gained from the buying and selling of other human beings. He also seems to have cheated his business partners and tried to defraud his creditors. Bigamy and bastardy seem to be rather light garnishments on that pile of dishonour. Adding murder to the family achievements surely wouldn't redeem this family.

"Also it seems a harsh reaction to your father's letter. We don't know what was in that letter. Did it include details? Did it include a demand? The typical reaction to such a thing would be to appoint some intermediary to ask your father how much money he wanted to go away, not murder.

"I think that the person or persons behind this had their own particular reason for this harsh reaction. How had they known about it? We know from the burnt scrap that Mary Ross complained of being hidden somewhere before they moved to Killeigh. Where? Perhaps he brought her back to Lancashire in hopes of introducing her to his family and then something caused him to change his mind. You suggested she was already with child when they married. Perhaps so. Perhaps he thought it would be better to wait so he took Mary to Killeigh in Ireland."

"Your father's note suggests that he visited Mary and her sons until his namesake son died. Are those events related? It was also about that time that he became involved with the slave trade. Is that relevant or am I wandering too far afield?" Holmes said.

All this time, as he was answering her question, Holmes was speaking more to himself than to her. He now looked across the table at her. She was leaning over her teacup with her hands grasped around it. He saw tears dropping into the tea.

"I am sorry. When I am working out problems I forget that it is not just a puzzle or a mathematical problem; there are real people involved."

"I understand," she said. "I'm going to my room."

She stood up and walked out. As he stood and watched her walk up the stairs to her room, a young girl came to clear the table.

"Do you know where I could find a large map of Liverpool?" he asked her.

"They've some at the bookstore two doors down."

"I don't really want to leave her, even to go that far. If I gave you some silver would you go down and buy one for me, the biggest you can find. Also a book on local history and something like a city directory, a book that lists where people live, if they have something like that."

"Yes, sir. I'll just tell me mum," she said.

She ran back to tell the proprietress of the tea room where she was going. Holmes waited at the foot of the stairs that led up to the hotel rooms, which was where the tea room adjoined the hotel. The girl was back shortly with a large map and some books. He mounted the stairs to his own room next to Miss Tarleton's.

The room was small. It contained a tiny writing table that was far too small for the map so he spread it out upon the bed. Among the papers collected by Liam Tarleton that Holmes had retained were deeds to properties in the Liverpool area. He began reading their metes and bounds descriptions and comparing them to the map. When he found the location that seemed to match that on a deed he marked it in pencil on the map.

There was also a lease by a Tarleton to an Aigburth Hall in 1771. That must have been his father who died two years later. Then Thomas, his elder brother, and primary heir to his father's estate, purchased Aigburth Hall. There was a pencilled note on that deed: Demolished 1830s or 1840s.

Holmes lit his pipe and sat down with the local history books, thumbing through to the mid-18th century. He paused to read a section on local buildings with priest holes and other places that Roman Catholics hid during the 15th through 16th centuries, when failure give up their religious beliefs to conform to the Church of England was considered treason. People who did not conform were called recusants. Several of the owners of the properties Liam Tarleton had been interested in were known recusant sympathisers.

The Tarleton family was mentioned in the part of the history book that discussed the economic prosperity of area during the 17th and 18th centuries. He marked some places that might be of interest on the map. Then he compared the names of the living descendants of John Collingwood Tarleton to the names in the directory. Some were listed. Some were not. He also made note of the address of the *Liverpool Mercury* and the nearest livery stable.

He spent the rest of the night turning over in his mind all the possibilities. By morning he had a plan of investigations. He knew he could proceed faster without Miss Tarleton along. However, he did not feel it would be safe to leave her behind. She possessed memories of things her father said and did that might come forth as they visited some of the sites he had taken her to. Fortunately Holmes found her in better spirits in the morning. Over breakfast he explained the itinerary.

"I have arranged with the cook here to refill our basket. Sally, the girl who works here in the tea shop, was good enough to take a note over to the livery stable for me and they will be delivering a trap and pony for our use in about an hour."

"We are going to pay a visit to a local newspaper so I can make some enquiries. Then we shall visit some locations in and near the city proper before visiting the farming areas you mentioned. I am hoping that you will remember things your father said when he was giving his tour."

"I'll tell you anything that comes to mind."

The clouds had broken overnight and the sun peeked in and out of them. The air was still brisk, much cooler than expected for June. They dressed warmly with the thought in mind that the rain might return in the afternoon. The trap arrived on schedule and Holmes loaded the basket and some blankets.

The *Liverpool Mercury* wasn't far. Inside the newspaper office he was able to review a copy of Jane Tarleton's obituary. It listed the current residences of her surviving relatives. It mentioned that two of her daughters, Margaret and Mabel Rose, had been living with her at the time of her death. Her married daughter Isabella and her husband had come to town for the service, as had her children living in other counties. It mentioned that Turner and Thomas resided locally which he had also discovered from the directory.

Holmes enquired whether they had a person who wrote a society column and was directed to a small plump woman with silver hairs escaping the bun on the top of her head. She had small, round spectacles perched on her nose. She was quite a contrast to Langdale Pike's flamboyant personality.

"Miss Richmond, I have been told you are local authority on society."

"Is that a polite way of saying I'm in on all the natter?"

"You are familiar with the Tarleton family?"

"Yes."

"Are any of them expected to receive any honours soon?"

"Not that I'm aware."

"My understanding is that most of their current holdings are in real estate?"

"Most, but not all. They've some involvement in cotton an' sugar trades still."

"Have they purchased or sold any property recently?"

"Not that I've heard."

"Have any engagements been announced recently?"

"No. However—"

"Yes?"

"Stanley Walker has been after Mabel Rose for ages. While her mum was poorly she wouldn't consider it. Folks reckon that after a proper mourning period they might announce, unless Mabel Rose thinks of another excuse."

"Do you think that she will continue to hold him off?"

"I'm not a fortune teller."

Sherlock Holmes smiled.

"Why d'ya wanna know all this, eh?"

"That, I'm afraid, is confidential."

Miss Richmond scowled at him.

The first few places he drove Miss Tarleton prompted no reaction from her. Then he drove her to a large whitewash mansion out in the country.

He pulled the trap up to the edge of the road.

"We were here," she said.

Holmes turned to a section in one of the history books.

"The original Aigburth Hall was abandoned for a hundred years before John Tarleton Senior became obsessed with restoring 'the family homestead.' He leased it and his son Thomas bought it after his death and tried to restore it, but the condition was too poor and he sold it again. The next owner demolished it and built a new one," he read. "That's the one you see there."

"So the John Tarletons never lived there?" she asked.

"From what I have read, Thomas might have lived there a short time. They weren't really country folk. John Senior had a large house on Water Street in Liverpool. That's where his sons were born and grew up. Thomas lived there for a while after senior died. Then he sold it and it was converted to an inn and then a bank. John Junior and Clayton lived on Duke Street. Clayton died young and then John moved to a big house on Finch Street."

"They're all gone now," said an old man walking with a dog.

"Are you the local historian?" Holmes asked.

"Oh, more likely the collector of local bits and bobs," he said with a laugh. "When I was a nipper, the Tarletons were a focus of much talk."

"You aren't a Tarleton yourself, are you?" Holmes asked

"Oh, no relation. I live down the street."

"Miss Tarleton here is from the Irish branch of the family. Her father was very interested in the English branches of the Tarletons. He died recently and she came over to see where they lived to honour him."

"That's a nice thing to do. There are still some Tarletons about, but I doubt any of them live in any manor houses. The city directory might help you find them. There are some proper old buildings around here that you don't wanna miss if you are interested in the history. Over there's what's left of the Monks' Grange," he said pointing behind them. "They reckon it's over 400 years old. It used to be part of a farm belonging to the abbey what was across the Mersey before the dissolution of the monasteries. If ya head down to the waterfront, ya can still spot the ruins of the old abbey over there. They had fields n' pastures all over this area."

As they turned the direction the man indicated, Miss Tarleton grabbed Holmes' arm. He looked at her.

"Perhaps we will," Holmes said to the man and bid him good day.

Dark grey clouds were assembling as Holmes and Miss Tarleton walked toward the Monks' Grange buildings.

"We were here. Me father was very interested in the Grange," she said.

"The burnt note also makes reference to a 'monk's cellar,'" Holmes said. "It could be here or at the abbey that man mentioned."

They stood for a moment looking at the buildings making up the grange complex. At the centre was a cottage with a massive oak door held together with oak pegs. The walls were red sandstone stacked and cemented with red clay. A mullioned window to the left allowed light in. The roof was thatched and in need of rethatching. Barns sat on either side of the cottage. An open cart-way ran through one of the barns. The ceiling of that passage was formed of saplings covered over with a mixture of red clay and straw. Farm implements lay around the yard suggesting it was still part of a working farm. No one seemed to be about and there was no fence encircling it. They walked up to the cottage.

"What was your father interested in here?" Holmes asked.

"He was looking for something. 'E kept tapping the walls an' stamping his foot."

"He thought the 'monk's cellar' was here?" Holmes asked.

"I suppose."

"Perhaps after the monks were expelled from the abbey some of them remained here at the Grange incognito, tended the farms, and held secret masses."

Thunder rumbled.

Holmes pulled out a tape measure. With Miss Tarleton's assistance he measured the length, height, and depth of the buildings. A flash of lightning tore through the air not far away. As rain began to fall they pulled open the door of the cottage.

Inside there was no furniture but stacks of crates and tools. The earthen floor was hard-packed and covered with straw. Above they could see that the beams of the roof were not made of sawed lumber, but cruck arches like those in the passage way, looking much like the natural branches of a tree. The interior was broken into rooms with walls that looked newer than the exterior, but were not really new at all. Holmes measured the rooms in that building.

"We are missing about four feet."

"Where?" she asked.

"Here."

In one of the rooms there was a part of the wall that extended out from the rest. There was a stone fireplace in the middle of that section. Most would assume that was space for the fire box. Holmes bent down and looked up the chimney.

"There is no chimney for this fireplace. It is false."

Holmes began feeling about the stones. He pushed them and pulled them but nothing happened. He did the same to the bricks along the bottom. When he pulled on one he heard a loud click and the corner of the wall extension opened. He grabbed it and pulled it the rest of the way. Another lightning stroke lit the inside as he did so. There was a staircase leading down.

"He was right," Miss Tarleton said.

"He was indeed," Holmes said.

Holmes lit a match and started down. Miss Tarleton was right behind him. Then he stopped.

"What's wrong?"

"I thought I heard something,"

"Maybe it was the wind," she said.

"Perhaps."

Then an unseen hand pushed against Miss Tarleton's back and

she tumbled against Holmes. He extended his arms against the walls of the staircase to keep them from falling but he dropped the match in the process. The light from the opening above disappeared with a click.

"Squeeze past me," he whispered to her and she did.

Holmes felt his way to where the opening had been. He could feel no crack at all. He tried to dig into it with his fingertips to no avail. He turned around and descended the steps to where Miss Tarleton still stood. He lit another match and told her to continue down.

At the bottom of the staircase there was a doorway that opened into another room. It was as long as several of the rooms upstairs combined. At the far end stood an altar. In the space between were crude wooden benches. Some had rotted through. He made his way to the altar and found an old stub of a beeswax candle. He lit it before the match went out. With the feeble light he explored the room. The remains of straw was scattered on the ground. In an alcove to the right was a makeshift crib. Under it were boxes and empty bags. He looked through them and under them. In a corner of the floor under them he found a child's rattle and a piece of blanket.

"A child was here," he said.

"I smell smoke," she said.

He sniffed the air.

"Very wet smoke. Perhaps he tried to start a fire and the rain put it out."

"He?"

"Your follower," Holmes replied.

Holmes turned his attention to the altar. There was debris scattered on and around it. There seemed to be the remains of an altar cloth, too. On the right side it looked as if the altar cloth was caught under the altar. He bent down to examine it and discovered it was true. He also found corresponding semi-circular scrapes in the debris on the floor, partially obscured, but still visible if you were looking for them. He pushed on the altar and it swung around to reveal another staircase.

They descended into an earthen tunnel. It curved around and they followed. At one point they encountered loose dirt on the floor that had fallen from the ceiling. They stepped over it. They continued on but saw no light ahead. At last they found themselves up against a wooden door. Air was coming through the desiccated slats in the door and blew the candle stub out. Holmes leaned against the old wood in the middle of the door and it splintered and gave way. Dim light from the cloudy sky filtered through. There were stacks of crates in front of the door. Holmes helped Miss Tarleton through the hole in the door and then they squeezed past the crates. They found themselves outside in a far corner of the Grange lot. As they walked toward the corner of the building, a bullet whizzed past them.

"Down," he whispered. "Stay behind me."

Holmes had the Colt .45 in his hand. It had been in his coat pocket since they had left London. He looked around the edge of the building again and another bullet flew. He saw the shooter this time, or at least a hat—the same he had seen at the railway station—a coat and some trousers protruding from the front of the middle building for a moment. He aimed and fired. There was a yelp and the figure hobbled off. The hat fell as it did. It was clearly a man, a man small in stature, and perhaps now with a bit of a limp. Holmes signalled to Miss Tarleton to follow him.

The rain had stopped. They walked across the Monks' Grange yard. Holmes picked up the hat. They went back to where they had left the pony and the trap in front of the new Aigburth Hall. Holmes was surprised that the horse had not bolted with the thunder and the gun fire. Miss Tarleton was shivering. He had her climb up into the trap and wrapped a blanket around her. He urged her to eat something from the basket. He took another of the blankets and rubbed the pony down. Then he climbed up and turned the horse towards Liverpool.

After they were back at the hotel and Miss Tarleton had consumed a cup of tea and retired to her room, Holmes examined the hat. It was a fairly ordinary, well-used black felt hat with a little bit of a feather in its band. It was small in size. Its owner was not well-to-do, but tried to make an appearance of being so, or at least of having prospects. Most of its wear was from over-brushing. He asked the hotel clerk to send a telegram he wrote to Miss Mabel Rose Tarleton in Cheshire asking if they could call on her the following afternoon. She acquiesced by return telegram.

The following day Miss Charlotte Tarleton seemed to have overcome the reaction to the ordeal at the Monks' Grange, whether it had been due to the weather or being shot at. They drove to Cheshire where Mabel Rose Tarleton greeted them cordially. Holmes asked her directly if she had seen the letters Liam Tarleton had written to her mother.

"I did. I found the first letter going through me mum's things. I showed it to me friend, Stanley Walker. He thought it was a bit dodgy. Me sister Margaret weren't keen on it either. I reckon we should've discussed it with our brothers, but we didn't. We decided just to ignore it.

"Then another letter came after mum died sayin' he was comin' here to Cheshire. We were proper worried. I thought we should show the letters to the police, but Stanley weren't keen on them prying about our business. He said it'd be a right scandal. Margaret said we should just tell him she had passed, and maybe he would go away. That's what we did. We heard nowt more."

"Does Stanley have some possibility of an inheritance?" Holmes asked.

"Why, yes. He has an elderly aunt who has a substantial sum that will be divided between himself and a cousin."

"Is that aunt of a rather conservative bent?"

"Oh, yes. She's all proper-like. He's always saying that any time he and Robert—that's his cousin, Robert—got into any bother she'd go on about leavin' her money to her dog. Recently she has been giving him the nudge to marry, settle down, and start a family."

"Has he proposed to you?" Holmes asked.

"Numerous times!" Mabel Rose cried. "I proper love Stanley. He makes me laugh. But I couldn't leave Mum when she was so poorly, could I? And if I did Margaret'd be all alone! Stanley says Margaret doesn't like him."

Just then another woman entered the door attempting to keep the rain out. It was immediately clear she and Mabel Rose were sisters.

"I don't dislike him. I don't trust him. Who've we got here, Mabel Rose?"

"Would you believe it? She's another Tarleton from Ireland. Meet Charlotte Tarleton. My sister, Margaret."

"Oh, how interesting!" Margaret said.

"Pleased to meet you," Charlotte said.

"An' this is Mr Sherlock Holmes. He's a detective from London helping Charlotte. May I call you Charlotte? It would seem silly to call you Miss Tarleton since we're all Miss Tarleton!"

"What have you been detecting, Mr Holmes?" Margaret asked.

"I hope that will be clear in a moment," he replied.

"Has Stanley been out of town recently?" Holmes asked.

"He said he had to go up to London to take care of business. He's been taking a few business trips recently. Why?" Mabel Rose said.

"Do you recognize this hat?" Holmes asked

"That's Stanley's hat. I gave him that feather," Mabel Rose said.

"Unfortunately, this hat was dropped by a man who was shooting at Miss Charlotte and myself yesterday afternoon."

"Oh, no. How could he do such a thing!" Mabel Rose exclaimed.

"I believe he was trying to stop our investigation," Holmes said.

"What's the investigation about then?" Margaret asked.

"The murder of my parents two days ago!" Charlotte exclaimed.

"Oh, dear, you poor thing!" Margaret said "This is proper grim. I think we need a pot of tea to settle our nerves," and she bustled off to the kitchen.

"Mr Holmes, do you reckon Stanley did that as well?" Mabel Rose asked.

"I think he or his cousin or both of them together did it."

"Why?"

Before Holmes could answer, the front door flung open and a man with straw-coloured hair stepped in brandishing a gun. Holmes leaped in front of Miss Charlotte and Miss Mabel Rose and was holding his own gun.

"Get out of me way!" the man yelled.

"Stanley! Stop that!" Mabel Rose cried.

"No, Mabel Rose, she is an Irish fiend! Her and her dad were wreckin' all me plans I've been workin' on for ages!" Stanley cried.

From where he was standing Holmes could see something that

neither Stanley in front of him, nor Charlotte and Mabel Rose behind him, could. Out of the corner of his eye he observed Margaret Tarleton come quietly to the doorway from the kitchen to see what was going on. Slowly she began creeping up behind Stanley. Holmes was careful to keep his eyes directly on Stanley so as not to expose her.

"You read Liam's letters. You understood them better than the ladies," Holmes said.

"Mabel Rose didn't understand at all," Stanley said. "If that man's research was made public it could result in a huge financial loss to her and her sisters and brothers. There would be a public scandal. Robert said that if I didn't stop him, then I couldn't marry Mabel Rose or auntie would disinherit me."

"Why?" Mabel Rose asked.

"Liam Tarleton was me father," Charlotte said. "He discovered that your grandfather married my great grandmother before he married your grandmother."

"You have proof of this?" Mabel Rose asked.

"Yes," Holmes said.

"Her father was trying to ruin you!" Stanley said.

"'E wasn't thinking of it in that way. He kept saying he was doing it for me," Charlotte said, defending her father.

"How would you benefit?" Mabel Rose asked.

"She is also descended from Margaret Collingwood," Holmes said.

"I don't care about any of that," Charlotte said. "I just wanted to find who killed my parents."

"He is standing right there," Holmes said. "Mabel Rose identified the hat. You can also see the blood on his trousers where my bullet creased him yesterday. You can't get out of this, Stanley. You need to put the gun down."

Margaret Tarleton had picked up a large vase and lifted it high. At that moment she slammed it down on his head. Stanley fell to the floor and dropped the gun. Holmes picked it up as he put his own away as well.

"Goodness!" Mabel Rose cried.

"I've never been keen on that vase," Margaret said.

"The sad thing is that his cousin, Robert, probably goaded him into this so he could get all of their aunt's inheritance," Holmes said, as he tied Stanley's hands with a sash cord. Margaret dashed next door to ask a neighbour to go the constabulary and have them send someone out. Once the local police had taken statements and hauled Stanley off to the station house, Margaret went back to making tea. Mabel Rose helped her bring the tea and biscuits to the sitting room.

"Charlotte," Margaret began as she poured the tea, "Mabel Rose and I have talked about it and we would like to invite you to visit as long as you like. It won't be exciting."

"First time either of us has seen a gun, let alone two!" Mabel Rose said.

"It won't be glamorous. We lead a right quiet life. We have a little money our mum left us. Our brothers sort the rest. We'll share what we have. We also have lost someone not long back, same as you, and we can share those losses and make the burden lighter."

"We are family," Mabel Rose said giving Charlotte a hug.

"I think that is a lovely idea. Thank you," Charlotte Tarleton said.

Sherlock Holmes took the next train back to London and slept the whole way.

292

Chapter 15

The Wine Merchant

"I dabble with poisons a good deal.
Sherlock Holmes, *A Study in Scarlet*

On July 26, 1879, Bart's summer session ended. The results of Sherlock Holmes' experiments on the corrosion of the various metals had not been as illuminating as he had hoped, in part due to the limited number of weeks he had to access to Bart's laboratories in December and January. Even the continuation in the jars in his bedroom had yielded less information than he expected. Therefore he applied to Dr Russell to repeat them over the longer break in August and September. As he was hoping clients would bring him problems to solve, he limited his time at the chemistry lab to a few hours in the morning and spent the rest of the day in his rooms.

As Holmes entered the rooms at Montague Street one afternoon in early September, he met Mrs Denton with the tea tray.

"Well, as you have returned, then perhaps this won't go to waste," she said setting it down on the table. "A man was here for a bit," Mrs Denton continued. "He left his card."

Holmes picked up the card from the table.

William Gazey
Wine & Spirit Merchant

The Wine Vault
5, Parson Street, Banbury, Oxfordshire

What mystery could a wine merchant be bringing to him?
He turned the card over. There was nothing written on the back.

"He's a ways from home. Did he say when he was coming back?" he asked.

293

"Not to me, he didn't. I asked if he would like tea. He said yes, but when I returned with the tea things he was gone."

"What did he look like?" Holmes asked.

"He was short, stout, bald man with a sallow face."

Holmes remained in his rooms the rest of the day but the Banbury wine merchant did not return. When Mrs Denton offered him supper he declined and satisfied himself with his pipe. Shortly thereafter she told him she was leaving for the day.

At quarter past seven there was a knock at the door and he thought perhaps his visitor had finally returned. He opened the door expecting a repentant, prospective client and instead found the little ferret-faced detective, Inspector Lestrade, to their mutual surprise.

"Well, well," the Scotland Yard detective said. "What are you doing here?"

"I live here," Holmes said.

"That's an interesting development."

"Come in and tell me about it," Holmes said, hoping to exchange the mystery of the delinquent client for something more stimulating.

Inspector Lestrade entered and took the seat offered.

"It's like this, Mr Holmes: Someone reported finding a dead body in the British Museum. I went to the scene and I found a slip of paper in the man's pocket with this address on it."

"What part?" Holmes asked.

"What part of what?"

"The museum."

"What difference does it make?" the inspector asked.

"It may mean nothing or it may make all the difference."

"Where they had some things about Queen Elizabeth and some mad astrologer friend of hers."

"John Dee?"

"That was the name."

"Was the scene disturbed?"

"Not that I noticed."

Nor would you if a herd of elephants have been driven through it, Holmes thought to himself.

"Who was it?" he asked.

"Eh?" Lestrade said, clearly lost by the divergence in the conversation.

"The corpse," Holmes said.

"Oh. He had no identification on him. Hey, I'm asking the questions here. Why would a dead man have your address in his pocket?"

"Any number of people may have my address in their pocket at any time," Holmes said. "I run advertisements for my services in the daily papers."

"Has anyone recently come requesting your services?"

"Perhaps," Holmes said.

"What does that mean?" Lestrade asked suspiciously.

"A man called here this morning while I was out and left his card, but he was gone when I returned," he said, producing the card from his waistcoat pocket. "So I don't know if he needed my services or hoped to sell me a case of champagne."

Inspector Lestrade examined the card.

"You'd never met the man before?"

"Nor yet. Was he a short, stout, bald man with a sallow face?"

"How would you know that if you never met him?" Lestrade asked squinting at Sherlock Holmes.

"My housekeeper spoke to him. She told me."

"Then I will need to speak to her."

"She won't be back until tomorrow."

"Then I suppose I shall have to interview her tomorrow."

"How did he die?" Holmes asked.

"We don't know that yet. There were no marks on him. The police surgeon is taking a look at the body now over at Bart's. Since I can learn nothing more from you, I'd best be going."

As the door closed Holmes grabbed his hat and coat. Lestrade had no sooner cleared the street than Holmes was out the back way. Holmes had been torn between going to the museum to look over the undoubtedly trampled scene or to Bart's to examine the body that had been removed, but a glance at his watch told him the museum was closing soon.

It didn't take long to find a member of the staff who could lead him to where the body had been found. There was nothing to be seen now if there ever had been. Too many people had come and gone since the body had been found.

"Not had any corpses before in my time here. I suppose that will add to our ghost collection."

Holmes raised his eyebrows.

"You have ghosts in the museum?" he asked.

"So people say. Not seen one myself."

"Do you know what he was looking for?" Holmes asked.

"This here," the man said pointed to a few discs and some pamphlets related to the notorious alchemist and spiritualist who had been an adviser to Queen Elizabeth.

"He wanted to know if we had anything on John Dee. I showed him, then left him alone, and next time I comes by there he was on the floor. My understanding is that Dee believed in spirits and was always trying to talk to them. So I guess he came here to converse."

Holmes sighed, thanked the man, and left. Outside the museum he hailed a cab.

"St Bartholomew's Hospital," he told the driver.

He headed directly towards the post-mortem room. On the way he encountered Stamford.

"Have you seen a police surgeon this afternoon?" Holmes asked.

"One just left," Stamford said.

"Do you know what he found?"

"No, I was not present when he examined the body."

"Is it still here?"

"I presume so," Stamford said.

"Can I see it? It is probably labelled as a John Doe, though I suspect he is a man named William Gazey."

"A friend of yours?"

"Not precisely. He stopped by my rooms this morning while I was out and then left and died somewhere else before I had an opportunity to speak to him. It makes me rather curious as to how he died."

As Stamford walked to the post-mortem room with Holmes, he wondered about this man. He had been in his teens when he had first met Sherlock Holmes, who was then a student at Cambridge. He had seemed highly intelligent and diligent in his chemistry studies at Bart's that summer. They spoke occasionally, though Stamford would not say they were friends. Since Holmes had reappeared at Bart's a few months ago he seemed far more eccentric. Initially he had expressed a desire to use the chemistry laboratory for some experiments related to the corrosion of metals, but while he was doing those experiments he had convinced Stamford to permit him to experiment on a fresh corpse. Now he wanted to look at another body that the police were obviously interested in. Curious.

The new corpse that Stamford showed to Holmes was indeed short, stout, bald, and rather jaundiced. The eyelids were slightly open and yellow in the eyes was also visible. Holmes ran his hands over the body. *Rigor mortis* was fairly well along. The abdomen was also swollen and hard. There was swelling in the arms and legs.

"No discolouration about the lips or in the mouth. Do you think the police surgeon plans to do a full post-mortem examination?"

"Usually only if the police or the coroner requests it."

"Yes. Do you think anyone would mind if I draw off a bit of blood?"

"I don't see why. He's obviously not using it."

Holmes found a syringe and drew some from the lower extremities where the blood was already pooling. He transferred it to a vial which he placed in his pocket.

Stamford started to ask what Holmes intended to do with the blood, but he stopped himself. Did he really want to know?

Back at the chemistry lab where he had metals corroding in sealed containers, Holmes began to set up another space to work. He set up test-tubes, retorts, Bunsen burners, and other equipment. In a new section of his notebook he recorded his observations of the corpse. No obvious trauma. No signs of strangulation. No needle marks before the one he just created. He pulled from the laboratory library several books on poisons, and began to test the blood he extracted. The blood showed no signs of the typical poisons. He detected no alcohol in the blood. The oddest result was that he could detect no albumin at all. That was only likely if the liver had ceased to function some time before death.

Was he poisoned before he appeared at Montague Street? The only potential sign of poisoning that Mrs Denton reported was that he looked "sallow." If he had felt ill or he had eaten before why would he accept Mrs Denton's offer of tea? If he had gone out to eat why not tell her so?

Holmes stared at his metal-on-metal experiments where he was trying to determine if metal corrosion could be used to create a delayed reaction. There were some poisons that killed by a delayed reaction. The victim recovers from an initial bout of indigestion only to die days later of liver failure. He did find signs of liver failure, which was consistent with the jaundice. Liver failure could also be the result of habitual over indulgence of alcohol by the wine merchant.

Had the man who appeared in his rooms left to die of natural causes, excessive consumption of alcohol, or poisoning?

He did not know. He also did not know whether the man's death was at all related to his appearance at his rooms, and the not knowing was annoying.

However, since he had no clue as to the man's activities in London before he appeared in Montague Street his investigation must move to Banbury. Dawn was breaking as he came to this conclusion.

Holmes wrote a telegram to Inspector Lestrade telling him that the police surgeon needed to check for liver damage, and look at the contents of the stomach and intestines for poisonous substances, if he had not already. After dropping it at the post office, he took the train to Banbury.

When he arrived there he sought out the Wine Vault which had been listed on William Gazey's card as his place of business. The sign was prominently displayed and the wide door opened to revealed barrels and crates and men moving merchandise. A small young man with abundance of curly, chestnut-coloured hair and a narrow nose that supported a pair of round spectacles asked if he could assist.

"I understand that this is Mr William Gazey's place of business."

"It is indeed, sir. I am afraid he isn't in today. I am his business partner and I assure you I can handle matters for him."

"An equal partner?" Holmes asked.

"Junior partner. Three years now with expectations."

"Your name?"

"Martin Ellington Potts, at your service, sir."

"Well, Mr Potts, if your expectations included Mr Gazey's return, I have some unfortunate news for you."

"News? What news?"

"Mr Gazey was found dead in the British Museum in London yesterday."

Mr Potts was very agitated by the news.

"Dead? In the museum? In London?" Mr Potts sputtered.

"Had he told you he intended to visit London?"

"No. Nothing of the sort. He had been a bit secretive recently. If he had been a married man I would have thought he was sneaking out on his wife."

"He wasn't married?"

"No."

"Could he have been involved with a woman?"

"I don't know. I can hardly believe this. What was he doing in London?"

"I was hoping you could tell me about that. He stopped by my rooms while I was out," Holmes said, "and next I heard of him a police inspector was tell me he was dead."

"Did you know him?"

"No, but in my business many strangers come to consult me."

"What is your business?"

"I am a detective."

"Why would he consult a detective?"

"That is what I am attempting to discover."

"How did he die?"

"I believe he was poisoned. I am not certain the police have made up their minds about it yet."

"Poisoned?"

"If you could direct me to Mr Gazey's home address, I would like to make enquiries there."

Potts gave him the address and Holmes left. At Gazey's home address he found the housekeeper, Mrs Kenric, in possession. She was very disturbed by the news and called it out to the cook, who joined in the mourning.

"Your master was a kind man?"

"Indeed, sir. Indeed."

"Did you know he intended to go to London?"

"No, sir."

"But you know he would be gone?"

"He was often gone, sir. He travelled a lot for business. It was more like he would tell me when he would be here."

"He had not?"

"No, sir."

"Did you have any idea where he was?"

"No, sir. Nothing unusual about that."

"Do you have any idea why he would consult a detective?"

"None, sir."

"Would anyone would have wished him harm?"

"Oh, no, sir!"

"He was not married?"

"No, sir."

"Any prospects?" Holmes asked.

"No. He was always so busy with his work."

"Had he been acting oddly recently?"

Mrs Kenric hesitated.

"Not, exactly him that's been acting odd, but it did trouble him, sir."

"What?"

"He received a letter from Mr Matthew Piers Ashwell some days back wanting to consult him about stocking a wine cellar, collecting wines."

"Is that unusual?"

"To come to the house rather than his business, yes, and who it came from. Might not mean anything to folks in London, but Mr Ashwell's the richest man in Oxfordshire."

"I've heard the name."

"He's something of a recluse. Has a wife, his second, and a flock of young'ens but they are the only ones who see him. Doesn't entertain or socialize. He's free enough with his charity, but I've heard that even when folks want to honour him for it, he doesn't show up to accept. Why now the interest in collecting wines? At least that's what Mr Gazey was saying. Not that he was going to turn down the opportunity. No, sir. The man has plenty of money. His father became rich on steam engines and factories. After his father died, he sold the business and purchased real estate and now he owns most of the land around Great Tew, including the quarry and most of the farms. Mr Gazey'd take his money, sure enow."

"Did Mr Gazey meet with Mr Ashwell?"

"I believe he did. He sent back a letter and another came. That's the last I've heard of it. But Mr Gazey became very close about it. That's not like him. A garrulous sort he is, or was."

"Did Mr Gazey drink at home?"

"No, sir, he was not much of a drinker in private. He had an appreciation of good wine and spirits like an art dealer appreciates paintings. It was business."

"Has the cook served mushrooms recently?"

"No, sir."

Sherlock Holmes walked back to the Wine Vault.

"Mr Potts. Did Mr Gazey tell you he was consulting with Mr Ashwell about collecting wines?"

"This is the first I have heard of it. However—"

"Yes?"

"I noticed in the ledger that Mr Gazey withdrew a case," Mr Potts began thumbing through the ledger, "from stock on September 2nd for his personal use." He looked up at Holmes. "It was a very expensive vintage."

"Did he often withdraw wine from inventory for personal use?"

"Never. Sometimes he withdrew a bottle as a gift to a client. This is different."

"Is there a livery stable close by?"

"Behind the White Lion Inn on High Street."

"Thank you."

At the stables Holmes hired a horse and carriage and obtained directions to the manor house at Great Tew. As he was about to mount the carriage, a hand grasped his shoulder from behind. He turned to see it was the ferret-faced Inspector Lestrade.

"There you are, Mr Holmes. I received your wire. I also spoke to your housekeeper. When she told me that you had not been in since she arrived this morning, I suspected you had come to Banbury. How did you know he was poisoned?

"Because he was not killed any other way."

"How did you know that?" Inspector Lestrade asked.

"I examined the body at Bart's—"

"Interfering with police business—"

"After the police surgeon, Inspector. I tested some blood I drew off. I tested it for some poisons and found none. There was no alcohol in his blood either. There were signs of severe liver damage which could also be a sign of poison. The only way to be certain was to examine the digestive tract. I left that to you and the police surgeon and came here to investigate why he had come to see me."

"Once more interfering with police business. I encountered reports of you questioning witnesses all over Banbury."

"There was no interference. I gave you everything I had."

"Be that as it may, you were right. The police surgeon found the liver to be severely atrophied. He said that combined with the jaundice and swelling, his opinion was the man died of liver failure. He found nothing in his stomach. In his intestines were the remains of some mushrooms. However, he stated they would have been eaten about a day before."

"If you wish to come along, Inspector, I will share what else I have found."

"Where are you off to?"

"Just an eight-mile ride to Great Tew, to call upon the illustrious inventor, Mr Matthew Piers Ashwell."

"What has he to do with all of this?"

"That is what is we are about to discover."

Inspector Lestrade scowled but hopped on.

They were soon out of Banbury and heading into the countryside. It was an easy drive amidst a picturesque landscape.

"Now explain to me about the poison," Lestrade said.

Sherlock Holmes inhaled and exhaled. He knew he was dealing with someone with no scientific training, much like most of his clients.

"As you saw yourself, Inspector, there was no obvious cause of death visible on the body," Holmes said.

"True."

"There were no signs of vomiting at the place where he was found."

"Correct."

"He could have died of natural causes, but he had gone to visit a detective the same morning before. Seems a strange coincidence."

"I agree that it seems like more than a coincidence," Inspector Lestrade said.

"I tested the blood I drew from the body and found no sign of any of the usual poisons. That suggested the possibility that, either he was not poisoned, or he was not poisoned in London. There are some poisons which cause an initial period of indigestion from which the victim seems to recover. However, what the victim does not realize is that the poison has destroyed his liver which will result in his death days later. I found indications in the blood of liver damage."

"So how did you know he was not a tippler and that didn't kill him?"

"I did not. I also did not know that he had not died of natural causes. Many things can cause liver damage," Holmes said. "From his housekeeper I learned that he did not drink at home, only if necessary in his work. I also learned from her that he recently began consulting with Mr Matthew Piers Ashwell, and from his business partner that he had withdrawn a case of wine from the company stock four days ago. Therefore, our enquiry draws us to Great Tew Manor House."

They were approaching the village of Great Tew. It was a pleasing cluster of ironstone cottages with thatched roofs on the north facing slope of the valley. Passing by the village they came to a large park which surrounded the manor house. The house itself seemed a mixture of ages and styles, some original and some revival. It was, like the village, built primarily of the local ironstone.

When they presented themselves at the manor house, a servant enquired and then directed them to the library. It was a large and exquisite library of a gothic revival style, housing perhaps thousands of volumes. Before them was the man himself, tall, and gaunt, with large eyes and a shy smile. He had just touch of grey to suggest his sixty years. He was well-dressed but not stylishly so. He sat before a desk littered with lenses, mechanical parts, blueprints, and schematics. He rose as they entered. The servant introduced them.

"Inspector Lestrade and Mr Sherlock Holmes."

"Have a seat, gentlemen. How can I help you?" Mr Matthew Piers Ashwell asked.

"Are you acquainted with Mr William Gazey?" Lestrade asked.

"Yes, I am."

Holmes wandered around the room examining books, scrolls, and bound papers as the inspector questioned Mr Ashwell. Ashwell glanced at him occasionally but made no comment.

"When was the last time you saw him?" Inspector Lestrade asked.

"Two days ago. September 4th."

"He was found dead in London yesterday," Lestrade said.

"Oh, dear."

Holmes turned from the shelves he was examining and looked directly at Mr Ashwell.

"In the British Museum," Holmes said, "next to some artefacts of John Dee."

Ashwell blanched.

"An odd coincidence. I have some of John Dee's papers here in my library that I showed to Mr Gazey not long ago."

"Did he tell you he was going to London?" Lestrade asked.

"Oh, no. I knew nothing of his plans. We weren't really intimate. I was consulting with him because I was considering starting a wine collection and knew he was an expert in such things. You see, there are substantial underground vaults on the property, under the house and beyond. I thought it would be an excellent place for the purpose."

"And perhaps to grow mushrooms?" Holmes asked.

"Why yes. I have started growing mushrooms down there as well. I showed Mr Gazey the mushrooms and some of my other collections and projects."

"What kind of mushrooms?" Lestrade asked.

"A variety. I shouldn't be able to tell you all of them. It was really the idea of a friend of mine. He knows all about them."

Sherlock Holmes thought the oddest thing was that Ashwell was allowing this interrogation to continue and even expand. Most men of power and wealth would have cut it off already. Most certainly any member of the aristocracy would have. Perhaps as the son of a wealthy industrialist rather than a business man himself, Mr Ashwell did not have that same need for control. Or perhaps he was hiding something. People desperate to hide a secret often talk obsessively around the hidden topic, and try too hard to appear to be cooperative until they trip.

"A friend? We heard you were a bit of a recluse," Holmes asked.

"Well, I don't socialize much but I do have a few visitors now and then. Anton, that's his name, Anton Kreuzen. Anton was also interested in the John Dee papers. Before we met he wrote to me about them. We corresponded for a while and I invited him here to examine them in person. We also got talking about Lucius Cary, 2nd Viscount Falkland and his wife, prior owners of this estate a couple of hundred years ago, and the Great Tew Circle of intellectuals that he and his wife drew here. That line had died out and the papers were left in the old manor house. When that house was demolished, about seventy-odd years ago, the papers were moved to the library here. I was telling him about the prior manor house and the changes to this one over time. It was then I mentioned the vaults and showed them to him. Anton was excited by the vaults and proposed the mushrooms and the wine cellar and some other projects."

Lestrade, obviously bored by the history lesson, asked "Are any of the mushrooms poisonous?"

"Well, nearly anything can be poisonous in sufficient quantities—Yes, some of them have the reputation."

"Could you show us the mushroom vaults?" Lestrade said.

Ashwell blanched again.

"Yes, I suppose. I don't know why you would want to see them, but come along."

"You showed them to Mr Gazey?" Holmes asked.

"Yes. A few days ago we had a little gathering. Mr Gazey and some other people Anton invited."

"Did Mr Gazey bring wine to this gathering?"

"He did indeed and excellent wine it was."

"Is Mr Kreuzen staying at the house now?"

"Yes, but I believe he went into the village. Down these stairs here. Watch your step."

After they descended the stairs, Ashwell lead them down a passage lined with ironstone to a massive iron door on which was emblazoned a seal with a background outline of flames and a goblet surround by grapes and mushrooms in the foreground and water flowing underneath. Above it was written: *Templum Aeternae Scientiae et Sapientiae.*

"Eternal Temple of Knowledge and Wisdom," Holmes translated. "This door is a recent addition."

"Yes, the inscription was—"

"Kreuzen's idea," Holmes said.

"Yes."

A small crate sat against one wall.

"Did this contain the wine Gazey brought?"

"It did, and does, there are still some bottles left in it."

Ashwell did not approach the door, but rather went to a small recess to one side. He pressed some button and pulled a switch, and the doors swung open slowly. A musty odour reached them as they entered the dimly lit room. As they walked straight ahead elbow high tables stretched to the right and the left in rows. On top of the tables were wooden boxes with glass tops containing mushrooms of different sizes and colours. He led them down the rows. Each container had a label identifying the mushroom species. As they completed the tour and reached a second closed door identical to the first, which still stood open behind them, they heard a sound and turned toward the open door. A man stood there. He was short, dark-haired, and pale. His eyes were wild.

"Anton," Ashwell said. "These men are Inspector Lestrade of Scotland Yard and Mr Sherlock Holmes."

"What have you told them?" Kreuzen said harshly.

"They wished to see the mushroom vault—"

Holmes watched the interaction between Ashwell and Kreuzen with interest. Here was the wealthiest man and the largest land owner in the county who probably could get any number of men to do his will, yet he seemed to be under influence of this young man. Ashwell seemed torn between the desire to please him and fear, mortal fear.

"They are here about Gazey, aren't they?

"What do you know about Gazey?" Inspector Lestrade asked, but Kreuzen ignored him and continued addressing Ashwell.

"It was a mistake to involve him. He wasn't one of us. I told you there would be a price to pay for the wisdom. Immortality does not come cheap."

"Anton, please. Let's talk about this," Ashwell said, and started forward with Holmes, and Lestrade behind him, but Kreuzen pulled a gun from a pocket and pointed it at him.

"You don't understand the sacred rites! You've never understood! Don't come any closer," he cried and moved toward the alcove.

"Anton!" Ashwell cried.

"Back in there!" he shouted waving the gun and directed the three of them to stay in the mushroom vault as the door was closing.

When the door had closed, the three of them rushed forward. There was no handle on the inside of the door. Sherlock Holmes pushed on the door. It did not move in the slightest. He examined the seam around the door. Not even a fingernail could be wedged between the door and the sill.

"There is no way to open that door from inside this room?" Inspector Lestrade asked.

"No," Ashwell said.

"What about the second door?" Lestrade asked.

"Yes, there is a way to open it, but you won't like it," Ashwell said.

"Why not?"

"Because that leads to the Ritual Room. To reach the Ritual Room you must pass through the other three Element Rooms."

"What does that mean?" Lestrade asked.

Holmes looked around the room.

"Here is Earth. The other rooms must contain Water, Wind, and Fire," he said.

"Precisely," Ashwell said, "and they must be passed through at a certain pace, neither too slow, nor too fast."

"What type of madness is this?" Lestrade said.

"There is no other way. The master controls are in the Ritual Room and there is no other route there."

"You have done this before, I presume?" Holmes asked.

"Many times. You must follow me precisely. The first is the Water Room. You must walk through the water and not attempt to resist the drenching. The next is the Fire Room. The water will protect you from the fire as long as you maintain a steady pace. Too slow and the water may evaporate from your clothes before you reach the end and they will catch fire. Too fast and you may create turbulence wrapping the fire around you in such a way as to scald you alive."

"So we risk being fried or poached?" the inspector said, not looking happy in the least.

"Yes. The last is the Wind Room. It would seem to be the least dangerous, but that is deceptive. The wind that blows down from above is pure nitrogen. There is no oxygen in that room. Too long in there and you will die. Inspector Lestrade place your hand on my back so you can track me and Mr Holmes you should do the same behind the inspector. Breath slowly through you nose in the ordeal rooms. Do not speak."

"What is the distance across each room?" Holmes asked.

"The same as this one: twenty feet. Ready?" Ashwell said looking at them earnestly.

"Yes," Holmes said.

Lestrade nodded.

The door swung open to reveal a torrent of water falling from the ceiling. They stepped into this waterfall, one after the other. Then door swung closed behind them. Very soon they were all soaked to the skin. It was difficult to see much through the fluid surrounding them. The water seemed to drain away beneath them because it never rose up their shoes. The constant onslaught of water awakened the fear of drowning, a very real danger if one breathed too deeply.

Any urge to run forward was quenched as before them a glow appeared through the water as the next door swung open. As they passed through that door, they left the water behind, but were surrounded by tall jets of flame with a narrow path between them. Steam billowed from their clothes as the door to the Water Room swung shut behind them. Ashwell's warnings of the dangers in this room were apt. It was necessary to resist the primal urges to dash away from the flames. They kept to the pace set by Ashwell.

Then another door opened. A gust of air from the ceiling nearly staggered them as it pushed back the flames and the door to the Fire Room closed. They kept up the pace until the last door opened and they passed through it. It closed behind them and they felt a fresh circulation of air and inhaled deeply.

"My God," Lestrade said and sat down on a couch nearby.

The Ritual Room looked like a small auditorium sloping downward. There were couches arranged in arcs on the descending levels. At the focal point was a structure that seemed too large to be a podium, more like an altar. The altar was also decorated by the same seal that was on the doors.

"Much like a Mithraeum," Holmes said.

"There are similarities."

"Your friend Anton is a student of ancient religions?"

"He is a student of many things."

Ashwell ran around the back of the altar and manipulated controls there.

"So this Eternal Temple of Knowledge and Wisdom is a form of religious syncretism," Holmes said.

"You could call it that. I have shut down the Elements. We need to wait a few minutes for fresh air to circulate into the Wind Room and then I will open all the doors."

"So when the 'elements' as you call them are on, no one can leave this room?" Lestrade asked.

"Essentially, yes," Ashwell confirmed.

"You engineered these rooms?" Holmes asked.

"Yes. Anton helped with the design."

"You decided the order of the rooms so the Water Room protected against the fire and the wind extinguished any flames that might have arisen despite that protection?" Holmes asked.

"Yes."

"But there is the risk of death in each room by drowning, burning, or suffocation!" Lestrade grumbled.

"Even the Earth Room contains death in the form of poisonous mushrooms," Holmes pointed out.

"Yes, it is about facing and overcoming mortality. But, now, gentlemen, it is safe to leave," Ashwell said as the door swung open.

"Then we should be after Mr Kreuzen," Lestrade said.

They walked back through the Wind Room that was silent and breathless, the Fire Room that no longer burned, and the Water Room which no longer rained. The doors to and from the Earth Room, where the mushrooms resided, were open. As they exited Ashwell closed the outer door while Inspector Lestrade and Sherlock Holmes rushed up the stairs.

They met a servant in the main part of the house.

"Have you seen Mr Kreuzen?" Inspector Lestrade asked.

"Yes, he came this way about a quarter hour ago."

"That long ago?"

"It could be a little less."

"Which way did he go?"

"He went out the front door."

"Was he armed?"

"Armed?"

"Did he have a gun?"

"Not that I saw. He was carrying a bottle of wine."

"He must have taken it from the case," Ashwell said.

"Come along," Holmes cried.

He was out the door in an instant. They found him bending down to examine the ground with his magnifying lens.

"He went that way," Holmes said.

Like a pack of hounds the three men ran across the drive, through the grass-covered park, through a fringe of hundred-year-old trees, across a lane and onward. Now and then Holmes lost the trace, but nosing about like a draghound, he quickly recovered it.

The summer sun was low in the sky as they followed the man's trail. The traces lead them toward a rounded hill. As Holmes was about to mount it, he looked back and saw his companions catching their breath.

"Come along," he said.

"He will be at the top," Ashwell gasped between pants.

"Why?" Holmes said.

"It's a barrow, an ancient burial site, one of many that dot the Cotswolds. He said they were sacred. He had a particular interest in this one. I should have known."

"What kind of interest?"

"Before I built the Ritual Room, Anton would hold his meetings on the top of this barrow. He lectured on the means to gain the knowledge of life and death and seek immortality. He was very convincing."

With renewed inspiration the three men clambered up the side of the hill to the rounded top and there in the middle lay Kreuzen, his arms and legs spread out and his face towards the setting sun. Dead. Next to him lay the bottle of wine. His fingers were blackened and there was some of the same black substance around his mouth. Pieces of something black lay in his left hand and had fallen to the ground next to it.

"Don't touch it," Ashwell said as Inspector Lestrade grew close to it. "It looks to be dried ink cap."

"One of the mushrooms," Holmes said.

"Yes, one that is harmless, unless consumed with alcohol."

"Suicide then," the inspector said.

Ashwell looked across the body to where the sun had set. An evening star winked near the horizon. He seemed shaken.

"Or an escape. At least in his mind," he said.

For a moment the detective and the inspector stood watching him as he stood over his friend in the twilight. Then he shook his head as if waking from a dream.

"He was right. I never understood."

Ashwell turned towards them.

"Unless you gentlemen object, I suggest we return to the house. I will send some of my servants up here with a tarpaulin and a cart to bring the body down."

Together they proceeded down the hill and back among the living.

As they entered the manor house a woman rushed forward with her arms outreached.

"What has happened, Matthew? Are you alright? When the children and I returned, the servants said you had run out with some other men."

"Yes, yes. I will explain later. This is Inspector Lestrade of Scotland Yard and Mr Sherlock Holmes, a private detective. This is my wife, Sylvia."

The men nodded their greetings.

"I have some bad news. Anton is dead."

She seemed at first startled and then relieved.

"Then I say 'thank God!' Excuse me, gentlemen. I know it is not a kind thing to say, but he has had such a hold over my husband that I hardly recognized him."

"I understand, dear. We will talk later. I am sure these men have many questions, and I owe them more than I have told them."

They entered the library and sat down.

"Can I offer your some brandy or water? Or I can ring for something else. I suppose I should want something stronger. I feel as if a spell has been broken. Looking back at it, I find it difficult to believe that I accepted the things he said. He was so charismatic. You were correct when you said I was a recluse. I am not fond of going out in society. A life of study and invention, the quest for knowledge was all I desired from life. My wealth sheltered me, and my wife and children pleased me.

"Then came Anton. He wrote a letter to me about the Dee papers, and the way he spoke of his search for knowledge I thought he was a kindred soul. I invited him here. He read the papers here in this library, and told me of the others he had read, and showed me his notes. He was convinced—and convinced me—that Dee had reached the spirit world and learned from the spirits the secret to infinite knowledge and eternal life. Anton doesn't—didn't—even think Dee died. He said he was translated to another world and could travel between worlds.

"His studies of John Dee had led him to study many of the ancient religions, as you surmised, Mr Holmes. His interpretation was that there was one truth, one path, but when humans had discovered the secret, and become gods themselves—that forbidden fruit—the truth had been split into many fragments and the keepers of the fragments were set against each other. That kept them from seeing that the true path required them to combine the elements of their faiths. Anton said that there were many teachers who had come to lead people back to the truth, to their destiny among the gods, but that they had been misunderstood, and the misunderstandings had further fragmented the religions of the world.

"Anton felt he, too, was a teacher to lead humans back to the true path. I suppose you could say I was his first disciple. I was enthralled. Ultimate knowledge for eternity? He began to recruit others and they would join him, as did I, on the top of that barrow. He would lecture or should I say preach? As we awaited the setting of the sun and then into the twilight. It was intoxicating.

"He said the elements were the most fundamental: earth, wind, fire, and water. They held doorways to the spirit world. We had to lose our fear of entering those doors.

"He spoke of the Mysteries of Dionysus and Persephone and Demeter. He spoke of soma, the drink shared to gain wisdom of the ancients. He had long been researching the recipe and he believed it was a combination of wine and mushrooms. In fact he had come upon this esoteric theory that at the last supper Jesus explained to his disciples that he was a part of all creation, even the earth beneath their feet. Then he took up a mushroom, and told them 'This is my body' and told them to eat, and they laughed. Anton said it was the same lesson, but it fell on their ears as babble and they did not understand."

"And that's what he said to you in the Earth Room?"

"Yes, and he was right. I was enthralled. I was sleepwalking. I would do nearly anything he said. In fact, I think at one time if he had said the secret was to walk across a lake or into a flame, I would have done it. Not—and you have to understand this—not because I had any desire to die, but because I believed I would not—not because of some great spiritual faith in some higher being but only—and I must emphasize this—ONLY because I believed in him. It seems incomprehensible now that the spell is broken.

"On the other hand, he believed in this path he was seeking and he saw there in the Earth Room that I did not believe it. What I think you gentlemen saw there as anger, was in fact betrayal. I had betrayed him. Anton had always chosen the followers. When I showed Gazey the mushrooms and I had invited Gazey to join us that night Anton was horrified. I don't know if there is any other word for it. He said I would regret it. He said there would be a price to pay. I was frightened. I thought he was going to leave. As I said, I was enthralled, intoxicated by his presence and his message. I hadn't realized until that moment that he had been living with us for years. Imagine how a drunk looks at the prospect of being denied the bottle.

"But Anton was there as usual for the ritual. As I said he had helped design the Ritual Room and the Element Rooms, but I had the technical knowledge to create them and make them work. I thought this was my great contribution to the advancement of mankind. Anton said that the rooms helped us face our fears and grow in wisdom. You were right when you said that each room contained death and it was death we were facing. I knew the science. I could make them safe. Did I also betray him when I trusted the science when I walked through those rooms, rather than pure faith? I had not thought of it that way.

"Wednesday night which was the fourth time we had held the ritual in the rooms, Anton was there with me and his ten followers and Gazey,"

"Thirteen of you?"

"Yes."

"Anton led the way through the Element Rooms. I had explained them to Gazey and followed him. He did alright through the elemental ordeals, though I think he was a bit shocked by them."

"These followers of Anton's had they all been through his lectures before?"

"Oh, yes, many times. Most had been coming over a year."

"Gazey had not?"

"No."

"None?"

"None."

"So he was not enthralled as you say?"

"No, definitely not enthralled. He had merely been curious and I believe it was curiosity that made him want to continue.

"Anton was always officiant at these rituals. He spoke again of the path of truth and how it led to eternal wisdom and eternal life and how the gods had felt threatened and had scattered the truth among people and divided them. He explained that we were finding our way back by combining those truths and following the old rituals. Then he handed out mushrooms to each of us and we drank wine from a single cup that was passed around and around. Between the mushrooms and the wine we saw amazing things and felt a profound kinship. The rituals lasted for hours. In fact we lost all sense of time and eventually consciousness."

"Were the Elements turned off before or after consciousness was lost?" Holmes asked.

"After we revived. It was understood that no one could leave until then."

"Who turned them off?"

"I did."

"Anton could have?"

"Yes. He knew how. No one else.

"It was mid-morning on my watch when the gathering revived," Ashwell continued. "I turned off the Elements in the outer rooms and the men prepared to leave. Nothing seemed amiss at that time.

"However, after we had returned to the main floor of the manor house, Gazey complained of feeling ill. I asked if he would like me to send for a doctor. He said no, it was probably just the aftereffects of the intoxication. He said he just needed to lie down and he was shown to a room. I told him to ring if there was anything he needed. The others headed toward their homes. An hour later I had a servant check on him and he seemed to be resting comfortably.

"Later he joined me in the library. I asked how he was and he said he felt much better. I offered him breakfast. He said he thought his stomach was not yet up for it.

"Then he said he had a serious matter he needed to discuss with me. He proceeded to accuse Anton of poisoning him. He said it was clear that Anton did not like him. He could tell from the way he looked at him. He was extremely upset. He enquired what I knew about Anton and accused me of harbouring dangerous foreigners.

"While I had personally only met Gazey twice, I knew him by reputation to be a very social and amicable man and this seemed entirely out of character. I assumed it was a result of his illness and attempted to calm him. I asked him again if I could call a doctor for him. He said no and left the house.

"Left alone, a seed of doubt crept into my mind. Would Anton have done such a thing? Perhaps no harm was intended, only a little bellyache to discourage him from returning? Then I caught myself. Of course he could not have done such a thing. It was preposterous.

"The library door had been open during my exchange with Gazey, and it turned out Anton had come down the hall in time to hear the accusations against him. He came into the room after Gazey left. He looked at me. I felt like he sensed my doubts of a moment before. He shook his head and reminded me that he had said I would regret it. He said no more and left the room.

"When you came and told me of Gazey's death, the doubts grew. I was lost between the fading dream and the incomprehensible reality. Had I been duped? Was Anton a false prophet? Was he a murderer? Had he made me an accomplice? These were the thoughts swirling through my mind when we first spoke in this room."

"But Gazey died two days later in London," Inspector Lestrade protested. "Are you saying Kreuzen followed him to London and poisoned him there?"

"That would not be necessary," Holmes said, "if Kreuzen fed him part of a death cap mushroom. The initial symptoms are gastric distress that passes. The insidious action of its poison is to destroy the liver which is not manifest for thirty-six to forty-eight hours later. Gazey was a dead man before he left Great Tew Manor. He didn't know it yet."

"So you are saying Kreuzen poisoned Gazey before Gazey made any accusations against him? What reason would Mr Kreuzen have had to do that?"

"I don't know," Ashwell said. "I am still having difficulty accepting that he did, but no one else handled the mushrooms. Anton himself picked them and prepared them."

"And no one else was harmed?" Holmes asked.

"I sit here before you having consumed what Anton gave me that night. I had no different reactions than I've had before: intoxication, visions, insights. To the best of my knowledge the others experienced the same. If any of them had become ill or died after leaving this house, I expect that I would have heard about it. But I can give you their names and you can enquire."

"We will need those names," Inspector Lestrade said.

"You shouldn't be surprised if they deny the whole thing. While Anton planned to eventually share with the whole world, he said we must initially keep our practice secret due to fear of public ridicule. Perhaps once they hear of Anton's death they will be shocked into reality, though they are still going to fear that exposure."

"And you?" Holmes asked.

"It will do me no harm. I care not what society thinks of me or says about me, and it will not affect my financial wellbeing at all. Others though, could be harmed in their professional practices if it comes out. If necessary, I will do what I can for them, for I feel somewhat responsible for lending credence to Anton's following."

"Yet you still have not explained his motivation," Lestrade said.

"I can think of several possible motives for someone in Kreuzen's mental state, Inspector," Holmes said. "Kreuzen may have felt that Gazey, as a non-believer, was not worthy to share the mysteries, and not only had to be denied the full experience, but had to die lest he share the secret with others. Perhaps in part his death was to punish Mr Ashwell for inviting an outsider to take part in the rituals. It is likely he expected Gazey to return to his home in Banbury, and die there where it might be set down to natural causes. He did not anticipate Gazey travelling to London to consult me about his suspicions, and then walking the few blocks to museum when I was not in, and dying there."

"Which attracted the attention of the Yard."

"Yes. Even then it could have been set down to natural causes if I had not suspected poison and then traced his steps back to Banbury and then to Great Tew."

"While I admit that you were at times a few steps ahead of the Yard, we would have found our way," Lestrade insisted.

"Perhaps," Holmes conceded with a twinkle in his eye.

"Well, that's as good a motive as any," Lestrade said rising. "I suppose he killed himself to avoid a hanging when he saw the law was on his trail."

"I'm not sure he thought of it as suicide so much as moving on to another plane of existence," Ashwell said. "That's what I had never understood. I think now he always meant death to be a gateway to those other worlds. That had never crossed my mind. Death was there in everything, and yet I thought that we were going to avoid it, as we did in the Element Rooms, not go through it. Perhaps he had planned for us all to die by suicide one day and my betrayal waylaid his plans."

"He could have killed you all that night," Holmes said.

"But he believed we weren't yet ready for the passage. Perhaps that night he thought he could bring me back to the fold after eliminating Gazey, but when he confronted us in the vault he knew it would not be possible and he must go alone."

"And what will become of the Ritual Room and the Element Rooms?" Holmes asked.

"I will dismantle them," Ashwell said. "I have had enough of ordeals."

"Thank God," Lestrade said with a shiver. "I don't know how I am going to write this report."

"Inspector," Holmes said, "I doubt it is necessary to go into much detail. Gazey died of liver failure. Even if you could prove Kreuzen poisoned him, Kreuzen is dead by suicide. There is no need for you to include the more exotic details of this adventure."

Inspector Lestrade rubbed his chin.

"I guess not. No one would believe it."

There was a tap on the door.

Ashwell said "Come" and the butler entered.

"The evening newspapers, sir."

"Just lay them here on the desk," Ashwell said, and the butler did and departed, leaving the three men to stare at the screaming headlines left in his wake.

"British Residency in Kabul Attacked!"

"Envoy Massacred!"

"Renewed War in Afghanistan!".

320

Chapter 16

The Musgrave Ritual

*"Very curious, and the story that hangs round
it will strike you as being more curious still."*
Sherlock Holmes, "The Musgrave Ritual"

It was a rare crisp, clear morning in late September of 1879 when Mrs Denton rapped on Sherlock Holmes' bedroom door. When he emerged he found a telegram leaning against his cup of coffee. He tore it open. Reginald Musgrave was coming to consult him that morning directly from the train scheduled to arrive at Victoria at 10.05. He had less than an hour to prepare. Holmes downed the cup, dashed to his room, washed, and dressed. He removed his papers—which Mrs Denton was under orders not to touch—and other stray items from the sitting room to his bedroom.

A little before half past ten, there was a knock at the door and Holmes answered it. It had been over four years since Holmes had seen Reginald Musgrave. He had changed little. He was dressed like a young man of fashion and preserved the same quiet, suave manner which had distinguished him at the university.

"How has all gone with you Musgrave?" Holmes asked, after he had entered and they had shaken hands.

Holmes offered him a seat and a cigarette case.

"You probably heard of my poor father's death," Musgrave said. "He was carried off about two years ago. Since then I have, of course, had the Hurlstone estates to manage, and as I am member for my district as well, my life has been a busy one. But I understand, Holmes, that you are turning to practical ends those powers with which you used to amaze us?"

"Yes," said Holmes, "I have taken to living by my wits."

"I am delighted to hear it, for your advice at present would be exceedingly valuable to me. We have had some very strange doings at Hurlstone, and the police have been able to throw no light upon the matter. It is really the most extraordinary and inexplicable business."

"Pray, let me have the details," Holmes said.

Musgrave sat down opposite to Holmes and lit a cigarette.

"You must know," said Musgrave, "that though I am a bachelor, I have to keep up a considerable staff of servants at Hurlstone, for it is a rambling old place, and takes a good deal of looking after. I preserve, too, and in the pheasant months I usually have a house-party, so that it would not do to be short-handed. Altogether, there are eight maids, the cook, the butler, two footmen, and a boy. The garden and the stables of course have a separate staff.

"Of these servants the one who had been longest in our service was Brunton the butler. He was a young schoolmaster out of place when he was first taken up by my father, but he was a man of great energy and character, and he soon became quite invaluable in the household. He was a well-grown, handsome man, with a splendid forehead, and though he has been with us for twenty years he cannot be more than forty now. With his personal advantages and his extraordinary gifts—for he can speak several languages and play nearly every musical instrument—it is wonderful that he should have been satisfied so long in such a position, but I suppose that he was comfortable, and lacked energy to make any change. The butler of Hurlstone is always a thing that is remembered by all who visit us.

"But this paragon has one fault. He is a bit of a Don Juan, and you can imagine that for a man like him it is not a very difficult part to play in a quiet country district. When he was married it was all right, but since he has been a widower we have had no end of trouble with him. A few months ago we were in hopes that he was about to settle down again for he became engaged to Rachel Howells, our second house-maid; but he has thrown her over since then and taken up with Janet Tregellis, the daughter of the head game-keeper. Rachel—who is a very good girl, but of an excitable Welsh temperament—had a sharp touch of brain-fever, and goes about the house now—or did until yesterday—like a black-eyed shadow of her former self. That was our first drama at Hurlstone; but a second one came to drive it from our minds, and it was prefaced by the disgrace and dismissal of butler Brunton.

"This was how it came about. I have said that the man was intelligent, and this very intelligence has caused his ruin, for it seems to have led to an insatiable curiosity about things which did not in the least concern him. I had no idea of the lengths to which this would carry him, until the merest accident opened my eyes to it.

"I have said that the house is a rambling one. One day last week—on Thursday night, to be more exact—I found that I could not sleep, having foolishly taken a cup of strong café noir after my dinner. After struggling against it until two in the morning, I felt that it was quite hopeless, so I rose and lit the candle with the intention of continuing a novel which I was reading. The book, however, had been left in the billiard-room, so I pulled on my dressing-gown and started off to get it.

"In order to reach the billiard-room I had to descend a flight of stairs and then to cross the head of a passage which led to the library and the gun-room. You can imagine my surprise when, as I looked down this corridor, I saw a glimmer of light coming from the open door of the library. I had myself extinguished the lamp and closed the door before coming to bed. Naturally my first thought was of burglars. The corridors at Hurlstone have their walls largely decorated with trophies of old weapons. From one of these I picked a battle-axe, and then, leaving my candle behind me, I crept on tiptoe down the passage and peeped in at the open door.

"Brunton, the butler, was in the library. He was sitting in an easy-chair, with a slip of paper which looked like a map upon his knee, and his forehead sunk forward upon his hand in deep thought. I stood dumb with astonishment, watching him from the darkness. A small taper on the edge of the table shed a feeble light which sufficed to show me that he was fully dressed. Suddenly, as I looked, he rose from his chair, and walking over to a bureau at the side, he unlocked it and drew out one of the drawers. From this he took a paper, and returning to his seat he flattened it out beside the taper on the edge of the table, and began to study it with minute attention. My indignation at this calm examination of our family documents overcame me so far that I took a step forward, and Brunton, looking up, saw me standing in the doorway. He sprang to his feet, his face turned livid with fear, and he thrust into his breast the chart-like paper which he had been originally studying.

"'So!' said I. 'This is how you repay the trust which we have reposed in you. You will leave my service to-morrow.'

"He bowed with the look of a man who is utterly crushed, and slunk past me without a word. The taper was still on the table, and by its light I glanced to see what the paper was which Brunton had taken from the bureau. To my surprise it was nothing of any importance at all, but simply a copy of the questions and answers in the singular old observance called the Musgrave Ritual. It is a sort of ceremony peculiar to our family, which each Musgrave for centuries past has gone through on his coming of age--a thing of private interest, and perhaps of some little importance to the archaeologist, like our own blazonings and charges, but of no practical use whatever."

"We had better come back to the paper afterwards," Holmes said.

"If you think it really necessary," Musgrave answered with some hesitation. "To continue my statement, however: I relocked the bureau, using the key which Brunton had left, and I had turned to go when I was surprised to find that the butler had returned, and was standing before me.

"'Mr Musgrave, sir,' he cried, in a voice which was hoarse with emotion, 'I can't bear disgrace, sir. I've always been proud above my station in life, and disgrace would kill me. My blood will be on your head, sir—it will, indeed—if you drive me to despair. If you cannot keep me after what has passed, then for God's sake let me give you notice and leave in a month, as if of my own free will. I could stand that, Mr Musgrave, but not to be cast out before all the folk that I know so well.'

"'You don't deserve much consideration, Brunton,' I answered. 'Your conduct has been most infamous. However, as you have been a long time in the family, I have no wish to bring public disgrace upon you. A month, however, is too long. Take yourself away in a week, and give what reason you like for going.'"

"'Only a week, sir?' he cried, in a despairing voice. 'A fortnight— say at least a fortnight!'

"'A week,' I repeated, 'and you may consider yourself to have been very leniently dealt with.'

"He crept away, his face sunk upon his breast, like a broken man, while I put out the light and returned to my room."

"For two days after this Brunton was most assiduous in his attention to his duties. I made no allusion to what had passed, and waited with some curiosity to see how he would cover his disgrace. On the third morning, however he did not appear, as was his custom, after breakfast to receive my instructions for the day. As I left the dining-room I happened to meet Rachel Howells, the maid. I have told you that she had only recently recovered from an illness, and was looking so wretchedly pale and wan that I remonstrated with her for being at work.

"'You should be in bed,' I said. 'Come back to your duties when you are stronger.'

"She looked at me with so strange an expression that I began to suspect that her brain was affected."

"'I am strong enough, Mr Musgrave,' said she.

"'We will see what the doctor says,' I answered. 'You must stop work now, and when you go downstairs just say that I wish to see Brunton.'

"'The butler is gone,' said she.

"'Gone! Gone where?'"

"'He is gone. No one has seen him. He is not in his room. Oh, yes, he is gone, he is gone!'

"She fell back against the wall with shriek after shriek of laughter, while I, horrified at this sudden hysterical attack, rushed to the bell to summon help. The girl was taken to her room, still screaming and sobbing, while I made enquiries about Brunton.

"There was no doubt about it that he had disappeared. His bed had not been slept in, he had been seen by no one since he had retired to his room the night before, and yet it was difficult to see how he could have left the house, as both windows and doors were found to be fastened in the morning. His clothes, his watch, and even his money were in his room, but the black suit which he usually wore was missing. His slippers, too, were gone, but his boots were left behind. Where then could butler Brunton have gone in the night, and what could have become of him now?

"Of course we searched the main house and the outer buildings, but there was no trace of him. It was incredible to me that he could have gone away leaving all his property behind him, and yet where could he be? I called in the local police, but without success. Rain had fallen on the night before and we examined the lawn and the paths all-round the house, but in vain. Matters were in this state, when a new development quite drew our attention away from the original mystery.

"For two days Rachel Howells had been so ill, sometimes delirious, and sometimes hysterical, that a nurse had been employed to sit up with her at night. On the third night after Brunton's disappearance, the nurse, finding her patient sleeping nicely, had dropped into a nap in the arm-chair, when she woke in the early morning to find the bed empty, the window open, and no signs of the invalid. I was instantly aroused, and, with the two footmen, started off at once in search of the missing girl. It was not difficult to tell the direction which she had taken, for, starting from under her window, we could follow her footmarks easily across the lawn to the edge of the mere, where they vanished close to the gravel path which leads out of the grounds. The lake there is eight feet deep, and you can imagine our feelings when we saw that the trail of the poor demented girl came to an end at the edge of it."

"Of course, we had the drags at once, and set to work to recover the remains, but no trace of the body could we find. On the other hand, we brought to the surface an object of a most unexpected kind. It was a linen bag which contained within it a mass of old rusted and discoloured metal and several dull-coloured pieces of pebble or glass. This strange find was all that we could get from the mere, and, although we made every possible search and enquiry yesterday, we know nothing of the fate of Rachel Howells or Richard Brunton. The county police are at their wits' end. I have come up to you as a last resource."

"I must see that paper, Musgrave, which this butler of yours thought worth his while to consult, even at the risk of the loss of his place," Holmes said.

"It is rather an absurd business, this ritual of ours," Musgrave answered taking out his pocketbook and extracting a piece of paper. "But it has at least the saving grace of antiquity to excuse it. I have a copy of the questions and answers here if you care to run your eye over them."

He handed the paper to Holmes who read the words on it aloud.

"Whose was it?"

"His who is gone."

"Who shall have it?"

"He who will come."

"What was the month?"

"The sixth from the first."

"Where was the sun?"

"Over the oak."

"Where was the shadow?"

"Under the elm."

"How was it stepped?"

"North by ten and by ten, east by five and by five, south by two and by two, west by one and by one, and so under."

"What shall we give for it?"

"All that is ours."

"Why should we give it?"

"For the sake of the trust."

"The original has no date, but is in the spelling of the middle of the seventeenth century," remarked Musgrave. "I am afraid, however, that it can be of little help to you in solving this mystery."

"At least it gives us another mystery," Holmes said, "and one which is even more interesting than the first. The solution of the one may prove to be the solution of the other. You will excuse me, Musgrave, if I say that your butler appears to me to have been a very clever man, and to have had a clearer insight than ten generations of his masters."

"I hardly follow you," said Musgrave. "The paper seems to me to be of no practical importance."

"But to me it seems immensely practical, and I fancy that Brunton took the same view. He had probably seen it before that night on which you caught him."

"It is very possible. We took no pains to hide it."

"He simply wished, I should imagine," Holmes said, "to refresh his memory upon that last occasion. He had, as I understand, some sort of map or chart which he was comparing with the manuscript, and which he thrust into his pocket when you appeared.”

“That is true. But what could he have to do with this old family custom of ours, and what does this rigmarole mean?”

“I don't think that we should have much difficulty in determining that,” said Holmes, “with your permission we will take the first train down to Sussex, and go a little more deeply into the matter upon the spot.”

The same afternoon they arrived at Hurlstone. A splendid park with fine old trees surrounded the house and the lake lay close to the avenue, about two hundred yards from the building.

“As you see, Holmes,” Musgrave said as they drove up in a dog-cart. “The house is in the shape of an L, the long arm being the more modern portion, and the shorter the ancient homestead. There is a date of 1607 chiselled in the old part, but experts are agreed that the beams and stone-work are really much older than that.

“Well, it is grand for history, but the enormously thick walls and tiny windows of the old part drove the family to build the new wing in the last century. The old wing is used now as a store-house and a cellar, when it was used at all.”

Right in front of the house, upon the left-hand side of the drive, there stood a patriarch among oaks, one of the most magnificent trees that Holmes had ever seen.

“That tree was there when your ritual was drawn up,” said Holmes as they drove past it.

“It was there at the Norman Conquest in all probability,” Musgrave answered. “It has a girth of twenty-three feet.”

“Have you any old elms?” Holmes asked.

“There used to be a very old one over yonder but it was struck by lightning ten years ago, and we cut down the stump.”

“You can see where it used to be?”

“Oh, yes.”

“There are no other elms?”

“No old ones, but plenty of beeches.”

“I should like to see where it grew.”

Musgrave led Holmes at once to the scar on the lawn where the elm had stood. It was nearly midway between the oak and the house.

"Was it a pollard, like the oak?"

"Oh, yes, my family extracted much useful wood from the trees of the park. There are oak and elm furnishings in the house that are hundreds of years old."

"So the oak and elm did not vary a lot in height."

"Just between harvest years."

"I suppose it is impossible to find out how high the elm was," Holmes said.

"I can give you it at once. It was sixty-four feet."

"How do you come to know it?" Holmes asked in surprise.

"When my old tutor used to give me an exercise in trigonometry, it always took the shape of measuring heights. When I was a lad I worked out every tree and building in the estate."

"Tell me," Holmes asked, "did your butler ever ask you such a question?"

Reginald Musgrave looked at Holmes in astonishment.

"Now that you call it to my mind," he answered, "Brunton did ask me about the height of the tree some months ago, in connection with some little argument with the groom."

Holmes looked up at the sun. It was low in the heavens, and he calculated that in less than an hour it would lie just above the topmost branches of the old oak. One condition mentioned in the Ritual would then be fulfilled. The shadow of the elm must mean the farther end of the shadow, otherwise the trunk would have been chosen as the guide. He had, then, to find where the far end of the shadow would fall when the sun was just clear of the oak.

Holmes went with Musgrave to his study and whittled a peg, to which he tied a long string with a knot at each yard. Then he took two lengths of a fishing-rod, which came to just six feet, and he went back with Musgrave to where the elm had been. The sun was just grazing the top of the oak. He fastened the rod on end, marked out the direction of the shadow, and measured it. It was nine feet in length.

He knew that if a rod of six feet threw a shadow of nine, a tree of sixty-four feet would throw one of ninety-six, and the line of the one would of course be the line of the other. Holmes measured out the distance, which brought him almost to the wall of the house, and he thrust a peg into the spot. Within two inches of his peg he saw a conical depression in the ground. He knew that it was the mark made by Brunton in his measurements, and that he was still upon his trail.

From this starting-point Holmes proceeded to step, having first taken the cardinal points by his pocket-compass. Ten steps with each foot took him along parallel with the wall of the house, and again he marked his spot with a peg. Then he carefully paced off five to the east and two to the south. It brought him to the threshold of the door of the old wing. Two steps to the west meant now that Holmes was to go two paces down the stone-flagged passage, and this was the place indicated by the Ritual.

Holmes felt a chill of disappointment. The setting sun shone full upon the passage floor. The old, foot-worn grey stones with which it was paved were firmly cemented together, and had certainly not been moved for many a long year. He tapped upon the floor, but it sounded the same all over, and there was no sign of any crack or crevice. Musgrave took out his manuscript to check the Ritual again.

"And under," he cried. "You have omitted the 'and under.'"

"There is a cellar under this then?" Holmes cried.

"Yes, and as old as the house. Down here, through this door."

Musgrave led Holmes down a winding stone stair. As they reach the foot of the stair Musgrave struck a match and lit a large lantern which stood on a barrel in the corner. They looked around. The cellar had been used for the storage of wood, but the billets, which had evidently been littered over the floor, were now piled at the sides, leaving a clear space in the middle. In this space lay a large and heavy flagstone with a rusted iron ring in the centre. A thick shepherd's checked muffler was attached to the ring.

"By Jove!" cried Musgrave. "That's Brunton's muffler. I have seen it on him, and could swear to it. What has the villain been doing here?"

"I believe we should call in the police before we proceed further," Holmes suggested.

They returned to the new wing and Musgrave sent a servant to town for the police. With a pair of the county constables in attendance, Holmes attempted to raise the stone by pulling on the muffler. He could only move it slightly. With an effort he and one of the constables finally dragged it to one side. As Holmes and the constables peered into the black hole yawning before them, Musgrave, kneeling at the side, pushed the lantern down into it.

A small chamber about seven feet deep and four feet square lay below. At one side of this was a squat, brass-bound wooden box, the lid of which was hinged upwards, with a curious old-fashioned key projecting from the lock. The box was furred outside by a thick layer of dust. Damp and worms had eaten through the wood and a crop of livid fungi was growing on the inside of it. Several discs of metal were scattered over the bottom of the box, but otherwise it was empty. Crouched beside the box was the figure of a man with his forehead sunk upon the edge of the box and his two arms thrown out on each side of it.

"My God! It's Brunton!" Musgrave cried.

He had been dead some days, but there was no wound or bruise upon his person to show how he had met his dreadful end. When his body had been carried from the cellar Holmes was still confronted with a problem which was almost as formidable as that with which he had started. He sat down upon a keg in the corner. He drew forth and lit his pipe as he thought the matter over.

If Brunton had made his peace with Rachel Howells and engaged her as his accomplice to raise the stone how did they manage it?

Holmes rose and examined the different pieces of wood scattered round the floor. He found one piece, about three feet in length, had a very marked indentation at one end, while several were flattened at the sides as if they had been compressed by a considerable weight. As they had dragged the stone up they had thrust the chunks of wood into the chink, until at last, when the opening was large enough to crawl through, they propped it open with one placed lengthwise which became indented at the lower end.

Only one person could fit into the hole thus opened. Brunton went down and girl waited above. Brunton unlocked the box and handed up the contents.

Had the wood slipped and the stone shut Brunton into what had become his sepulchre? Or had she dashed the support away and sent the slab crashing down into its place?

Musgrave still stood with a very pale face, swinging his lantern and peering down into the hole.

"These are Triple Unite coins of Charles I minted at Oxford," Musgrave said, holding out a few of the discs which had been in the box. "No other coin has been made this thick. You see we were right in fixing our date for the Ritual."

"We may find something else of Charles I," Holmes cried. "Let me see the contents of the bag which you fished from the lake."

They returned to Musgrave's study, and he laid the debris before Holmes. The metal was almost black and the stones lustreless and dull. Holmes rubbed one of them on his sleeve and it glowed like a spark in the hollow of his hand. The metal work was in the form of a double ring, but it had been bent and twisted out of its original shape.

"You must bear in mind," Holmes said, "that the royal party made head in England even after the death of the king, and that when they at last fled, they probably left many of their most precious possessions buried behind them, with the intention of returning for them in more peaceful times."

"My ancestor, Sir Ralph Musgrave, was a prominent Cavalier and the right-hand man of Charles II in his wanderings," said Musgrave.

"Ah, indeed!" Holmes answered. "I must congratulate you on coming into the possession, though in rather a tragic manner, of a relic which is of great intrinsic value, but of even greater importance as an historical curiosity."

"What is it, then?" he gasped in astonishment.

"It is nothing less than the ancient crown of the kings of England."

"The crown!"

"Precisely. Consider what the Ritual says: How does it run? 'Whose was it?' 'His who is gone.' That was after the execution of Charles I. Then, 'Who shall have it?' 'He who will come.' That was Charles II, whose advent was already foreseen. There can, I think, be no doubt that this battered and shapeless diadem once encircled the brows of the royal Stuarts.

"It is commonly known that the crown jewels were ordered to be taken from the Tower and destroyed. What is less often remembered is that the crown of St Edward was not kept in the Tower at that time, but at Westminster Abbey."

"Yes, yes," Musgrave said, rising and looking through some books on a shelf. "I know I read about that in some book long ago. Due to the family connection, my ancestors were very keen on collecting books on the period, my grandfather especially. Here it is."

He spread one book on the table before Holmes.

"The Dean of Westminster Abbey refused to give up St Edward's regalia and they continued to reside there for years," Musgrave said, as Holmes looked at the page before him. "In August of 1649, after Charles I was executed, the regalia of St Edward were forcibly removed from Westminster Abbey and taken to the Tower to be broken up and sold."

As he spoke, Musgrave was thumbing through a second book until he found a page which contained a reproduction of a sketch of the original crown of St Edward. He laid it on the table next to the tangled mass. The sketch showed a double arch of wire-work decorated with filigree, stones, and little bells. Musgrave sat down before the blackened double ring and rubbed one spot with his handkerchief. The gold glinted. He held it up above the sketch and squinted at it.

"I can see now the similarity of the work, but how did it come from the Tower to our estate, and come to be in this condition?"

"For those I can only offer surmise and conjecture without more evidence," Holmes replied. "We can surmise the Royalists heard the crown had been taken from the Abbey and through various bribes were able to gain custody of it."

"Possibly from Sir Henry Mildmay, Keeper of the King's Jewel house," Musgrave suggested. "There is evidence that he exploited his position for profit."

"A likely candidate," Holmes agreed. "Since all the regalia was to be broken up and minted into coin, the small amount of gold represented here would hardly be noticed as missing. Even if it was, would those in control of the Commonwealth have admitted this treasure got away from them? The symbolism was greater than its weight in gold. I suspect the Royalists attempted to smuggle it out of England."

Musgrave turned a page in the first book and pointed.

"Here," he said. "I remember this man, George de Carteret, Lieutenant Governor and Bailiff of Jersey. He was a Royalist who was also a privateer in the Channel."

Holmes pulled the book closer and read the page Musgrave had indicated and the following page.

"'On the 17th day of February, 1649, Jersey proclaimed Charles II king in the normal manner in the Market Square. The proclamation was read in Elizabeth Castle after morning service the following day and at Mont Orgueil the following Wednesday. The Proclamation was signed by George de Carteret, Lieutenant Governor and Bailiff of Jersey and many of the most prominent citizens of the island.

"'Carteret maintained his estates and the government on Jersey through privateering, principally seizing the merchant ships of the Parliamentarians. He had twelve ships at sea, each carrying eight guns and about eighty men. In those days, seizing ships and taking their cargo as prize was piracy, unless sanctioned by a sovereign against enemy vessels during war by Letters of Marque.

"'In recognition of the loyalty of Carteret and the Isle of Jersey expressed in their declaration, Charles II sent to Carteret a bundle of Letters of Marque with the names of the captains and the vessels left blank to be filled in by Carteret, authorizing them to seize vessels and cargo of ships of nations not in affinity with Charles II.

"Ah, Musgrave, pay heed to this part," Holmes said. "'In early 1649 Carteret had gone to France to visit the Royal family in exile. On the 8th of September of that year—That would have been a few weeks after the crown was taken from Westminster Abbey.—Carteret returned to announce that King Charles II and his brother James were on their way to visit Jersey. They arrived on the 17th of September and were welcomed by a great discharge of guns from all the ships in the bay and Elizabeth Castle. It was a day of rejoicing and excitement in Jersey and the bells of the churches were rung and the hills were lit up by bonfires. Charles stayed over the winter in Jersey leaving on the

14th of February 1650.'

"The plan may have been to take the crown and the gold coins to Jersey to crown Charles II," Holmes said. "I can imagine a small sloop making its way down the Thames under the cover of darkness. It passed safely down to the Thames Estuary intent on crossing the Channel to Jersey. Perhaps it was pursued by Parliamentary ships in the Channel. Perhaps there was a storm."

"There are many tales of sunken ships in the Channel. Bits of things turn up on the shore after heavy weather," Musgrave said.

"If the ship sank off West Sussex," Holmes said, "It may have taken Sir Ralph sometime to locate the wreckage and find the box containing the crown and the hoard of gold. If it was deep he might have needed to find divers he could trust. By the time he recovered it, the interaction between the sea water and the different metals had created the effect you see. Despite the condition, he intended to preserve it for Charles II on his restoration. It was hidden in the house and the Ritual written to provide directions to the hiding place. Brunton found the box, decided to leave it behind, and handed up the treasure to Rachel Howells who threw it in the lake."

The twilight had closed in and the moon was shining brightly in the sky before he finished.

"And how was it then that Charles did not get his crown when he returned?" asked Musgrave, pushing the relic into its linen bag.

"Ah, there you lay your finger upon the one point which we shall probably never be able to clear up," Holmes said, "It is likely that the Musgrave who held the secret died in the interval, and by some oversight left this guide to his descendant without explaining the meaning of it. From that day to this it has been handed down from father to son, until at last it came within reach of a man who tore its secret out of it, and lost his life in the venture."

"Come, Holmes," said Musgrave as a maid appear at the threshold, "Supper is being served and I have had a room prepared for you. We can discuss this more in the morning."

"The inquest for Brunton shall be tomorrow afternoon," Musgrave said as they worked on their breakfast the following morning.

"They want us to testify. I invited the coroner to hold it here so the coroner's jury may view the space in which Brunton died. I doubt the coroner will come to any conclusion other than misadventure."

"It is likely Brunton suffocated in that small space," Holmes said.

"I suppose I must report the discovery of the crown to the Treasury. That's going to be a profound nuisance. We have had enough bother with the press over these disappearances and the discovery of Brunton's body."

"Before you do," Holmes said, "let me send a telegram to my brother. He works for the government and may know how to best to handle the matter quietly."

While Holmes enjoyed the hospitality of Hurlstone Hall, Reginald Musgrave gave him the liberty of his library and Holmes ploughed his way through books there. He was surprised that he had no return telegram from Mycroft and even further surprised when his brother appeared on the doorstep of Hurlstone Hall the following morning.

"Well, well, I did not expect my simple enquiry to have such a profound effect," Sherlock said. "Musgrave, this is my brother Mycroft. Mycroft, Reginald Musgrave."

"We are honoured," Musgrave said. "How do you do, Mr Holmes? Welcome to my home. Can I get you some refreshment after your journey?"

"A glass of water and a comfortable chair, would suit my needs of the moment," Mycroft said, handing his coat and hat to a maid.

"Easily solved," Musgrave said. "Come into the library."

"I have been authorized by Treasury to examine this relic my brother told me you have. Here is my letter of authorization," Mycroft said, pulling a paper from his inner pocket and handing it to Reginald Musgrave.

"Yes, of course," said Musgrave perusing the brief document with its attached seals. "I placed the relic in the safe."

When Musgrave turned aside to open the safe, the Holmes brothers exchanged a series of looks decipherable by no one other than the two of them. In a moment Musgrave turned with the linen bag in hand and laid it upon the table. Mycroft proceeded to remove the blackened relic from the bag.

"I note one odd authorization in this document," Musgrave said. "It says here that you are permitted to make any tests or experiments upon the relic that you deem appropriate. Perhaps I should have my solicitor present."

"No need," Mycroft said turning it over in his massive hands until he reached the small spot that Musgrave had cleaned the night before.

"Good heavens, sir, what are you doing?" Musgrave said as Mycroft gashed into the spot with a small metal tool.

"Performing my commission. It is as we suspected," Mycroft said. "It is fraudulent."

Mycroft turned the relic toward them.

"As you can see, there is base metal below the gold. This object is merely gilt. It may be some peer's coronet or some cheat's bait. But it is not the true crown."

They could now see brass showing through where Mycroft had made the small gash. Mycroft pulled a second document from his pocket which he handed to Musgrave before taking a seat.

"I am authorized to give you this document which permits you to retain this relic here at the Hurlstone Hall, but which denies that it is the crown of St Edward or any other king or queen who has sat upon the throne of the United Kingdom."

This was a slightly larger and more formal document than the first, also festooned with seals.

"Well, I don't suppose I could have expected it to be true, though your brother was quite convincing," Reginald Musgrave said with a slight chuckle. "I guess we can display it as a local legend and allow people to make up their own minds. Now if you gentlemen will excuse me, I need to see the cook about lunch, and deal with a few more domestic matters. You will be joining us for lunch, won't you, Mr Holmes?"

"I would be delighted," Mycroft responded with a slight bow of his head.

When they were left alone, Sherlock laughed.

"That was quite a performance, Mycroft. I could be angry for your coming here and undermining my conclusions in front of my client—with the government at your back—but I don't think even Musgrave believed it. He's not exactly an intellectual, but he's a Member of Parliament. He knows how political games are played. Why doesn't the government want this to be proven to be the Crown of St Edward?"

"Can you prove it is?" Mycroft asked.

"Not at this moment, no," Sherlock said.

"Do you believe St Edward and all those who came after were crowned with brass crown?"

"Oh, anything is possible that long ago, but as you most likely know the Crown of St Edward wasn't really worn by Edward the first or his father Alfred.

"And was it made of solid gold then?" Mycroft asked.

"We may never know," Sherlock said. "You see, I have been doing some reading," pointing to the stacks of books on the table. "And it turns out that the 'Crown of St Edward' was most likely lost by King John in the river Wash in 1216. We can't really confirm that the crown used thereafter was the same one."

Mycroft smiled.

"I've been aware of the base metal problem since I saw the blackened condition of the crown and the rust encrusted on the coins," Sherlock said. "Gold and silver do not rust, only iron does. Copper coins tarnish to green. Brass tarnishes green or blue or in more severe cases of corrosion the zinc may separate from the copper causing it to turn pink. Silver will tarnish grey or black or other colours depending on what it was exposed to, but gold does not turn black. The black is a coating on the gold from another source. That's why it rubs off so easily. It is not bound to the gold."

"And these," Sherlock said picking up a group of disks that had been lying on an open book on the table, "are quite remarkable. Like those in the box they are gold Triple Unite coins of Charles I minted at Oxford in 1643. No one knows how many were made. They are the largest gold coins minted in England. They are the same diameter as crowns of the time but much thicker. It may have been Charles' attempt to demonstrate that he still had sufficient resources to regain control of the country.

"The encrustation tells another story. It demonstrates that these coins were submerged in sea water in the proximity of iron for a length of time, most likely a shipwreck.

"My theory is that the government does not want to admit the Crown of St Edward was ever made of base metal even before the regicide. So they deny the authenticity of this relic, maintain the Crown of St Edward was destroyed during the Commonwealth—as all the history books say—and had to be recreated by Charles II. Of course, that does not explain that odd tale of Captain Blood absconding with the crown jewels from the Tower in 1671 only to be caught and arrested, and then, rather than being thrown in the Tower or executed, he was set free by Charles II, and given a life pension.

"Charles II had the same problem as earlier monarchs: shortage of funds. He wanted all the regalia restored by his coronation, but he didn't have enough gold to do it, in part, perhaps, due to the fact that hoards like this one were still missing. So the regalia were created out of base metals and gilt. Later when Charles II acquired enough gold, he had new ones made of gold and commissioned Blood to perform the dubious theft to hide the process of swapping the gold regalia for the base metal gilt ones. It is that second set created for Charles II that is now kept in the Tower."

"Bravo, Sherlock. Do you believe Musgrave will play along even if he believes it to be real?"

"Of course. He said as much. He would never do anything to embarrass Queen and Country. We are left with one more mystery."

"Which is?

"Why you came. I am surprised you could get away from London given the state of things."

"I volunteered. There is nothing I can do about the foreign situation other than remind them that I predicted this outcome and they refused to heed my warnings. As much as I dislike travelling, it is refreshing to be away from Whitehall at the moment. Besides I had an established relationship with one of the parties involved."

Sherlock chuckled.

After lunch the coroner arrived with his jury and the inquest was convened. As Musgrave had predicted the verdict was death by misadventure. Afterwards the Holmes brothers boarded the train for the ride back to London.

Chapter 17

The Old Russian Woman

The old woman faced round and looked keenly
at him from her little red-rimmed eyes.

Dr John H. Watson, *A Study in Scarlet*

It was early October and the morning frost had not yet melted from the window panes. Sherlock Holmes was transcribing the results of his metal corrosion experiments at Bart's during August and September when the post brought an envelope for him from Hurlstone Manor, West Sussex. It contained a bank draft and a letter.

Dear Holmes,

I cannot thank you enough for resolving the mystery, or rather myster-ies, at Hurlstone. Though I have not yet received your statement of account, I hope that the enclosed bank draft will cover your services. If I have miscal-culated, please advise me at once and I will send the difference.

Reginald Musgrave

Holmes looked at the draft and whistled.

"That will most assuredly cover my services and all my expens-es for the next six months," he said to himself and grabbed his hat and coat. After visiting the bank he met his brother Mycroft for lunch to tell him of the improvement of his finances.

"Excellent, Sherlock! I am sure there will be more of that."

"From here on I insist on paying my share of the rent."

"Agreed. I also think the time is appropriate to mention that I am looking for rooms closer to Whitehall and the Diogenes Club. I am tired of the drive."

"So you won't be renewing the lease next year?"

"No. Though I am sure the landlady would be glad to let you take it if you like."

"I shall give it some thought."

Holmes did give it some thought on the drive north and since smoking helped him think he had his driver stop by Bradley's for more tobacco before returning to Montague Street. As he was dismounting from the hansom, he caught sight of some movement out of the corner

341

of his eye. He paid the driver and mounted the steps to the flat. He was inserting the latchkey when he suddenly turned around and grabbed the arm of a young boy in need of a wash, whose clothes did not fit him well and showed signs of some amateur mending. But the most remarkable thing was that the boy looked somewhat familiar, yet he could not immediately place him.

"What is this?" he enquired. "Hoping to pick my pocket?"

"Remember me, Mr 'olmes? Don't ya?" the boy said.

The boy held out a very worn, creased, and stained copy of Holmes' calling card.

"You said if I e'er needed onny 'elp—"

It dawned on Holmes who this young Cockney was. He had given the card to the boy three years before at the climax of his involvement with the Scotland Yard scandal. Since then the lad had grown six inches taller, as boys that age do, and lost most of the cherubic look to his face. His fortunes seemed to have declined somewhat and he obviously was not as well fed now as he had been by the cooks of Canonbury when he was younger and more able to pull their heartstrings.

"Wiggins?"

"Sure eno', gov'nor."

"Do come in," Holmes said, turning the key in the lock and pushing the door wide.

The boy came in glancing about at the sitting room.

"Nice place ya got 'ere."

"Have a seat."

Looking at the slip of a lad, maybe now nine years old and growing fast, he rang the bell for the housekeeper.

"Have you had your tea yet?" Holmes asked.

"No, suh. Could go for spot."

"Mrs Denton? Could you please bring tea?" Holmes asked his housekeeper when she appeared.

Mrs Denton looked a bit askance at the dirty ragamuffin. She had been delighted to provide for the orphaned young lady a few months before. She was less sure of this one, but she did as requested.

"Are you in some kind of trouble?" Holmes asked Wiggins.

"No, I keep clear of onny of that," Wiggins said.

"What can I do for you then?" Holmes asked.

"It's a woman I met, an old woman. Not from this country. From Roosha maybe. I think wha' she said. She knows some English but I can't always understand her. She speaks it ginger beer."

Holmes remembered Wiggin's fondness for rhyming slang: "Ginger beer" was "queer" in Cockney rhyming slang. It was ironic that Wiggins was complaining about how well someone else spoke English.

"She was lookin' fo' her daugh'er who lives in London but no one would 'elp 'er. Here's the picture she gave me."

He pulled from some inner layer a worn, crumbled photograph with some writing in Cyrillic on the back and handed it to Holmes. The photograph was of a woman in a fancy dress, possible a wedding dress.

"You could bring her here and perhaps I could help her," Holmes said as Mrs Denton returned with the tray, which Wiggins eyed hungrily.

"I brought hot water for washing as well, Mr Holmes," Mrs Denton said as she carried that pitcher to the bedroom.

"Oh, come along, Wiggins. Mrs Denton won't be happy unless you wash your hands and face before eating. Just takes a minute."

"I know 'ow to wash clear enoof," Wiggins said, rolling up his sleeves and doing as requested.

"Would've brought 'er along if I could, Mr Holmes, but she's feelin' poorly. Couldn't get 'er to walk far enoof for a cab. She said she dinna 'ave the energy. She kept sayin' she needed to find 'er daughter. I told her I knew someone who might be able to help find her. That's when she gave me the photograph."

"Mrs Denton, wait a minute. I need to send a message to my brother."

As Wiggins was digging into the sandwiches on the tray, Holmes wrote out a note to his brother Mycroft asking if he could refer him to a Russian interpreter.

"I will see that your brother gets it promptly," said Mrs Denton.

Holmes poured tea for Wiggins and himself.

"Did she tell you her name?"

"Soffy or someten."

"Sophia?"

"Yea, Soffya Orlawv," Wiggins said, his pronunciation complicated both by his Cockney accent and the food in his mouth.

"Sophia Orlov?

"Got it, gov'nor."

"And her daughter's name?"

"Anna. Spliced to an English bloke, sounded like a dog. Barking or someten."

There were many English surnames that sounded something like "barking."

"Did she know where they lived?"

"Uh uh. On the docks someone stole her bag with address in it and 'er money. She 'ad the picture in 'er pocket. That's all she 'ad left."

"Did her daughter know she was coming?"

"I don't know."

Wiggins began to stuff an extra sandwich in his pocket.

"Wait," Holmes said, going to his room and bringing back some brown paper and string. "Wrap the rest in here and tie it up."

"So you want to hire me to find this woman's daughter?" Holmes asked.

"That's what you do, ain't it? Figure things out fer folk?"

"A succinct description, yes. I accept the commission," Holmes said holding out his hand.

Wiggins grasped his hand in his somewhat crumb-laden one and shook firmly.

"Don't 'ave any money on me, but next I get some, it's yours."

"Let's not worry about that," Holmes said. "Where is this woman?"

"Near St Katharine Docks."

There was a firm knock at the door. Holmes opened it to find a slender young man.

"Mr Sherlock Holmes?" he asked.

"Yes."

"Mr Mycroft Holmes told me you were in need of a Russian

interpreter. I am Demetri Panov, at your service."

Holmes shook the man's hand.

"Thank you for coming! How very much like Mycroft to send the man himself rather than a mere reference. Let me get my coat and hat. We are going out. We need you to interpret for a Russian woman. Come along, Wiggins."

Fortunately the interpreter had told his cabby to wait and they all piled in.

On their way, Holmes asked Mr Panov what the writing on the back of the photograph meant.

"It was written by someone named Anna to her mother begging her not be angry with her for marrying a foreigner. She asked her to come visit them."

They arrived at the docks as quickly as the press of traffic would allow, and all tumbled out of the cab. Wiggins led them to the spot where he had left the Russian woman, but she was gone.

"Gone! Left 'er sitting right 'ere," Wiggins said, pointing to a makeshift seat of bricks, slates, and an old board.

He starting to run forward. Holmes held out an arm to stop the boy.

"Stand back," Holmes said. "Let me see the soles of your shoes."

Holmes knelt down and picked up first one then the other of Wiggin's feet and examined the bottom of his shoes. He then walked carefully forward, bent over; reading the story the impressions in the dust told him.

"These are your tracks leaving her. Here is where you stood while you were talking to her. There is another print partially covering yours. Those are her shoes. Even though she was sitting she shifted her feet several times. After you left someone came—no, two people came. They stood talking to her, then urged her up. She seemed reluctant. One on either side, close, at her elbows, nearly dragging her."

"Blimey, y' can tell that from the dust?" Wiggins said.

"Yes."

"Peelers?"

"Not the shoes of constables. Women. Women in low-heeled sensible shoes. They went this way, but then I lose the traces among all the wheel tracks and other shoes."

Holmes looked up at the buildings on either side. They were mostly surrounded by warehouses. Some had windows but they were grimy, and inside were labourers moving the wares about, not staring out the windows.

"Unfortunately, this is not an area likely to yield a nosey neighbour who was looking out the window to tell us what happened."

"Wait!" Wiggins shouted and disappeared between the buildings.

He was back in a few minutes followed by five other street urchins, all smaller than he.

"We go everywhere an' see everything. Mostly people don't see us," Wiggins said.

"Did any of your friends see what happened?" Holmes asked,

"Oi did! Was some o' those women in black! Improvers!" one of them said.

"Improvers?" Holmes asked.

"Watt we call 'em. Women wearing black dresses an' bonnets thinking they know what's best fer folk. Snatchin' children off streets. We keep clear o' them!"

"We warn youngens not to listen," another said, "to their offers o' food cause once they get you...."

The small boy shivered.

"Why would they take an old woman?" Holmes asked.

"They take all kinds. Workin' girls. Folks in their cups. Most ne'er come back!" one of the boys said.

"At least if the peelers get ya, if ya ain't done nothin' they let you go," Wiggins said. "But the Improvers? Don't know what happens t' folks they get."

"You say they dress in black?" Holmes asked.

The boys nodded.

"Mostly. Sometimes in dark blue," one said.

"Thank you for your help," Holmes said and gave them each a shilling, which caused much excitement among them. "Keep a watch out here for the old woman or any of those Improvers. If you see anything, leave me a message at 24, Montague Street near the British Museum. You know where that is?"

They nodded.

"Come along, Wiggins and Mr Panov. I believe I know where to find our old Russian woman," Holmes said directing them back to the waiting cab. "Cabby, 272, Whitechapel Road."

When they arrived at the Mission House, Holmes told the cabby to wait again, and he marched boldly in and spoke to the first person who looked to be in charge.

"I am looking for Sophia Orlov. I was told that two women from this institution brought her here."

"Sophia Orlov? I don't know who that is," the woman he spoke to responded.

"She is an elderly Russian woman new to London. She does not speak English well. This man, Mr Panov, is a Russian interpreter."

Mr Panov gave a slight bow.

"Oh, now I understand. A woman was brought in. She seemed confused and could not answer questions. She had too much to drink. Some of our officers brought her here where she could get food and rest."

"Where is she? We must see her immediately."

"Well, I don't—"

"Otherwise we will have everyone involved arrested for kidnapping. This is a very serious international incident."

"Surely—Well, come along."

She led them to a room. Wiggins ran up to the old woman.

"She's worse," he said.

"Speak to her," Holmes directed the interpreter.

Panov spoke some words and she responded in kind.

"She feels very bad, thirsty, pain in her stomach," the interpreter said. "She doesn't know where she is. She wants to see her daughter."

Holmes drew nearer to Sophia Orlov. He took her hand gently in his. She looked up at him. She was breathing rapidly. Her hand was hot and dry. Her face was flushed.

"Why did you say she had been drinking?"

"Her stupor and the smell on her breath,"

He smelled it himself.

"That's not the smell of alcohol. It is acetone. This woman is ill."

"Tell her I will take her to a hospital, then I will find her daughter."

The interpreter did as he asked and the woman nodded.

Holmes scooped the old woman up in his arms. The others opened the doors of the building and then of the cab for him.

"Driver, to Bart's, quickly," he cried.

The driver pulled up in the hospital grounds. Holmes lifted Sophia Orlov out of the cab and handed her over to attendants with a stretcher. He turned to the interpreter.

"Please, go along with her," Holmes told Panov, "and explain to the doctors that she speaks Russian and you would need to interpret any questions."

"I will do as you ask," Panov said and followed the woman into the hospital.

Holmes turned to Wiggins.

"You should tell your friends that she was found."

"I want to see 'ow she is. Won't hurt them none t' keep a look out longer."

"Well, driver, this is for all the wear and tear. We don't have need of you right now, though if you are not busy in an hour or two, you might come back around to check."

The driver took the silver offered, tipped his hat, and turned the horse's head.

"What do we do now?" Wiggins asked.

"We think," Holmes said. "This bench under this tree looks to be a good thinking spot."

He walked to the bench with Wiggins trailing behind. Holmes sat down and pulled out his pipe and began to load it.

"Just going to sit 'ere and smoke your pipe?" Wiggins asked.

"The doctors are taking care of Sophia Orlov. The only way I can help is to find her daughter. To do that I need to think. The pipe helps me think."

He lit the pipe and took a few puffs.

"We are looking for a Russian woman named Anna who married an Englishman," Holmes began, speaking more to himself than the boy. "The Russian woman's family, at least her mother, was still living in Russia. How would an Englishman meet a Russian woman whose mother was still living in Russia? The interpreter said the writing on that back was from the daughter begging the mother to not be angry with her for marrying a foreigner. It is more probable that she met the Englishman in Russia than that the Russian woman travelled alone to England or another country. Why would an Englishman be in Russia? Just visiting? The relations between Russia and the British Empire are not very good at this time. It is more probable that the visit was for business rather than pleasure. What kind of business was it? Diplomatic? Trade? Import or export? What kind of goods does Britain import from or export to Russia?"

Holmes drew on his pipe and wrinkled his brow. Wiggins sat there scowling. After a while Holmes' train of thought was broken by the interpreter as he approached.

"She is sleeping more comfortably now," Panov said.

"Do you need to leave?" Holmes asked him.

"No, I will stay until she wakes up."

"Good. I believe there is a bookstore nearby. I need to consult some directories. When she wakes up you can tell her we are looking for her daughter."

The interpreter re-entered the hospital wing.

"Come, Wiggins, you may find the proximity of books educational."

At first the proprietor had a mind to chase the boy out, but Holmes assured him he would be responsible for his behaviour.

"No nicking any books," Holmes said. "Or anything else."

"Upon my word, guv'nor," Wiggins swore.

In the bookstore Holmes found a copy of the *Business Directory of London*. After reviewing a few sections he purchased it and returned to the bench under the tree on the grounds of the hospital. He resumed his silent contemplation, smoking his pipe, and thumbing through the directory now and then. At one point he paused and turned to the boy who still retained the ability to sit silently for hours that most children seemed to lack.

"Now, Wiggins, you know your way around the City," Holmes stated more as a fact than a question.

"As well as any cabby. Better'n most," Wiggin replied.

"How far is Crutch Friar Street?"

"Not far, in shadow o' the Tower."

"And Sipping Lane?"

"Crosses it close by."

"Excellent," Holmes said and returned to reviewing the directory.

"Ah, here comes our cabman again. Wiggins, go tell your friends they can stand down. Here's the shillings for the fare there and back and more for their troubles. Off you go. Tell the driver where to drop you."

"I'll be back," Wiggins called.

Holmes waved as the carriage pulled out. But when Wiggins returned he was nowhere in sight.

Shortly after he had seen the boy off in the cab, Sherlock Holmes had set out on foot eastward towards the Tower. It was not long before he came across Crutch Friar Street where he saw the shops of a number of wine and spirit importers. He began his enquiries at the nearest. He entered and assumed the identity of a buyer for a new restaurant enterprise who was contemplating what beverages their establishment should stock and who would be the best supplier. Obviously the man at the front desk was more than willing to sing the praises of their imports from France and Spain. Holmes took notes of the man's recommendations.

"Someone told me they were importing spirits from Russia," Holmes asked "Do you know anything about that?"

"Oh, the only thing I think you could get from Russia would be grain alcohol. Better for cleaning your machinery than your gut, if you know what ah mean. We don't import anything from Russia."

Holmes laughed and said he must have misunderstood.

The next importer emphasized their efforts to maintain their prices reasonable despite the pressures of the crop failures in vineyards of Sicily and parts of France due to the powdery mildew, and a nasty aphid named *phylloxera*.

"We've even imported some cases of wine from the States," he said.

"Any from Russia?" Holmes asked.

"I have not heard of significant vineyards in Russia. Mostly they distil alcohol from grain or potatoes. Not much of a beverage market," he said then looked around and leaned forward. "I have heard though that some importers might be importing raw grain alcohol from Russia and using it in their sherry and other fortified wines, to lower their costs. We don't do it and I am not going to name names."

"Ah, you have been very helpful. I may call upon you again," Holmes said.

Holmes was certain he was on the scent. His review of the listings and advertisements in the directory had convinced him that the majority of the imports from Russia to Britain were raw materials, mostly grain. None of those was the type of specialty item that would require a personal visit. But a wine importer facing the financial stress on the European wine market might investigate a new source of alcohol that would spread the more expensive imported wines a bit further. Having succeeded in this venture he might feel financially comfortable enough to take a wife. Holmes continued his enquiries down the street asking more questions related to sherries and fortified wines. Many merchants were willing to praise those that they offered but all denied using any ingredients from Russia. Then he stopped at Wulfric Cynewulf & Associates. The man at the front had turned to another man of sturdy Anglo Saxon stock, coming in from an office.

"Mr Cynewulf, this man wants to know if we use any alcohol from Russia in our sherry?"

Cynewulf smiled.

"We use the finest ingredients from throughout the world in our sherry. But here, allow me to pour you a sample."

The liquid he poured was dark red almost brown in colour but very clear. It had the body of a red wine with a smoky flavour and a hint of nutmeg.

"Is that not a warm, hearty beverage?" Cynewulf asked

"It is indeed. But I have another question for you that you

might find somewhat shocking," he said pulling the photograph from his pocket. "Is this your wife?"

"What is this? Why do you have a picture of my wife?" Cynewulf asked harshly.

"Please calm yourself. This photograph is one your wife sent to her mother. Turn it over and you will see the truth of what I say," Holmes assured him.

He turned it over and read the Russian on the reverse.

"How did you come by it?" Cynewulf asked.

"Your wife's mother travelled here to London to surprise your wife but her luggage was stolen containing your address. She became lost and fell ill. We have taken her to St Bartholomew's Hospital not far from here. I am sure she would be very happy to see your wife, if she would visit her there."

"Yes, I will tell her immediately. Thank you."

Cynewulf grabbed his coat and left the shop while Holmes turned on his steps and walked back to Bart's. He found Wiggins on the bench under the tree.

"Where'd you go?" Wiggins asked.

"I found the daughter, or rather the husband of the daughter, Wulfric Cynewulf"

"That's it!" Wiggins cried.

"I thought you said his name was like barking?"

"I said it sounded like a dog barkin'. Wooff woof."

Holmes laughed.

Soon a carriage drove up with Wulfric Cynewulf and his wife Anna inside. Mr Cynewulf introduced Holmes to his wife as the man who had found him.

"Thank you, Mr Holmes!" she said.

"This is the lad you need to thank," Sherlock Holmes said, "Wiggins found your mother ill near St Katharine Docks and came to me for help."

Mr and Mrs Cynewulf showered Wiggins with praise.

Chapter 18

Francesco Nicoletti

"When these fellows are at fault they come to me"
Sherlock Holmes, *A Study in Scarlet*

The cool, wet summer and autumn of 1879 had given way to a bitterly cold winter. It was mostly dry in London, though some other parts of England were hit by sudden storms. In January the winter sun hung deceptively inviting over London in a brittle blue sky. The cloudy breath of the passers-by on the street revealed the truth, as coal fires struggled to keep the cold at bay. Sherlock and Mycroft had put off their usual dinner on January 6th by mutual agreement for neither wanted to venture out.

Snowy weather lingered into spring and Sherlock Holmes had no particular urge to stir himself. He sat in his dressing gown surrounded by the newspapers from the last few days that wanted cutting, pasting and indexing, as he was reading from the stack of books he had purchased after the completion of the Musgrave case. Those combined with the Stradivarius, which lay nearby, had kept him occupied during the months of hibernation.

The cases he had handled in 1879 had brought him some mention in obscure corners of the daily press. Despite the Crown's efforts, the Hurlstone incidence had made a bigger splash. Enquiries for his services had increased. Three years from the time he had started out as a detective and now there were several clients approaching him each month; sometimes several in a week.

Many prospective clients brought cases he had no interest in. Most particularly he maintained a rule that he did not meddle in the domestic disputes between husbands and wives because that presented no intellectual challenge. In fact the increase in such enquiries had encouraged him to limit his newspaper advertisements. This had been a useful economy. Other persons brought trivial affairs that he solved from his armchair and for which the compensation was minimal. Nothing especially interesting had been presented to him so far in the spring of 1880 until there was a knock on the door in late March.

Holmes answered the door himself and found Inspector Lestrade standing on the other side of the threshold. That phenomenon had happened only once before at the commencement of the Banbury wine merchant case the previous summer. Holmes was immediately curious.

"Good day, Inspector."

"Mr Holmes, I wonder if you would mind if I came in for a minute."

"Welcome, Inspector, take a chair. What might I do for you?"

Inspector Lestrade sat down, scratched his head, and knit his eyebrows. He turned his hat around in his hands.

"I will admit there are some cases, Mr Holmes," he began, "that are beyond the police because there is no sign that a crime has been committed, or at least committed within our jurisdiction."

"Do you have an example in mind?" Holmes asked.

"I do. You have heard of Francesco Nicoletti?"

"The famous artist, yes. If I recall, his parents urged him toward a career in art at a very young age because his club foot made it difficult for him to get around. That was fortunate choice since it turned out he had much natural talent."

"Yes, yes," Lestrade said, "then his parents, who were very wealthy, died young, leaving him a substantial trust which he gained control of a few years ago, when he turned thirty. Shortly thereafter he married Gina Giuseppe who was supposedly from the old country. Mr Nicoletti's parents were from Italy as well, but he was born here in England. Gina is a devout Catholic and while Francesco was raised in the faith he had fallen away from it since his parents had died. Gina has been encouraging him, but she leans more toward the mysticism, miracles, and so on."

"I thought miracles were an essential part of the Roman Catholic faith."

"They are, as I understand these papists, but—"

"Who is the source of your information, Inspector?"

"His younger sister, Stella Nicoletti."

"Ah. Is she a sceptic?"

"At least as far as her brother is concerned. She claims he is missing and she thinks it has something to do with a priest his wife introduced him to."

"When did he go missing?"

"She is not certain."

"Where was he last seen?"

"She is not certain about that either. It could be here. It could be in Italy or anywhere else in-between. She says Francesco and Gina went on trip to Bari, Italy several months ago. She says something is wrong."

"Has she written to him?"

"Yes, and he responded, but she claims the letters aren't really from him."

"Do you have some samples?"

"I do, and some letters from him to her a few years ago, before he met Gina," Lestrade said pulling some envelopes from his coat and handing them to Holmes.

Holmes retrieved his magnifying lens from a drawer and sat down at the table and spread the letters out before him. He looked at the older letters and then at the more recent ones with his lens, then he examined the envelopes.

"She is correct. These are excellent forgeries, yet forgeries nonetheless. You can see the hesitation and the lifting of the pen between strokes in the forgeries which are not present in the natural writing. However, the cancellations on the envelopes seem genuine."

"There is my dilemma. If there has been a crime, it seems it wasn't committed here," Inspector Lestrade said.

"You could inform the police in Bari," Holmes said.

"Stella Nicoletti did that, but she says they are not taking her seriously. We have no evidence other than someone is intercepting her letters to him and forging responses. I don't even know if that would be illegal in Italy!"

"And yet...."

"And yet, I don't like the smell of it."

"Neither do I."

"There is little I can really do officially at this juncture but I'm afraid if I tell her there is nothing we can do that she will run off to Italy herself and get in trouble, or at the least be a nuisance to the Italian police, and they will send us a wire telling us to keep our crazy women home."

"How can I help?"

"Talk to her. Perhaps you can convince her there is nothing wrong."

"Or get to the root of the matter."

"Yes, I would appreciate it."

"The sister's address?"

Lestrade gave him an address in Clerkenwell.

"I will speak to her tomorrow."

Miss Nicoletti had greeted Holmes' note with enthusiasm and quickly invited him in when he called.

"Thank you, Mr Holmes, for coming. I didn't believe the Inspector was going to do anything."

"There may be little he can do if something happened to your brother in Italy."

"Something happen to my brother. I know it," she said.

"Tell me what you know."

"I am an artist myself, Mr Holmes. Not as well-known as my brother. This is true. I had a commission to complete in Scotland. While I was away Francesco and I wrote to each other nearly every day, as we usually do when we are apart.

"Here in Clerkenwell, we have a nice Italian Catholic church, St Peter's. Everyone knows the priests at St Peter's. They are like family. While I was gone, Francesco wrote that Gina had introduced him to a new priest. I was sceptical because Gina is a believer in much mysticism not approved by the Church. She had been trying to convert Francesco. Francesco wrote that this priest had a vision that if he—Francesco—performed certain prayers and rituals at the Basilica of St Nicholas in Bari, Italy, St Nicholas would heal his clubfoot as he has healed the lame before.

"Francesco sounded so very hopeful in his letter. I wanted to cry! He's had to wear those braces all his life! The doctors say that he should have had surgery when he was a child, but there was so much more danger of infection from surgery in those days that my mother wouldn't risk it. There are some doctors willing to operate on him now and he was considering it when I left for Scotland. Then this priest showed up and promised him a miracle.

"I will tell you something, Mr Holmes; Nicolettis do not give up easily. When the Turks overran Myra in 1087, it was Nicolettis who travelled there and took the bones of St Nicholas and brought them to Bari. I will do whatever I must to find out what happened to my brother. I don't mock the powers of the St Nicholas. But I don't believe this priest. This man—maybe he isn't a priest at all. In any case, I don't believe he knows anything of the powers of St Nicholas or the powers of God."

"Do you know the name of this priest?"

"No. I asked Francesco but the following letters were the forged ones. They did not reply to that question."

"Where is this priest now?" Holmes asked.

"Francesco said he was going with them to Bari."

"Did your brother describe him?"

"No, but I have a photograph."

She picked up a photograph lying on a bureau. It was a photograph of a priest and another man and a woman standing before a steamship. All three of them were bundled against the cold air.

"That is Francesco and Gina with him. It is the last photograph I have of Francesco. When I returned to London it was in the mail that had arrived here in my absence. The note from the photographer which came with it said they had paid for the photograph, and asked that it be sent to me, since I had been unable to see them off. I never received another real letter from Francesco. I gave Inspector Lestrade the forgeries that arrived later."

"Yes, Inspector Lestrade showed them to me. I agree they are forgeries."

Holmes turned the photograph over. The photographer's name and address was stamped on the back.

"May I borrow this?" Holmes asked.

"You can take anything I own if you can tell me what became of my brother. I will pay you, Mr Holmes, down to my last farthing, if that's what it takes."

The photographer's studio was in the City. Holmes took a cab there and showed the photograph to him.

"Yes, I remember taking that," he said.

"You sent it to Stella Nicoletti. She would like more copies."

"I can do that."

"I am curious. Where were the photographs taken?"

"St Katharine Docks."

"Do you regularly take photographs of passengers before they leave on a voyage?"

"No. That man there. The priest. He arranged for me to be there to take the photographs."

"What was the date?"

The photographer looked at his ledger.

"November 27, 1879."

"Did you stay until they boarded the ship?

"No. I just took a few plates and left. That's all I was paid to do and it was bloody cold out there."

"May I see the others?"

Holmes paid to have the photographer make prints of the other plates he had taken and send them to his rooms in Montague Street. The name of the ship is visible in one. He made a note of it. His next visit was to the shipping office.

At the shipping office he confirmed that ship was indeed at St Katharine Docks on the date that the photograph was taken but it was not bound for Italy.

From there Holmes proceeded to Scotland Yard and spoke to Inspector Lestrade.

"So they never went to Italy," Lestrade said.

"Not on that ship. But someone is mailing letters from Italy. Remember the envelopes."

"A confederate, perhaps?"

"I must go to Bari. I can see no other way. There are too many other loose ends there. But I will leave you two of these photographs. You can set your records people on the task of finding if these two have ever been convicted in England before or are wanted for any crimes."

"And the other?"

"To compare with any unidentified corpses found, especially since late November of last year. I am not certain Francesco ever left England. I will wire when I arrive and if I find anything useful."

The particulars of international travel having been dealt with, Holmes left Victoria station for Dover early the next morning. The train ran directly to Admiralty Pier where he boarded a steam ship across the Channel. He arrived in Paris by supper time and Marseille by the following day. The steam packet boat trip from Marseille to Bari was a tedious ordeal lasting several days but at last he found himself in Bari, Italy.

Bari was an old walled city of white and beige stone buildings with tiled roofs. The cobbled streets were very narrow, making walking the most efficient method of travel within the city. Holmes found a room at the Palazzo Calo hotel, a mere three minute walk from the Basilica of St Nicholas. He sent a wire to Inspector Lestrade telling him he had arrived. Then he walked to the Basilica with the photographs. No one who worked there remembered Nicoletti, his wife, or the priest. When he arrived back at the hotel, the desk clerk informed him that he had a telegram.

It was from Lestrade. The Criminal Registry Division had matched the photographs to some in the criminal records files. Gina Guiseppe was really Gina Lombardi who was born in Southampton in Hampshire. She had been previously convicted and served time for fraud and forgery. The priest was not a priest at all, but Benito Florio from Clerkenwell. He also had prior convictions. The news was not a surprise to Holmes. Now he had to find them if they were in Bari.

He began by visiting art galleries in the city. He found some of Nicoletti's paintings for sale in one and was told by the proprietor, with assistance of an employee who spoke some English, that the artist was now living in Bari. However, when Holmes presented him with the photographs, he pointed to the "priest" Florio as Nicoletti rather than the real Nicoletti whom he did not recognize at all. He said he had also met Gina Nicoletti. He, of course, had contact information in case one of the paintings sold. The address he had was to a hotel in Bari. Holmes thanked him and asked for directions to the hotel. The hotel confirmed that Gina and her false husband had stayed there a few days registered as the Nicolettis, but they had since moved to a villa outside the city, and mail for them was being forwarded to that address.

Holmes wired Lestrade with this new information. While Lestrade was communicating with Italian officials regarding this fraud and the theft and trafficking of the artwork, Holmes hired a local man to drive him out to the location of the villa. It was a lovely villa overlooking the sea. Holmes had his driver take him to the front door and wait. He boldly knocked at the door and introduced himself as himself to a servant. He was soon invited in.

"Thank you, Mr Nicoletti," Holmes said to the man who obviously was not Nicoletti standing on two very well formed feet. "I have long been an admirer of your work and when I heard you were here in Italy, I just could not resist the urge to meet the great man himself."

They spoke for a few minutes about art and he admired one of the Nicoletti paintings on the wall. Mrs Nicoletti joined them just as Holmes was leaving and he said good day to them both. He rode back to Bari satisfied that he had spoken to the real Gina Nicoletti and the imposter Benito Florio.

On his return to Palazzo Calo, the desk clerk informed him that he once again had a wire from Lestrade. The Italian police had agreed to pick up Gina and Benito and confiscate the paintings. Inspector Lestrade was coming down with warrants and proof of their identities and criminal records. He hoped to convince the Italian police to allow him to escort them back to London. Holmes wired back about his visit and said he would wait for Lestrade's arrival.

The following day the newspapers in Bari were full of the news of the arrests and the confiscation of the paintings. Three days later Holmes met the steam packet from Marseille. Lestrade stepped off the boat and greeted him more warmly than ever before.

"I am glad that there is someone else in this town who speaks English," he said.

"There are a few others," Holmes assured him. "How confident are you that the Italian government will release them to you?"

"While some of the crimes were committed here, they seem to

be glad enough for us to prosecute them in England."

"You are certain the evidence of the art theft and fraud charges is sufficient?"

"The crown prosecutor is confident. With the information you provided we were able to get search warrants for their homes in Clerkenwell. We found evidence in London that they emptied Nicoletti's bank accounts and took his paintings. The only defence to the art theft would be if his wife claimed he inherited them from her husband and then she would have to prove he was dead."

"Any sign of Francesco Nicoletti?"

"None."

The Italian authorities released Gina and Benito to Lestrade's custody a few days later. Holmes, Lestrade, and the two cuffed criminals took the steam packet boat back to Marseille and crossed France by railway. From Paris they took a train to Boulogne and a steamship from there directly to St Katherine Docks in London via the Thames Estuary.

Lestrade and his prisoners were met by constables who took the couple into custody. Holmes stayed behind when they left. He pulled the photographs out of his pocket. To the best of his knowledge the day the photographs were taken was the last day that anyone had seen Francesco Nicoletti alive. Perhaps if he could stand on the spot where the photographs were taken he could determine what became of Nicoletti.

While a ship took up most of the background in the photographs, some portions of the wharfs and warehouses were visible to varying degrees on the edges. He took out his magnifying glass, examining those details on the edges and then looked at the buildings surrounding him. St Katharine Docks was different that those he had seen in Rotherhithe. Here the docks had been built at one time as a single system rather than built up over time by competitors. The warehouses were built straight along the water of the inner pools. Cargo was raised to the warehouses directly out of the hold rather than being deposited on the wharf. But the view he saw did not match what he saw in the edges of the photographs.

"Mornin', gov'nor," a voice said.

He recognized it before he turned around.

"Good morning, Wiggins," Holmes said. "Perhaps you can help me with this. I am attempting to identify the spot where these photographs were taken."

The boy looked over the photographs.

"Come along, guv'nor," he said taking off, leading Holmes through the crowd of luggage, passengers, ships' crews and dockworkers all going about their business. Wiggins stopped on the other side of St Katharine Docks. He pointed to features in the view.

"Yes, you have found the spot," Holmes confirmed.

"Whatcha lookin' for?" Wiggins asked.

"This man," Holmes said pointing to the man in the middle of the photograph. "He has not been seen since these photographs were taken. His sister says she has not heard from him since that date. The other people in the photograph are not talking. They probably killed him but the police have not found his body."

"Could 'ave dumped him in the river," Wiggins suggested.

"But wouldn't the body have come up by now?"

"Most likely would have 'ere inside the docks. Out there in the river some float out t' sea; Some get stuck somewhere."

"Where do they get stuck?" Holmes asked.

"Under the wharfs, piers, and docks, round the pillars o' bridges. There's pots along the shore where a body could be dumped and it wouldn't float out. The fishies an' things pick 'em clean."

"Even if this man's skeleton was found it could be identified," Holmes said. "He had a severe clubfoot and wore a brace. But I doubt I could convince the police to spare the constables to search all along the Thames foreshore."

"My chums and I could," Wiggins offered "For a consi'eration, of course. We know the places."

"Well, if we can't get the regular police—" Holmes said.

"We'll be your irregulars," Wiggins said.

"Begin near St Katherine Docks, and spread out if nothing is found. A shilling a piece for each and a crown for the one who finds him."

"Yes, gov'nor," Wiggins said with a salute.

He ran off among the maze of shipping offices and warehouses and disappeared. Holmes walked out of St Katharine Docks towards the Thames and found some stairs down towards the foreshore. They were labelled the Alderman Stairs. The tide was coming in but there were still hours to go before high tide. The exposed shingle was littered with pieces of pottery, bricks, and lumps of chalk. He placed the photographs back in his pocket and took out his pipe. He lit it in part to help him think and in part to cover the stench of the river which was very strong along the foreshore.

There were wharfs here extending out into the river and older warehouses on piles. Looking at the undersides of them, it was easy to imagine a body dumped at high tide getting snagged beneath as the tide went out. The same must be true of the footings and pillars of the many bridges. From here the Thames flowed around the Isle of Dogs which contained the East India Docks, the West India docks, and Millwall dock. More places for a body to snag.

If there was flooding from rainstorms or melt from snow storms the higher volume might knock such snags loose and quickly push them downriver through the estuary and out to sea. It had been dry over the past few months so that was less likely. If, as Wiggins said, the flesh might be eaten away, wouldn't the bones just fall to the bottom where they might rest for centuries?

Sherlock Holmes began to mount the stairs again still thinking.

It was daylight in the photographs. The shipping office had confirmed that ship was docked there for only one day. If they had killed him in broad daylight they would not have done it on a wharf or anywhere else exposed to the public. Where would they have gone?

He looked left and right as he stood at the top of the stairs. People were bustling about their business. Suddenly a street urchin appeared, waving at him. He followed the boy down St Katherine Way and was led to a place where older warehouses were built right up to the river and even overhung it. He was not led into a building, but next to it where there was a narrow space between it and another warehouse. Wiggins stood there with some of the other boys.

"Pierce 'ere found it," Wiggins said indicating the boy next to him, and he and Pierce lead Holmes toward the river.

Both buildings reached over the foreshore a short distance and had supporting pillars there. The pillars of the two buildings did not meet flat against each other but rather approached each other at an angle over the foreshore with a space of a few inches at the furthest point. At the nearest point they were more than two feet apart. It was shortly after noon and the summer sun shone down into the triangular space between the pillars. There was a bright splash of white down below which could easily be the top of a skull. Some other bits of white could be seen lower down but were hard to make out. It was too far to reach and two narrow to crawl down. Some of the boys offered but Holmes declined their offers.

"I think we need to leave this to the regular police force," he said.

He sent one of the boys off to the nearest post office with a telegraph form addressed to Inspector Lestrade at Scotland Yard. He left Wiggins and his irregulars on guard and walked out to the place he had directed Lestrade to meet him. Lestrade and several constables appeared as promptly as they could assemble with ropes, nets, grappling hooks and other tools. The boys vanished as the police appeared.

Holmes, the Inspector, and a constable with a long narrow pole with a hook at the end walked around on the foreshore to view the space between the pillars.

"There is no doubt that is a skeleton," Lestrade said.

Holmes ignored the inspector's statement of the obvious. The constables above attached a small net to a rope and tossed it down. The constable below used the hook on his pole to pull the net around the skull so it could be lifted up. This process was repeated for each of the bones they could see below. After several of the largest bones had been lifted Holmes headed back up with Lestrade. He picked up the skull and held it out to the inspector.

"See this crack? A blow from a blunt instrument."

"Cause of death?" Lestrade said.

"Most likely. At the very least a contributing factor. There was no healing of the bone so it occurred near death."

The constables pulled up the net again. Inside was a metal framework encasing the tibia and fibula of the leg. The Inspector took it from the constable.

"I think we have our identification here," said Lestrade.

"Yes. Nicoletti's doctor can probably identify the brace," Holmes said. "The small bones of the foot may be down there or they may have all washed away."

"It means the rope for them. I will need to tell Nicoletti's sister."

"May I do that, Inspector?"

"It's my duty to, but you can come along if you like."

Inspector Lestrade and Sherlock Holmes shared a hansom to Clerkenwell.

"I appreciate your assistance finding them in Italy. I don't know how you found the body."

"I was convinced it was nearby. I consulted a local expert about where a body could be."

"Who is this local expert?"

"I don't believe he wants to be drawn into police business."

When they met with Miss Nicoletti, Holmes returned the photograph she had given him and the prints he had made of the others.

"The photographs helped us locate his remains," Holmes said. "There is little doubt in my mind that they are his remains."

"His wife Gina and Benito Florio—that's the fake priest—are being held awaiting charges," Inspector Lestrade said.

"Will they be convicted of murder?"

"That will depend on the jury, miss," Lestrade. "I believe we have convincing evidence."

"How did he die?" she asked.

"I'm afraid one of them struck him in the head and pushed him between two buildings that lean out over the Thames."

"They left him there to drown? How abominable!"

"If it is any comfort, the blow to the head may have been enough to kill him," Holmes said. "Still no less abominable."

Chapter 19

The *Matilda Briggs*

"We have not forgotten your successful action in the case of Matilda Briggs."
Morrison, Morrison, and Dodd, "The Adventure of the Sussex Vampire"

A knock at the door interrupted Bach's "Chaconne from Partita No. 2 in D minor." Sherlock Holmes set the Stradivarius and the bow on the table and opened the door. A messenger boy presented him with a letter from Jacob Morrison of Morrison, Morrison, and Dodd, solicitors. He opened the envelope and read the letter.

Dear Mr Holmes,

We have a client in urgent need of your services. A solicitor by the name of Michael Abrahams referred us to you. If you could come around to our offices this afternoon at 2 pm we could explain the matter to you.

Jacob Morrison

Morrison, Morrison, and Dodd

Holmes scribbled a quick response confirming the appointment and sent it back via the boy.

Holmes arrived at the offices in the City of London at the appointed time. He was lead into an office not quite as large as Michael Abrahams' and a bit more modern. Jacob Morrison stood and came forward to shake his hand.

"It is very good of you to come, Mr Holmes," he said. "Mr Abrahams said you were a man of discretion and intelligence who could be counted on in unusual circumstances."

"What are the 'unusual circumstances'?" Holmes asked.

"Well, you see, Mr Holmes, our client is Sir Walter Eliot—"

"The naturalist? Just named a Fellow of the Royal Society?" Holmes said.

"Yes. He is retired now after a long career in the East India Company Civil Service. He is a cousin of Lord Elfinstone and was his personal secretary when he was Governor of Madras. He has many friends in high places. That's what makes this so awkward.

"Yesterday he wired the foreign office for some assistance. The foreign office could not help him. They said there are international treaties and protocols that tie their hands. He was persistent and sent a string of telegrams to us this morning. It is really beyond our purview. However, he has been our client for a very long time and we wish to aid him, if possible. We approached the Dutch embassy on his behalf and they laughed at us, or as near as diplomats come to laughing at someone. The shipping office says they can do nothing. Perhaps you can come up with a solution, or maybe talk him out of it."

"What does he want?" Holmes asked.

"He wants a shipment stopped. It is coming from the Dutch East Indies by way of the Suez Canal. He says there will be dire consequences if it reaches England. However, the import documents all seem to be in order and it is on board a Dutch flagged ship called the *Matilda Briggs* bound for Liverpool."

"Is it a plague? Or a bomb?" Holmes asked.

"He hasn't said."

"What are the consequences he predicts if it arrives?"

"Civil war!"

"Good heavens."

"Yes. Serious if true, but rather incredible, I'm afraid. If he were a younger man, I think Sir Walter would try to stop the shipment himself. Unfortunately, he is now nearly blind and feeble and cannot travel. When you responded, we wired to Sir Walter to propose that we hire you to act on his behalf. He has authorized us to offer you £500 plus expenses to stop the shipment. However, I don't feel you can proceed until you travel to his home in Scotland and weigh the seriousness of his concerns."

Holmes sighed.

"And if a medical certification seems to be the most appropriate action?" he asked.

"Then please inform us, and we shall take the matter up with his family," Morrison said, "On the chance that you would accept the commission, we had one of our clerks examine Bradshaw. The most efficient way to reach Sir Elliot's home in Wolfelee, Hawick from London is to take the express to Carlisle and drive from there."

"Then you may tell your client that I will be on the first express to Carlisle."

"Very good. We will arrange for someone to meet you at the station."

It was a very strange commission, but Holmes' curiosity was piqued. He returned home, packed a bag, informed his housekeeper he was heading north for a day or two, and met the early train to Carlisle the next day. On the train he reviewed the stack of telegrams from Sir Walter and the notes the members of the law firm had made on the steps they had taken. The papers merely confirmed Jacob Morrison's summary.

Morrison had wired to Sir Walter to expect his arrival as promised, and a servant with a cart awaited him at the station. Sir Walter was a paunch man in his late seventies. He had wispy white hair on his head where he still had any hair at all and side whiskers of a similar nature. He couldn't seem to sit or stand still for long. He kept getting up and walking about and wringing his hands, then thinking better of it and sitting down again.

"Mr Holmes, thank you for coming. Please have a seat. Is there anything I can get you?"

"No, I would like to get right to it."

"What has Morrison told you?" Sir Walter asked.

"That there is a shipment from Sumatra that you want stopped because you believe it could cause civil war in England."

"He thinks I am mad, doesn't he?" Sir Walter asked.

"He does not know what to think."

"What about you?"

"I have insufficient data to come to a conclusion about either the shipment or whether you are mad," Holmes responded.

"Ha! An open mind? Well, at least you came all this way. That's something," Sir Walter said.

"What is this cargo you seek to stop?" Holmes asked.

"It is an idol of great power made two centuries ago as penance for a wrong done a Hindu goddess. Now an Englishman seeks it."

"Who is he and why does he want it?"

"I do not know who he is or why he wants it."

"Tell me about this idol. What does it look like?" Holmes asked.

"Easily done since I saw it myself in past years. It is three feet tall, two feet in diameter and cast in gold."

"Surely not solid gold?" Holmes said.

"No, not solid, but it weights nearly 800 pounds."

Gold in that quantity was the type of idol Holmes could imagine men fighting for. He suspected the plans for it involved a crucible. It would be worth over £48 000.

"What does this idol look like?"

"It was made in the form of a *Golundi elliotti* somewhat crouching. Much like this specimen here," Sir Walter said, pointing to a taxidermy specimen in a display.

Holmes looked and did not conceal his surprise.

"A rat?" Holmes exclaimed. "This idol is in the shape of a giant gold rat?"

"Yes. It has recently been painted over black," Elliot continued. "I presume they did that to hide the gold from the men who were handling it. They are simpletons if they think that will stop its power. But let me tell you the story of the shrine to Karni Mata and how it came to pass that Devilaal created the Golden Rat. Perhaps you will better understand.

"In the Rajasthan region of India there is a shrine to the goddess Karni Mata where thousands of rats live. It is located in a village called Deshnoke, less than 20 miles from Bikaner. I heard of the shrine when I was studying the rats of India and visited it. The local Hindu people say Karni Mata was born as a woman named Riddhi Kanwar in the late 14th century. Before her birth her mother had a dream that the goddess Durga appeared to her and told her the child would be an incarnation of the goddess herself. There are stories if her performing miracles from a young age. That is how she earned the name Karni Mata which means Miraculous Mother.

"When one of her sons died, Karni Mata confronted Yama, the Hindu god of death, and demanded that her son be returned. After much pleading he relented by reincarnating her son as a rat. He said that in the future all members of her clan would be reincarnated as rats before they die again and resume human form. They say Karni Mata lived to be over 150 years old, protecting the rats of her clan.

One day she vanished and the shrine was built to honour her and protect the rats. The shrine has stood since the 15th century. Visits to the shrine are supposed to bring luck.

"In the 17th century a wealthy Dutch trader, Cornelius van Beeck, visited the shrine at Deshnoke. When he heard that the rats at the shrine were supposed to bring luck he secretly captured several of them and took them away to West Sumatra where his mining and trading ventures were. Unfortunately the rats died during the voyage. van Beeck was haunted by dreams of rats and Hindu goddesses. They were relentless and he could not eat or sleep. Instead of good luck all his luck turned bad. Storms flooded his gold mines and sank his trading ships.

"Finally Karni Mata appeared to him in a dream and said she would forgive him if he built a shrine to her in Sumatra. She told him to return to Deshnoke where there was a talented artist named Devilaal of the Charan clan, who was a debt slave. Van Beeck must pay the man's debt and promise to free him after he built the shrine in Sumatra. He did as he was told. He brought Devilaal to Padang in West Sumatra and housed him in the best room in his house. He offered to provide any materials he required, and as many assistants as he needed. Devilaal began to work and van Beeck's luck began to change: the pepper harvest was good, the trade was profitable, and the mines dried.

"Devilaal first drew plans for a small but elaborate building to house the shrine. It had stone walls with carvings of the goddess on the outside. It had iron gates with representations of rats cavorting as if they were humans. Inside was an idol of a giant rat in tribute to those he had killed. Devilaal asked for stone masons, stone carvers, iron-workers, and casting materials. Van Beeck provided it all and the shrine began to take shape.

"But Devilaal also asked for gold, lots of it, for the idol was to be cast in gold. Van Beeck hesitated for he thought this was a trick. But the goddess appeared to him in a dream and reminded him of his promise. So he agreed to set aside a portion of the gold produced by his mines for the creation of the idol. He had it milled and smelted right there on Sumatra. Devilaal created the mold and the idol was cast. When it cooled and the mold was broken open the idol shined so brightly in the sun that it was hard for anyone to look at it. They covered it with a cloth and took it to the shrine where it was uncovered. It continued to shine brightly to show the goddess' favour.

"This shrine was built away from the cities, in the mountains of West Sumatra. Van Beeck freed Devilaal as he had promised, but Devilaal did not return to India. He built a house near the shrine and stayed to tend it. The goddess appeared to him in his dreams and taught him the mysteries of her many incarnations. Karni Mata told him that the golden idol of the rat drew her to the shrine and through it she would perform miracles as she had in life.

"Devilaal knew of a sick child in the Paganda hospital that was not expected to survive. He convinced the child's parents to bring the child to the shrine and ask the goddess for a cure. The child got better. Others heard of the cure and brought their ailments. Soon the forest was filled with a line of people.

One man visited many times. He tried to convince Devilaal to charge a fee to enter the shrine, and when Devilaal refused, the man pretended to people on the queue that there was a fee, and took money from them and kept it. Devilaal found out and forced the man to leave. Then the man plotted to steal the idol. The night he came for it a great storm arose. Devilaal said he saw the image of Karni Mata in the clouds, then it turned to Durga the goddess of power, and then to Kali the goddess of death and destruction. As the evil man touched the golden idol it was struck by lightning and he was killed.

"Karni Mata, the loving mother, came to Devilaal in his dream that night and told him that the idol focused her power for good, but it also could focus it for evil. It would cause great strife if evil men sought to use its power. The idol would magnify their corruption and destroy those around it. Devilaal knew he must tell all to stay away and let the memory of the shrine fade, for the idol was too powerful.

"Devilaal married a local woman of Sumatra. They raised many children. Devilaal watched his children as they grew and chose one to impart the mysteries of the shrine. His son did the same. Most of the children moved away, but one of each generation stayed to tend the shrine.

"Van Beeck visited the shrine from time to time to thank the goddess. He left instructions in his will that the land it was on was not to be sold, and the shrine was not to be destroyed. In his will he advised his heirs to thank the goddess for their good fortune. So for generations these two families protected the shrine in Sumatra. But in time van Beeck's family left Sumatra and returned to the Netherlands. Only the Charan family remained to protect the shrine."

Holmes tried to hide his impatience. He did not believe the man's supernatural poppycock. It was unnecessary that he do so. Sir Walter continued.

"After I retired, I travelled about Asia researching the flora and fauna. I visited the shrine in India. I heard there was another shrine in Sumatra. After much enquiry I found my way there and met Aatma Charan, the current guardian of the shrine. He told me the story of how it came to be, as I have just told you. He told me much about Sumatra and India that his fathers had passed down to him. We became friends. He told me many mysteries of the goddess and her many incarnations. He said she appeared in his dreams as she had to his forefathers. They believed, as he believed, that there was power in the golden rat idol, power that was sleeping and that his family's role had been to honour and assuage that power.

"After I returned to England, Aatma and I corresponded by letters. What I am going to tell you now I am summarizing from his recent letters.

"A few months ago Johannes van Beeck, the most recent descendant and heir of Cornelius van Beeck, died, and his son, and sole heir, Hendrik, inherited all his properties. While Hendrik was settling the estate he received offers for the land in Sumatra from mining interests that made no mention of the shrine, and seemed fair to him. About that time he received an offer for the idol in the shrine from an Englishman. The shrine, the idol, and the instructions in the will seemed to him to be the folly of old men passed down through generations. Since there were no other heirs there was no one who could stop him from ignoring the instructions in the will.

"Before he accepted either offer Hendrik van Beeck travelled to Sumatra to inspect the land and the shrine. He met Aatma Charan.

Aatma said Hendrik was a young, handsome man, dressed sharply in new clothes. Initially they spoke in a friendly manner. Then one day Hendrik told Aatma that he had two weeks to move because he was going to sell the land. He also told Aatma that he had sold the idol to an Englishman. Aatma asked who the Englishman was and what was the price. Hendrik said none of the mattered, he was selling it. He said he would have men pack the idol and take it down to Paganda where it would be stored at the office of the shipping agent until the ship arrived to take it to England.

"The next day other men came with Hendrik van Beeck. Some came with cans of coal tar and brushes. Some carried long guns. They painted over the golden idol with the coal tar to hide its glory. While the tar was drying, more came with tools and crates and saws. They knocked down the walls of the shrine. Aatma could feel the goddess' anger growing. He begged van Beeck to send him with the idol. The men pulled him away and tossed him to the ground. Aatma is an old man. His wife had died many years before. He was not well, but he did his duty to the shrine. His youngest son Chitranjan lived with him and helped him. Chitranjan was angered by the treatment of the shrine and his father. He struck out at Hendrik van Beeck and the men with the guns shot and killed him. Then they wrapped the dull black rat with blankets and crated it. It was so heavy that they built a sled for it and hauled it down the mountain.

Aatma placed his son's body in the remains of the shrine and set fire to it. He then headed down the mountain to follow the idol. He said that the winds rose as he walked down the mountain and the fire spread through the forest and the smoke filled the sky. When he reached Paganda he took up a seat next to the shipping office where the idol was stored. He found out the ship was a steam freighter in the pepper trade called the *Matilda Briggs*. It was loading pepper cargo in the islands and would collect the idol when it was done."

"Then I received a telegram that claimed to be from Aatma who never sends telegrams. I suspect he dictated it to someone who sent it: 'Idol loaded on ship. Ship leaves tomorrow. You must stop them or England will be destroyed.' You can imagine how chilling that was to me. I sent a wire back asking for more details. I received no response but a few days' later the letter came. You may see it if you like but it is written in the Charan family's peculiar mix of dialects from India and Sumatra that they developed over the generations. It will be easier for me to translate."

Sir Walter Elliot took up a large magnifying lens and squinted at the letter:

"The goddess came to me in a dream. Karni Mata cried for me and the death of my son. She promised me that he had already found a new human form and I would soon, too. But her grief was consumed with anger at the destruction of the shrine, and the removal of the icon. With the anger she transformed to Durga and Kali. Many do not understand these are all facets of the same being, though 'force' is a better word. Kali shrieked 'If the giant rat reaches England there will be war in the lands. Brother shall turn upon brother. Sister upon sister. They shall destroy each other and lay waste to the land.' This is a terrible prophesy. I cannot appease the goddess. I cannot stop them. The ship leaves Padang tomorrow headed for the Suez Canal and then to England. You must stop them or the land you love will be destroyed."

Sir Walter was silent for a few seconds.

"Have you ever believed something merely because someone you trust told you? I am a Christian. I do not worship Hindi gods. Yet—"

He paused again.

"Yet, I feel in my heart," Sir Walter continued, "that what Aatma wrote is true and I must do everything in my power to stop the idol of the Giant Rat of Sumatra from arriving in England."

Sir Walter got up to pour himself some brandy with a shaking hand.

A servant entered.

"A wire for you, sir," he said offering the yellow envelope on a salver.

Sir Walter took it and tore it open and took up his powerful lens again. His face fell as he read it and he dropped into a chair.

"It was from the manager of the telegraph office in Paganda, Sumatra. They were unable to deliver my last telegram to Aatma Charan because he is dead."

"Mr Holmes," Sir Walter said with a shaking voice, "I have promised you £500 if you stop that cargo. I now double that offer."

"I accept your commission on those terms. However, it is not so much the money that entices me, but the problem itself. I do not blindly accept tales of magical beings without evidence of their existence. I respect your trust in your friend's word and his belief, but all I have so far is a series of tales. I admit that no alternative theory explains the facts as you have stated them unless this is some elaborate ruse, or—"

"I am mad."

"Yes. But at the moment I have insufficient information to select among those hypotheses or to construct another. The best way to gain additional information is to meet the *Matilda Briggs* at the Suez Canal and board her. What I do next will depend upon the circumstances. I will take any steps necessary to prevent the idol from causing harm in England."

He had chosen his words carefully to include the circumstance in which he found the idol to not be a danger.

"Thank you, my boy, thank you," Sir Walter said. "Would you like to spend the night here and travel in the morning?"

"No. As you know, time is a critical factor. I must be certain that I reach the Suez Canal before the *Matilda Briggs* does. I will take the sleeper to London tonight and meet the boat train to France tomorrow. I will keep in touch with your solicitor since I may need him to do additional research while I am travelling. He will relay to you information he deems appropriate."

"Very good. Godspeed."

Holmes noted with irony the last word Sir Walter said.

Which god? he wondered.

Holmes returned immediately to the train station and sent a wire to Jacob Morrison confirming that he had met with Sir Walter and was travelling to intercept the *Matilda Briggs* at the Suez Canal. He asked Morrison to investigate the probate of the will of Johannes van Beeck in the Netherlands and any sales of property from the estate.

Sherlock Holmes travelled south by trains to Dover, and by the boat from there to France, and across France by train to Marseille. As the trains sped across two countries, Holmes smoked his pipe and turned over all the information in his mind. He was deeply sceptical that Hindi gods or goddesses were threatening to destroy England over a giant gold rat. He remained puzzled by the whole affair.

At the port of Marseille on the Cote d'Azure he had to wait sometime before he could get a boat over to Port Said. Having lived in France for a number of years when he was young, French was a second language to him. He changed some of his funds to francs, and used them in a second-hand clothing shop to purchase the pantaloons, blouse, cap, and boots of a French worker. A French wine bottle and the fact that he had not shaved for several days completed the costume of an unemployed Frenchman. Here he would leave the English detective behind.

From Marseille he also sent a wire to Jacob Morrison. Morrison quickly returned a wire confirming the death of Johannes van Beeck in the Netherlands in April and the probate of the will which contained the reference to the property and the shrine in Sumatra, and the advice to thank the goddess. There was only one heir, Hendrik van Beeck, who had also been named executor. There had been several sales of property from the estate. There was a contract for the sale of the Sumatra property to the Solok Mining Group, Ltd, as well as a contract for a statue measuring approximately three-foot by two-foot by two-foot through an agency in Liverpool. The ultimate buyer's name was not available. The Liverpool agency said it was confidential. There was one final detail in the telegram from Morrison: Hendrik van Beeck was on board the *Matilda Briggs*.

Holmes boarded the boat from Marseille to Port Said. The trip across the Mediterranean Sea was four days long. Physically he spent most of it leaning against the rail, working on his character of a drunken unemployed Frenchman hoping to find work in the canal. Mentally he was stripping away the veneer of the case. Ignoring all historical, religious, or mythological considerations, this was the case of a wealthy heir liquidating estate assets in a harsh manner. If this was fiction, he would be investigating the heir's murder, rather than attempting to stop one of the assets from being transferred in Liverpool. The story contained enough exotic misdirection to be fiction. Yet as far as he knew the heir was still alive, and Holmes and the golden idol were steaming towards a rendezvous.

When they arrived in Port Said, Holmes joined many others vying for a spot on a ferry heading south through the Suez Canal to Port Tewfik. The Canal was 120 miles long and the passage at an average of eight knots took twelve to sixteen hours depending on traffic and weather conditions.

At Port Tewfik he learned that the *Matilda Briggs* was scheduled for coaling there for the remainder of the journey to Liverpool, and then on to the Netherlands, but the officials at the coal fuelling depot had not seen her yet. He resigned himself to wait. There were hotels, cafes, and restaurants at Port Tewfik and the nearby town of Suez, but Holmes did no more than consume several cups of coffee.

Since turning the facts of the case, as he knew them, upside down and inside out had not proved beneficial, he bought some French newspapers to take his mind off it. He was shocked to learn of the massacre of British troops near the village of Maiwand in Afghanistan, and the forty-five mile retreat of the wounded to Kandahar ten days before.

It was then, as he was staring across the Gulf of Suez shaking his head at such senseless loss of life, that he saw the *Matilda Briggs*. She was not the pride of anyone's fleet. The freighter was small and dirty. It was an older style steamship which still had sail masts to conserve coal, or to replace it if they ran out. It had no paddlewheels, so it was screw propelled. The blue and white hull colours were peeling, rusty, and nearly hidden by the coal soot that covered her. But the name was visible on the bow, and the flag of the Netherlands flew on the mast.

The sun was low in the west as she steamed toward the coal depot at substantially below port limits. The ship was almost coasting. Perhaps the captain had underestimated the coal supply, or they had met bad weather or other causes for delay that had used up their fuel. Perhaps such economy was his habit since he had the sails to fall back on. Or perhaps he had not been told the true nature of the cargo and its immense weight.

Holmes watched as the depot men who were expecting the

Matilda Briggs launched a coal barge towards her. He had considered attempting to reach the ship in the disguise of a coal heaver. The coaling stations were always short-handed. However, he had noticed watching other vessels that those from the coal barge never boarded the ship, and an attempt to do so would raise suspicions.

No one at the coaling station would find his watching the coaling operation of the *Matilda Briggs* suspicious, as he had been watching coaling operations for several days, and she wasn't the only ship he had enquired about. He had left the impression that he was unemployed with a vague idea of getting a job on board a ship, but liking the bottle better than work. That had been confirmed in their minds when he had turned down their offer to do some coal heaving on another vessel. No one would be surprised if he continued to hang about or just disappeared.

Before the coaling had actually begun, a boat had been lowered from the *Matilda Briggs* with a few men on board. They docked the boat and headed into the town of Suez. Holmes assumed that Hendrik van Beeck was among them, hoping to get a decent meal and a comfortable bed for the night.

Coaling was a very dirty and noisy process. Holmes planned to take advantage of that fact. While it was proceeding Holmes made his way down to the shore at the nearest point he could to the *Matilda Briggs* that was not well lit. The sun was setting and twilight would last about an hour. He untied his boots, removed them, tied their laces together, and slung the boots on his back. Keeping to the shadows he crept out and plunged into the water. On the far side of the *Matilda Briggs* from the coal barge he found the ropes that had lowered the boat. He caught one in a hand and looked up. Then he scrambled up the rope quickly, peered over the side, and vaulted over. He landed next to one of the other boats on the deck and slid behind it. The banging, scraping and clattering of the coaling process on the other side and in the coal bunker below entirely covered any sound he might have made.

He shook out his boots to assure they contained as little water as possible. He removed his shirt and stockings and wrung them out. They would dry quickly in the summer heat and the dry desert air.

Even after sunset the air was quite warm and the dip in the water had been rather refreshing. He lay prone on the deck behind the boat with his head lying on one arm. He could not smoke. He dared not fall asleep due to his precarious position of being a stowaway. The constant noise of the shovelling of the coal from the barge to the baskets, and the calls of the coalers and the levellers in the bunker did not encourage sleep. He attempted to separate the different sounds he heard. He needed to have a better idea of the layout of the ship. He had hoped to speak to Hendrik van Beeck but since he had gone ashore that would have to wait.

In time the noise ended. The sounds from within the ship settled down and eventually he heard the barge moving away. Since the ship was anchored in the gulf few crew were needed for the watch overnight. Most shuffled off to their berths. The ship was silent except for some slight creaking as she gently rocked on the water. He heard no voices and no footsteps. No engines were running. Turning over and looking up he saw a dark sky pierced with stars.

Holmes crawled out from under the boat and began a tour of the vessel. He was still barefoot and was cautious about where he stepped, not wanting to add any creaking to the night. Someone was assigned to the watch even though the ship was at rest, and he could not depend upon them being lulled to sleep by the easy motion of the ship. Most of the crew were probably exhausted from the coaling operation and fast asleep but they were trained to snap awake quickly if need be.

He looked for the cargo holds but found they were padlocked. As he continued to explore the deck he came across a crate about four feet tall and three feet wide on its sides. It was tied to the deck with several wide straps. A label readable even by starlight said it was bound for Liverpool. This must be the legendary Giant Rat of Sumatra.

As he made this discovery, he heard a creak from a staircase. He quickly concealed himself. A man walked by carrying a rifle. By starlight he seemed to have dark hair and swarthy features. Holmes wondered if this was one of the men Aatma had seen in Sumatra, perhaps even the man who had killed his son. He held his breath.

Holmes was unarmed, barely clothed, and alone. He had notified Jacob Morrison when he had arrived at Port Tewfik. The solicitor knew he intended to board the Matilda Briggs, though he might not have understood (intentionally or unintentionally) that Holmes planned to stow away. The solicitor's job would be to protect their client. It would be left to Mycroft to determine what had become of him if he disappeared at this moment, and Mycroft undoubtedly would. The letter from Jacob Morrison was still lying on the table in the flat where he had left it. That was one of many bread crumbs that Mycroft could easily follow. But neither justice nor vengeance is comforting, when you are considering your own mortality, as Sherlock Holmes was in that instant. The instant passed, as the man had, and Holmes made his way back to his hiding place under the boat.

It was just after dawn that he heard a commotion on board. Running, shouting, a splash. More running and shouting. "Man overboard" in Dutch was not very different from the English equivalent.

Several hours later he had some uncomfortable moments when the boat that had departed the previous day was hauled up very close to his hiding place. He heard several men speaking in Dutch as those in the boat came aboard the ship.

He knew very little Dutch, but he heard the words *zelfmoord* which seemed to refer to the earlier event and *een andere* which suggested it was not the first. He deduced it was Hendrik van Beeck who said the latter and the man he was speaking to was the captain. Van Beeck seemed tired and annoyed. Among the words Holmes heard him say thereafter were *Engelsman*, *geld*, Liverpool, and *vervloekt schip* which did not seem very complementary to the *Matilda Briggs*.

From the conversation Holmes concluded that the journey from Sumatra had not been a smooth one. Perhaps his theory that something had caused them to burn more coal than expected was correct. Several crew members also seemed to have gone overboard. Voluntarily or involuntarily? He had heard no gunshot when the one had gone over earlier. He could not tell from the sounds whether the others were chasing him to stop him from jumping or whether he was trying to escape them.

The *Matilda Briggs* started her engines not long after and began the approach to the canal. Several other ships were ahead of her and she joined the queue. From time to time crew members passed his hiding place going about their business. Once that morning he heard footsteps going both directions. One crew member seemed to be asking another a question. The other responded that van Beeck *is ziek*. Holmes could not decipher the response of the other. He took the risk of taking a peek and saw one of them with a tray heading off. Holmes followed him at a distance and watched from the stairs. He saw which cabin the tray was delivered to and swiftly returned to his sanctuary.

The journey north through the Suez Canal was not as scenic as the journey south since he spent it lying on his back beneath a boat. His clothing had dried out and he had put his shirt back on but left his stockings and boots off for it was easier to move silently about the ship without them.

The sun set before the *Matilda Briggs* reached Port Said. The twilight showed clouds gathering. As daylight faded away Holmes saw lightning in the distance. He waited a bit longer for darkness to deepen then made his way up the stairs. He approached the cabin door where the crew member had delivered the tray for van Beeck and opened the door slowly. There was a small lamp lit in the room. Light spilt out the doorway. He slid in the gap between the sill and the door and closed the door behind him.

He saw a thin man with red hair leaning over a small desk. He poured a clear liquid from a bottle to a glass and gulped it down. The man was sweating profusely. He seemed to shiver then he walked over to the berth and sat down. It was then he noticed Holmes standing at the door.

Wie ben je? Ik zei tegen de kapitein dat ik niet gestoord wilde worden, he said.

"My name is Sherlock Holmes. I am sorry but I do not speak Dutch."

"You are an Englishman. You are not one of the crew," Hendrik van Beeck said in English.

"I am not."

"A stowaway," van Beeck said before flopping back on the pillow.

"You have malaria," Holmes said.

"That's what the doctor in Suez said. He said I should stay at the hospital until I get better. I want to go home."

"You are drinking quinine water."

"Yes. Doctor said it might cure it."

"You caught malaria in Sumatra?" Holmes asked.

"Most likely. I thought that place held my fortune—"

"The rat."

"You know about that? No, this is all probably a fever dream."

"I am real," Holmes said.

"Then what do you want from me, Mr—whatever it was,"

"Sherlock Holmes."

"What do you want, Mr Holmes?"

"I want the giant rat," Holmes said. "Or rather my principal wants it."

"I already have a buyer," van Beeck said.

"The man I work for will pay twice as much if the idol never reaches England," Holmes said.

"Where does he want it?" van Beeck said feverishly puzzled.

"Just push it overboard in the Mediterranean Sea."

"And then he will pay? Now I know you are a hallucination. Go away."

Van Beeck pushed the button of a call bell.

"Mr van Beeck—" Holmes began but his words were drowned in a clap of thunder.

There was a knock at the door.

"*Kom binnen. Deze man is een verstekeling,*" van Beeck called.

The door was thrown open. A sailor stood there with a knife in his hand.

Holmes grabbed the chair and swung it at the sailor. When he dodged it, Holmes grabbed his knife arm and forced it backwards and knocked his hand against the wall. He snatched up the knife and ran past him out the door.

Van Beeck yelled something in Dutch.

On deck Holmes could see that they were approaching Port Said. It was raining and the winds were rising, tossing up waves. The ships ahead were increasing speed to reach the Mediterranean Sea before the storm overcame them and *Matilda Briggs* did the same. The lights of Port Said slid past.

Sherlock Holmes ran to the golden idol's crate and began sawing away at the bands that held it to the deck with the knife he had taken from the sailor. Perhaps if he could release the crate, it would disembark on its own in the rising storm. He could hear shouts of the crew looking for him. As he was working on the last band, a flash of lightning revealed his location to his pursuers. He ran in his bare feet across the wet deck and found a new hiding spot. Another lightning stroke revealed him again and a bullet sailed over his head. He ran.

Matilda Briggs picked up steam heading northward into the open sea away from Port Said and with luck away from the storm. Another bullet sailed past Holmes and he ran. He found himself beside the mast. He could not hide behind it long before they would find him. So he climbed, as he had climbed the buildings at Cambridge as an undergraduate. The mast made for easier climbing than the drain pipes or lightning conductors he'd climbed in college. He climbed rapidly. As he gained altitude he saw the frothing sea was glowing. Lights in the waves seemed to pulse and form spoked wheels that rotated, some clockwise, and some counter clockwise. He saw his pursuers on deck staring at the sea as well. They seemed to be arguing with each other. But he also saw the storm was surrounding the ship. Lightning illuminated swirling clouds. The wind rose and the seas heaved. He clung to the mast. Below the argument reached a crisis and one man shot another and two of the men threw him overboard. The rest spread out once more searching for him.

Ice began pelting from the heavens. It tore at his shirt and slashed at his flesh, but still he clung. The men were too close to the base of the mast for him to come down. Waves splashed over the deck taking some of the men with them. The thunder was deafening. The storm, now directly above the ship, was a fearful aspect of darkness and blinding ionized gas. For an instant, it seemed to take the form of a woman of kindly aspect, then a warrior woman of power, and then a woman with many arms reaching towards the ship. Then a gigantic wave overtopped the mast. Sherlock Holmes held on with all his might as the mast splintered below him and fell. Even the stunning impact with the sea did not loosen his grip. That saved his life.

In the light of the dawn, some fishermen found him, half-conscious, still clinging to a portion of the mast. They dragged him aboard their boat and took him back to Port Said, Egypt. He met with the British Consulate which helped him arrange for funds from London to book passage back to England. Nothing more was ever seen or heard of Hendrik van Beeck, the *Matilda Briggs*, her crew, or the Giant Rat of Sumatra.

On the deck of the passenger ship back to England Holmes sat scribbling mathematical figures with a pencil on a pad of paper. Sometimes he stopped and stared out across the water, remembering the things he had seen and heard. Then he would do more calculations.

Two gentlemen were walking along the deck speaking French.

"Voici, Jules! C'est une belle journée."

"Vraiment! Tu sais à quel point j'aime être sur la mer."

As they passed Holmes, the one called Jules stopped and said in English to him, "I have noticed before that you are an Englishman. Excuse me for being rude but I am curious what you are doing there."

"Calculating the source of some unusual meteorological phenomena," Holmes responded.

"I suppose therein hangs a tale?" Jules asked.

"Not one the world is prepared to hear."

"Why not?" Jules asked.

"Do you believe that we live in a world where the majority of the population places more confidence in science than supernatural intercession?"

"No," Jules responded.

"That is why not," Sherlock Holmes said.

"Ah. You fear they will attach a supernatural significance to the phenomena rather than accept the scientific explanation?"

"Precisely."

"You may be right about that, young man. What are you going to do about it?"

"Keep it to myself for now."

"Come along, Jules. Leave the man be," his companion said.

"Good day!"

Holmes looked down at his figures. His calculations might explain the rotating lights he had seen in the ocean, but they did not explain what he had seen in the clouds. Was it a hallucination caused by days without sleep or nourishment? Had he dreamed it as he floated on the sea? He did not know.

He did know that if word spread of what he thought he had seen in those clouds, it would not be believed in serious scientific circles and would be latched onto by occultists. It could significantly harm his budding detective career. Thus no word of it should cross his lips. That the *Matilda Briggs* sank in a storm in the Mediterranean Sea was all that he reported to the solicitor Jacob Morrison who in turn informed their client. Sir Walter Elliot was satisfied that the idol never reached England and paid as he had promised.

Chapter 20

Connections

"I had already established a considerable,
though not a very lucrative, connection."
Sherlock Holmes, "The Musgrave Ritual"

In Holmes' mind the *Matilda Briggs* case overshadowed everything that occurred in the autumn and early winter of 1880-1881. Clients came with petty problems that Holmes solved, but they were hardly worth noting by comparison. Yet he had sworn to himself that he would not reveal the details of that most peculiar case to anyone, which is why it remained so much on his mind.

The most noteworthy event of a personal nature that autumn was Mycroft moving to new rooms that had come available across from the Diogenes Club. Yet that seemed nearly anticlimactic given that Mycroft had rarely been present at their shared rooms for years.

Another event of import to Sherlock Holmes himself was his use of some of the funds he had received from Sir Elliot to purchase scientific equipment of his own, as well as standard chemicals that would be needed for most analysis. He had hesitated to do it before Mycroft moved to separate lodgings for several reasons, not least of which was that the only space for them in the small flat was either on the table in the sitting room used for meals or in the room Mycroft had previously occupied. Mycroft would not have approved of either.

January of 1881 was once again a cold one. However, on the 6th of January the Holmes brothers resumed their tradition of dinner and a play to celebrate Sherlock's birthday.

"Happy Birthday, Sherlock!"

"Thank you, Mycroft."

"Twenty-seven years, and to think I remember the day you were born."

Sherlock laughed.

"I raise a toast: May 1881 bring you many challenging puzzles to which to apply your unique talents!"

They raised their glasses to the toast, and then Mycroft pushed

"

a large envelope across the table toward his brother.

"This might seem an unusual birthday gift but I know how your tastes run. This copy of the October 28th, 1880 issue of the journal *Nature* came to hand. You will see on page 605 a letter from Mr Henry Fauld, a British surgeon at Tsukiji Hospital, in Tokio, Japan, about his investigations into the skin-furrows of the hand and how they may be used in the identification of criminals. I thought you might find it interesting."

"Indeed," Sherlock said taking the journal in one hand and turning the other over to examine the ridges on his own fingers. "Fascinating."

The following day Sherlock Holmes re-examined Fauld's article and made prints of his own finger tips and studied them with his magnifying glass. Of course, without more samples the conclusions he could make were limited. Mrs Denton, already irked about the laboratory set up in the other bedroom, was unwilling to participate.

A blizzard raged from January 18th through the 20th, with gale force winds combining with a high spring tide to cause severe flooding from the estuary up past London, drowning the ports of Rotherhithe, and causing extensive damage. This was followed by heavy snow falling on London, piling up to ten inches in most places, with drifts over three feet in some spots.

Initially Sherlock Holmes spent time at chemical analysis but the storm outside made it difficult to air out the small rooms without inviting it in. So he turned to the recent accumulation of newspapers.

There were, of course, the usual collections of petty thefts, burglaries, and deaths by person-or-persons unknown. On January 14th, a bomb had exploded at the military barracks in Salford, Lancashire. A young boy was killed. It was thought to be the work of Irish or Irish-American radicals. Perhaps Lestrade had been justified in his suspicions on the Tarleton matter though he had been entirely wrong in that case. Holmes added the clippings concerning the bombing to his collection and to the index.

The newspapers continued to report on troop movements from Afghanistan. What remained of the 66th (Berkshires) Regiment had marched from Kandahar on October 1st, 1880, en route for India, and arrived at Quetta on the 18th. After a fortnight's rest at Quetta, they had marched to Pir Chowki, arriving on November 3rd. From there the regiment proceeded by rail to Kurrachee, where it arrived on November 7th. These notices were added to the pile which the housekeeper was permitted to use for fire-starting.

No clients came requesting his assistance during the storm and the immediate aftermath. By early February London was beginning to dry out and Holmes was becoming restless. Even his beloved Stradivarius was insufficient to settle his nerves. He walked over to the British Museum and began reviewing their latest scientific acquisitions. As was not unusual, references in one treatise led him to another, and another, and he spent weeks reading at the museum until the weather improved.

On the evening of March 16th, 1881, Sherlock Holmes was absorbed in a book at the British Museum when heavy tread and the call of his name pulled him from his studies. He looked up to find Inspector Gregson of Scotland Yard.

"Mr Holmes, I need you to come with me."

Usually such a summons from a Scotland Yarder is followed by the application of handcuffs. While Holmes did not expect that was the case, the next sentence was even more thrilling to the young detective.

"We need your assistance."

The fact that the Scotland Yard detective had tracked him down at the museum was not at all remarkable since he had told his housekeeper where he would be on the off chance a client did call, and the museum was around the corner from his flat. The fact that the official detective had gone to the effort of tracking him down was remarkable.

When they arrived at Scotland Yard, Holmes was led to a room he had never been in before. There were tables and chairs in the room, and maps on the walls. He deduced it was some type of planning or strategy room. There were several other people present. Some did not seem to be happy he was there. None were in uniform and no introductions were given. Several were obviously other police detectives. He also recognized the Chief Inspector of Explosives, which reflected on the seriousness of the situation.

"A time or two you have given us a clue that has set us on the right track," Inspector Gregson said. "I think in those cases we would have gotten there eventually, but in this case time is critical. Likely to be a matter of life or death. Anything that can speed up our investigation even a little would be helpful. I suggested that we consult with you to see if you could offer a clue. Regardless of the outcome, you are not to repeat anything about this meeting to anyone else. Do you understand?"

"Yes."

"You are aware of the bombing at the Army barracks in Salford, Lancashire in January?"

"Yes. I read the newspaper reports," Holmes said.

"We believe that was just the beginning. We recently raided a house where some of the Fenians were living. We believe we have found a cypher message that might indicate the time and place of the next bombing but none of our people can decipher it."

"Let me see it," Holmes said.

A man set a roll of paper in front of Holmes. The paper was about an inch wide and the roll was approximately two inches thick. He picked it up and began to unroll it. He noticed something tacky on the back and turned it over.

"You are looking at the wrong side," someone said.

"Patience," Holmes replied.

He turned the paper tape so the sticky substance caught the light. It ran down the length of the paper. He felt it and smelled.

"Some type of gum or other adhesive," he said.

"Is that significant?" someone asked.

"Perhaps," Holmes said.

He turned it over and examined the other side. There were letters and numbers with spaces between them. They were written in simple block form but often seem to curve slightly at the bottom. They responded to none of the standard substitution or shift types of cyphers.

"Would you expect the message to be written in English or Irish Gaelic?" he asked.

"We believe they are Irish-American and thus English is more likely."

Holmes curled the paper tape around his finger a couple of times then increased the size of the loops.

"Do you have a broom handle?" he asked.

His audience seemed surprised and annoyed by the request, but one of them fetched a broom and handed it to Holmes.

He took the broom and stuck the paper to the top of the handle and the spirit gum held it. It took a couple of attempts to get the wrapping angle right, but soon he had wrapped the roll around the handle so that the letters and numbers lined up on either side of the broom handle running its length. English words were formed.

"Mansion House. Tonight," Holmes said holding the broom handle out for Inspector Gregson to see. The others gathered round trying to see the message.

There were more words, but Holmes figured they could read for themselves.

"It is an ancient form of cypher invented in the 5th century BC called a Spartan Scytale," he continued. "They used spear shafts but I figured the common broom was the most likely device today."

As he was talking the room emptied as the men scrambled for the exits.

"Thank you," Inspector Gregson said before leading Holmes out to the street where he hailed a cab back home.

The following morning Holmes read the headline: "Scotland Yard Foils Attempted Bombing at Mansion House." The article underneath said: "Quick action by the Metropolitan Police found and diffused a bomb outside the Mansion House at 10 p.m. last night. Sir Vivian Dering Majendie, Chief Inspector of Explosives says the bomb would not have damaged the structure but could have injured passersby." There was no mention of his name. Holmes chuckled.

As the weather warmed more clients brought their problems to Sherlock Holmes. In late May a woman sat turning over her handkerchief in her gloved hands in his sitting room in Montague Street. Holmes observed her in silence. Her hat, dress and gloves were powder blue with white accents. Her coat matched. The ensemble was simple, but of fine fabric and well-tailored. It was not new. She was matronly, yet graceful. She was past the first blush of youth, but her career as a young wife had been interrupted by tragedy. It was there in her eyes. She had no husband, parent, or sibling to advise her. She had the experience to know she needed help, but not quite the confidence to ask for it. He broke the silence.

"Mrs Forrester, I understand that you are a young widow left to manage your household on your own. You have no living family in England, other than your two boys. You are well-enough off to have household staff, yet you cannot afford extravagances. You are seeking my advice on some matter."

"Yes. My husband, Cecil, died last year—struck by an omnibus, but I don't suppose you need to know that. How did you know I had no family and have two boys?"

"Because your son, the eldest, I presume, sensed something was concerning you and that your excursion this morning was related to your concern. So he inserted a tin soldier in your right coat pocket to protect you. I saw the outline of it bulging as you entered."

She reached into her pocket and pulled out the soldier. She smiled.

"And despite the immaculateness of your attire and coiffure, there is a spot of jam on the handkerchief that you have been showing to me. I infer that you saw the jam on your younger son's face when you were telling him goodbye and instinctively wiped it off with the handkerchief."

She smiled down at the handkerchief.

"If you had other family who could advise you why would you have come to me?"

"Yes. I see. All that is true. I can manage the usual things like dealing with greengrocers and tradesmen and maintaining the house, but this is something out of the ordinary. It is a delicate domestic complication that could cause such a disruption to the household. I don't want to call the police. Even if they could solve it, and I am uncertain they could, the embarrassment if they falsely accused anyone—I am sure some of the staff would turn in their notice. You understand?"

"Certainly."

"I mentioned it in confidence to a friend of mine whom I have known forever. She said that her younger brother had known this clever fellow in college—I hope you recognize yourself—who might be able to help. She got your address for me and you were kind enough to see me. But I am not really getting around to the matter, am I? I should just tell it to you straight."

"Please do."

"Someone is stealing things in my home and I don't know who."

"You believe it is someone in the household?"

"Yes."

"Tell me about the household."

"There is myself and my two sons, Ham and Alex. Ham is Cecil Jr, but when his father was alive we called him by his middle name, Markham, and it was gradually shortened to Ham. He's the oldest, now seven and Alex is five. There is their governess, Joan Sanford. The cook is Mrs McDowell and there are two maids, Betsy and May."

"Any groundskeepers or gardeners?"

"There is one man who tends the gardens but he only comes around once a week and is rarely in the house. The grounds are not extensive."

"What day of the week?"

"Thursdays."

"And regular tradesmen or deliverymen?"

"No."

"Does any of your staff have sweethearts who visit?"

"Not that I am aware of."

"Does the staff live in?"

"Joan Sanford and May do. The house is large enough to accommodate additional live-in staff, but it is just not the situation at this time. Mrs McDonald is married and goes home to her family in the evening. Betsy lives with her parents."

"What items have gone missing?"

"The first thing I noticed was my husband's watch and then some of his cuff links, a tie pin, and some of my jewellery. It happened gradually over several months. My first reaction in each case was that they had merely been mislaid. I was trying to be generous. No one should be going through my husband's things.

"Have you questioned your staff about them?"

"I have asked them if they had seen the items. I did not want to accuse anyone without some idea of who may be responsible."

"Quite so. What was their response?"

"Betsy and May said they did not know anything about those things. Miss Sanford said she saw May admiring the jewellery one day while she was supposed to be dusting. Mrs McDowell said that was likely the boys, but I think she is annoyed at them because they are at the age that they like to play pranks on people and she does not appreciate it. But I can't completely rule that out either."

"Boys can be mischievous at that age."

"Yes. And they miss their father. Maybe one of them wanted some tokens from their father to remember him. But why would they take my jewellery?"

"Did you ask the boys?"

"They were adamant that they knew nothing about it."

"Has anything else unusual happened in the household recently?"

"Well, I don't think it is relevant."

"Let me be the judge of that."

"A week before the end of the last quarter, Mrs McDowell asked for an advance on her wages for the following quarter. I had to tell her that I could not do that. The dividends weren't in for the quarter. Mr McFarland, my accountant, clips the coupons and deposits the dividends to my account each quarter. Near the end of the quarter money can be a little tight, and I need to keep some to spare in case there is an emergency. I just didn't have as much as she wanted. I offered a few pounds, but she said that was not enough. She never spoke of it again."

"Did she tell you why she needed an advance?"

"No."

"Do you have any suspicions yourself?"

"I don't know what to think. I would not invite someone into my house if I thought they would steal from me, yet someone has."

"When did the thefts occur?"

"I am not certain. It is not like I saw something one day and it was gone the next. Some of these things might have been missing for weeks before I noticed. I do know they didn't disappear all at once but rather gradually over time."

"How often are you away from home?"

"Not all that often. Some friends and I play whist once a month. Some of us went to see Gilbert and Sullivan's new musical, *Pirates of Penzance* at The Opera Comique in March.

"Did you search the house?"

"I have looked everywhere, the kitchen, the nursery, the parlour, even the unused bedrooms."

"Do your servants have any days off?"

"They have Sundays off."

Holmes was thoughtful, then he asked, "Do you perhaps need new curtains?"

Mrs Cecil Forrester was somewhat startled by the question.

"I suppose it is possible. They have not been replaced for a few years. Is this important?"

"What I propose is that I come into your house in a few days as a curtain maker. I will come with the proper accoutrements, measuring tape, samples—do you have a ladder?"

"Yes," she replied still puzzled.

"Very good," he said and continued. "It will give me an excuse to enter every room and linger a while taking measurements and considering the proper material for the room, so I can both examine the rooms and observe the persons."

"Oh, I see."

"Don't tell anyone I am coming before Tuesday morning. Then tell them to expect the curtain maker, a Mr Lockhart, about 10 o' clock on Wednesday and he will be about the place all day long."

After Holmes saw her out, he sat for a moment and thought, then he grabbed his hat and coat and walked out to the street to hail a cab. He asked the cabby to take him to St Katharine Docks. After he had sent it on its way, he walked back among the warehouses. He sat down and lit his pipe and smoked for a few minutes.

"Good to see ya gov'nor," said a voice behind him and Wiggins joined him on the makeshift seat.

"I wasn't sure I would find you here," Holmes said.

"Word got to me ya were 'ere. So I came."

"I have some work for you and your friends."

Wiggins smiled.

"Always could do wi' some extra bob," he said.

"There might be more opportunities in the future. Perhaps there should be some way I could signal that I would like to speak to you. I can't exactly send you a telegram."

Wiggins smiled.

"Might work. I know some o' the telegraph boys. Just stick a paper in your window with a W on it. I'll hear and come."

"Excellent. I need you and the others to do some surveillance beginning today and continuing over the next few days. You will be my Irregulars again."

"Who and where?" Wiggins asked.

"There is a nice lady named Mrs Cecil Forrester who lives in Lower Camberwell. She thinks someone in the house is nicking her things and selling them. She doesn't know who."

Holmes proceeded to explain to Wiggins who the persons in the drama were.

"I want you and the rest of the Irregulars to follow any of them who leave the house in the next week. Report back where they go and who they might see. There are also two boys in the house. Ham is seven and Alex is five. They might be more forthcoming about goings-on in the house to someone near their own age. I'll meet you near the house in Camberwell when I want a report."

He handed Wiggins a handful of shillings and pence.

"For expenses. Plus I'll pay each boy a shilling per day."

"Thank you, gov'nor!" Wiggins said and promptly disappeared.

Holmes did not tell his client of the additional resources he had deployed. He was well acquainted with the street urchins' abilities to remain invisible, unless they chose to reveal themselves.

On Wednesday Holmes appeared at Mrs Forrester's house as Mr Lockhart promptly at 10 o'clock in the morning with his tape measure and fabric samples. He borrowed her ladder and went about measuring rooms, poking and prodding here and there and doing much sighing and tisk-tisking. He even managed to have a look at the pantry on the excuse of having gotten lost in an unfamiliar house. He also listened to all the chatter around him. He was soon convinced that Mrs McDowell was an honest woman and her request for an advance was prompted by an illness in her family and she had found another way to handle the situation.

He took a break in the early afternoon and strolled down the street. A few blocks down Wiggins appeared at his side.

"Have your boys spotted anything?"

"The lady with the yellow hair was walking with a man on Sunday. He was sayin' they needed more and she was saying was too soon."

"Anything else?"

"She keeps looking out the window at the back o' the house. Loik she is watchin' fo' someone."

"Which floor?"

"The first."

"Very good. Keep a sharp eye out tomorrow. I think she is watching for that man she was walking with. He might come today and if not he will come tomorrow."

When he returned to the house, Holmes paid special attention to the rooms at the back of the house. One of those was the nursery where the blond Miss Sanford spent most of her time. She was there with the boys when he came in with the ladder. She blushed.

"Surely, you don't mean to come in here?" she said.

"I need to measure all the rooms for new curtains, miss," he responded.

"Come boys, it is a nice day out. We will take our work out into the garden."

Once she was gone, he closed the door and searched every inch of the room, poking up the fireplace and looking through books. Then he went up on the ladder and checked light fixtures and vent covers. In a vent he found a small bundle about the size of a woman's fist wrapped in a piece of cloth and tied with string. Inside were pieces of jewellery and a silver spoon. He wrapped it back up and replaced it.

Early the next morning the gardener began his work trimming the flowers. In a short time he was below the nursery window and a bundle fell out. He quickly stuffed it in his pocket. He was immediately grasped by a multitude of small hands. In a trice they had him bound tighter than a peeler's cuffs. In a moment Mrs Forrester, Miss Sanford, and Sherlock Holmes joined them in the garden.

"I don't understand what this is all about," Miss Sanford said.

Holmes walked over to the bound gardener and pulled the bundle out of his pocket.

"I just saw you throw this out the window to your confederate," he said as he untied it.

Mrs Forrest gasped.

"Those are mine!"

"Miss Sanford has been stealing your things, hiding them in a ventilator in the nursery, and then tossing them out the window to the gardener. I saw the bundle in the ventilator yesterday and these boys saw Miss Sanford walking with the gardener on Sunday. She attempted to throw suspicion on May to divert it from herself."

"Well," Mrs Forrester said, "Thank you, Mr Holmes and your assistants. I guess I need a new governess."

Chapter 21

Studies

"It seems to be a very delicate test,"
Dr John H Watson, *A Study in Scarlet*

It was a morning a few weeks past midsummer when a telegram arrived for Sherlock Holmes from Theodore Darnell asking to consult with him. It said he would be arriving about one o'clock. Holmes recognized the name. Teddy Darnell had been an undergraduate at Sidney Sussex College at Cambridge a year ahead of Holmes. They had fenced together and Darnell had introduced him to night climbing. They had climbed the Old Library and King's Chapel together at Cambridge.

When Darnell arrived Holmes immediately understood that the matter was one of a personal nature from the man's haggard look. The dark circles under the eyes spoke of many sleepless nights. His clothes fit poorly as if he had lost weight recently.

"Thank you for seeing me. I am really beside myself. No one seems to be able to help me. Maberley said I should talk to you. He said you helped him with a family problem. Then I remembered getting a letter from you a few years back announcing that you had opened a consulting detective practice."

"Yes, I have. People come to me in precisely the kind of situations you mentioned, where the police are at loss and can do nothing for them."

"I hope you can help me."

"Have a seat and tell me about it. Do you smoke?"

"No, thanks, but feel free."

Holmes pulled a small pouch of tobacco from the Persian slipper which had been thrown at him a couple of years prior and refilled and lit his pipe as he listened to Darnell tell his story.

"It is about my younger brother, Charlie. He's always been somewhat impetuous. When an idea strikes him, he acts upon it. Sometimes in the past it has gotten him into trouble. I remember once

399

he came home with a black eye and wouldn't tell anyone who gave it to him or where or why it happened. There was never any more to that as far as I ever knew. I guess he settled his differences with the other fellow.

"My parents and I have been hoping he would settle down. My father tried to talk him into going to university as I had done, but he wanted no part of that. My father offered to set him up in business. Charlie was thinking about it, but wasn't quite sure what he wanted to do or where. Given his rather impetuous nature I fully expected him to suddenly announce what business he wanted to go in for and believe he could plunge into it immediately, which I suspect you know isn't always possible, and even if it is, it may not be immediately profitable."

"I know it well," Holmes said.

"What I hadn't expected is what did happen,"

"What was that?"

"He disappeared!"

"Did he leave any note?"

"No."

"Did he take his clothes?"

"Perhaps. His room was all disarranged. It looked like someone had been searching for something. Drawers rifled through; clothes on the floor. Charlie was never a tidy person but this was beyond his usual casual housekeeping. I thought perhaps a burglar had come in through the window and Charlie had tussled with him."

"The window was open?"

"Yes."

"Was anything of value missing?"

"Not in the rest of the house. All the other rooms were undisturbed. Maybe Charlie had something that someone else wanted? I don't know. We looked around the property and beyond. We couldn't find any sign—"

"How long ago was this?"

"Four weeks ago," he said.

"It would have been best if you had called me at once. Much of the evidence I could have found is probably gone now."

"I didn't know. We didn't find any sign until we had crossed a neighbour's property. We found this on the fence along the railway line."

He held out a brown paper packet. Holmes unwrapped it. It was a tan shirt with long sleeves. There was a large dark stain on the back of the shirt. The centre of the stain was very solid, but beyond the edge of the primary stain were spots and splotches.

"Are you certain this is Charlie's shirt?"

"My mother is."

Holmes took out his magnifying glass and examined the stain closely. It was not a crust on top of the threads but had soaked into them. Whatever it was had either been liquid or suspended in liquid at the time it had come in contact with the shirt. Yet it had stiffened the shirt after it dried.

There were gashes in the shirt on both the stained side and the front. They were not cuts like a knife would make. However, if that stain was blood, a lot of it had been lost. There were also small rectangles that had been cut from the outer reaches of the stain.

"You have had tests done?"

"Yes. After we found this we called the police. They said there was no way for them to tell if it was blood and unless we found more evidence—"

"Like a body?"

"Precisely. They said without something like that, they could do nothing. We approached some chemists and other scientists, but all of them said it was impossible to determine if it was blood. Someone suggested Alfred Swaine Taylor, but we discover he had died last year."

"Yes, he was a great scientist."

Holmes looked at his pipe and shook his head.

"Come along," he said setting down the pipe. He led Darnell into the room that had been Mycroft's bedroom which now functioned as a small laboratory. "I doubt this will be of any use but we should eliminate the simplest tests first."

He lit the lamp on the table then chose a portion of the stain that was solid, cut a very small piece, placed it on a slide, and added a drop of water. He slid the slide under his microscope and adjusted the lamp and the mirror. He looked through the microscope and shook his head. Then he picked up a small bottle among the many on the table and shook it. It foamed. Then he applied a drop to the fabric piece on the slide then slid it under the microscope again. He watched for a few seconds and shook his head again.

"No reaction."

"What is in the bottle?"

Holmes smiled.

"Sodium stearate, commonly known as soap. Dried blood sometimes reacts to it. The fact that it did not react does not say it is not blood. Blood that is too old or has been exposed to heat or sunlight may no longer react."

"Is there no test that can determine if it is blood?"

"It is difficult. I am not saying it is impossible," Holmes said.

"Everyone else said it was impossible."

"May I keep this a while to do more tests?" Holmes asked.

"Yes, of course," Darnell said.

"Let's return to the sitting room."

Holmes picked up his pipe and relit it.

After a few puffs, he asked, "How tall was the fence?"

"About four feet."

"Which side of the fence was the shirt on? The side facing the railroad tracks or the side facing away?"

"Most of it was on the side away from the tracks but part of it was over the top of the fence."

"What was the fence made of?"

"It is wooden post and rail fencing."

"Was it new or old?"

"Rather old."

"Smooth or rough?"

"Rough."

"Were there any ponds or streams nearby?"

"Yes."

"Had it rained recently?"

"It rained very hard early that evening."

"So the ground was wet?"

"Very wet."

"Has it rained since?"

"Several times."

"Had your brother been associated with any young women?"

"Do you mean of good reputation or other?" Darnell asked.

"Either."

"To my knowledge he did not have any interactions with women of bad reputations. He has been interested in some local girls from time to time. We kept hoping he would marry one and settle down."

"Any recent interest in anyone in particular?"

"Not very recent. The most recent was Sarah Gooding. They seemed to be quite sweet on one another for a while but her family moved away two years ago and he has not mentioned her since then."

"Has he ever received any letters from her?"

"Not to my knowledge."

"You said he was impetuous and at least once got into a fist fight. Has he ever been involved with shady characters?"

"He hangs about the public house sometimes, and likes to get to know strangers who appear there. So from time to time I would say I have seen him with people that I'd consider to be of questionable morals, but most of the time they pass on through and I never see him with them again."

"Do you think he would do anything illegal?"

"I want to say no, but perhaps if he had some sudden inspiration, he might do something without thinking through the legal ramifications."

Holmes paused thoughtfully, drawing on his pipe.

"Answer a question for me," Darnell said. "Do you think Charlie is alive?"

"If that stain is blood, then no. If the stain is not blood then I think there is strong possibility he is."

"Do you have a theory as to why we found the shirt where we did?"

"Yes, that is fairly obvious. The shirt was placed there to help Charlie over the fence to reach a train. The question is was Charlie alive or dead when he went over the fence. So many weeks have passed since the event occurred any evidence on the ground is long gone, washed away, blown away, or trampled."

"You have some hope?"

"Hope is what you must cling to until science gives facts."

"Thank you. I will cling to the hope that Charlie is alive and well somewhere. Let me know if you discover anything."

Holmes saw Darnell out the door of the flat and met a postman with a letter from Mrs Nugent, the landlady, at the same time. She was asking if they intended to renew the lease. Another puzzle to consider.

He sat down in the sitting room to smoke and consider, but at the end of a half hour he had no new theories about Charlie Darnell or a decision as whether to renew the lease or find new lodgings. However, one problem might apply to both: he did not have the facilities here to do the chemical experiments necessary to solve the problem of the dried stain on the shirt. He grabbed his hat and descended to the street and hailed a cab to take him to St Bartholomew's Hospital.

He requested once more to use the chemical laboratory to do experiments during the break between sessions. He was granted permission on the same terms as before. Having made those arrangements he was riding back to Montague Street when he suddenly told the driver to drive around the block. Holmes looked about as he did. Due to the proximity to the British Museum most of the people in this area were scholars, philosophers, or curiosity seekers. While he had found the closeness to the museum occasionally useful, it was not where one necessarily expected to find a consultant of crime. Perhaps a more commercial area?

His driver must have thought he had gone mad because he now started directing him to drive in larger circles about the area. There were some streets that seemed more conducive to what he had in mind. Then he saw the office of an estate agent. His driver must have sighed with relief when he asked to be set down. He wished him a very good day when he saw the coins Holmes had given him.

The discussion with the estate agent was not fruitful. The agent's idea of what Holmes might need was very different than his own, and primarily limited to his currently available housing stock. He left and walked about and visited some others with similar results. He picked up some newspapers as he walked back home.

By the time he arrived back at Montague Street he had definitely made up his mind to find new lodgings. Having spent so much time making do with what was available he had not previously considered the two factors that now decided him: the location and the small size of the sitting room. He had hopes he could improve upon both.

Once inside the flat, he immediately sat down and wrote back to Mrs Nugent, advising her that he and Mycroft were not going to renew the lease come September, and would be vacating the premises by Michaelmas. As he was sealing the envelope, the housekeeper entered to ask if he would like tea. He said yes, because having made the decision suddenly gave him an appetite.

"Before you go, Mrs Denton, a word. I have decided that I will not be renewing the lease on this flat when it ends at Michaelmas. I will not be needing your services after that time. If you should find another position before the time comes please let me know and I will fend for myself for the remaining."

"Thank you for the consideration of the advanced notice," Mrs Denton said with what Holmes thought was a sigh of relief. While he and Mrs Denton had been on good terms, he suspected she was tired of his irregularities, but had been hesitant to give notice.

After tea Holmes played some spritely airs on his violin as he considered the chemical researches he intended to embark on the following morning. He was going to start by reviewing the literature on blood tests to determine if anyone had discovered a new test he had not heard of. Then he planned to examine the basic chemistry of blood and how one would go about testing for it from a purely chemical point of view. He also planned to test the stain on the shirt to determine if it was consistent with the basic elements one would expect in blood or if there were others that pointed to another result.

He slept well that night and set off for Bart's early.

His searches through the literature revealed that most recent studies were variations on the principles of either the Teichmann test or the Guaiacum test to find a process that was easier, faster, and more sensitive. Hudson produced the characteristic hematin crystals using potassium and ammonium salts of bromides and iodide. Struve had recently published about his experiments using ammonia, tannic acid, and acetic acid with ammonium chloride rather than sodium chloride. Neither of these were improvements.

The list was growing longer of the contaminants that could interfere with the tests. The test would fail even if the stain was blood, if stains were subjected to excessive heat, light, or some organic solvents. The presence of iron or iron oxides would result in a positive result when no blood was present.

Human blood was primarily composed of hydrogen, oxygen, nitrogen, carbon, and iron. The iron in haemoglobin was the discriminating factor most chemists targeted. He set about testing the chemical composition of the shirt stain. It contained all of those elements as well as potassium, sodium, and calcium, which were to be expected in bodily fluids. But he also found something else: silicon dioxide. The iron present was principally in the form of iron oxide as well. What it told him was that clay was a major component of the stain. He knew from the way the stain had soaked into the fibres that the clay had been in solution at the time the shirt came in contact with it.

On a rainy night Charlie Darnell fell into a stream, a pond, or even a puddle, containing iron rich clay. But did he fall or was he pushed? Was there a slip or a struggle? Was he beaten by fists or by rocks? Were the tears in the shirt caused by the fence or the fall?

Holmes had found few wood particles, but the shirt had been through so many hands before his that he did not know if that was significant.

Was there blood in that clay solution?

He did not yet know and that annoyed him.

Leaving Bart's he had the cabby drop him at Bradley's on Oxford Street to buy more tobacco. He had no doubt that it was going to take a few pipefuls to solve the problems on his mind. For the moment he was going to concentrate on the other problem.

He walked west on Oxford Street and surveyed the cross streets and near neighbourhoods. He explored from Regents Street to Marylebone High Street as far north as Euston Road, turning right or left at each intersection as the whim struck him and eventually found himself back on Tottenham Court Road which he followed to Great Russell Street and then on back to Montague Street. He had seen some "to let" signs and had knocked for a look. Too small or too dingy. To grand or too pricey. One woman renting out rooms in her house had a handful of children tearing about the house and he knew that was not the place for him. He needed to find a more scientific method.

By the time he arrived back to the rooms on Montague Street, Mrs Denton had gone for the day. He settled down with some newspapers he had collected on the way home. He went through the advertisements for flats to let and looked the locations up on a map of London. He made note of the addresses that looked interesting. He would use that list for his searches the following day.

Then he relit his pipe and settled on the couch to consider the blood stain problem. Unfortunately most of the researchers had concentrated on detecting the haemoglobin. They dealt with potential reactions to other substances as an afterthought rather than considering their elimination as part of the initial criteria.

He mentally reviewed the chemicals that he theorized would create a visible reaction to some component of blood, but nothing else, to create his new plan of research. The following day he was once again at Bart's chemistry lab early. He set up four test areas. In each of the he added a drop of his blood to water. He went through one experiment after another. When he found a test that would change the colour of the fluid or result in a precipitant he then tried it again with another suspect substance. Unfortunately, many tests that reacted positively for haemoglobin also reacted with other forms of iron or even some plant derivatives. The only progress he made was in eliminating possibilities. He became obsessed with finding the solution and stayed later at Bart's chemical laboratory than he had intended.

While his mind was not entirely into the pursuit of lodgings he fulfilled his plan of the previous evening, and visited the lodgings on the list. He was again disappointed, and it drove home the fact that people were not always truthful in their advertisements. The "scientific method" of flat hunting could only work if the data was good.

Weeks proceeded in this manner with Holmes spending his days at Bart's doing chemical tests and wandering the streets of London for an hour or two looking for a new home. He gradually worked his way further into Marylebone and one evening found himself on Baker Street.

Baker Street was a busy thoroughfare with a mix of flats and commercial enterprises. As he walked down the street considering if this was a prospective location he came upon a "to let" sign in one window. He braced himself for the results and rang the bell.

"I saw the 'to let' sign, and wished to enquire," he said to the woman who answered.

"Come along then," she said and guided him to a sitting room at the back of the house.

"I'm Mrs Hudson. My husband and I bought this house years ago, but now there is just me, so I rent out the rooms in the front. There is a nice sitting room on the first floor overlooking the street with a bedroom attached. There is a second bedroom up the stairs from there if you'd need two. They will be available Michaelmas—I hope."

"Can I see the rooms?"

"Well, some students have been renting them and they won't be out for a while. They are a frightful mess. Perhaps if you come back in a week."

"What are the terms?"

She reeled off some numbers for the sitting room and the one bedroom alone, for both bedrooms and the sitting room, and for cooking and housekeeping. The terms were quite reasonable based on his experience. Even without having seen the rooms to be let, her own rooms were nicely arranged and the fact that she was embarrassed to show them when they were, in her words 'a frightful mess' was a good sign of her housekeeping standards.

His concern was the old one: could he afford the terms on a consistent basis. He was currently rather well placed financially. While the majority of the cases this year had provided him with little or no income, he still had the cushion from Sir Walter's payment from the Sumatra case. He could not predict when the next big case would come along. Of course, he knew Mycroft would always be willing to tide him over if there was a shortfall, but he wanted to make a clean break from that once he moved from the rooms at Montague Street. It would be prudent to find a flat mate, one with a steady income.

"Then I shall stop by next week," he said to Mrs Hudson, "Here's my card."

He continued his stroll down Baker Street. He could imagine living here. It would be more conducive to doing business.

Now with at least a prospect in hand he had to resolve the subsidiary problem. He needed a flatmate. Holmes decided to advertise in some of the newspapers for a potential flatmate. He requested that they respond by letter to the newspaper explaining their personal circumstances.

The responses were not encouraging. He'd read them after a long day of chemical experiments and tossed them in the fireplace. He received a number of responses from young women with small children willing to keep house for him in lieu of rent which was very far from what he had in mind. There was one elderly couple with a similar offer. Several men responded that if he could provide them with an accommodation for the first few months they would reimburse him once they found employment. Unfortunately, most did not have the steadiest of handwriting which suggested that their record of employment was not of the steadiest either. Not one response came from a junior clerk or a barber's apprentice or similar occupations where the wages might be low yet steady.

The summer dragged on into autumn without a solution to the test for blood or the quest for a flatmate. He was quite convinced the Baker Street rooms were the best option. He had gotten a peek at them the next time he called and met the current occupants, who were randomly tossing books and clothes into boxes. The sitting room was nearly twice the size of the one in Montague Street, and the bedroom was sufficient for his needs. He explained his situation to Mrs Hudson and told her that he would take the sitting room and the single bedroom in any case, but he was still hoping to find someone to go halves with him.

Back at the flat at Montague Street, he began making preparations to move. He was going to need to evacuate Bart's chemistry lab soon, before the next session of classes began, but he was going to use every day there he could and recommence in Baker Street if necessary.

On September 27th, Stamford came in to the laboratory as another test failed.

"Any luck?"

"No," Holmes said sitting back on the stool. "In theory it should be possible to find the right formula that reacts with blood and nothing else. Haemoglobin is the most obvious target, but anything I have found so far that reacts with haemoglobin reacts with other things. Perhaps I am just too distracted by the other problem."

"What is that?" Stamford asked.

"Whether it is possible to get comfortable rooms at a reasonable price. I found this nice set of rooms on Baker Street that are a bit too much for my purse. In theory, it should be possible in a city of over four million people to find someone to go halves with me on a flat. But all the responses to my advertisements for a flatmate did not have the income to pay their...."

Holmes' voice trailed off as a new potential solution to the chemical puzzle came to him. Stamford left him alone.

"Perhaps I need something that binds two components of blood together...." Holmes mumbled thumbing through the reference books and setting up a new experiment.

That experiment also failed. He tried another idea. This time the fluid turned a dull mahogany colour, and a brownish dust was precipitated to the bottom of the glass. He could hardly believe it. He repeated it with the same result. He repeated his test multiple times on fresh blood and dried blood. Even blood he had heated reacted in the same way. He tried it with several different iron compounds and even a scrap of cast iron. No reaction. He proceeded to check the test against other metal and organic compounds.

When Stamford returned Sherlock Holmes was bending over the table absorbed in his work. At the sound of footsteps he glanced round, saw Stamford and another man entering the room, and sprang to his feet with a cry of pleasure.

"I've found it! I've found it," Holmes shouted to Stamford, running towards him with a test-tube in his hand. "I have found a re-agent which is precipitated by haemoglobin and by nothing else."

"Dr John Watson, Mr Sherlock Holmes," said Stamford, introducing them.

Holmes gave Dr Watson the quick introspective gaze he gave to all he met. While Stamford had introduced Watson as a doctor, he had the air of a military man, an army doctor then. His face is dark, and that is not the natural tint of his skin, for his wrists are fair. His haggard face said clearly that he had undergone hardships and sickness. He held his left arm in a stiff and unnatural manner. Where in the tropics could an English army doctor have seen much hardship and been wounded recently?

"How are you?" Holmes said cordially. "You have been in Afghanistan, I perceive."

"How on earth did you know that?" Dr Watson asked in astonishment.

"Never mind," Holmes said chuckling to himself. "The question now is about haemoglobin. No doubt you see the significance of this discovery of mine?"

"It is interesting, chemically, no doubt," Dr Watson answered, "but practically--"

"Why, man, it is the most practical medico-legal discovery for years. Don't you see that it gives us an infallible test for blood stains? Come over here now!"

Sherlock Holmes seized Dr Watson by the sleeve in his eagerness and drew him over to the table at which he had been working.

"Let us have some fresh blood," he said, digging a long bodkin into his finger, and drawing off the resulting drop of blood in a chemical pipette. "Now, I add this small quantity of blood to a litre of water. You perceive that the resulting mixture has the appearance of pure water. The proportion of blood cannot be more than one in a million. I have no doubt, however, that we shall be able to obtain the characteristic reaction."

As he spoke, he threw into the vessel a few white crystals, and then added some drops of a transparent fluid. In an instant the contents assumed a dull mahogany colour, and a brownish dust was precipitated to the bottom of the glass jar.

"Ha! ha!" he cried, clapping his hands, and looking as delighted as a child with a new toy. "What do you think of that?"

"It seems to be a very delicate test," Dr Watson remarked.

"Beautiful! Beautiful! The old Guaiacum test was very clumsy and uncertain. So is the microscopic examination for blood corpuscles. The latter is valueless if the stains are a few hours old. Now, this appears to act as well whether the blood is old or new. Had this test been invented, there are hundreds of men now walking the earth who would long ago have paid the penalty of their crimes."

"Indeed!" Dr Watson murmured.

"Criminal cases are continually hinging upon that one point. A man is suspected of a crime months perhaps after it has been committed. His linen or clothes are examined, and brownish stains discovered upon them. Are they blood stains, or mud stains, or rust stains, or fruit stains, or what are they? That is a question which has puzzled many an expert, and why? Because there was no reliable test. Now we have the Sherlock Holmes' test, and there will no longer be any difficulty."

Holmes' eyes fairly glittered as he spoke, and he put his hand over his heart, and bowed as if to some applauding crowd conjured up by his imagination.

"You are to be congratulated," Dr Watson remarked.

"There was the case of Von Bischoff at Frankfort last year. He would certainly have been hung had this test been in existence. Then there was Mason of Bradford, and the notorious Muller, and Lefevre of Montpellier, and Samson of New Orleans. I could name a score of cases in which it would have been decisive."

"You seem to be a walking calendar of crime," said Stamford with a laugh. "You might start a paper on those lines. Call it the 'Police News of the Past.'"

"Very interesting reading it might be, too," remarked Sherlock Holmes, sticking a small piece of plaster over the prick on his finger. "I have to be careful," he continued, turning to Dr Watson with a smile, "for I dabble with poisons a good deal."

Holmes held out his hand as he spoke. It was all mottled over with similar pieces of plaster, and discoloured with strong acids.

"We came here on business, Holmes," said Stamford, sitting down on a high three-legged stool, and pushing another one in Dr Watson's direction with his foot. "My friend here wants to take diggings, and as you were complaining that you could get no one to go halves with you, I thought that I had better bring you together."

Holmes looked again at his new acquaintance and saw a man of courage, education, and good breeding. The look in Dr Watson's eye said he felt broken inside, but his stance and his speech said he was going to marshal on. That and his army pension quickly determined Holmes that this was just the man to share rooms with.

"I have my eye on a suite in Baker Street," he said, "which would suit us down to the ground. You don't mind the smell of strong tobacco, I hope?"

"I always smoke 'ship's' myself," Dr Watson answered.

"That's good enough. I generally have chemicals about, and occasionally do experiments. Would that annoy you?"

"By no means."

"Let me see—what are my other shortcomings? I get in the dumps at times, and don't open my mouth for days on end. You must not think I am sulky when I do that. Just let me alone, and I'll soon be right. What have you to confess now? It's just as well for two fellows to know the worst of one another before they begin to live together."

Dr Watson laughed at this cross-examination.

"I keep a bull pup," I said, "and I object to rows because my nerves are shaken, and I get up at all sorts of ungodly hours, and I am extremely lazy. I have another set of vices when I'm well, but those are the principal ones at present."

"Do you include violin-playing in your category of rows?" Holmes asked, anxiously.

"It depends on the player," Dr Watson answered. "A well-played violin is a treat for the gods—a badly played one—"

"Oh, that's all right," Sherlock Holmes cried, with a merry laugh. "I think we may consider the thing as settled—that is, if the rooms are agreeable to you."

"When shall we see them?" Dr Watson asked.

"Call for me here at noon to-morrow, and we'll go together and settle everything," he answered.

After they had gone Holmes unwrapped the stained shirt, cut a small piece from the stain, placed it in water, as he had his own blood a few minutes before and stirred. When he was certain the majority of the stain had separated from the fabric he removed the fabric from the water and added the chemicals as before. Nothing happened.

Before making his announcement to Stamford and Dr Watson he had repeated his test multiple times on fresh blood and dried blood. In each case the reaction had occurred. Now there was none. He tried it again and the result was the same. He placed a piece of the stained shirt on a slide, added the chemicals, covered the slide and slid it under the microscope. Nothing. He had run every blood test including his own on the stain on the shirt. At this point it was highly improbable that it was blood. He wrapped up the stained shirt and put the equipment away.

On his way back to his rooms in Montague Street he stopped at a post office and sent a telegram to Darnell:

Stain is not blood. Most likely iron rich clay. Look for your brother alive in the company of Sarah Gooding. SH

Sherlock Holmes and Dr John H. Watson met the next day as had been arranged and inspected the rooms at No. 221B, Baker Street. Mrs Hudson, finally rid of the former lodgers, had cleaned the rooms, and now beamed as she showed them to the gentlemen. They consisted of a couple of comfortable bedrooms and a single large airy sitting room, cheerfully furnished, and illuminated by two broad windows. The bargain was concluded upon the spot, and they at once entered into possession. Dr Watson moved his things over from the hotel that evening and the following morning Holmes followed with several boxes and portmanteaus.

THE BEGINNING

Acknowledgments

I am grateful to Sir Arthur Conan Doyle for introducing the world to the greatest detective of fact or fancy. I strongly urge anyone reading this book to read the original four novels and fifty-six short stories written about Sherlock Holmes by Sir Arthur Conan Doyle, for you cannot truly appreciate any imitation until you have read the originals.

I am thankful to William S. Baring-Gould for his biography, *Sherlock Holmes of Baker Street*, not only because some ideas herein are based on that book, but because it was that book that first introduced me to the Sherlockian world beyond the Canon.

I also thank Sherlockians everywhere for keeping green the memory of Sherlock Holmes.

I am especially grateful to Peter E. Blau, Alexander E. Braun, Erica Fair, Danna Mancini, Steve Scott, and Diane Zike, for critiquing and commenting on the manuscript.

Due to the length of this book and the extensive amount of research done for it, I have decided to publish the usual list of sources separately. However, I must acknowledge that this book uses a number of characters, as well as some actual text, from Arthur Conan Doyle's works which are now in the public domain. It also uses some ideas first established by William S. Baring-Gould and other Sherlockians.

Escott

"William Escott" was an alias Holmes used in the case of "The Adventure of Charles Augustus Milverton." In his book *Sherlock Holmes of Baker Street*, Baring-Gould suggested that it was Holmes' stage name, and I used it as such in this series.

Mycroft Holmes

Mycroft appears in "The Adventure of the Greek Interpreter" and "The Final Problem," "The Empty House" and "The Adventure of the Bruce-Partington Plans." Mycroft appears throughout this series.

Langdale Pike

Langdale Pike is the name of a character mentioned in "The

Adventure of the Three Gables." Baring-Gould suggested it was also a stage name. I combined the two ideas when I identified that stage name in Part II of *The Consulting Detective Trilogy* with the character of Lord Cecil Hamley which I created in Part I.

Stamford

Stamford introduces Holmes and Watson in *A Study in Scarlet* as is shown in chapter 21 of this book, which uses parts of Conan Doyle's text. I gave Stamford a first name and a backstory in Part I of the *Trilogy* and expand his role in chapters 8, 12, 15 of this book.

Gregson & Lestrade

Inspectors Gregson and Lestrade were both introduced by Conan Doyle in *A Study in Scarlet* and reappear in a number of other tales. I had Gregson first meet Holmes in Part II of this series. Lestrade was introduced in Part III. Some Sherlockian scholars have proposed that Gregson became a member of the Special Branch that concentrated on Fenian activities. I used that idea in the Mansion House case. Scotland Yard did thwart the bombing of the Mansion House.

Wiggins

Conan Doyle created Wiggins as the head of the Baker Street Irregulars in *A Study in Scarlet* and *The Sign of the Four.* In this book, Wiggins first appears in chapters 4 and 5, in late 1876, then reunites with Holmes three years later in chapter 17. They begin forming the Irregulars in 1880 and 1881 in chapters 18 and 20.

Reginald Musgrave

Reginald Musgrave is featured in chapter 16 which uses parts of Conan Doyle's story "The Musgrave Ritual" with some original writing interspersed.

Old Sherman

Conan Doyle introduced the character of Old Sherman in *The Sign of the Four.* I expanded Holmes' relationship with Sherman in *The Crack in the Lens.*

Mortimer Maberley

Mortimer Maberley was mentioned as a prior client of Holmes' in "The Adventure of the Three Gables." He is a fellow student in Part I of *The Consulting Detective Trilogy*.

Dr. John H. Watson

Parts of the final chapter are based on *A Study in Scarlet*, Doyle's first novel in which Holmes and Watson meet.

Wilson Hargreave

Conan Doyle mentioned Wilson Hargreave in the "Adventure of the Dancing Men." Holmes met Hargeave in *Part II* and helped him investigate corruption in the New York City police.

Bradley's

Bradley's tobacco shop was mentioned in the *Hound of the Baskervilles*. Holmes's publication 'Upon the Distinction between the Ashes of the Various Tobaccoes' is mentioned in *The Sign of the Four*.

Baron Dowson

"Baron" Dowson (aka in this series as Baron Von Marienburg) was mentioned in "The Adventure of the Mazarin Stone."

Sherrinford

Conan Doyle originally considered naming his detective Sherrinford Holmes. Baring-Gould suggested that Sherriford was the eldest Holmes brother who was the country squire while his younger brothers worked in London. I greatly developed Sherrinford's character in Parts I & II of this *Trilogy*, and in *The Crack in the Lens*.

The Cabman's Story

I borrowed three pieces from Sir Arthur Conan Doyle's "The Cabman's Story," which was first published anonymously in the May 17, 1884 edition of *Cassell's Saturday Journal*, including the story about coal torpedoes in chapter 8, the criminal John Malone in chapter 10, and the corpse in the cab in chapter 12.

The Producers

The theatre fraud is a homage to Mel Brook's *The Producers* with a few different plot twists.